Playing Harry

Nick Wastnage

Other titles – all e-books

~~~

Electronic Crime in Muted Key
Murder He Forgot
The Wrong Menu
Killing Sam Forever
The Bloodied Black Heart
Death in The Fishing Net
Oh, What a Night
Harry and His Unfinished Business
Love, Life, and Loss

~~~

http://www.nickwastnage.com
http://nickwastnage.blogspot.com/

Playing Harry

Nick Wastnage

Edited by Katy Sozaeva
Cover by Anna Arianova

Playing Harry is the first story in The Harry Fingle Collection

Published by New Generation Publishing in 2012

Copyright © Nick Wastnage 2012

First Edition

www.newgeneration-publishing.com

 New Generation **Publishing**

Thanks to Katy for editing this book and for the many hilarious comments she made in the margins of the proof copy. They made me laugh.

Thanks also to Justin, Carol and Margot for the help they gave me while I wrote Playing Harry.

Threads

Chapter One

HARRY FINGLE became certain the jury would find him guilty and that he'd go to prison for several years. At the beginning of the trial he had no doubt that his case would be thrown out of court; dismissed as a shameful case of trumped-up evidence manipulated by someone he'd upset in the past who'd convinced a corrupt policeman to press charges. But as the case dragged on and he listened to lie after lie, convincingly told by the prosecution witnesses and then highlighted by the skilful and eloquent prosecution barrister, Harry became more and more depressed and demoralised. He eventually doubted his own innocence and gave up any hope of walking free. Philip Stacey, his friend and boss, gave a powerful testimony in his favour. He told the judge and jury that Harry had only been doing his job. But Harry didn't believe it convinced them.

'Please stand,' said a court official. The large, wooden door that led from the judge's chambers creaked loudly as it opened. The noise rippled through the stifling and expectant silence of the courtroom. Harry stood up with his head down, and stared at his shoes as he heard the judge walk back to his seat on the bench.

The judge motioned for everyone to sit. Harry, with his head still bowed, lowered himself slowly down onto the hard, wooden seat he'd sat on every day for the last month. He looked up and glanced across to the seats directly behind his defence team's table: to where his girlfriend sat. She wasn't looking his way. He returned his gaze to the ground around his feet, and thought back to moments during the trial. The times when he'd thought she'd shown sympathy and belief in the untruths and downright fabrications peddled by the prosecution witnesses; he decided not to look her way again.

It'll be over shortly and then she'll be rid of me.

~~~

The trial judge, his white wig covering his hair, and dressed in his red robe with thick, black edging, proceeded at a slow pace to his seat, followed by the other court officials. **AMIE LAU** touched her straight, black hair and watched the deliberate and well-practised ritual. She turned to look at Harry. She kept her eyes fixed on him for some time, waiting for him to turn and see her so she could give him a sign of support. But he didn't glance her way. She felt nervous, a bit sick, a touch unsteady, and was sure all colour had drained from her face. She turned back to watch the judge adjust his glasses to sit on the end of his nose. He looked over the rims towards the foreman of the jury, who stood next to and slightly forward from the other eleven jury members. The judge leant forward. He rested his robed arms on the bench and motioned for all in the courtroom to take their seats. He turned back to the foreman of the jury. Amie found the tension difficult to bear. She shook.

'Members of the jury. Have you reached a verdict?' the judge asked.

'Yes, your honour.'

'Is that a unanimous verdict?'

'It is, your honour.'

The judge nodded to one of the court officials.

'Will the defendant please stand,' the court official said.

Amie gripped the sides of her chair. She turned again to look as Harry slowly stood up. He didn't look her way. His gaze focused on something on the wall above the judge's head.

'Do you find the defendant, one Harry Nicholas Fingle, guilty or not guilty under the Criminal Justice Act 2003 of being in possession of indecent images of children?'

Amie looked away. She took a deep breath. She hoped she wouldn't pass out.

~~~

Amie sat in a side room of the court waiting for Harry to appear. Words could not describe the elation she felt. She never doubted his innocence, but had found the four-week-long trial, the gradual sapping of his confidence, and his increased negativity and despair difficult to cope with. She looked up at the door. She expected Harry to come through at any time.

It's all over, she thought. *We can start to get our lives back on track.*

They'd been a pair for seven years. They had met at a friend's party when she'd been doing her MA. Both had gone alone. They bumped into each other when, by coincidence, they went to get a drink at the same time. They hit it off immediately. Three weeks later Amie moved in with Harry. They became inseparable – with many common interests and mutual friends – and like oxygen to each other: the air they both needed to survive. 'Rock solid' was how their friends described their relationship – both of them clearly in love. Amie knew they'd eventually marry. She wasn't worried about it. They'd get round to it at some time.

While she waited, she thought about the pressure Harry had been under and how he had become remote and snappy. She looked at her watch and wondered what was keeping him. *How will he be*?' she asked herself. Would he be elated, like her, or just pleased it was all over and wanting to get away? Maybe they could go somewhere they liked – Devon, Cornwall, or the Yorkshire Moors? She heard a noise coming from behind the door.

The door opened and he came in, alone. His face was grey and ashen, almost the same colour as his suit. His blue eyes looked red, as though he'd been crying. He didn't rush to greet her as she'd expected. She smiled. 'Oh, poor darling. I love you so much.'

He stood and looked at her, his expression distant and remote. They remained one or two metres apart.

'What's up? You were acquitted. We can go home.'

He didn't move. He shook his head. 'No. I want to split. I need some space.'

Amie felt bewildered. She couldn't understand what Harry was on about. 'Harry? What are you saying?' she exclaimed.

'I can't explain. We'll stay friends. I have to go now. I'll call you.'

He turned and walked out of the room.

~~~

RICHARD MORECOMBE was known as a media mogul. He owned many companies worldwide. One of them was The Morning Times Newspaper Group, the parent company of *The Morning Times*: the much-respected daily, and the paper that employed Harry Fingle.

The day after Harry was acquitted Richard hosted a lunch party in a private room in his favourite restaurant near Covent Garden. It was the one-year anniversary of a small advertising company he'd bought off the receiver for a knockdown price. On the first day of his ownership, exactly a year earlier, he and his team had gone in, assessed the employees, fired those they thought useless, doubled the salary of the people they wanted to keep, appointed a chief executive, and promised everyone huge bonuses if they turned the business into profit within a year. The newly invigorated team did just that. The lunch was to celebrate and Richard, who relished any excuse for a party, felt in his element. He made a fuss of congratulating everyone, giving out the bonus cheques, toasting the company, and kissing most of the girls. He couldn't have been happier.

'Great news about Harry,' Pat Faulk, one of the assistant editors of

The Morning Times, said to Richard. They'd bumped into each other while everyone changed seats between courses.

'Yeah, it's good,' Richard replied in an instant. He'd been taken by surprise. He'd flown in that morning from New York and had stopped only for ten minutes at his London office for a quick shower and a change of clothes. He hadn't read the papers or caught a news bulletin.

'I don't know how the case got so far. The judge said it was a complete travesty of justice,' Pat added.

'You're right; but don't think me rude. I've only just got in from New York and I should circulate. See you at next week's meeting.'

Richard touched Pat on the shoulder and moved quickly away. He didn't talk to anyone else. Only one topic occupied his mind: to obtain a copy of any newspaper and read about the Harry Fingle case. He found one. Not one of his papers – a rival's – but it covered the case on the front page. He took it to the gents' room and locked himself in a cubicle. He read the account of the trial from the beginning.

'Fuck,' he said aloud when he came to the end. He discarded the paper and went straight back to the party.

~~~

Later, when alone for the first time since the lunch, he pulled out his phone and made a call.

'What the hell happened? I thought the Harry Fingle thing was a done deal. Who screwed up?'

~~~

KATE FISHER had been the commercial director for Ritzler Pharmaceuticals, one of the world's largest drug companies, for three years. Ian, her husband was a lawyer. They both had come home early from work to meet with their sixteen-year-old son, Jack. He'd just been excluded from school for being in possession of cannabis. They sat on opposite sofas in their period-style sitting room and waited for him to come in. Kate flipped through a magazine and fiddled with her fingers. Ian corrected a document he'd brought home from work. Neither had spoken for some time.

'That's him,' Kate said as she heard the front door slam. She looked across at Ian. 'Aren't you going to go and meet him?'

Ian looked at Kate and shrugged his shoulders. 'If you want me to.' He stood up and went to the hall.

'What's this all about?' Kate heard him say in an aggressive tone.

'Let me get in. I'll explain. Don't have a go at me as soon as you see me.'

'What do you mean, have a go? You've successfully ruined your chances at school. Don't you know how much we're paying for you to go there?'

'Call yourself a fucking lawyer. Don't you know a man's innocent until…'

'Don't swear at me and tell me what to do. Come in here and listen to us.'

'Ian, give him a chance. You jumped down his neck before he's even tried to explain.' Kate's gaze flashed between Ian and Jack as they burst through the door. Ian looked flushed. He sat in one of the upright chairs. Jack sat in another one. He wore scruffy jeans and a well-worn T-shirt. He dumped his rucksack on the floor and took out his phone. He started to fiddle with it and check his text messages.

'Jack, could you put that down and speak to us,' Kate said.

'What about?' Jack had his head down. He continued to play with the phone.

'About fucking getting suspended for drugs,' Ian yelled. He looked down and turned back one of the cuffs of his crisp, blue shirt.

Jack dropped the phone onto the top of his rucksack and looked up at his father. 'What the hell? You just had a go at me for swearing. Now you're doing it.' Jack glared at his father. 'Hypocrite.'

'Stop it, both of you.' Kate rubbed a hand through her spiky blonde hair. 'Don't say another word, Ian. Let me handle this.' She glowered at her husband and turned to Jack. 'Tell us in your own words what happened. I want to hear it from you.'

Jack's eye flashed between his mother and father and then settled on Kate. 'As long as *he* doesn't interrupt.'

'Just get on with it,' Kate said. She shot Ian a quick glance. Her nose pointed upwards. The silhouette of her face showed her fine, distinct bone structure.

'I never had any of the stuff. It was planted on me.'

'Who by?' Ian snapped.

'I don't know, do I? But I didn't have any of it.'

'Truthfully?' Kate asked.

'Yes, Mum, truthfully.'

'But what about those boys you go around with? I bet they have it,' Ian said. He looked at Jack with a snide expression.

'What boys? What are you talking about?' Jack, with scorn in his eyes, glared at his father.

'You know, the black boys in those gangs you go around with.'

11

Jack jumped up. He stormed over to where his father sat. 'You're just a fucking racist. You just don't understand. I hate you.' He turned and ran out of the room.

'Jack, come back immediately. I haven't finished…'

'Leave it. Let him calm down. I'll talk to him later. We're getting nowhere like this. I've got to make a work call.' As Kate rose she heard the front door slam. She ran and opened it.

'Where're you going, Jack?' she yelled. Jack had disappeared down the street and out of sight.

~~~

GARY LESTER woke early. He felt shaky and had a thumping headache, as had become his norm every morning. He rolled out of bed. He knocked over the empty bottle of scotch lodged against the side of his bed, ignoring the dregs that dribbled onto the dirty carpet, and rushed to the bathroom. He grabbed the sides of the stained washbasin for support and vomited. He retched a few times, sluiced some water around his face, and attempted to clean his teeth. He showered. He dressed quickly and packed his small rucksack with a newspaper, a toothbrush and toothpaste, a couple of breath-freshening, aerosol sprays, some Polo mints, a new packet of Nurofen, and half a bottle of whisky. He closed the door on his small apartment and started to walk the short distance down Shepherd's Bush Road to Hammersmith tube station. He had to be in early that day. He was due to meet Margaret Hudson, head of human resources, at nine. He had no idea what it was about.

'Come in, Gary. Sit down,' Margaret said, as he arrived at her office door a few minutes after nine. She stood up from behind her desk, and motioned to a spare chair around a low-level table in front of where she'd been sitting. She joined Gary in the adjacent seat.

'How's it going? Like some coffee?' She took hold of a fresh-looking cafetière and held it over an empty, white cup. She waited for his reply.

'Thanks. Black please.' Gary watched Margaret pour. He felt glad he'd taken the precaution of a few, quick sprays from his mouth freshener before he'd entered her office. They sat quite close.

Margaret poured some coffee for herself. She added a little milk and turned to Gary. 'Push the door closed, will you?' He did as she asked; beginning to feel it was no ordinary progress meeting that was about to start.

'Is there anything you want to talk to me about, Gary?' Margaret said as soon as the door had fully shut. She looked straight at him.

'No. Should there be?' He was concerned and unsure where the discussion would lead.

Margaret sat up straight. She moved the pencil that rested upon the A4 pad on the table to one side and looked up. 'I understand you may find this difficult to accept, but I believe you have a drink problem. Can we talk about it?'

Shit, thought Gary. *She knows*. He'd worked for Ritzler Pharmaceuticals for twenty-six years. He joined them as a junior at sixteen after he'd left school with no qualifications. He'd done well and worked his way up until he was appointed IT research manager some seven years previously. It was all going fine until about two years earlier when his wife walked out on him with their children. She'd been having an affair with his best friend. It was then that the drinking started.

He shook his head. 'I don't know what you're talking about.'

'I know it's not easy. But I think it would be helpful if you and I discussed it – just the two of us – to see if we can come up with a solution.'

'There's nothing to talk about.' Gary shrugged his shoulders. 'I told you, I don't have a drink problem.' He spoke in a raised tone.

'Come on, Gary. I really want to help, but you're making it difficult.' Margaret reached forward to pick up the A4 pad. She turned over the front sheet.

'There's nothing to discuss. I've told you I don't have a drink problem.'

Margaret looked into Gary's bloodshot eyes. 'Are you sure?'

'Absolutely,' he said. He hoped his persistence would prevail.

Margaret pulled out three separate sheets of typed, white paper from the bottom of her pad, placed them on the table, and looked up. 'I'm sorry. I'd hoped we could have handled this in an amicable fashion.'

'What do you mean?' Gary looked down at the top sheet of paper and tried to read it upside down.

Margaret picked up the three pieces of paper. 'These are three statements from your colleagues. They…'

'What do they say?' Gary asked in a flash. He'd become worried. He'd realised his bluffing tactics hadn't worked. He feared the meeting would end badly.

Margaret looked at him with a serious expression. 'They say that on Monday 1 October, Wednesday 3 October, and Friday 12 October you came to work smelling heavily of alcohol.' She paused, looked down for a second at the papers in her hand, and took a deep breath. 'And that on certain other days you came back from lunch and behaved as though you were drunk.' She paused again for a moment. 'I'm afraid we can't tolerate that.'

~~~

Gary left Ritzler later that day.

~~~

MOHAMED 'JIMMY' ALI – known as Jimmy to his friends and his sister – heard the big, studded, wooden door of Pentonville prison slam closed behind him. He'd just served eighteen months of a three-year sentence for drug dealing. His good behaviour had earned him remission.

I'm never going back inside that shithole, he vowed, and headed off down Caledonian Road. He was due to meet his sister, with reluctance, in The Hemingford Arms. He remembered making the same promise to himself after his previous spell inside.

I mean it this time.

Jimmy's family fled from Somalia to London in the late eighties, when he was five. Shortly after he started secondary school, his father, whom he'd admired and looked up to, died. He'd been devastated. He blamed his mother for his father's death, and rebelled at all authority. At school he mixed with the other boys from single-parent families with absent fathers. He started to become involved with them in petty crime. When his mother passed away on his sixteenth birthday, he dropped out of school and renamed himself Jimmy. After a few months with no work and no money, he joined up with a small, drug-dealing gang. He earned enough to pay the rent and see that his grandmother was okay until she died a year later.

'Hi.' Jimmy found Sahra, his sister, sitting alone in the garden. He noticed she'd changed her hairstyle since he'd last seen her. He wasn't sure if he liked it. She stubbed out her cigarette and stood up to greet him. He thought she seemed nervous.

'It's good to see you, Jimmy.' She leant forward, and gave her brother a quick peck on the cheek.

'So what's this all about? Reconciliation, your guilt? Some'ing like that?' Jimmy asked, towering over his sister's petite frame. He was furious. He had a grievance with his sister and wanted to deal with it. He'd only agreed to meet with her after the prison prerelease team had pressed him to do so. As a routine, they always pushed offenders who'd served their sentences to meet up with family or friends. That way, most of them found immediate accommodation.

'You cross with me?'

'What you think? Been locked up in that hellhole for the last eighteen bleeding months and didn't hear a peep from you. Never answered my calls, letters, nothing. What's wrong with you? Of course I'm angry.' He stopped and rubbed his right hand across his mouth a few times. 'I thought you were dead. That's what I thought. I had to ask the screws to check you out. What the hell?' Jimmy turned away and scratched his shaved head. The early spring sun shone on his brown-skinned arm.

'It wasn't my fault. Look, go get us both a drink.' Sahra took hold of Jimmy's arm. She held out a twenty-pound note. 'I'll explain when you...'

'I don't want a drink and don't want to listen to your excuses. I'm your brother. Don't you know that?'

Jimmy looked into Sahra's deep-brown eyes. He'd become incensed. Sahra was his next of kin and hadn't visited or tried to contact him in any way while he'd been inside. He became so worried he asked the prison staff to check on her. After they told him she was alive and living in London, he become depressed and despondent, unable to comprehend why his sister, who'd he'd always believed was his soul mate and someone he could rely on, had suddenly disowned him.

Both of them stood. Sahra stared at Jimmy's angry and troubled face. 'Please, Jimmy. Get us a drink. Then we can talk. People are looking at us.'

Jimmy returned five minutes later with a pint of beer and a glass of white wine. Sahra had found a table under a tree in a quiet corner of the garden. He plonked her drink down, spilling some of her wine in the process. He took a slurp from his drink and sat and faced her.

'Go on, then. It had better be good.'

Sahra leant down and pulled up two carrier bags. She held them out for Jimmy.

'What's this?'

'Stuff you'll need. A phone, some money, clothes, a few other bits and pieces.'

Jimmy looked away. 'Come on. Tell me.'

'I need a ciggy. Do you mind?'

Jimmy nodded. 'Don't bother me. Get on with it.'

Sahra lit up and inhaled. She blew out the smoke then took a large sip from her glass and looked at her brother.

'I'm married, Jimmy.'

15

'You bleeding what? You got married without telling me.' Jimmy jumped up. His expression changed. His head jerked towards Sahra. His eyes seemed to grow bigger. He couldn't believe what he'd heard.

'Who to?'

Sahra looked up. She seemed nervous. 'Steve.'

'You what! That candy-ass white trash who called me and my mates low-life black scum?

'I ain't putting up with anymore of this shit. I'm out.' Jimmy turned and stormed out of the pub without saying another word.

~~~

Six months after Jimmy had left prison he'd become desperate. He'd kept clear of drug dealing, but finding work had been difficult. The jobs he did get had been sparse and sporadic. He shared a room in Stockwell with another ex-con. One night he was sitting alone in the room wondering what to do next. He picked up a book he'd been given by another inmate in prison. He opened it at page thirty, where he'd left off. A torn, dirty card he'd used as a bookmark fell out and dropped to the floor. He picked it up and stared at the details.

THE MORNING TIMES
Harry Fingle
Senior Reporter
Morning Times House, 21 Pennington Street, London, E98 1XY
020 6642 5000
07786 567043

'Hello, Harry. Remember me? It's Jimmy Ali. Can you call me when you get a moment? My number is 07976 602498.'

~~~

ED JAMES saw his opportunity and pulled out from behind the large van where he'd been hiding. He overtook it, and pulled in behind the navy Fiat Punto. He was driving his blacked-out BMW M3 convertible, and had tailed the Fiat for some time, waiting for the right moment. He travelled on a straight, single-carriageway road, with no other cars around apart from the Fiat and the van. The Fiat moved at about 80 mph. If he kept up with it, the two cars would leave the van behind in no time. The weather conditions were perfect; heavy rain after a dry spell. The road would be slippery. Not the sort of surface on which to suddenly push down hard on the brake pedal. He kept close to the rear of the Fiat. In the distance, he saw a fully laden car transporter coming towards them at speed on the other side of the road.

'Bloody marvellous,' he whispered and thought he couldn't have asked for better.

He guessed the transporter was about a minute away. When it neared him, he changed down to third gear, swerved out and drove on the wrong side of the road towards it. The driver flashed him several times. Ed ignored him and carried on. As they closed, Ed saw the look of panic on the lorry driver's face. Ed accelerated hard. His speedometer touched 120 mph. He edged in front of the Fiat and passed it quickly. He flipped the steering wheel to the left and pulled hard across the front of the Fiat, then straightened up and accelerated away. He hit nearly 130 mph.

In his rear mirror he saw the Fiat skid. It overturned and crashed sideways into the front of the lorry. Ed slowed to see the lorry slice through the Fiat and crash into the oncoming van that he'd hidden behind earlier. The pileup was massive.

Job done. He changed down a gear and accelerated away.

~~~

Harry Fingle was preparing his supper when his phone rang. He put down the wooden spoon he'd used to stir the tomato sauce. He turned off the gas under the pan of pasta, and went to answer the call.

'Hello.'

'Is that you, Harry? It's Clare.'

Bloody hell. This will be important, Harry thought. Clare was married to his brother, Joe. He didn't have a good relationship with either of them. They rarely spoke.

'Yeah, it's me. What's up?'

'Joe was killed today in a car accident. It was awful, Harry. I can't tell you how awful.' Clare broke down in tears.

Chapter Two

There had been no lovers in Amie's life in the twelve months since Harry had walked out on her. She'd immersed herself in her work as a language tutor at the University of London, where she taught Japanese and Chinese. As well as fulfilling her contractual obligations, she'd taken on extra tuition for many students, volunteered to stand in when other tutors were off sick or unable to take a lesson and joined a drama society. She been out on a few dates and entered into the university social activity, but had not struck up a relationship with anyone. She'd flown back once to Hong Kong to see her folks who'd been stunned by Harry's uncharacteristic behaviour.

She opened the front door of her ground-floor flat in Ealing and froze.

'Hello. Can I come in?'

Amie stood and stared. Her mind and body had become disconnected in an odd way. She felt unable to say or do anything. She hadn't seen or heard from Harry since the court case. She'd thought about him plenty, and had even considered calling him on one or two occasions, but had passed on the idea. Now, in the murky dusk, he stood on her doorstep, no more than a metre away.

'Hi,' she managed, mesmerised by the pouring rain that had drenched the leather jacket she'd bought him for his last-but-one birthday.

He smiled in the way he'd always done. 'It's bloody wet out here. May I?'

'Yes, of course. Come in.' Amie stepped to one side for Harry to squeeze past. She didn't notice the wet splodges forming on the carpet, or the leaves that blew in with him. 'You could have warned me.'

'I'm sorry. I had to see you.' He looked around the small hall. His wet jacket dangled from his left hand. 'Can I put this somewhere?'

There was much Amie wanted to say and ask, but she held back for fear of sounding stupid. Harry's sudden appearance had unsettled her. She sensed a mood of urgency about him and, for the moment, would let him take the lead. She followed him down the hall with her fingers tucked into the top of her jeans' pockets.

He looked around the small kitchen. 'Hope I'm not disturbing you?' he inquired. He'd noticed the lettuce leaves and half-cut pepper sitting on the chopping board.

'Not really. I'd been preparing some supper. Can I get you something? Tea, coffee, something stronger?' They faced each other. Harry stood about sixteen or seventeen centimetres taller than Amie.

She remembered how she'd always had to look up at him.

'Tea would be nice. Mind if I talk while you fix it?'

'Go ahead.' Amie turned away. She had no idea what he was about to say.

She listened while he told her about the sudden death of his brother, Joe, in the road accident, how the funeral had been strange and difficult, and his surprise when his sister-in-law asked him to deal with Joe's estate.

'And that's why I'm here.'

They sat around the wooden table in the kitchen. Both clasped their hands around their mugs of tea. Amie looked down at her drink and swirled it around. He'd come for a reason and she began to think it was not just to see her. 'You going to tell me, then?'

Harry reached into his pocket and pulled out a memory stick and flashed it at Amie. 'Clare asked me to go through all the files on Joe's PC in case there was anything important. I came across these.' He waved the memory stick around. 'One's named "ccc.doc". The rest are in Chinese.'

Amie brushed her hand through her dark, black hair and touched her forehead. She felt upset.

'I get it.' She snatched the memory stick from Harry's hand and headed towards her laptop, which sat in the corner of the room. She didn't want him to see the expression on her face or the wetness she felt in her eyes. 'So you want a translator, then.'

~~~

On Sunday morning, Ed James finished the last of his press-ups. He took several seconds to lower himself onto the beech-wood floor of his bedroom. He lay flat on his stomach and took a few deliberate, slow breaths before he rose to his feet and pulled a white T-shirt over his taut chest. He'd just completed his regular morning exercise routine.

He wandered over to the sliding-glass window, and looked out at South Quay and the few people walking around Canary Wharf. He checked his watch. It was eleven-thirty. In an hour's time he'd arranged to meet his long-term girlfriend for lunch. He needed to be ready and turned to walk back to the kitchen.

'How you doing?' he said to the young, blonde girl, dressed in a short bathrobe, who sat on one of the high stools around his granite-topped breakfast bar. He spoke with an East London accent, occasionally missing an h here and there.

'Good. How about you? Want some OJ?' she replied, holding a

carton of Tropicana in her hand.

'Just 'alf a glass. I'm in a bit of a hurry. Got a business partner coming round here soon. I need to shower.'

'You want me out, I suppose.' The blonde put her left hand up to Ed's cropped grey hair and slid it to the back of his head. 'That's a shame. I was hoping to stay all day. I understand, my love.' She pulled Ed's head towards hers. They kissed for several seconds.

'I'll go and dress, and get my stuff together.'

Ed saw the girl off twenty minutes later. He promised he'd call her soon to arrange a longer weekend. She was one of several girls he slept with to top up his insatiable appetite for sex. Carla, his regular, Italian girlfriend of several years, had no idea about his philandering. She was a flight attendant for Virgin Atlantic and frequently stayed away. They didn't live together, but she often slept over at his apartment. On that Sunday, she was going to work immediately after they had lunch. He'd have time to clear away the traces of his cheating before she returned the following weekend.

He showered and dabbed himself with Hugo Boss aftershave. He pulled on a pair of black, Ralph Lauren slacks and a black shirt and took out a beige, Armani jacket from his wardrobe and left it on his bed. He was ready by twelve. There was time to have a quick look at the paper, he thought, and picked up the *Sunday Mirror*. His phone rang. It was someone he needed to talk to.

'What do you want?' he said in a brusque manner.

'Got another job for you, connected to the last one. Need to meet you.'

'You haven't paid me yet.'

'Don't worry. I've got it. Give it to you when we meet. Tomorrow night at ten. Same place as last time. Okay?'

'Look, mate. Listen to me. If you don't 'ave the dough it's no deal, and you'll wish you'd never met me. Understand? Don't mess with me.'

'It's okay. I've got it. Will you be there?'

'I'll be there to pick up my money. I'm not agreeing to anything new until I've told you how much I want. It'll be more than last time because you've screwed me around. Get it?'

Ed switched his phone off.

~~~

After closing the door after Harry left, Amie sat down on the sofa in her small living room and cried. *Fuck you, Harry Fingle. I still love you.*

When they'd split a year earlier she'd been devastated. She'd been unable to function for some weeks. Eventually, to rid Harry from her thoughts, she decided to work all hours possible. It had worked somewhat. Exhaustion and tiredness dulled the awful loss and regret she'd felt. Her guilt in not pressing Harry to talk about his difficult childhood and the abuse he'd suffered from his stepfather diminished. No longer did she feel any responsibility for the breakup.

But she had missed him more than she could have imagined. The end of the day was the worst. It was the time, when she'd been with Harry, which she'd most looked forward to. They'd get home, have a drink and then cook together while they talked about each other's day. Sometimes they'd meet up with a few friends or go out for a meal or a movie.

He'd left a huge hole. Yet, in the weeks prior to his unannounced visit, she'd begun to feel she'd gained some control back in her life. She even considered starting up a relationship with someone else. But after Harry's unexpected visit, she was confused: her emotions in turmoil yet again.

~~~

Harry dismounted his bike and took it into the hall of his house on Marlborough Road, Chiswick. It was the house he'd lived in with Amie. He owned it. He'd bought it before they became a couple. When they parted, straight after the court case, he went away for a couple of weeks. He sent Amie an e-mail asking her if she could move her stuff out of the house before he returned. He offered her some money for the things in the house they'd bought together. She didn't reply, but removed most of her belongings by the time he came home.

~~~

Four years earlier, when Harry was thirty-three and a war correspondent in Afghanistan, he witnessed, firsthand, the violent death of a close friend in an assault operation on the Taliban. It wasn't the first time he'd experienced war's brutal fatalities. He'd covered both the Iraq and Afghanistan invasions, but that particular incident had left a deep and painful mark on him, so much so that he asked never to cover a military conflict again. His editor at the time, an admirer of Harry's journalistic skills, was sympathetic and moved him on to other projects. Harry was grateful and believed he'd never be so emotionally drained as he was in Afghanistan. It came as a shock when his trial affected him the way it did.

It left him cold. He felt empty of any emotion or feeling, unable to function as a normal human being. He knew all along he was innocent and the charges laid against him were false, manufactured by someone who wanted him to go to prison and be out of the way. Nevertheless, towards the end of the four-week ordeal, he started to think he could have been guilty. He'd been abused by his stepfather and still carried the mental scars. In moments of irrationality, he believed he might easily have slipped into the same behaviour. When the jury found him not guilty, he was so stunned he couldn't walk free of the dock. He asked to go back down to a cell to settle his thoughts.

It was then he decided he had to split with Amie. It was only fair. He found he had no feelings for her at all, as though the past had been wiped away. If they stayed together she would suffer more and be exposed to his aloof and distant self. He was incapable of loving her the way he knew he'd done before. And so he decided to end it the way he did. He spent the next year alone, working all hours, socialising little, and becoming introverted. His brother's mysterious death shook him out of his stupor and forced him to engage with the outside world again.

~~~

Once inside his house, he hung the wet, leather jacket he'd worn to Amie's on the back of a stool in his kitchen and called up Clare, his sister-in-law.

'Hi, Clare. Sorry to bother you, but you know that computer file of Joe's I found. The one named "ccc.doc".'

'Yes. What about it?' Clare answered. She sounded disinterested.

'Do you know what Joe was working on?'

'Why?'

'The file was encrypted and the document with it was in Chinese, which Amie translated, but it was little use.'

'I thought you two had split.'

'Yeah, yeah. We have, but she just did me a favour.'

'Do I need to know any of this? Joe's dead and frankly I couldn't give a toss. And, if you want to know, I really couldn't give a toss about you, either. If you want my opinion, I think you were lucky being acquitted. Joe and I always had our doubts about you.'

The line went dead. Clare had cut Harry off.

Taken aback, Harry rubbed his stubbly chin, put his phone in his pocket, and made for his drinks cupboard. He wasn't a regular drinker, but always had a small stock of wine and spirits. At the back of the cupboard, where the bottles were kept, he caught sight of a half-empty bottle of Ardbeg malt whisky, and reached in for it. He poured a large slug into one of the cut-glass tumblers Amie had given him. He took it into his sitting room, put on some music, and dropped onto the sofa with his legs up in front of him.

Mmm, that's better, he thought as the whisky took effect, and his mind returned to his sister-in-law's erratic comments and unhelpful attitude. At first he blamed his brother's death for her odd behaviour, but after a while he wondered if the CCC file was connected in some way.

His phone rang. He reached into his pocket for it and looked at the screen. 'Hi, Amie. I was going to call and thank you for your help and the supper. I was too preoccupied with the file stuff to say thanks properly. Sorry.'

'That's okay. It was good to see you again. Come round again anytime. Listen. I've been studying the backup document again. I've found out quite a lot more.'

'Go on.' Harry sat up.

'Do you know what Joe did: work, I mean?'

'Huh. I just tried to find that out from Clare. She told me to piss off.'

'Don't worry about her. She's a bitch. Did you tell me once that Joe was a scientist?'

'Yes, he was. He worked for Vantiche, the big drug company. That's as much as I know. Why?'

'Well. This file is about a major, new drug. Sounds like something that will be a cure for a fatal disease, widespread in some of the poorest parts of the world. But I can't find out anymore. The file, as you know, is encrypted.'

Harry rubbed his chin again. He was silent, thinking about what Amie had said.

'Harry. You still there?

'Yeah. I was thinking. It's all strange.'

'Why?'

Harry sat back in the chair. He looked ahead and held the phone to his ear. 'Because what I didn't tell you earlier is that the police are not entirely sure Joe's death was an accident. The driver of a van, who survived but lost both his legs, has said that he thought he saw another vehicle swerve deliberately in front of Joe's car and then speed away.'

'My God. That's awful, quite scary.' Amie paused. 'What're you doing to do?'

'Dig around a bit and investigate. That's my job. You know that.'

Amie didn't respond.

23

'You still there, Amie?'

'Yes, I'm here.' Amie was then silent for a moment before saying, 'Don't do anything silly, will you?'

'Would I? You know me.'

'Yes I do.' Amie paused again for several seconds. 'And I still...'

'No, Amie. Don't. It was great seeing you, but don't try to go back. Thanks for your help. I'll be in touch.'

'Harry.' Amie sounded indignant. 'Don't jump down my throat. I wasn't trying to go back. I just wanted to say I don't want you to come to any harm.' Amie paused. 'And anytime you want any more help, just call.' She moved the phone away from her ear for a split second and gazed at it. Tears had started to roll down her cheeks.

'Take care, Harry.'

~~~

A year after Gary Lester had been fired from Ritzler, he received a call from Margaret Hudson. It wasn't the first call she'd made since he'd left. She'd called several times to see how he was getting along with Alcoholics Anonymous. This time she called with some good news. She knew he'd been sober for several months and contacted him to offer some work on a consultancy basis. Margaret asked him to go and see Alex Goad, the chief executive, at nine the following morning.

~~~

ALEX GOAD was fifty. He'd been in the pharmaceutical industry since he graduated with a first-class honours' degree in science from Cambridge. He was ambitious, and had worked for several drug companies before being headhunted to join Ritzler when he was forty-five. He was considered to be good at his job, with a reputation for decisiveness and strong leadership.

'Good to see you, Gary. Margaret tells me you're doing fine,' he said as Gary Lester entered his office and took a seat. Gary wore a new, navy suit and an open- neck, cream shirt. He'd bought both items immediately after Margaret's call. All his other suits felt too tight on him.

'That's right.' Gary nodded. He felt nervous, a little unsure, and tried his hardest to stay calm and sound measured in his responses. He needed the job badly, and wanted to make a good impression.

'Not drinking, I understand?'

'Yep. Haven't touched a drop for five months and don't want to.'

Alex pushed a cup of coffee across the large, square, wooden table in front of them both and looked up and directly into Gary's eyes.

'Okay. Let's not hang around. This is a big one, Gary. We'll ask you to do it on a consultancy basis to start with and see how it goes. Margaret will sort out the details with you. Do you want to do it?'

'I don't know what it is.'

'I'm coming to that.' Alex covered his mouth for a few seconds with his right hand.

'Gary?'

'Yes.' Gary was eager to find out what Alex wanted him to do.

Alex glanced around the room and then focused again on Gary. 'I'm told your computer-security skills are excellent. Better than anyone else we have. Is that so?'

'You mean, am I good hacker? You know I am. That's what I did before. As far as I know, you don't have any other hackers in the business.'

Alex Goad's expression remained deadpan. He stood up and walked around his desk and sat down in his chair. He looked across at Gary.

'Could you hack into Vantiche, our biggest competitor's system?'

Gary was puzzled. He wasn't sure why Alex asked him the question.

'Of course I can. I did it for you before, all the time.'

Alex smiled. He rose and walked towards where Gary sat. He put out his hand for Gary to shake. 'Good. I just needed to check. You're hired. You'll report directly to me.' He stopped, and turned to face the door to his office. He pointed to a sliding-glass door on the back wall. 'There's a small office behind that door. It's yours so you're close to me. We'll set you up with whatever you need. I want you to start this afternoon.'

~~~

Two weeks after the sudden, traumatic death of her husband, Clare Fingle decided the time had come for her to return to work. Joe and she had lived in a large house alongside the Thames at Marlow. She could walk from there to her office. On Friday 1 October, paying no attention to the heavy rain and strong wind, she set off at eight along her usual route. The towpath was deserted. She was the only person who braved the atrocious weather. Well wrapped up, she hurried along the muddy track. She wanted to be in early to begin to pick up the pieces from where she'd left off before Joe's death.

She thought about her brother-in-law, Harry, and the call he'd made to her the previous evening. It wasn't her rudeness to him or that she'd put the phone down that worried her. It was her lies; blurted out on the spur of the moment to cause harm and upset. Joe had never told her that there was anything strange or inappropriate about Harry, and she had no reason at all to believe he should have been found guilty. She'd just made it all up to ease her own failings.

Harry's mention of the CCC file had triggered her outburst. She'd had no idea that Joe had brought it home from his office, or that he'd put a copy on his home PC. If she'd known, she would never have asked Harry to check Joe's computer. Not in a million years. *Now there'll be trouble*, she thought, unaware of the cyclist who had passed her, or that he had stopped a little ways down the path and turned in her direction and started to peddle hard towards her. The sudden whooshing noise as his bike neared made her look up and gasp. He seemed to be almost on top of her. His face was covered with a scarf. He had a hood around his head.

'Look out. You're going to hit me,' she shouted.

The bike came straight at her and knocked her headlong into the Thames. It flowed fast that morning towards the big weir that sluiced and directed the waters to cascade under Marlow Bridge. She disappeared, broke the surface a few seconds later, flung her hands around, and shouted out. No one heard her. Now and again the top of her shiny, waterproof hat appeared as the powerful current dragged her towards the fast-flowing weir. Only one person saw her – the lone cyclist. He watched from behind a tree some distance away. He waited until she was engulfed and no longer appeared, and then cycled away at speed.

Chapter Three

Kate Fisher wiped her fingers on her paint-stained apron. She dropped the handle of her brush into the pot where she kept all the other ones, and stood back to examine her work. She had painted all her life: from her early childhood through both primary and secondary school, and at university. She'd graduated with a fine-art degree from The Slade School of Art. After she broke up so acrimoniously with her husband, Ian, following Jack's death, she found painting to be a way of taking her mind off the almost-continuous pain and upset she was going through.

Jack had been stabbed the night he ran from his home after rowing with his parents over his suspension from school. The next day the police came and told Ian and Kate that he'd died. They rowed loudly and continuously all that day, sometimes resorting to violence. Each blamed the other for their son's death. They kept up their hostility until both became so tired and upset that they just walked away and slept in different rooms.

After Jack's funeral, they agreed to divorce. Kate left the same day to stay with a friend until she'd found somewhere to live. Two weeks later, she went back to Ritzler to see Alex Goad, and handed in her notice. He was sympathetic, but pleaded with her to stay in touch to do some occasional consultancy work. Her low emotional threshold, and desire not to be subjected to a bout of Alex's well-known persuasive powers, influenced her agreement to his proposal. She hoped he wouldn't call her.

She picked up another brush, and filled it with some of the blue she'd mixed to make the sky more vivid and intense: dabbing and touching here and there to create the effect she wanted. She stopped. Somebody had rung her doorbell.

Shit. Who the hell's that?

The sight of two police officers – one male – one female – standing outside her front door made her shiver. As she approached, she could see them clearly through the four glass panels that formed the top half of the door. She thought back to the time when they'd come and told Ian and her about Jack's death.

She held the edge of the opened door in her left hand and peered through the gap. 'What is it?'

They left after ten minutes. She'd told them she wanted to be alone. They came to tell her that her sister Clare had been drowned in the Thames at Marlow. Clare and Kate didn't have a good relationship, but her sister's sudden death in such a horrific way, and just after Clare's husband had been killed, was too much. The police told her that Clare's body had been dragged through the weir and had been seen bobbing in the water under Marlow bridge by a walker. Kate didn't return to her painting.

~~~

Alex Goad had only one meeting planned for the morning of 14 October. It was with Kate. She'd agreed to work on a special project, and he'd come in on a day off to see her. It would be the first time he'd met with her for just over a year. He looked forward to it. Eleven years earlier, when she'd been at university, she did a three-month internship with the pharmaceutical company he worked for at the time. They'd had a torrid affair. It lasted only a few months. Kate found out he was married and blew him out. Her post-affair histrionics became legendary within the company.

When Alex joined Ritzler as chief executive and found that Kate was the head of the development department, he'd expected trouble. But he was surprised. Kate's behaviour and work ethic were beyond fault and highly professional. Within a year he promoted her to commercial director. Neither spoke of the past, nor did he believe anybody in Ritzler knew about it.

She was due at ten. Five minutes earlier, he had visited the private bathroom adjacent to his office and splashed cologne on his face, and checked that his shirt sat tidily within his jacket. He didn't wear a tie.

He smiled when he saw her sitting on one of the reception chairs just outside his office with her grey cardigan draped over one of the chair's arms. 'Kate. It's good to see you.' He moved towards her with open arms.

The glass door to Gary Lester's office slid open. 'Alex,' Gary yelled with his laptop cradled in his hands. He rushed up to where Kate and Alex greeted each other.

'Sorry to butt in. I must see you.'

Hi, Gary,' Kate said as she turned to smile at him. 'Great to see you back.'

'And you,' Gary said. He smiled back. 'How's things?'

'They're fine.' Kate glanced at Alex and Gary. 'Why don't I just sit here and let you two get on with whatever it is that's so urgent. I've plenty of time.'

'You sure?' Alex said.

'Sure.' Kate smiled and nodded. She turned and walked back to the seat where she'd been sitting and picked up a magazine.

Minutes later Alex and Gary sat around Gary's laptop. He showed Alex the entire internal IT network of Vantiche Pharmaceuticals, Ritzler's biggest rival. Gary navigated between employees' work files, departmental reports, and individuals' incoming and outgoing e-mail messages. He highlighted sales data on existing drugs and status reports on new drugs in the development stage. He showed Alex the drop-down menu that indexed medicines, personnel, and Vantiche's latest products.

'Here we are. This is the CCC file.' Gary pointed with the computer's cursor. He looked up at Alex. 'Look. It's encrypted.'

'So? Break the code.' Alex glared at Gary. 'Is that all you came to show me?'

Unruffled by Alex's obvious irritation at being interrupted, and the lack of any praise for what he'd done, Gary closed down the Vantiche network and brought up a personal e-mail inbox.

'This,' Gary said with confidence, 'is Harry Fingle's e-mail inbox.'

'So? Who's he?'

'Isn't he the brother of Joe Fingle, the scientist who worked for Vantiche who was killed in a horrific car accident?' Gary turned to look at Alex.

Alex didn't answer. He'd looked up from the screen and gazed out of the window.

'Did you know his wife was drowned in the Thames at Marlow a couple of weeks back?' Gary asked.

'My God. No. How awful.' Alex glanced at Gary and then looked at his watch. 'How do you know?'

'I read it in the paper.'

'That's tragic. I don't think they had any children.' Alex turned his attention back to the screen. 'Go on. What's the significance?'

'Look. Read this.' Gary scrolled down through Harry's inbox until he came to an e-mail from Amie. 'Harry Fingle has the CCC file.'

~~~

Kate Fisher eventually saw Alex two hours later than planned. After he'd finished with Gary, he apologised to Kate again and said he needed to make some calls and would she mind coming back later. Kate told him she had things to do and agreed to return at noon.

'How long's Gary been back working for you?' she asked as she closed Alex's office door.

'Oh, he's just back doing a special project.' Alex filled the two glasses on his table with mineral water and placed one in front of Kate

29

while, with his other hand, he nudged the white plate full of smoked-salmon sandwiches towards her. 'Help yourself.'

'Thanks,' Kate said. She straightened the skirt of her black, sleeveless dress that hugged her tall, slim figure. It made her blonde, spiky hair and striking face more noticeable.

'What's this all about?' Kate picked up one of the small sandwiches and took a bite, her eyes fixed on Alex. She waited for his reply.

When Alex had called Kate a couple of days earlier, he'd used the death of her sister and brother-in-law as the reason for his call. He'd said he wanted to express his sympathy. 'It was terrible, Alex, but I can't be a hypocrite,' she'd replied. 'You know I didn't get on with either of them. Thanks for calling, but please leave it. I've had enough death talk to last me.'

Alex had seized on the opportunity, and quickly changed the subject to ask her if she wanted to work on a special project for him. She agreed to come in and discuss it. After Clare's death she had decided to immerse herself in her painting. With no salary, the money from whatever Alex wanted her to do would come in handy.

'I want you to keep an eye on Harry Fingle. You're sort of family. I...'

Kate stopped eating. She looked aghast. She held the half-eaten sandwich in her hand and stared at Alex. 'What're you on about? I hardly know him. He's not family.'

'Well he's your sister's husband's brother, isn't he?'

Kate dumped the remainder of the sandwich on the plate. She glared at Alex. 'They're both dead. I'm not related to him in anyway. What is this?'

Alex shuffled a little in his seat. He looked Kate in the eyes. 'You know him, surely?'

'Hardly. I met him at their wedding and on one or two other occasions.' She stopped and put a finger up to one of her eyes and brushed away a small tear. 'He came to Jack's funeral and was very nice to me. It was just after he'd been acquitted from that awful, trumped-up court case against him. I thought it good of him to have bothered. He'd said it was because he vaguely knew me and felt so sorry for parents of youngsters caught up in the stabbing epidemic.'

'There you are, just your opening. You can call him and find some way to strike a friendship.' Alex smiled in a smutty way. 'You know what I mean.'

Kate leapt to her feet. She picked up her handbag and looked down at Alex. 'What the hell? I can't believe you said that! What's got into you? Are you insane? You can't believe I'd do that, can you?' She turned and walked quickly towards the door.

'Think about it. It'll be good money.'

'No way. Get someone else to do your dirty work.'

~~~

Harry mooched around his kitchen. He'd just come back from an early visit to his gym, and was thinking what to have for a quick breakfast. He'd been called for a meeting with Philip Stacey, his boss and the editor of *The Morning News*. He wondered what it was about. A new assignment, he guessed, after he'd been taken off the rent-boy investigation so abruptly. They'd said they wanted a newly appointed female journalist to put a different slant on it. Since then, three weeks earlier, he had worked on a few small assignments: growing obesity, illegal sale of fireworks, and overcharging in health clubs. He hoped Philip would give him an interesting project, one that would fully involve him.

But the CCC file concerned him most. Amie and he were sure it linked to a groundbreaking drug, possibly even the formula for the drug itself. He felt certain his brother and sister-in-law's deaths were no accidents, and suspected they were connected. His experience and instincts told him all was not as it seemed and powerful organisations were at work. He decided to talk to Philip about it. He'd ask him if the newspaper would take it up and allow him to investigate.

Harry heard the sound of his mail dropping through his letter box. He went to collect it, and sifted through the envelopes as he walked back down his hall. A couple of handwritten ones caught his attention. Once back in the kitchen, he pushed his half-eaten toast and mug to one side and opened one of them. It was from two friends of Joe and Clare. They'd written to express their sympathy. 'So sudden and so close,' they'd said.

That's kind, he thought. He tossed the letter to one side and checked his watch. If he was going to make his meeting with Philip on time, he needed to leave. He reached for his jacket. The other letter would be similar, he guessed. He figured he could read it later, when he came home, and he made for his front door. Halfway down the hall he stopped. He turned, dashed back to the kitchen, scanned to the bottom of the opened letter, and read the last few lines again.

'Please convey our sympathy and best wishes to Clare's sister, Kate. She must be devastated. It must be so awful for her after the tragic death of her son last year. We wanted to tell her ourselves, but she wasn't at the funeral and we don't have her address.'

Why wasn't she there? Harry asked himself.

~~~

The previous evening, as Richard Morecombe had left the theatre with his wife and another couple, Alex Goad had called him. He'd said he needed to see Richard urgently. Richard had to excuse himself from the dinner arrangements. He left his blonde wife Sam – ten years his junior – to go alone to the other couple's house for supper. Sam was a TV presenter on one of the morning shows and didn't want to hang around waiting for Richard. She told him she'd spend the night at their friends' house and go directly from there to the TV studio in the morning.

Her plan pleased Richard. Although he knew his discussion with Alex would be short, he didn't tell Sam. Her absence gave him the opportunity for which he'd longed for some time. After he'd left Alex at The Institute of Directors' Club in Pall Mall, he made two calls. One was to Philip Stacey, the editor of *The Morning News*: the second call was to a man he knew only as Sanjay.

'That you, Sanjay?' he said, with a touch of urgency.

'Hello, Mr Morecombe. What can I do for you tonight?'

'Who's available?' Richard waited. He hoped Sanjay's reply would be what he wanted.

'It's quiet tonight. You can take your pick. Who do you want?'

Richard felt himself becoming aroused. 'Good. Is Ramiro there? And, emm, Felipo?'

'They're both here. Shall I send them round?'

~~~

Harry bounded up the stairs to Philip's office. He never used the lifts. He tried to keep himself fit, and would always use stairs. Philip was more than a boss to Harry. They'd known each other for some time, and played squash together and often socialised. Before Harry's trial, Philip and his wife and Amie and Harry would often eat together at each other's homes. Philip had been instrumental in Harry's acquittal. When Harry had been charged with being in possession of indecent images of children, he'd been working on an investigation for the newspaper on paedophiles in high places. Philip had made that clear to the judge and jury.

Harry leapt off the top step, swung off the brass handrail, and bounced into Philip's office. He came to an abrupt halt. Philip wasn't there. Sitting in Philip's chair was John Edwards, the finance director, generally regarded as the dullest, greyest man in the organisation. Someone Harry and the crowd he hung around with avoided at all costs.

'Good morning, Harry. Philip has left the company. I'm acting editor until Richard Morecombe appoints a new one.' John Edwards motioned with his hand to the one empty chair in front of Philip's desk. 'Take a seat.'

'What're you on about? Philip's left the paper? Why? What the hell? Are you crazy?' Harry stood. He hadn't moved from the spot where he'd first entered the office.

'No. I'm not crazy. And if you don't mind, I'd prefer less of the emotion and a more cool and rational understanding of what I have to say to you.' John Edwards undid the middle button of his jacket. He fiddled with his tie and looked down at a single sheet of white paper sitting on top of the desk.

Harry, who wore a suit jacket over jeans and an open-neck shirt, felt stunned. Philip had been the editor for three years, in which time the circulation of *The Morning News* had become the highest among the quality papers. Philip had been given much of the credit. He was held in high regard by the news media circle. His name had been bandied around as a potential editor of *This Week's World*, the internationally renowned weekly news and current-affairs journal.

'This is crazy. What's the explanation? Why has Philip left in such a hurry? Is he ill, a family problem or something?'

Edwards shuffled in his seat and looked uncomfortable. 'I can't say.' He looked down at the sheet of paper on the desk and then up at Harry.

'I've been asked to speak with you about your employment with The Morning News Newspaper Group.'

'What about it?' Harry snapped. He was dazed at Edwards's unbelievable coldness and his refusal to offer any explanation for Philip's sudden disappearance.

'I'm afraid the company is terminating your employment forthwith. We'll pay you...'

'Fuck off. You little shit. What the hell are you talking about? Are you out of your tiny mind? You stupid...,' Harry stopped. He was aghast. John Edwards had stood up from behind the desk. He held out the white piece of paper that had been sitting on the desktop for Harry to take.

'You'll find all the details in this letter. Now I must go, if you'll excuse me.' Edwards dropped the letter back on the desk and slid it towards Harry. 'Please have your belongings out of the office by midday.'

33

Harry watched as Edwards buttoned up his jacket, then picked up his pen and tucked it into his inside pocket. He started to walk away without giving Harry a single glance.

'You're fucking incredible.' Harry stood in Edwards's way. 'Sit down and start talking sense. You're not going anywhere.'

'I wouldn't be difficult, if I was you. You don't want us to rake around and see what we can dig up amongst all the evidence from your trial, do you?'

Harry became enraged. He stuck his head out and pointed his right index finger at John Edwards so it was no more than a few centimetres from his face.

'That's blackmail. I promise you, you'll regret ever saying that.'

John Edwards ignored Harry. He moved to one side to avoid bumping into him and walked out of the room.

Harry snatched up the letter. He turned around and rushed back down to his own desk, a floor below, grabbed a few things and then left the building immediately. He didn't stop to say good-bye to any of his workmates.

'What's up, Harry? You look angry,' the security guy on the front desk asked as Harry sped past him.

'Dead right. I am angry, very angry. Tell them all up there I'll call.' Harry stormed through the revolving doors, almost crashing into them, and headed straight out to the street.

He arrived home at eight. Amie had called and left a message. She'd heard the news from a girlfriend who'd worked with Harry.

'Harry, this is so wrong. They can't do this to you. Call me. I'll come round straightaway with a bottle of wine and some food.'

The only other message was from Jimmy Ali. It was the second time he'd called Harry since he'd been released from prison. In his message he reminded Harry of the help he'd given him once before, when Harry had done an investigation into the street-drug scene. He'd called to ask if Harry wanted help on anything else. Harry didn't return Amie's call, but he did call Jimmy. He arranged to meet him the next day. After Harry spoke with Jimmy he called Kate Fisher.

Chapter Four

Ed James never knew his parents. He'd been brought up in a children's home, and left school at sixteen with no qualifications. The authorities that ran the home gave him three months to find a job, after which he'd be thrown out on the street to fend for himself. He was physically tough and able to look after himself, and although where he had lived violence and abuse were common, nobody had bothered him. With no affection or attachment to the home, he moved out, with just one bag, on the same day he'd left school.

At first he found it hard. He lived rough on the streets for a month and then teamed up with some addicts involved in petty crime to fund their habits. He never touched drugs, and believed he never would. He tagged along with them to learn their methods and routines, and to share their squat. It wasn't long before he realised he could make more money by going it alone.

Eight weeks after he'd left school, he moved out of the squat and into a disused warehouse, and started up on his own. At first he shoplifted, mugged, stole cars, and broke into houses until he'd made enough money to move into a flat and figure out his future. He decided to steal luxury cars to order. He could earn £5k for a quality, top-of-the-range BMW or Mercedes. He stole one every ten days to two weeks. But after his nineteenth birthday, his run of good luck changed. He had just stolen a black Porsche 911 and was on his way to deliver it to the client when a motorcyclist jumped the lights and careered into the offside of the car. Ed made the wrong decision. He fled from the scene of the accident and was picked up by a nearby patrol car. The judge sentenced him to two years.

Since then, at the age of forty, he'd been to prison on only one other occasion. It was for GBH. He served four years of a six-year sentence. When he came out, he gave up car theft and became a specialist in extortion and contract killing; jobs he believed he could control and execute well. In the five years that preceded his fortieth birthday, he earned several hundreds of thousands of pounds for murder, violent punishment, and the collection of debts. He became feared and regarded as the best in his area of speciality. He owned a pub in London's East End, and used it to launder his criminal earnings.

On the evening of 16 October, Ed was due to meet a man he knew only as Dave in a bar in the Docklands. Ed knew little about Dave, only that he acted as the link to the client – a sort of go-between. Ed never knew who was behind the hit jobs he did, and didn't want to. He would receive a call from Dave, meet up with him to be briefed, and then carry out his own research and devise his plan.

Dave and he were due to meet in their normal place, but on this occasion Ed wanted somewhere quieter. He needed Dave to understand what he was going to tell him.

Ed strode into the bar and up to where Dave sat on his own in a corner. Loud music blasted from the many speakers. The bar appeared busy. Ed zipped up his short leather jacket a little more, and touched the small bulge above his right pocket.

'I don't like it 'ere,' he said as he touched Dave on the shoulder. 'I want somewhere quieter.'

Dave turned his head slightly in Ed's direction. He was overweight and not someone whom Ed would have had any trouble with in a fight, but Ed had never pushed it with him. He learned a long time back to respect people in the business, regardless of their appearance.

'What do y'mean quiet. We've always agreed to 'ave lots of noise, stops people eavesdropping.'

'I mean really quiet, like outside. I've something serious to tell you.'

Dave turned fully to see Ed's face. 'Serious? How serious?'

'Like police serious, mate. Follow me. We'll find a quiet spot outside and talk there.'

A few minutes later, they walked, with Ed leading the way, to the West India Quay, and stopped at the edge. It was 10:00 p.m. and the area was almost deserted. About twenty metres away, a few people walked towards the door of a pizza restaurant. Ed waited until they had gone inside, and placed one hand on the ornamental, wrought-iron balustrade, and turned to wait for Dave. His other hand, tucked inside his jacket, gripped his pistol.

'Come on, tell me then. What's with this police business?' Dave, who looked worried, stopped a few paces in front of Ed.

In less than a second, Ed whipped out his revolver and stuck the barrel into Dave's ample stomach. 'Turn around. One beep and I'll blow your guts out.'

Dave did as he was told. In a well-practised move, Ed pushed Dave onto the balustrade with the gun shoved up against his ribs.

'You won't get away with this. I've contacts you know.'

'We'll see.' Ed pushed a sheet of photos in front of Dave's face. Dave tried to move one of his feet back and behind Ed's foot.

'Argh.' Ed's steel-tipped boot smashed into Dave's left ankle.

'Don't try and be clever, sonny. See that dark, black water down there? If you mess with me, your body will be floating in it. I'm told it's fucking cold at this time of year, not that you'll worry. You'll be dead. Get it?'

Ed manoeuvred himself so his body was pressed hard against Dave, who he'd pushed against the railings. With his free hand, Ed held the photos close up to Dave's eyes so he couldn't avoid seeing them. Dave retched and vomited into the water.

'That's what people look like when they cross me. I keep these pictures to let smartarses like you know they can't get one over me.' Ed pushed the barrel of his gun harder into Dave's ribs. He stuffed the photos back into his pocket, and spun Dave around to face him. He stuck the gun in Dave's stomach again. 'Now. Where's me money?'

Dave's face had turned ghostly white. He sweated and looked terrified. 'I'll 'ave it next week. Promise. Gimme a bit'er time. The client's a bit difficult.'

Ed's free hand shot up to cover Dave's mouth. He jerked his knee hard into Dave's groin. Dave's body buckled. His face twisted and contorted with the pain. Ed released him and let him slump to the ground in a heap, moaning and dribbling. Ed checked to make sure no one was around and leant over. He put his pistol in Dave's ear.

'I warn you. Fuck with me and you'll be another image in my photo collection.

'Next week. No messing.' Ed stood up, kicked Dave hard in the groin, and walked away.

~~~

The morning after Harry had been sacked for no reason from *The Morning News* he woke at seven, as usual, after an unbroken night's sleep. He felt surprised. After the unbelievable events of the previous day, he'd been sure he'd be in for a sleepless night. Grateful for the rest, he stretched his arms, swung his legs over the side of the bed, and thought about the meeting with John Edwards. He remembered the raging anger and the wish for violent revenge that had taken hold of him afterwards. He had wanted to go and find both Edwards and Morecombe and inflict some painful and terrible act of retribution so ghastly that they'd suffer for the rest of their lives. Eventually, he'd figured he was being stupid, out of character, and irrational. He decided to go to his gym, work off his crazy mood, and try to find a reason for his dismissal.

After he filled his mug to the top with a second black coffee, he left his breakfast bowl and the glass he'd used for the orange juice on the worktop and took his notebook and pen to his sitting room. He sat in the big, comfy, square armchair that Amie had bought him after he suffered a long bout of back pain, and opened up his notes. He'd placed his mug on the stripped-pine floorboards next to his bare feet.

Richard Morecombe/Ritzler – the connection?
this ccc file – what is it?
Clare's funeral/Kate Fisher – not there?
Clare – arsy/difficult – why?
today's fiasco – why Edwards? who's driving him ?
dig up the shit – he's fucking joking!!!
who fixed it?

Harry scanned down the list of questions he'd jotted down the previous evening and wondered where to start. The letter John Edwards had given him fell to the floor. It had been tucked in the back of his notebook.

Dear Harry

I know you must be aware of the severe economic downturn and will understand that we have been forced by the circumstances to make certain harsh decisions.

Unfortunately, we have decided that we must make some redundancies. I regret that I have to inform you we are dispensing with your job as a senior reporter and are making you redundant forthwith. In view of your past service with The Morning News, *we will pay you £200,000 as redundancy payment and a goodwill gesture.*

In view of the circumstances and sensitive nature of what you have been working on in the past, I have to tell you that you are obliged, in accepting this arrangement, not to speak to anyone about any of the investigations that you've been involved with. I have to inform you that if you do talk about or inform anyone on any matter concerning the former, you will be in breach of this agreement and The Morning News Newspaper Group will instruct its lawyers to recover the aforementioned sum of money from you.

I wish you all the best in the future.

Please sign at the bottom of this letter indicating your agreement, take a copy for yourself, and return the same to us as soon as possible.

Yours sincerely

John Edwards

Acting Editor
The Morning News

'Bollocks,' Harry said aloud, and tossed the letter onto the floor.

They're trying to buy my silence. They can go to hell. I'm not falling for that. Two hundred thousand pounds, that's four years' salary; they don't have to pay me that much. Do they think I'm mad? It's obvious they're hiding something. I'm bloody well going to find out what it is.

Harry reached down and picked up his coffee. He drained it and picked up his phone, which lay on the floor next to his mug.

'Is that you, Penny?' he said when Penny Stacey, Philip's wife, answered his call. 'Is Philip there?'

Penny didn't answer immediately. For several seconds all Harry could hear was the sound of their two small children shouting at each other and running around the kitchen.

'Harry. Sorry. I was miles away.'

Harry thought Penny sounded strange, almost as though she'd been crying. 'You alright, Penny? You sound a bit upset.'

'No, I'm fine. Just not fully awake yet. Emm, sorry. No he's not here. He's gone out.'

'What? So early? It's only seven. Where's he gone?'

'I'm sorry. I'm not being very helpful. I don't know. He was picked up by a car at six-thirty this morning. He just said he'd be back as usual tonight.'

Harry thought about his next question. 'Has he gone to work?'

'I expect so. I don't really know.'

'I see. Well thanks, Penny. 'Bye then.'

Harry cut off. He made another call.

'Welcome to *The Morning News*. Please listen carefully to the following options and use your keypad to be connected to the extension you require.' Harry pressed to speak to the helpdesk.

'Can you give me the name of your editor, please?'

'We have an acting editor at the moment. His name is John…'

Harry ended the call and went to take a shower. Afterwards, he put on the same pair of jeans he'd worn the day before, pulled on a black T-shirt with a grey, crew-neck jumper over the top, stepped into his navy Converse trainers, and grabbed a canvas jacket from his wardrobe. He ran down the stairs, dropped a piece of bread into the toaster, and filled up his espresso maker. He was due to meet Jimmy Ali in Hammersmith at eight. As Harry's toast popped up he heard the ringtone from his mobile. He looked at the screen. It was Amie.

'Hi. Look, I'm in a bit of a hurry. I've got to go out in a minute to meet someone. Can you call tonight?'

'I called you last night and you didn't even bother to call me back. You don't have to ignore me. I was worried about you. Surely you got my message.'

'Look, I'm really sorry. I wasn't ignoring you. I'd had enough yesterday and just wanted to go to bed. I appreciate your call, but I really do have to go now. Call me tonight.'

'Why don't you call me?'

'Hey, what's this all about? Why are you being difficult?'

'I'm not.' Amie paused. 'I just want to know you're alright, and to be able to talk to you.'

'Thanks. That's kind. I will call you. But I do have to go. I'll speak to you later. Okay?'

'Okay. 'Bye.'

Harry chucked his toast into the bin, switched off his espresso machine, and ran out of his front door.

~~~

Jimmy Ali leant on the handle of a floor mop and looked up at the big clock on the wall above the lifts. He stood in the entrance hall of an office block above Hammersmith tube station. Every morning, between 6:00 and 8:00 a.m., he cleaned the floor, the reception desk, the revolving, glass entrance doors, the lift doors, and the male and female WCs in the vast lobby area. He wasn't paid well and hated the cleaning company, who he believed screwed him. They'd told him if he didn't do the job properly, they could easily find someone to take his place. Since leaving prison, he'd lived in a ramshackle room in Stockwell with another ex-con. After paying his rent and travelling costs, he had little left to live on.

When his roommate told him he had a reliable supply of good-quality, Russian cannabis and would he like to earn a bit by dealing, he'd said no. After two spells in prison, the brutality and dark times had left vivid and painful memories. To risk another and longer period of incarceration would be foolhardy. Whenever he weakened, he'd cast his mind back to the anguished screams and cries that pierced the long nights on a regular basis. Other inmates – not as strong and powerful as he was, and unable to look after themselves – were being attacked or raped by the prisoners who shared their cells. Often, it seemed, the authorities turned a blind eye.

But after a while, his memory faded. He saw the jewellery, clothes, electrical goods, and other consumable items that his flatmate bought, and the good time he enjoyed, and weakened. His resolve broke. He wanted the same, and started to sell marijuana to one or two people until he'd built a lucrative business, one that he depended on.

As he rushed to put away his cleaning stuff, he wondered what

Harry Fingle wanted. He'd agreed to meet him in Starbucks in Hammersmith at ten past eight. He ran out of the building in the hope Harry had something good and he could jack in the cleaning job.

'Good to see you again, Jimmy. Can I get you a coffee?' Harry stood up to meet Jimmy and shook him by the hand. 'You looked rushed.'

Jimmy looked down at his wet tracksuit, his soaked trainers, and the blobs of perspiration on his T-shirt. 'Sorry. I was in a bit of a hurry this morning to finish. I didn't want to keep you waiting.'

'No problem. Relax. Good of you to make it. Coffee?'

~~~

'What do want?' Jimmy asked after they'd spent several minutes catching up.

Harry reached into his pocket and pulled out a newspaper cutting. He unfolded an advert for an office-cleaning company that wanted cleaners for the Ritzler Pharmaceuticals building. He'd found it the previous evening.

Harry knew Richard Morecombe was a director of Ritzler, and that the company was a direct competitor to Vantiche Pharmaceuticals. Joe, Harry's brother, had been working for Vantiche on the CCC file when he'd been killed. Harry figured that someone on the inside of Ritzler could be a smart move. He pushed the cutting over to Jimmy. 'I want you to get that job.'

Jimmy looked bemused and crestfallen. 'Cleaning? That's what I do now.'

Harry looked up. He held a spoonful of froth from his coffee in his hand. 'Not for them, I hope.' He put the spoon in his mouth. 'Here. Let me tell you about it.'

Chapter Five

Kate had converted the back part of the living room of her small, terraced house in Barnes to a studio. The glass-panelled French windows at the end of the room opened out onto a little patio that overlooked the minute garden and the Thames at the bottom. On a clear day, the rays from the early morning sun lightened up the normally grey water, turning it into a view, sometimes so spectacular that it made Kate gasp. The day she expected Harry Fingle was one such day. It was late in October. The sun had risen low in the east, and a mist hovered over bits of the river like puffs of cotton wool. A lone rower pushed upstream. A police riverboat, as it crossed to the other bank, left ripples in the still water. A man and his dog ambled along the river's edge. Elsewhere was empty and eerie.

So stunning and beautiful, Kate thought as she pushed back the doors to smell the early autumn air. She wanted to finish the painting she'd been working on before Harry arrived. She stood back to check on it and thought about the last time she'd seen him. He had come to Jack's funeral. She remembered him being attractive, and quite tall and slim. She figured he was a little older than her, maybe mid-thirties.

After a few strokes, she put her brush down and dabbed away the small drop of moisture that had welled up in her right eye. She cried whenever anything about Jack entered her mind. She couldn't help it. His memory was so vivid: his death so painful. She didn't know how long the hurt would last. *Perhaps forever,* she told herself, as she picked up one of the many pictures of him she had dotted all around the house.

I'd better go and change and check my makeup. He'll be here soon. She wiped the rest of the paint off her brush, cleaned up her hands, and left the room. She closed the two big doors that split the room in half and, by doing so, turned the small area at the front of the house into a cosy sitting room.

She'd split with Ian six months earlier. Jack had been dead for the same amount of time. Ian and she had sold their big house in Putney, and each bought something else. She didn't know where Ian lived, and didn't want to. She blamed him for the tragedy and never wanted to speak to him again. The solicitor handling her divorce knew, and kept it to himself as Kate had instructed.

Her new home, small with only two bedrooms and a miniscule kitchen, felt cute. It'd been built around 1850, with a long living room that stretched from the front of the house to the back. It overlooked the garden, with the river at the bottom. Many of the old, original features –

the knobbly, wooden floors, the alcoves and intricate plastering, and the original door furniture – remained. Wherever possible, Kate intended to keep them all. She found the layout and the feel of the house good for her painting. She liked being there.

While she changed, she noticed a few drops of rain on the windowpanes, and felt a little cold and shivered. She thought how quickly the weather had changed, and hoped she'd remember to close the French windows from her study. She came back downstairs wearing dark-navy jeans; a red, long-sleeved T-shirt, and white plimsolls, and started to get out the mugs for coffee. Her doorbell sounded, and she turned to walk down the hall towards her front door. She stopped to pick up her post.

'Hi,' Harry said as she opened the door. 'Sorry I'm a bit late. I just met a guy in Hammersmith and it sort of overran.'

'No problem. I've been lost to the world, deep into my painting. Come in.' Kate led the way to her sitting room, next to the front door.

'What room are you decorating?'

Kate laughed. 'Not that sort of painting. I'm an artist.'

'Arr. Okay. I didn't know.'

'Have a seat. I'll bring some coffee.' Kate quickly moved away to fetch the tray she'd prepared. She regretted she'd mentioned her painting, sure it would lead to her having to explain that she no longer worked in a nine-to-five-type job, and why she'd quit. *Then he'll ask me about Jack.*

I'll tell him up-front, she thought, as she glanced at the unopened letters she'd dumped on the chopping board next to the kettle. They looked like bills, and she tossed them to one side and poured boiling water into the cafetière.

'I want to say something first before you start,' she said, as she put the tray with coffee and biscuits on the small table between the two sofas and sat down to face Harry.

'Go ahead. It's your house. I'm your guest.'

Kate took a deep breath. She waited for a few seconds and then looked up at Harry and directly into his blue eyes. 'Don't ask me anything about Jack. I couldn't cope. I'd break down and probably burst into tears.'

Harry scratched the side of his head. He smiled a little and nodded a few times. 'Of course.'

Kate didn't notice him lean forward and pick up the cafetière. She'd looked away. She bit her bottom lip and tried hard to take control of her emotions. Saying what she'd said had been hard. She put her finger up to her right eye again and wiped away a tear.

'How do you like your coffee?'

'Oh. Black, please,' Kate replied. 'Have a chocolate biscuit. They're bloody good and really fattening.' Kate hoped she sounded normal. 'They're made here in the village. I eat tons.' She laughed nervously and looked up at Harry. The moment she'd dreaded had passed. She'd managed to come through it okay.

'Go on. Ask me what you want. I don't know if I can answer. I wasn't at all close to Clare or Joe. Hardly ever saw them.'

Harry smiled again and sipped at his coffee. 'That makes two of us. I hardly spoke to Joe in the last year. Look. Let me start by explaining where I'm coming from.'

It took Harry fifteen minutes to describe all that Amie and he had deduced about the CCC file. Kate didn't interrupt. She remained still and patient and transfixed by Harry's words. When he came to the end, she finished her coffee, stood up with the tray, and went to the kitchen without saying a word. Harry watched her go.

'So what do you think the drug is?' she asked as she returned with a refilled jug of coffee.

'We don't know. But it did say that trials had been carried out in the African countries most affected by HIV and AIDS.'

'But isn't that being sorted with the antiretroviral drugs?'

Harry rubbed his cheek and swept his hand a couple of times through his thick mousey hair. 'I don't know. I'm not a scientist, but it seems that in the testing they were using a one-off vaccine, not a lifetime's course of drugs with nasty side-effects.'

'My God. If this is true, it'll be wonderful.' Kate looked away.

If what Harry's saying is true, it would be a financial catastrophe for Ritzler, she thought, and realised why Alex had been so insistent and determined to have her help.

'You're right. It would be. But not worth the death of two innocent people.' Harry leant forward and looked Kate in the eyes.

She felt shocked, and didn't understand what Harry meant. She met his eyes. 'What're you on about?'

'Someone's behind this and it's not just drug companies. The police think that Joe's death was not accidental and...'

'And what?' Kate feared what he would say. He looked concerned, as though he held something back. 'Come on. It's about Clare, isn't it? Tell me!'

'I don't know. But I think her death so soon after Joe's was not an accident either.'

Kate put her hands up to her mouth. She wondered if she could take anymore. She bit her bottom lip again and asked Harry to continue.

'That's it, really. I came to see if you knew anymore. Do you know what Joe maybe was working on before he was killed?'

'Hardly. I told you I didn't get on with them. You're more likely to know that than me. He was your brother.' Kate looked down and then up and across the room to Harry. 'Isn't this all guesswork and a bit circumstantial?'

'Could be. But I don't think so. Listen, I missed something out. I was made redundant yesterday from *The Morning News* on some trumped-up reason: the recession and all that. I simply don't buy it. It all stinks.'

'And you intend to find out?'

'Yes, I do.'

'Why.'

'Because that's what I do. Expose the truth.'

'What, and the bad guys?'

'Something like that.' Harry stood up. 'But I guess I'd better be going.' He picked up his jacket, which he'd draped over the edge of the sofa. 'Call me if you think of anything.' He started to walk to the door.

'Oh, by the way. Some friends of Joe and Clare wrote to me. They asked me to pass on their condolences...'

'Don't.' Kate burst into tears. 'I asked you not to mention him.' She sobbed and ran upstairs. Harry let himself out.

~~~

At 3:00 p.m. Harry saw Richard Morecombe walk past the coffee shop in South Kensington, where he'd sat for three hours, and peer in. He covered his face with his newspaper, and hoped Richard hadn't noticed him. He'd gone there directly from Kate's house. He'd arrived at midday, and bought several coffees and a sandwich to keep the manager happy. Richard looked away, crossed the road and went into his office.

Harry waited for half an hour, then walked across Pelham Street to the discreet head office of The Blue Group, Richard Morecombe's holding company that controlled all his businesses. Richard had a large penthouse suite on the top floor that overlooked South Kensington tube station. Harry had been there on one previous occasion for a reception after *The Morning News* had won the Best Factual Newspaper of The Year award. The first and only time he'd met Richard.

Shit, he thought as he looked at the small entrance. By the left of the door a security camera pointed down to capture anyone who waited to enter. He tucked his shirt into his jeans and straightened up his navy linen jacket and pressed the buzzer.

'I've a personal letter for Richard Morecombe. Can I come in and give it to him?'

'Who're you from?' a woman with a refined accent said.

'Sorry. It's personal. I can't say. I have to give it to him myself.'

'That's not allowed,' she replied in an authoritative tone. 'We'll send someone down to collect it.'

'That's no good. I'm not permitted to give it to anyone else but Mr Richard Morecombe.'

'I can't authorise you to do that. Unless you tell me who you're from, I can't let you in. Anyway, it'll be given straight to Richard. Let me just check if he's in.'

I know he's fucking well in. I've just seen him enter, you snotty-nosed bitch, Harry said to himself as he considered his next move.

'Listen. I'm not supposed to do this, but I'm from St James's Palace. I have a personal invitation from the Prince of Wales for Mr Richard Morecombe. His Royal Highness has invited him to one of the special dinners he gives for prominent people. I've been told to give it to Mr Morecombe personally. I'll lose my job if I don't.'

Immediately the buzzer on the door sounded, and Harry was able to walk straight in. He strode to the lift and took it to the top floor. It stopped directly in front of Richard's office. The door stood slightly open. Harry pushed it back and walked in without knocking.

'Who the hell do you think you are, barging in like this?' an elderly, grey-haired man, wearing a dark suit and light-grey tie, said as he looked up. He was tidying the large desk and putting papers and files away into the drawers. He wasn't Richard Morecombe.

'Where's Richard Morecombe?'

The man looked down his nose and over his glasses at Harry. 'He's not here. Who are you?'

'Where is he? He must be in the building somewhere.'

The man pressed a buzzer on the desk. 'I'm getting you evicted immediately.'

As Harry turned to leave, a security man and woman rushed in through the office door. 'Who are you?' the woman said. She stood in Harry's way.

'Just leaving.' Harry smiled. He held his hands up in the air and executed a smart rugby swerve to avoid them both and ran out of the door.

~~~

PHILIP STACEY lived in Pimlico. Harry knew the house well. He'd been there many times, often with Amie and more recently on his own. Harry had waited for Philip since four-thirty. He'd gone there after being chased from Richard Morecombe's office. He sat in one of the espresso bars in Tate Britain, just around the corner from Philip's house. He looked at his watch. It was six-thirty. He reckoned there was a good chance Philip would be at home. He finished his drink and left. The house was in Moreton Street, off Belgrave Road, a street of large, terraced houses, all painted in alternate light-pink and light-blue pastel washes. Most of them were at least 120 years old.

'Harry, what are you doing here?' Philip held open the door: his right hand gripped its side and barred Harry from entering. He wore trousers from a blue, pinstriped suit, held up by red braces, a crisp, white shirt, and a spotted, blue tie.

Striped, blue suit, white shirt, tie, black shoes, his uniform, Harry thought.

'What the hell is going on, Philip? Penny told me you were going to work this morning. Yesterday, that creep Edwards told me you'd left the company and then fired me. When I called the switchboard this morning they confirmed you'd left. I need some answers and I hoped you'd be able to give them to me.'

'Emm.' Philip turned and looked behind him, down the hall. 'Let's go for a drink. I'll get my jacket and tell Penny I'll be back later.'

They didn't get to a pub or a bar. Harry started to question Philip on the street as soon as they'd left his house.

'I've known you for ten years as a friend, regularly played squash with you, been at the christening of one of your children, and always thought of you as someone I could turn to in a crisis. Now I find I can't get the fucking truth out of you.' Harry stood still on the street corner. He faced Philip.

'Look. I got the sack yesterday and no one will tell me what the hell is going on. I thought at least you'd tell me what the fuck it's all about.'

Philip looked shattered, as though he'd not slept for days. He swept a hand through his flowing, white hair and pulled the two edges of his suit jacket together. A cold blast of wind had whipped around the corner. He stood taller than Harry, and looked down on him. 'I can't. I can't tell you anything. I'm sworn to secrecy. You'll have to trust me.'

Harry looked away down Victoria Street. A large fall of leaves swept across the road and blew into their faces. Harry brushed them away and turned back to face Philip.

'Why the fuck are we going for a drink then? If you can't tell me anything, I'm going. Thanks, mate.' Harry turned and started to walk away towards Pimlico station. He stopped and twisted around to face Philip. 'One question, one simple answer, please.'

'I'll try.' Philip looked crestfallen.

'Do you still work for The Morning News Newspaper Group or any of Richard Morecombe's other companies?'

'No I don't. That I can confirm.'

'Well, who the hell do you work for?'

'Can't tell you. Sorry, keep in…'

Harry didn't hear the end of Philip's sentence. He'd become angry and upset and had turned away quickly and headed for the Tube. Over an hour later, by the time he'd reached Gunnersbury station – his stop – he felt shattered and depressed. It was ten past eight. It had been a long day, and he hadn't discovered anything of consequence. Kate Fisher had been pleasant enough and a bit dramatic, but no use at all: Richard Morecombe managed to avoid him, and Philip had hid the truth. Philip had been a good friend. His behaviour left Harry with an ill feeling. He'd been deceived and let down, and by someone he'd always believed he could trust and rely on.

I'll go to the pub, he thought as he stopped on the corner where Chiswick High Road joins Marlborough Road. His phone rang.

Oh shit. It's Amie. I said I'd call her.

'Hi, I'm sorry. I haven't got home yet. I was going to call later. I've only just got off the Tube.'

'I know. I'm inside your house. I've bought a takeaway and a bottle of wine.'

'How the hell did you get in?'

'I've still got a key. You never asked for it back.'

Chapter Six

Kate collected the used coffee cups and the plate of biscuits and made for the kitchen. She thought back to the short meeting with Harry and her sudden outburst of emotion. She'd been oversensitive. Harry hadn't mentioned Jack. He'd referred to her sister, but she still lost it and turned into a blubbing wreck. She became embarrassed and turned her thoughts to Harry's conspiracy theory.

I get it. That's why Alex wants me to snoop on Harry, she thought as she put the tray down on the worktop and flipped through the mail she'd dumped earlier. One was from her solicitor, Tomlinsons. She tore it open.

Re Fisher versus Fisher

Dear Kate

I feel I should draw your attention to the enclosed letter I have received from your husband's solicitors, Palmer, Palmer and Johnson.
You will read that your husband is disputing the ownership of the property, Flat 9 Peabody Estate, which you told me you both own jointly. He says he is the sole owner, having purchased it outright with a one-off bonus he received from his employers four years ago. You'll see he's enclosed a copy of the land registry deed of title.
Notwithstanding his title or its authenticity, it is quite possible that in the final settlement to be agreed between both parties, you may well be entitled to a share, if not half, of the value of this property or its residual income. However, as I know you appreciate, this will take a little time.
You will see in the final paragraph of Messrs Palmer, Palmer and Johnson's letter that your husband has instructed his bank to stop paying you the 50% share of the monthly rent you receive from the tenant. I regret, until the divorce agreement has been finalised, there is little I can do about it.
Please call at your earliest.
Sincerely

Kate fumed. *The little shit. How can he? He can't do that. No way. He's not getting away with it.*

Ian bought the flat with his money. He owed Kate some money from way back and to repay her, they agreed to put the flat in their joint names. From the day the first tenant moved in they always shared the rent 50/50. It hadn't occurred to her he had put the flat in his name only.

Incensed, she tore open the second letter. It was from her investment bank. They said that, due to the recession, the value of her investments had halved.

'Oh my God.' She tossed both letters onto her worktop. She pushed open the French windows to her garden and stared for some time at the grey Thames and the pouring rain.

~~~

Later that day, Kate pulled her car into the car park at Ritzler Pharmaceuticals' head office on the Great West Road close to Hammersmith Flyover. It was a tall, glass building, rising forty floors and clad in smoked glass. Kate grabbed her big, leather handbag. She climbed out, slammed the car door closed, and strode across the tarmac to the revolving door. Dressed in a knee-length, black skirt and a short, green jacket with large, black buttons and broad lapels, she paced across the marble-covered floor towards the round, central-reception desk. The sound of her high heels clicked on the stone surface and resonated in her ears.

Alex Goad sat with his back to her when she entered his office. He was working at his laptop. Kate closed the door with a bang. He continued with what he'd been doing. She stood still and waited.

'Alex,' she said in an emphatic tone after ten to fifteen seconds.

He put his hand up in the air and waved at her backwards. 'Have a seat. I won't be long.'

'No. You listen to me. I want to get a few things straight. Turn around. I don't like talking to someone who's not looking at me.'

Alex touched the computer's mouse and swung his chair around. 'What's got into you?' He looked confused.

Kate took one pace forward so she stood over his desk. 'I don't like this at all. I'm only agreeing to do this because I have to and don't intend to do it for long. As soon as I've agreed on the financial split with Ian, I'm off. I don't want you thinking this is long-term in any way. You have to understand that I'm no longer a corporate person. In fact I hate everything about corporate life.'

'Me included?'

'I'll ignore that. I just want to make things clear to you. I was repulsed by the way you said I should approach Harry Fingle, and had no intention of doing what you said.'

'Okay. Okay, Kate. So you've changed your mind, but I don't need a lecture. Look, I've offered you a great deal – snoop on Harry Fingle, and I'll pay you a couple of grand a month. Okay. Yes or no?'

'No. It isn't okay.' Kate felt muddled. She knew she had no choice, but despised the idea and had wanted to vent her feelings.

'Why are you here? I'm a busy man and haven't time to listen to your illogical ranting just because you've got the hump. Are you on board or not? Alex moved his head forward and stared at Kate.

'Just say yes or no.'

Kate sat down. She rested her elbows on Alex's desk and put her hands up to her cheeks and looked at him. She felt a little better. The tension and apprehension she felt earlier had eased.

'Okay. I'm not going to apologise. I will help. But I wanted to get things straight and level beforehand. I'll tell you what I know about Harry Fingle out of loyalty to Ritzler.' She spoke in a forthright and serious way.

'You mean because you'll get a pension from us when you're fifty.'

'Shut it. If you carry on like that, I'll walk.'

'No you won't.' Alex smiled a little. He stroked his chin with his left hand and swung from left to right in his chair. 'I had a call from Ian's solicitor this morning.'

Kate recoiled sharply. 'Why's he calling you?'

'Because I know him,' Alex replied in a measured tone. 'He told me off the record that Ian believed he had evidence that you and I had been having an ongoing affair throughout your married life and that he was going to use it against you in the divorce.'

'That's preposterous. It's a load of bollocks. You know that. He hasn't got a shred of evidence.'

Alex rocked back. He looked at Kate and smiled again. 'Yeah. But I could give him some.'

Kate felt all the colour in her face drain away in a rush. She could not believe what she'd just heard.

'Now, shall we talk about Harry Fingle?' Alex sat upright.

Kate looked at Alex's mean, thin face, his neatly manicured hands, poised so perfectly over the large A4 pad on his desk. She glanced at his crisp, white shirt and immaculately knotted tie and thought, *I hate you, you slimeball. How could I ever have slept with you?*

~~~

'Oh shit.' Amie dropped her phone into her bag. In about five minutes Harry would walk through the door. She felt nervous and not at all sure she should be there, in his house, uninvited. In the four weeks since he'd crashed back into her life, she felt uncertain and at a loss as to how to respond. Her common sense had told her to walk away, leave him to sort things out himself.

So why am I here, standing in his kitchen? She heard Harry's keys turn in the lock. He tossed them on the side table as he'd always done and dumped what sounded like a bag or something in the hall.

'Hi,' she yelled.

'Hi.' Harry's tone sounded cheerless and dejected.

Amie waited and listened as his footsteps drew close. He appeared at the entrance to the kitchen. He stopped and looked around. He looked tired and deadbeat. He started to shake his head.

'This is not a good idea. I'm shattered. I've had a goddamn awful day.'

'I understand. But I thought you might appreciate a...'

'Look.' Harry put both his hands in the air. He hadn't moved a centimetre and was still wearing his jacket with a scarf tied around his neck. 'I appreciate what you've done. I don't know what your angle is, but I can't handle it tonight. Please take it all home. Let me pay you for the food.' He reached into his back pocket and pulled out his wallet.

Amie took a couple of paces forward, and stood about a metre in front of him.

'Okay. Tell me I'm wrong coming here uninvited; but Harry Fingle. Listen to me.

'Just over a year ago you walked out of my life. You said you needed your space and would call – no other explanation. After seven years living as a couple, crossing all our bridges together, and saying you'd love me forever, how do you think I felt?

'No thanks for supporting you during your trial. Nothing. Not even a letter – just a fucking e-mail asking me to clear my stuff out of this house by the time you returned from your precious "time on my own", as you called it.

'"We'll stay good friends," you said, and what happened? I didn't hear a word from you in a year. Not a bloody squeak.'

Harry took a step back. 'Amie, please...'

'No, Harry. I haven't finished.

'You had it all your own way. Fucked up my life, and then what do you do? You turn up after a year, unannounced, because you want a translator: that's all. Didn't bother to ask me how I'd been or how I was.'

Harry looked away. He clenched his lips.

'I help you. I try to find out as much as I can, and call you several times, and you don't even bother to return my calls. I was upset for you

52

when I heard you'd lost your job. It was wrong. I told you so, on the message I left. But no, nothing.

'Now I come round with a meal. Yes, I may be wrong using the key I should have returned, but I was trying to be helpful.' Amie looked away for a moment, and then back at him. He appeared shocked and surprised.

'And what do you do? Tell me to fuck off.'

'I didn't.'

'Okay, no you didn't. But as good as. "Take it all home – let me pay you…," you said. Okay. Bloody hell Harry. It may not be fuck off, but it means the same.

'Don't you get it? Can't you understand how I feel?' Amie stopped. She knew she was about to lose it. She closed her eyes and bit her bottom lip.

'Oh shit. Why do you do this to me?' She burst into floods of tears.

Harry stroked the back of his head and said nothing. Amie sobbed and sniffled a couple of times, and looked up at Harry.

'Okay. I'm sorry. What do you want me to do?' Harry said. He looked at Amie's sad, tear-stained face.

'Nothing. I don't want you do anything just because I say so. Let's drink the wine.'

Harry opened the wine. Amie laid out the Chinese takeaway she'd bought. Neither of them spoke. Harry pushed a glass in front of Amie. She looked up at him and smiled.

'Thanks. Come on. Sit down, it's ready.'

Harry pulled up a stool. He took a sip from his glass and looked at Amie. 'Do you want me to tell you all about my shitty day?'

'Only if you want to. If it helps.'

Using the chopsticks Amie had put out, Harry picked up some food and started to eat. When he'd finished his mouthful, he laid his chopsticks down and looked up at Amie.

'Okay. It goes like this.' Harry explained in detail about Clare's suspicious death. He told Amie about his meeting with Kate Fisher, and the arrangement he'd come to with Jimmy Ali. Amie looked at him and listened, occasionally glancing down to refill her chopsticks.

'Then I went to find Richard Morecombe.' Harry stopped to collect some more food and a sip of wine. They both ate for a couple of minutes in silence.

'He'd gone: scarpered. Must have known I was around. I went on to find Philip: had to hang around a couple of hours in Tate Britain before I could see him.' Harry paused and looked at Amie. 'He was absolutely useless. He wouldn't say anything about why I was made redundant.

Pretended he didn't know.'

Amie looked astonished. 'He must have known.'

Harry shook his head. 'Nope. Wouldn't even tell me who he works for. I walked away.'

Amie's expression changed. She looked worried. 'Didn't you tell me once that Kate Fisher was a big cheese in a drug company?'

Harry looked up in the air and then at Amie. 'Shit. She told me today she was a painter, you know: arty-type painter.'

'Come on.' Amie grabbed Harry by the hand. 'Where's your laptop?'

They googled Kate Fisher. They were directed to a quote on Ritzler's website.

Ritzler's record of being the first to deliver lifesaving drugs that spare millions from death is unsurpassed. We remain, and always will be, the world's leader in drug development. **Kate Fisher**. *Commercial Director, 2008.*

'Bloody hell,' Harry said. 'I told her everything I know about the CCC file.

Amie turned and looked into Harry's eyes. 'I'm scared. For you.'

Chapter Seven

Gary Lester found his first week back at Ritzler tough. Alex Goad hadn't left him alone for a minute. He'd wanted a constant update on all e-mails Harry Fingle sent and received, and a continuous bulletin on Vantiche's private IT network, particularly any mention of the CCC file. Gary worked long hours. Often he stayed in the building until well past midnight and returned shortly after six the following morning. When, at the end of the week, Alex left early at 5:30 p.m., Gary decided to do the same. He was exhausted, and craved an alcoholic drink more than at any time in the past eight months. He resisted and headed for Starbucks.

'Large Caramel Macchiato and that danish,' he said when he'd reached the front of the queue. He accidentally bumped into a tall, black guy in front of him. 'I'm sorry. I didn't see you there.'

'No problem, mate,' Jimmy Ali said. 'Just waiting for mine. Same as you. Their Macchiatos are the best, man. I love 'em.' Jimmy stopped. He peered into Gary's face. 'Haven't I seen you somewhere else?'

'Don't know. I've just come out from work.' Gary pointed down the street. 'Down there. I work for Ritzler. I've worked my nuts off this week.'

'That's it. I knew it. I work there as well.'

'What do you do?'

Jimmy smiled and looked upwards. 'Me, I just keep the place clean. How about you?'

Gary looked away for a second. 'Oh. I work for Alex Goad, the chief executive, on special projects.'

'Hey. You're important, mate. I must bow to you.' Jimmy mimicked bowing his head a couple of times. 'Goad's the big god, ain't he? What's a big man like you doing 'aving a coffee here? What's yer name?'

'Gary. What's yours?'

'Jimmy.' Jimmy pointed to the counter. 'Look, our stuff's ready.' He reached for the two mugs of frothy coffee. 'Mind if I join you?'

'My privilege. Nice to have someone to talk to.'

~~~

Harry rose early. After Amie had left the previous evening, he'd spent several hours on the Internet. He'd trawled through the websites of Ritzler and Vantiche Pharmaceuticals, and then dashed off nearly forty e-mails to friends and colleagues, asking them various questions in the hope he'd get a lead. At three-thirty he had felt too cold and too tired to continue, and went to bed. He woke at seven and made for his kitchen.

She's right and I'm wrong and I should have contacted her, he thought as he waited for the kettle to boil. *But there's not much I can do about that now. The trial almost destroyed me. I just wanted to get away, lose all my baggage and be on my own to sort things out. Then, when I felt okay, I discovered I still didn't have any feelings for her and couldn't face telling her. I chose, instead, the cowardly route of avoidance, telling myself I was doing her a favour and she would move on.*

Harry filled up his mug. *But she hasn't.*

I guess I was wrong asking her to help with the file. But she was the only person I knew who spoke Chinese. So I'm a shit. Not much I can do about it now.

His mind moved on to when he'd returned to work a few weeks after the trial. Philip had called him into his office and said he wanted to give him something to get his teeth into. 'Take your mind off the trial,' he'd said. He was putting Harry onto an investigation into how some men in high places and spheres of influence pay for rent boys.

'Isn't that a bit close to the paedophile thing that landed the newspaper, and particularly me, in so much trouble?' Harry remembered asking.

'Exactly,' Philip had said. 'If you're up to it, we might really get somewhere this time.'

Harry took a sip from his drink. He stood up in his kitchen and leant against his worktop, wearing the boxer shorts he'd slept in and a black T-shirt. He held his mug in one hand: the other hand rested on the work surface. *And then Philip took me off it. Just as I was getting somewhere. Why?*

He refilled his mug and went to his laptop. It sat on a desk, in the corner of his living room that he used as an office.

Hello Jackie, he typed.

How's the rent-boy investigation going? Have you found anything and are you going to publish and when?

Best

Harry.

He then dashed off a message to Philip Stacey.

Philip.

You probably thought I was rude last night, but I was cross and upset. Sorry.

Why did you take me off the rent-boy investigation?

Harry.

And a quick e-mail to Amie.

Hello Amie.

Sorry.

I've been a bit of a shit. I should have called you in the last twelve months and explained my feelings, and I've taken advantage of you in asking for your help. If I try to explain, it'll all come out wrong. I do want to stay friends, and I promise I will call you from time to time.

I don't know what you want from me, but it's only fair to say I can't go back to where we were before the trial. Sorry, but I don't have that feeling anymore.

Thanks for bringing the meal and wine last night and your help.

Best wishes

Harry.

He pressed send and stood up. He drained his coffee, and was about to take a shower when his laptop pinged. Amie had replied.

Harry

I guess I'm no longer on your wavelength and can't figure you out anymore.

Take care.

Amie.

Harry looked at the screen for a moment. *I guess you're right*, he thought, and turned to make for his shower.

He stood still for several minutes while the jets of warm water pulsated down his body. He thought back to the events of the last few weeks and months. He was sure Joe and Clare's suspicious death, his own dismissal from *The Morning News* and Philip Stacey's shadowy departure and subsequent unhelpfulness were connected. He rubbed shampoo into his hair and closed his eyes. *It's all about the CCC file,* he told himself, as he rinsed away the last of the soapy suds.

~~~

Jimmy Ali knocked on Harry's front door as he dressed.

'Hold on,' Harry yelled from a window above his porch. He hurried to pull his clothes on, and raced down the stairs.

'I got it, man. The job at Ritzler. I got it. Must tell you about it.' Jimmy jumped around from foot to foot. He looked pleased with himself. 'I go for this interview with the cleaning company yesterday afternoon, man. You know, the one on the bit of paper you give me. Guess what? They take me over to the Ritzler building and show me all around.'

'Come in. Keep talking.' Harry beckoned Jimmy inside with his hand.

Listen,' Jimmy said, as he followed Harry to the kitchen. 'That boss man, Alex Goad. The bloke you told me is the big boss. Well I get to see his office, like. They've only gone and put me on his floor. I have to look after his office and a few of the other top people's offices. Smart, yeah?'

'Want a drink?' Harry asked as Jimmy sat down on one of the high kitchen stools.

'Thanks. Tea'd be good. But listen, I've more.' Jimmy stroked his head and caught Harry's gaze. 'Bit of a result, man.'

'Go on,' Harry said, as he made Jimmy's tea and another coffee for himself.

'I met this bloke last night in Starbucks called Gary. He's some'ing to do with the Goad bloke. Works for him. Says he has to do special work on computers for him.'

Harry sat on the stool opposite Jimmy and pulled it close in to the worktop. 'Good stuff. This is the best lead so far. How come he told you all that?'

'Well. It's a bit of luck, really. I bumped into him in Starbucks, as I said, just after I'd been taken round Ritzler's office. I think I saw him in the building, walking around. Well, over our Macchiatos...' Jimmy smiled. 'You had one? They're the coolest, man.'

'No, I haven't, but I believe you. Go on.'

'Well, we got talking.' Jimmy stopped and drummed his right hand on the table. His left hand shielded his lip. 'He seemed a bit lonely. Wanted to talk, like. We ended up across the road having a pizza.'

'You've done well. Like some toast or something?'

'Thanks.' Jimmy looked into Harry's eyes. 'What is it you want me to find out?'

Harry put a couple of pieces of bread in his toaster and started to fill Jimmy in on all the details. He told him that, as well as Alex Goad, he wanted him to keep an eye out for Richard Morecombe and Kate Fisher. He lent him a camera, and showed him how to use it to take pictures of any documents relating to the CCC file. He also gave him several memory sticks for copying information from computers. When he'd finished, he took Jimmy out and bought him a mobile phone, and had a spare set of front-door keys cut. He told him to make himself at home anytime, and use the laptop whenever he wanted. Before they parted, he gave Jimmy £400 in cash and agreed to pay him £200 per week. He also promised a bonus of £5k, dependant on how much information he provided. Harry didn't know how he'd fund the payments, but he'd figure it out somehow.

~~~

At 10:30 a.m. Harry returned home. Several e-mails waited for him.

Hi Harry

Nice to hear from you.

Sorry you left the company in such a hurry. Maybe you can come back and have a good-bye drink with a few of us and tell us who you're working for. No doubt you've managed to hook a fab job with one of our rivals, hence your speedy exit.
Re the 'little boys for big boys' investigation, as I've christened it. Well that's another story!! Too long to e-mail. We must meet and I'll tell you all.

Finally, Harry. What's the lowdown on Philip disappearing in such a hurry? Nobody here knows a thing. He was here one minute, gone the next.

Call me, and I'll get the gang together for a few glasses.

Cheers

Jackie.

The next message was from Philip Stacey.

Harry

Thanks. No offence taken. All I can say is that it wasn't my decision. Stay in touch.

P.

It was the last two messages Harry found the most interesting.

Harry.

Good to hear from you after all this time. Rumour tells me you've left

59

The Morning News, *and in somewhat of a hurry. What was that all about? Also, I hear Philip Stacey has gone as well. What's up? Some sort of takeover or something?*

You asked me about Vantiche's main suppliers. They have many, but the one you may be interested in is Moon Pharmaceuticals, Ltd, based in Mumbai. They are one of the biggest drug companies in India and seem to be good at producing high-quality medicines at volume prices. What makes me think they may be the one you're after is that my sources this end tell me they are about to announce a new deal with Vantiche to produce a new and revolutionary drug. If you're right about Vantiche having something up their sleeve, then the two stories seem to tie up.

Finally, a word of warning: Vantiche, like Ritzler its main competitor, is now almost completely funded by foreign capital. Vantiche is over 50% owned by Chinese, and Ritzler is owned, by the same percentage, by Russian businessmen. Some of my sources say a lot of the money comes from the Chinese and Russian governments respectively. I mention this not because I have any evidence or knowledge of unlawful or inappropriate dealings, just that the Chinese and Russians, as you know, are not always transparent in their business ways, and have a reputation for getting their own way!

If I can be of any more assistance, don't hesitate to contact me. We should have a catch-up drink some time.

Until then

Regards

Bill Saunders

PHARMACUETICAL INDUSTRY SPECIALIST
BERGOFF NEWS INTERNATIONAL

The last message came from an old university friend Harry hadn't seen for some time who worked for another drug company. Harry wasn't sure what his friend's role was in the company and hadn't expected a reply.

Hi Harry.

It's great to hear from you. I must apologise for being brief but I'm really busy. I agree: we must catch up sometime.

All I can tell you is that the only drug-producing company able to manufacture a volume drug at the price and in quantities you describe is an Indian-based company called Moon Pharmaceuticals, Ltd. I think they are based in Bombay, or Mumbai. Sorry, I can't be any more help.

Best wishes

Tom.

Harry sat back in his chair and gazed at the wall for a moment.

Jackie, he scribbled on a small pad next to his laptop. *I need to see her today. She's got something on the rent-boy investigation.*

He twiddled his pen around, a Mont Blanc given to him by Amie, and thought about the short one-liner he'd received from Philip. Clearly he was being gagged, he figured, and decided to leave him for later.

The two messages about Moon Pharmaceuticals, the Indian drug company, kick-started his adrenaline. He stood up and started to pace around his living room. He stopped. He reached a decision. He'd have to go to India and visit Moon, and find out as much as he could. He returned to his desk and started to search for flights to Mumbai. While he waited for the flight options to come up, he thought he heard a car draw up outside, and a door slam. He stood up and went to the window to check. A tall man, wearing a black mackintosh, approached the house. Harry waited in his hall until the man knocked on the door.

~~~

Kate Fisher strode past the security desk and straight up to the bank of lifts at the back of the marble-floored reception hall. She ran to a door that was just closing and forced her way into the packed car. 'Sorry,' she said to the ten or more other occupants, who all seemed to be annoyed. 'Got an early meeting with Alex.'

The man directly in front of her moved his foot back so it was almost on top of one of hers, making her stand on one leg. Another person shoved their briefcase into her back, and a third occupant lifted up his arm a little so his elbow dug into Kate's ribcage. Kate didn't say a word. She was too busy concentrating on what she was going to say to Alex. She didn't have an appointment with him. She didn't even know if he was in. But she'd take a chance.

'Thanks, guys, for being so welcoming and such pleasant company.' She walked out of the lift on Alex's floor, and marched towards his office.

'Is he in?' she asked the guy who washed the floor outside Alex's office. Alex's PA wasn't at her desk.

Jimmy looked up from his mop and bucket. 'I think so. He's got Julie in there with him.' Jimmy smiled at Kate. 'You Kate Fisher?'

'Yes. Why? How do you know my name?'

Jimmy put out his hand. 'I'm Jimmy Ali. I'm the new cleaner on this floor. Anything you want, just tell me. I'll do my best to get it done.'

'Thanks, Jimmy. Nice to meet you.' Kate shook Jimmy's hand and passed him to enter Alex's office. Jimmy watched as she pushed open the door and charged in.

Alex looked up from his desk. Julie, his PA, swung round in the chair opposite. Both stared at Kate.

'I need to talk to you, Alex. *Now.*'

'Can't it wait? You can see I'm busy.'

'No. I have to see you *immediately.*' Kate's tone left no doubt about the urgency of her visit. She fumed, and had done so ever since the call she'd received from her solicitor late the previous afternoon. Her short journey from Barnes had been a nightmare. She'd been caught up in traffic and torrential rain. At one time, she'd feared her old Alpha 147 was about to give up on her. Luckily she was on her own. Many times the appalling weather conditions and the traffic, combined with her inner rage, made her scream out as though she was a madwoman.

'Are you going to sit down?' Alex said to Kate as she stood in front of his desk. 'Or is this going to be one of your Oscar performances?'

'You have no right to do this. No right at all. It's all absolute lies. How can you do this to me? You're quite the most revolting man I've ever met. How can you possibly believe I'll help you? There are no words to describe how much I hate you.

'You're a fucking little shit!' Kate stopped and stared at Alex. Her face was bright red. She still stood.

Alex sat still while Kate ranted on. He looked up at her. 'I was right. An Oscar performance.' He shook his head. 'I haven't a clue what you are talking about.'

Kate took a pace forward and placed the palms of her hands flat on Alex's desktop. Her face was a few centimetres from his.

'You know very well what I'm on about. My solicitor called me last night and told me they'd received a letter from Ian's solicitor. It said you'd admitted to sleeping with me regularly in the last four years.'

'So?'

'*So*. It's that all you can bloody well say? *So*.

'*Alex*, it's a downright lie. How can you sink so low? What is it you want out of me to do this?'

'If you sit down, I'll tell you.'

'You don't get it, do you? I'm here to tell you what I think of you. Nothing else.'

Alex's expression didn't change. He seemed unmoved. He clasped his hands together and looked at Kate, who still stood in front of his desk.

'I need some more information from Harry Fingle, urgently.'

'You must be out of your tiny mind. I can't believe you said that.'

Alex looked down for a moment and then back up at Kate.

'I want you to find out everything that Harry Fingle knows about the CCC file, even if it means sleeping with him.' Alex stopped for a moment and smiled at Kate. 'Then we can discuss how I'll withdraw the information I've given to Ian's solicitors.'

'My God. You're unbelievable.' Kate turned and started to head towards the door.

'Remember Ian's solicitor is a friend of mine,' Alex called after her.

Kate stopped in her tracks. She twisted her head around and glared. 'I detest you, Alex Goad. You couldn't sink any lower if you tried. You're a repugnant, odious creature and not worthy of any further thought.' Kate paused.

'I never want to set eyes on you again.'

Chapter Eight

Mr Fingle,' said the tall man, wearing a black mackintosh, who Harry had watched as he'd walked towards his door. He held out a police ID card for Harry to inspect. 'Can I come in for a minute? I need to talk to you.'

Harry examined the man in more detail. *Probably in his mid-forties*, he guessed. He thought the policeman seemed serious, and looked quite senior.

'Sure. Follow me.' Harry turned and led the way into his living room. The officer followed. His shoes tapped against the vanished floorboards.

'Can I get you a tea, coffee, glass of water?' Harry gestured to the chairs and sofa, and stood and waited for the man's reply. 'Excuse the mess. I was doing some work.' He pointed to the pile of notes and papers he'd dumped on the floor around his desk.

'No thanks, I'm fine.' The policeman dropped his raincoat over the arm of the chair. He wore a dark suit and tie. 'Okay if I put my coat here?'

'Sure.' Harry sat on the sofa. He was anxious to know the reason a stony-faced police officer, with a stern, unyielding expression, sat opposite him. 'What can I do for you?'

'Let me introduce myself. I'm Deputy Assistant Commissioner Banks. I want to talk to you about the sad deaths of your brother and sister-in-law.'

He is senior. And this is serious. 'You're going to tell me their deaths were connected.'

Commissioner Banks looked down at his trousers and rubbed his hands slowly up and down each thigh before he looked up to face Harry. 'No. What makes you think that, Mr Fingle?' The expression on the policeman's face remained sombre and unfriendly.

'Come on, Commissioner Banks...' Harry shot the Commissioner a quick glance. 'Is that what I should call you?'

The policemen nodded.

'Your lot have already told me there was a third car involved in Joe's collision, and it was being driven recklessly.' Harry looked directly into the policeman's eyes. 'And people don't just fall in the Thames, do they?'

'You're referring to the drowning of your sister-in-law, Clare Fingle, I assume?'

'Who the hell do you think I'm talking about? You said, when you came in, you wanted to talk to me about both their deaths.'

Banks turned one of his hands over and clenched his fist. He looked down at his fingernails for a second before looking up at Harry. 'Has it occurred to you she might have jumped?'

'What; suicide?' Harry had never considered the possibility.

'Did you know that your brother and sister-in-law had been having marriage counselling, Mr Fingle?'

'No, I didn't. I wasn't close to either of them.' The policeman's antagonistic manner had begun to irritate Harry.

'Could you tell me why you're here?'

'It's a courtesy call, Mr Fingle. We have concluded our investigations into the untimely deaths of your brother and sister-in-law and believe; in both cases, that no foul play was involved.'

'No foul play. Oh, come on.' Harry jumped up and started to walk around the room. 'You must be joking. Surely you don't think I'm going to go with that, do you? That's completely at odds with what the police told me previously.'

'That's why I'm here. We were wrong to tell you about another car. It was a mistake. There wasn't one. We needed to inform you of that.' Commissioner Banks stood up next to Harry. He picked up his raincoat and draped it over his right arm.

'I don't get it.' Harry stood about a metre away from the policeman. He stared into his face. 'Why is somebody of your rank sent round to tell me that? Surely an ordinary police constable could have done it?'

Banks had turned to walk towards the door. He stopped and glanced over his shoulder to look at Harry. 'We don't like misunderstandings. Where there is a possibility one might have occurred, we always send someone of my rank to talk to the families involved.

'I'm sorry, but I must go now. Thanks for your time.' He started to walk towards the front door.

'That's crap. You haven't explained a thing.' Harry stopped. He'd become speechless. Banks opened Harry's front door himself and walked out.

'What is this? Some cover-up?'

The policeman didn't hear Harry. He slid into the back seat of the black saloon car that had waited for him, and closed the door. Harry watched as he was driven away. He pushed his front door closed and sat down on the bottom stair of his staircase.

That guy's crazy or I'm going nuts. He thought back to the phone conversation he'd had with a police officer shortly after Joe's funeral. He could clearly remember the PC telling him that the driver of the van, who had lost both his legs in the accident, saw a car swerve violently in front of his brother's car.

65

Joe had been killed on a desolate stretch of road in Wales. The Dyfed-Powys Police dealt with the crash. It took Harry thirty minutes to get through to somebody at the police station to talk about the accident.

'I have the file relating to the road accident in question up on the screen now, sir. What's the nature of your enquiry?' an administrator with a strong Welsh accent asked.

'A policemen, whose name I can't remember, called me on 20 September and said that a car had been seen swerving violently in front of my brother's car shortly before he crashed head-on into a car transporter and was killed.'

'My condolences, sir. What is it you want to know about it?'

'Well. Can you tell me more? Did you follow it up?'

The administrator didn't reply. The line sounded as if it had gone dead. 'Are you still there?' Harry asked.

'Yeah, I'm here, sir,' the man answered. He sounded bewildered and unsure. 'I'm sorry, Mr Fingle. There's no mention of another car. Only your brother's car and the car transporter are listed as being involved. Do you know the name of the policeman who called you?'

'I told you before. I've forgotten.'

'Well then, I'm sorry. I can't help you sir. The officer-in-charge closed the case.'

'What! You're taking the piss. What's the name of this officer-in-charge, please?'

'Well, it was signed off by Chief Inspector Hamilton, head of the traffic section.'

'Can you put me through to him?' Harry tapped his pen hard on his pad several times while he waited for a reply.

'That won't be possible, sir. I'm afraid she's not here. In fact she won't be around for a while. She's had a baby and...'

Harry cut off and dialled *The Morning News*.

'Jackie Sentence, please.'

'Is that Harry? How you doing?' the switchboard operator asked.

'I'm fine, thanks.' Harry paused. He tried to hold back any sign of his growing sense of frustration. 'Don't want to be rude. But I'm in a bit of a hurry, can you put me through to Jackie.'

'She's not in. Hasn't been in all day. I think she's on holiday.'

'That can't be.' Harry sounded indignant. 'She e-mailed me this morning. She knew I'd left the paper.'

'Maybe. But not from here. I've just checked. Her extension's switched to an *Out of office 'til Monday* message.'

'Thanks then Paula. Take care. 'Bye.' Harry put his phone down on the step next to him. He leant forward and covered his face with his hands.

This is all crazy. He rubbed his eyes, and slowly rose to his feet and went to make another coffee.

~~~

The day after Amie had been to Harry's house uninvited, the day she received his short, unsympathetic e-mail, she got drunk and slept with a colleague. It wasn't a memorable experience; in fact, it was quite unexceptional. Both of them had consumed too much alcohol to make love in any meaningful way. But it was cathartic, and the beginning of closure on Harry, Amie thought.

The next morning, Amie's wish for more closure drove her to enter Harry's house, again without an invite and in his absence. It was the second time she'd been there in three days. She'd wanted to collect the CDs she'd left behind, her books, the few kitchen utensils she owned, and some of the paintings that she brought to the house when they first moved in together. Things that she'd left a year earlier in her haste to clear out before Harry returned. She felt confident she could remove her belongings with ease, and with no feelings of remorse or regret. Yet the opposite occurred.

Within minutes of closing his front door, she played their favourite CDs, rearranged photos, and even lit the old incense sticks they'd collected and used most Friday and Saturday nights when alone. She discovered the pictures of her that Harry had hidden away in drawers and cupboards, and took them out. She placed them in obvious positions. She knew what she did was wrong. Her feelings and emotions would slide backwards to a state she thought she'd left behind. But she wasn't in control and was unable to stop. She enjoyed being there and the warm glow she experienced: the memories of happier times gone by. Upstairs, in Harry's bedroom, she rearranged his shirts, and ran her fingers down his towels and linen in the airing cupboard. She changed the position of a couple of paintings to make the ones she had given him more prominent. Eventually, she lay on his bed for several minutes before she undressed and slid between the sheets until the music, the memories, and the familiar smells took over. She sobbed and sobbed onto Harry's pillow. She ran to the shower, turned it full on and stepped in. She let the powerful streams of warm water drench her long, black hair and wash away her tears and mascara.

'I shouldn't be here without his permission,' she yelled through the steamy mist that surrounded her. *What am I doing? I'm insane. He could be home soon.*

She ran out of the cubicle and left the water running. She dripped all over the wooden floor and grabbed one of the big, white towels she'd given Harry for Christmas one year, and dabbed it against her chest.

I'm so wrong. I've got to go, she thought as she dropped the towel and struggled to pull her clothes on over her damp body. She left within minutes. The shower still flowed. Her wet towel lay on the floor. She left the bed unmade. Music played, and the CDs and their cases lay untidily on the floor by the system.

~~~

Harry put on his cycle helmet and started to undo the padlock on his bike. He'd been to his gym in King Street, Hammersmith for a couple of hours and wanted to return home. He'd sent out several e-mails after Commissioner Banks had left earlier and he needed to check the replies. One had gone to Jackie Sentence to try to find out where she'd been when she'd e-mailed him. Another message went to the High Commission of India with a list of specific questions about Moon Pharmaceuticals. He'd decided to go to Mumbai to investigate Moon, but wanted to read the Commission's replies before he booked his seat.

Not long after he'd started peddling down King Street towards Chiswick, he felt his phone vibrate in his pocket. He pulled in on the left opposite The Polish Club to take the call. The caller was Jimmy. He said he had to see Harry urgently, and couldn't explain on the phone. Harry agreed to meet him in the Italian café in Hammersmith that they'd been to before. He turned his bike around to point in the opposite direction. He didn't own a car. He always cycled or used public transport. Occasionally, he'd take a taxi.

Harry arrived at the café at twelve-fifteen. He padlocked his bike to a lamppost that he could see from inside and went to find Jimmy. He found him sitting on his own at a corner table away from any other customers. He wore dark-navy jeans, a navy top, a hooded, fleece jacket, and trainers.

'Hungry?' Harry asked as he put a hand on Jimmy's shoulder.

'I can wait, man. Sit down and listen.'

Harry pushed the empty cup another customer had left to one side, and sat in the wooden, wicker chair opposite Jimmy.

'Come on. Tell me what's up.'

Jimmy looked around and leaned forward. 'Listen.' Jimmy spoke quietly. He almost whispered. 'The Kate Fisher woman.'

'Yeah. What about her?'

'Well, she was in today. Early this morning, and I introduced myself.'

'Okay. So what's so urgent about it?' Harry asked.

'Listen. I ain't finished. She burst in on Goad, unannounced, and they had a bust up. She swore at him like a good 'un.'

'How do you know?'

'I listened. I was in the office next door. Guess what the row was about?'

'I don't know, do I?'

'You, Harry. It was about you. Your name come up many times. Some'ing about a file. "Find out as much about it from him as possible," the Goad bloke said to her.'

'Did you catch the name of the file?'

'No, mate. Didn't hear that.'

'So what was the row about?'

'Don't know. But the Kate woman didn't seem that much keen on what Goad was saying. She yelled at him. Called him "a fucking little shit." Filthy language for a doll, ay.'

Jimmy raised his head and caught Harry's eyes. 'Then she stormed out.'

'Did she see you?'

'No way, mate. I was doing my cleaning work. Nobody takes no notice of the cleaner, do they? Particularly if they're black.'

'You've done well, Jimmy. I'll buy you some lunch. What do you want?'

'I don't know. I'll have a look.' Jimmy picked up the menu card. He looked down at it quickly and then back at Harry. 'What's this all about? You know – the whole thing. Me snooping on these people, like?'

They both ordered the same. Harry asked for a glass of wine; Jimmy a beer. Harry figured he could trust Jimmy. While they waited for their food to arrive, he told him as much as he knew, and all that had happened. He included the spooky visit he'd had from Commissioner Banks earlier that morning. When he'd finished, he placed his hands on the table and waited for Jimmy's reaction.

'Bloody hell. Sounds mighty scary to me. What you gonner do?'

Harry looked to his right. Two waiters approached their table with the food. Harry and Jimmy sat back and watched. The first waiter placed a plate of steaming pasta in front of both of them, and stood aside. His female colleague put the green salad and the garlic bread on the table. Both waiters stood back and next to each other. They opened their arms, smiled, and said, '*Buon appetito*!'

'Thanks,' Harry said. He smiled back.

'Some parmesan?' the male waiter asked. Harry nodded. Jimmy looked at Harry and nodded as well.

They watched him sprinkle the cheese on each of their meals and smile at them both again. 'Enjoy,' he said.

'Thank you,' Jimmy said. They both picked up their forks. Harry waited a few more seconds to be sure the two waiters couldn't hear him.

'This CCC file is the key. I'm waiting for a reply from the High Commission of India to a few questions about this Moon company I told you about. If they confirm what my other two contacts have told me, I'm getting on the first plane to go out there.'

'What you gonner do there?' Jimmy gathered some pasta onto his fork.

'Ask them about CCC.'

'Will they tell you?'

Harry put his fork down and smiled. 'I've been at this game long enough to know how to get information out of people. Once they know you're a journalist, they tend to talk. Want to keep their image clean.' Harry shrugged his shoulders. 'They may drop a few lies in, but I can usually suss that out.'

'But you just said *The Morning News* gave you the heave-ho, didn't yer?'

'Moon don't know that, do they?' Harry said with a smile.

~~~

Harry slowed as he cycled past the black car, parked a few metres down on the opposite side of the road from his house. He noticed a man who sat inside and read a paper. He thought nothing of it, and dismounted. He pulled his bike up onto the pavement, and pushed it the few metres to the small, metal gate at the end his path. The man in the car watched. He waited until Harry walked up to his front door, and then he took out his mobile phone.

'Grigoriy,' the man in the car said a few seconds later. 'He's gone inside the house.'

~~~

It was the sound of the Jack Johnson album and the smell of incense that told Harry he been visited again.

'Why are you here again, Amie?' He rushed in through his front door. He left it wide open, and his bike outside. He saw the burning incense sticks and the twenty or thirty CDs spread around the floor by his music system. He noticed one or two pictures of Amie staring at him. But she wasn't in the room.

'Amie, where are you?' He ran upstairs and found the unmade bed, the discarded towel, and heard the water from the shower. *What the hell?* He hurried to check the other rooms.

Amie, he typed minutes later, when he was sure she wasn't in the house. He felt angry, and typed hard and wrote fast.

I can't believe you. Words fail me. I've told you. We're over, past tense. Surely you understand that? What on earth possessed you to invade my privacy and do as you did? Amie, you are out of order. I can't explain how angry and cross I am.

Don't ever, ever do that again, and send the key back – NOW!!!

He stopped for a second, and looked around for a scrap of paper, and scribbled a note: *the locks – change – urgent.* He turned back to his screen. He scanned the hurried e-mail and decided not to add his name. He was about to press *send* when his phone rang. It was from an unknown number.

'Hello.' He stood up and started to walk around his living room.

'Hi, Harry. It's Kate Fisher.'

Harry stopped and stood by the large window that overlooked the road outside. He turned around and leant against the wall. He rested his backside on the window sill. 'How did you get my number?'

'Oh. I found it amongst Clare's stuff.'

Bloody liar, Harry thought. *I never gave Clare my mobile number.* 'What can I do for you?'

'Can we meet? I've something important to tell you.'

'What about?'

'Can't tell you, Harry: not over the phone. Just that I think you'll be interested.'

Harry thought back to the conversation he'd just had with Jimmy. 'Okay. Do you want to come round here?' He was suspicious, but wanted to discover what Kate was up to.

'Sure. When?' Kate asked.

'About half an hour.'

'Fine. See you then. 'Bye.'

Harry said good-bye and switched off his phone and turned around. He started to think about how he'd approach their meeting. The black car that he'd passed by earlier pulled out. It slowed in front of his house. The driver turned and held up a camera and snapped Harry as he looked out.

What is going on? Harry asked himself as the car accelerated and sped away.

Chapter Nine

Vantiche Pharmaceuticals' head office was located a mile outside Reading, just off junction 13 of the M4. It was an older and less glitzy building than that of their main rival, Ritzler, thanks to the prudence of their long-standing chief executive, David Masters. He was a traditionalist at heart, who ran the company in a frugal manner and who didn't believe in spending the company's profits on showcase architecture, as he called it. He'd worked for Vantiche for thirty-five years, and was due to retire. Having survived a hostile take-over by the giant Chinese drug company, Ning, he looked forward to his exit.

David had an impeccable track record. He'd kept Vantiche at the forefront of the international drug industry for most of the eleven years he'd been their managing director. The sudden death of Joe Fingle, their best scientist – who'd been behind the trials and development of the CCC drug – came as a devastating blow. Once his masters in China had made it clear that any possible leaks of the file's information to competitors or the media would cost him his pension, he decided to own up. He told Ning he believed Joe Fingle had taken the file out of the building and copied it onto his home PC. For that reason, on a wet, windy evening in late October, he waited with some concern in the boardroom for the arrival of Grigoriy Nabutov syn Yegor, Ning's head of security and special projects.

At 7:00 p.m. Grigoriy Nabutov pushed open the boardroom door. He'd come alone. He wore an expensive, leather jacket, a black shirt and well-tailored, black trousers. He stood about 1.85 metres tall. He looked lean, with a thin, mean face, and sharp, sallow features, and a six-centimetre scar on his right cheek. He had thick, black hair, swept back to show his forehead. His eyes were dark and penetrating, with small eyebrows. He had a pronounced, pointed jaw. David had been told he was thirty-seven, and had once run the largest mafia setup in Moscow. He'd been nearly killed in a shootout with the Russian FSB. He escaped by faking his own death.

~~~

When Nabutov recovered from the incident, he heard Ning was looking for a security expert. He contacted them. They hired him immediately. They wanted someone with extensive Russian contacts who understood the workings of the Russian government, and its connections with the country's mafia. Ritzler's owners were Zeum, a Russian company jointly owned by a group of Russian businessmen and the Russian government. They were ruthless, and would do whatever it took to ensure Zeum and Ritzler dominated the world pharmaceutical industry. Ning, Vantiche's Chinese owners, believed Grigoriy to be the person to safeguard their interests from Ritzler's onslaught.

~~~

'A drink?' David asked. He flexed his hand after Grigoriy's bone-crushing handshake.

'You have vodka?' Grigoriy spoke with a heavy accent.

'Russian Standard?' David said.

'That's good,' Grigoriy answered. David reached to take out the empty glass from the fridge and the vodka bottle from the freezer, and started to pour, while Grigoriy pulled out some papers and a file from his black-leather bag. David opened a low-alcohol beer for himself.

'This him?' Grigoriy asked in a gruff voice as David pushed the vodka across the table towards him. Grigoriy pointed to a large photo of Harry that he'd withdrawn from his case.

David leaned over and took a long look at the photo. He sipped on his beer. Grigoriy downed his vodka in one and reached for the bottle.

David turned to look at Grigoriy. 'I think so. I've only met him once. At the funeral of his brother, Joe. Where was the photo taken?'

Grigoriy stared down at a typed card he'd laid next to the photo. 'My man, he take photo and say he lives at 13, Marlborough Road, Chiswick, London West. He see Fingle enter house. Snap him. He look out of window. My man, he drive away.' Grigoriy looked up and directly at David. 'The address. It correct – yes?'

'I don't know. But I can check it. I wrote him a letter after Joe's death.'

'How long it take you?' Grigoriy turned away and picked up his glass.

'I have a copy next door in my office. Wait here. I'll go and get it.'

'Good. I wait.' Grigoriy downed his vodka and filled his glass up for a third time.

~~~

Harry had expected Kate to arrive by four-thirty. She called and asked if she could delay her visit by an hour. He agreed. It gave him time to check the e-mail he'd received from the High Commission of India. Their trade department had sent him a list of Moon Pharmaceuticals' main customers. Vantiche was at the top of the list, and consistently the company who had the highest US dollar spending with them over the previous three years. Harry couldn't be certain that Moon would manufacture the new CCC drug, but felt he had enough indicators to warrant a flight to Mumbai. He'd booked an Air India flight for 2230. He needed to check in two hours earlier.

At five, when he'd nearly completed his packing, his phone rang. It was an unknown number.

'Hi, Harry, can you talk? It's me, Jackie.' She sounded upset.

'Of course. What's wrong?'

Jackie didn't reply immediately. Harry could hear her sniffle and sob a little. 'Are you okay?' he asked.

She sniffled again. 'No. I'm not okay. I've been fired.'

'Why? Who by?'

'I wasn't fired, but made redundant. That creep John Edwards did it this morning. He said it was because of the recession, cutbacks, etc.'

'But I thought you weren't in this morning? The switchboard told me you were on holiday when I called.'

'I was there. I sent you an e-mail, didn't I? Then I got the chop.'

Harry rubbed his hand through his hair. He pushed the suitcase he'd been packing away a bit to make some space and dropped back onto his bed. *This is all getting crazier by the second*, he thought and said, 'That's bloody baloney, Jackie.'

'Call it what you like. But they bloody well did it.' Jackie sniffed loudly. 'And you know what? I'm not allowed to tell anyone anything about what I worked on. If I do, I'll lose the redundancy money.'

'That's what they tried to do with me, but I didn't take the money and told them to stuff it.'

'I know you did, and I wish I'd been able to do the same. But listen. I can't risk talking to you about anything at all. I'm a single mum. I can't afford not to take the money, but...' Jackie paused. 'Listen. End the call. Now.'

The line went dead. Harry dumped his phone on the bed next to his suitcase. 'What is this all about?' he murmured as he received a text message. It was from Jackie. He opened it.

RICHARD MORECOMBE

Thanks Jackie. Just as I thought, Harry noted and smiled.

A few minutes later, after he'd thrown the last items into his case, Kate arrived.

It was dark when he opened the front door. The dim light from his porch shone onto Kate's spiky hair and her face. Harry noticed her unusual beauty.

'Hi. Come in. Let's go in there.' Harry pointed to his living room.

Kate wore a knee-length, black skirt, a white blouse and a short, beige jacket, and brown, lace-up shoes. He followed her. He caught the light scent of citron and apple.

'Have a seat.'

Kate looked around and took one of the chairs. Harry stood near to where she sat. 'Can I get you a glass of wine?' He noticed Kate turn her head and look around. 'Sorry about the mess.' He hadn't been able to clear away all the stuff he'd been working on earlier.

Kate smiled at him. Her hands were clasped in her lap. 'Thanks. That would be nice. Have you some white wine? But don't fill it up. I have to drive.'

Harry returned after a few minutes with the drinks. He placed Kate's on a small table next to her chair, and his on the large, rustic table in the middle of the room. He sat down on the sofa and looked at her. 'So what's the big story, then? I haven't got long. I've a plane to catch.'

'Where you going?'

'Oh, just a short break away. Nothing special.'

Kate took a sip from her glass and placed it on the table next to Harry's beer. She looked up and smiled. 'Just wanted to be friendly. We didn't get very far last time we met. I thought maybe you might like some help. Did you know I used to work for Ritzler? I might be able to help you with that file you said you found on Joe's PC.' She stood up and looked down at Harry. 'Mind if I take my jacket off? It's warm in here.'

'Go ahead.' Harry thought back to his last conversation with Jimmy about the row between Kate and Alex Goad. 'I didn't know you'd worked for Ritzler. I thought you were an artist.' He picked up his glass. 'How do you think you can help?'

Kate dropped her jacket on the sofa next to Harry's thigh. Her arm brushed past his as she returned to her chair. He caught another whiff of her perfume.

'Well – I could look and see if any of it makes sense to me,' she said as she sat down.

Harry frowned. 'It's encrypted. You don't know the code?'

'In the pharmaceutical industry, we tend to use the same codes.'

Harry leant back on the sofa. He stared out of the window for a couple of seconds and bit on his thumbnail. He sipped on his beer before turning back to Kate.

'What? That's so lame. I can't believe you said it.' Harry looked away again for a moment.

'Alex Goad sent you, didn't he?' Harry spoke in a soft, deliberate voice. He stared directly into Kate's eyes.

She sat up sharply in her seat. 'What the hell, Harry? What do you think I've got to do with Alex Goad? I left Ritzler over a year ago. I came to see if I could help you.'

'When you called me earlier, you said you had something important to tell me. What is it?'

'I have. But first, why do you think Alex Goad put me up to seeing you?'

Harry didn't reply. He turned again to the window and thought about the lies she'd just told him. *She could be useful*, he thought, and decided to appear vague, and play along and humour her.

'I don't know,' he said after some time. 'There's so many screwy and odd things going on at the moment, I figured he might have asked you to find out what I was up to.' Harry turned away and glanced at the window.

'Do you know someone is watching me?'

'Watching you? What do you mean?'

'I mean just that. A car was outside earlier and the man inside it took a photo of me and drove off.' Harry turned back to face Kate.

'Come on. What is that you came to tell me?'

Kate crossed her legs. Her skirt slid up above her knees so the lower half of her long thighs was visible.

'Did you know that Vantiche is owned by the Chinese, possibly the Chinese government?' she said.

'How do you know that? And so what, anyway? Is that all you came to tell me?'

Kate stood up. She picked up her jacket and tossed it over the side of the sofa. 'Mind if I sit next to you? It'll be easier to explain.'

'Okay.' Harry shrugged his shoulders and shoved up a bit to make more space. Kate moved closer. Her skirt rode higher up her legs. She turned and looked at him. Their eyes locked.

'Harry, Vantiche was taken over by Ning, the biggest Chinese drug company who is bankrolled by the Chinese government. We watched it all go on when I was with Ritzler.'

Kate gazed in front of her for a few seconds. She rubbed her knee with her left hand, and moved closer to Harry so their legs touched. She turned back to look at him. He twisted around to face her, and found he was starring into her big, open eyes.

'If this CCC drug is a cure for AIDS, as you think it is, Vantiche will go to any lengths to get it back from you.' Kate shifted and turned, her knee and thigh pressed hard against Harry's leg.

'You're not safe.' She shook her head. 'Why do you think you're being watched?'

'Maybe I'm not safe. But how do they know, whoever *they* are, that I've got the file?'

'Who've you told about it? Anyone at your newspaper?'

'I told you. I was made redundant. I haven't seen or talked to anyone about it, except Amie.'

'Amie? Amie who?' Kate snapped.

'Amie Lau, my old girlfriend.' Harry sat back. He moved away from Kate. 'She wouldn't have said anything to anybody.'

He became aware again of Kate's perfume. She had leant forward so her face was not far from his, her mouth a little open. Inviting warmth shone from her eyes. She put a hand on Harry's knee. 'You need to be careful. Where is the file now?'

He moved away. Kate withdrew her hand. He looked at his watch. It was nearly six-fifteen. He'd copied the file onto his laptop, and needed time to transfer it to a memory stick and delete it from his computer. He'd booked a taxi to take him to the airport for seven-thirty. There were a few more things he needed to do before he left.

'It's in the bank.' He stood up.

'Look. I'm really grateful for you coming and warning me about Vantiche, and I *will* take care. I don't want to appear rude, but I have to go shortly.' He looked down. He noticed the top button of Kate's blouse was undone, and he could see her cleavage and the top of her breasts.

'In the bank? What you mean? You must have a copy?' Kate sounded concerned.

I get it, he thought. *She's come to get the file. She'll sleep with me if that's what it takes.*

'That's right. It's in the bank, and no – I don't have a copy. What's wrong with that?'

'Nothing. That's your choice.' Kate looked away for a second and then stood up close to him. Her breasts nearly touched his chest. She looked up into his eyes and smiled.

'Look. If you want someone to look after it while you're away, I'll be glad to do it. I've a safe.'

Harry grinned. He moved away and reached down to finish his beer. 'Thanks. That's kind of you. But it's safe in the bank. Now, I'm really sorry, but I'll have to ask you to leave. Perhaps we can have a drink when I get back.'

Kate bit her bottom lip. She finished her wine, and looked across to where Harry was standing by the door. She seemed flushed.

'You okay? You look put out.'

She smiled. 'I'm fine. Take care, and thanks for the wine.' He saw her to the door, closed it behind her, and hurried to his laptop.

~~~

Kate drew into the car park at the Ritzler building at seven. She'd driven there straight from Harry's house, all the while bothered by how she'd deal with Alex. She knew he'd be angry. Somehow she had to face him. She hated him more than she possibly could have imagined. She believed she easily could have killed him if she had the chance. But he was in control. He'd threatened to compound the lies he'd already told Ian's solicitor. She had no option. For the time being, she had to do what he asked.

As the lift climbed near to his floor, she prepared herself for what she knew would be a difficult meeting. The lift slowed and came to a halt. The shiny, metal doors slid open. Alex's office door, immediately opposite the lift, appeared wide open. He stood and waited for her.

'Have you got it?' he shouted across the passageway.

'No, I haven't.' She walked into his room at a deliberately slow pace. 'But I think he's going to India to see Moon. You know, Vantiche's biggest supplier.'

'You mean you've failed. I told you to get it. Whatever it took.' Alex had shouted from the other side of the room. Both of them stood and looked at each other.

'I couldn't. He's put it in the bank.'

'The bank? Surely he's got a copy?'

'He said not.'

'And you believe him?'

Kate sensed herself shake. Alex was being aggressive and completely unreasonable. She wanted to throw something at him. 'Short of holding a gun to his head, there was not much more I could have done.'

'Has he told anyone else about it?'

'Just his ex-girlfriend, someone called Amie Lau.'

'Who's she?' Alex growled.

'I don't know anything about her. Harry told me before – when he came to see me in Barnes – that she'd helped with the Chinese translation.'

Alex had turned around and had his back to Kate. He seemed to be scribbling something down on the pad on his desk. He twisted back to face her and said, 'You didn't tell me that.'

'I forgot, okay. Sorry. Is it important?'

'What else haven't you told me?'

'What's wrong with you? You're behaving as though you're demented. There's nothing I haven't told you about Harry, apart from the Amie thing.'

'I told you to sleep with him. Did you try?'

'I did my best. He didn't respond. What else do you expect me to do? Walk in there and rip my clothes off and run up to him?'

Alex Goad looked away for a moment. 'You could have tried. You've got a good body. Most men…'

Kate took a pace forward so she was within a few centimetres of Alex and raised her hand to slap him across the face.

'Shut it. You're the pits.' She thought better, and lowered her hand to her side.

'Harry's a highly intelligent man. He would have thrown me out on the street if I'd tried that. Look. I told you, he's going to India to see Moon. That's important, isn't it?'

'Not really, but how do you know? Did he tell you?'

'No. Quite the opposite. I read the tag on his hand luggage in the hall when he went to get me a drink.'

Alex Goad stroked his chin. 'How do you know he's going to see Moon?'

'I don't, but I've guessed he is. He was being secretive about his movements.'

'Okay. So let's say he's going to meet up with Moon. What do you expect me to do about it? Blow them up?'

'Don't treat me like a fool. I thought it would be helpful if you knew what he was up to. We think it's Moon who is manufacturing the CCC drug for Vantiche, don't we?'

'Sit down. I need you to understand how serious this is.'

'I don't need a lecture. I'm not stupid. I know what's at stake. Look, I've done my best and I want to be paid. I've kept my part of the agreement.'

Alex had walked around his desk while Kate had been talking, and sat in his chair. He looked up. 'I said sit down,' he shouted and looked down.

Kate stood still and looked at him for a few seconds. Her loathing and hatred of him had built to such an extent that she wasn't sure she'd be able to contain it much longer, and feared she'd do something she'd regret. For a brief moment she thought about turning and running, but knew she couldn't. With reluctance, she dropped into one of the three soft chairs in front of the large, beech-wood desk, and waited for Alex to speak.

He looked up. The expression on his face was serious.

'Everything we know and have subsequently found out confirms that the CCC file contains information on a new and highly successful vaccine for HIV. It could eliminate the disease from Africa, and the world, within a decade. We understand Vantiche were close to bringing it to a limited-trial production process. As you know, if they're successful, their legal people would make sure nobody else in the world would get a look in. If they bring it to market, Kate...' Alex stopped to check he had her full attention. 'They'll clean up. We would miss out on the most important medical breakthrough since penicillin. The estimated revenue from it over ten years runs into trillions of dollars.'

'Alex. That's so patronising. You know damn well I understand all of that.'

Alex pushed back in his seat. 'You might understand it. But what you do not know is that Zeum, our Russian owners, have made it quite clear to me that if we do not get hold of this file and stop Vantiche bringing it to market, they'll pull out. That means they'll withdraw all their capital and sell us. In today's climate, I don't think there would be a ready buyer. In short, Kate, if we don't get the file, we're washed up, screwed, on the heap. All of us, not just me: you included.' He paused and glared at Kate.

'Understand now?'

Chapter Ten

The evening Harry travelled to the airport, Ed James went out on a different mission. He still hadn't been paid for the hits he did on Joe and Clare Fingle. Dave, the intermediary, had disappeared. Ed had been unable to contact him, and had to ask around for his whereabouts, an approach he didn't favour. He always worked solo, and carried out his assignments without the involvement of anyone else. However, he had no choice. He was owed fifty thousand pounds, and needed to collect it.

Ed parked his black BMW under a tree, still with a few leaves attached, across the road from Dave's house. It was a quiet street in Acton lined with large, well-maintained houses. The BMW didn't look out of place. Ed arrived at five when it was dark. He turned off the engine and lights, pulled the hood of his jacket over his head, selected some music on his iPod, and waited. He knew Dave would return that evening. He'd checked it out. He'd called his house and pretended to be a salesman offering a not-to-be-missed TV deal. Whoever answered the phone volunteered the information about Dave's movements.

At 9:00 p.m. Ed saw Dave's silhouette amble around the corner. Ed had become cold and stiff, and wanted to urinate, but ignored his discomfort. Dave approached the side of Ed's car and walked past. He crossed the road, and started to walk towards the front door of his house. He didn't enter. He didn't hear Ed creep up behind him, clamp his powerful arm around his neck, and gag him with a chloroform-drenched cloth. Dave passed out without a struggle. Ed bundled him into his car, and took him to a garage he owned in Stepney, attached to an empty house at the end of a run-down street where few people walked past. He used it to store some of his equipment. Nobody but Ed knew about it. He'd bought it cheap a while back and registered it in a false name.

Ed opened the door in the dark. He heard a familiar, scurrying noise at his feet and guessed he'd disturbed a mouse, or maybe a rat; he'd seen both in the past. He dragged Dave into the garage, dropped him on the floor, and closed the door. He went to the back wall and plugged in a large power-torch that flooded the building with light. A dirty, large, canvas bag lay next to his feet. He opened it up, and started to remove the contents and place them in a line on the floor, next to where Dave lay. A dirty pair of pliers, several bloodstained knives with long, serrated edges, thin wire used to cut cheese, rusty-looking chains, a wooden mallet, and several broken-ended, old screwdrivers made up the assortment. Once Ed had arranged them as he wanted, he stripped Dave of all his clothes. He tied him up and moved him so the scary objects were close to his eyes. Then he rubbed a rag covered with peanut butter over his hands.

He checked the time: ten-thirty. *Dave will wake soon*, he thought, and took a couple of paces to the left wall and picked up a hose attached to a tap. He turned it on and aimed a blast of cold water at Dave's naked body.

'Good. So you're awake,' he said a few minutes later. 'I've been waiting to start.'

Dave coughed and spluttered and tried to look around. He attempted to raise his head. He couldn't, and let it fall back onto the cold, concrete floor. A rat ran over his left hand. He moaned, and started to shiver and shake.

'I told you not to mess with me.' Ed picked up one of the serrated-edged knives. He kneeled down next to Dave's face, and pressed the flat side of the blade against his cheek. He forced Dave's other cheek against the dirty ground, next to the line of terrifying items.

'See my tools? I'm going to show you what I do with them.'

~~~

Gary found his second week back at Ritzler worse than the first. He began to think Alex Goad had gone crazy and was out of his head. Apart from his insatiable demand to be updated on Vantiche's every movement, and to be given a running commentary on Harry Fingle's e-mails, he asked Gary to do things he considered illegal. Gary knew hacking into other companies' systems was wrong and probably against the law, but everyone in the industry did it. For Ritzler to stay ahead of their competitors, they had to do the same. But when Alex asked him if he could sabotage and disable Vantiche's entire IT system, Gary doubted Alex's sanity. He even considered quitting. Hacking was one thing; bringing down a company by deliberately causing their computers to crash for a lengthy period was a different matter. He could end up in prison.

His downtime wasn't much better. Most evenings he fell out of the office between eight-thirty and nine-thirty. He grabbed a takeaway and just managed to crawl through his front door in time to catch snippets of the ten o'clock news. There was a pub on the corner of the street where he lived. Every evening he crossed over the road to avoid the smell. He found staying sober hard, and wondered how long he'd be able to keep it up.

One night, when he was able to leave early, he took a bus to Kensington High Street and started to look around the shops. He saw in the window of a clothes shop a dress that he thought his teenage daughter would like, and he bought it. He found a present for his son, and caught another bus to where his two children lived with his ex-wife. He became excited. The last time he saw them both was several weeks earlier. His daughter had been difficult. She told him she hadn't much time and could only spare him a few minutes for a coffee. His son wouldn't go with them. He preferred to stay at home with a friend. While Gary waited for the door of their house to open, he thought about how much he missed them both. He hoped, in some way, his gifts might help to bring them closer.

'They're not in,' his wife said in a sharp and dismissive way. She held the door barely open. 'I'll take them.' She grabbed the presents, and shut the door in Gary's face.

~~~

The following evening started better. Gary bumped into Jimmy again at Starbucks.

'How's things?' Jimmy smiled. He clasped Gary around the shoulders. 'You look a bit down. Anything I can do to help?'

'I'm shit. Work's crazy, my kids don't seem to want to know me, and I feel exhausted and washed-up most days.'

Jimmy thought back to one of the conversations he had with Harry. 'The more information you can give me, the more I'll pay you,' Harry had said, and then talked about a bonus.

'Want to fill me in?' Jimmy asked. 'Look. I know you don't do booze, mate, but we could nip over to the pub, grab a quiet corner, like, and I'll just sit and listen. Might make you feel a bit better.'

Gary bit on his fingernail and looked into Jimmy's eyes. 'Yeah, why not?' He drained his coffee.

They went around the corner to Edwards Bar, an old pub with a modern makeover on the corner of Hammersmith Broadway. They found a couple of seats in a quiet, dimly lit alcove away from the main bar area. Jimmy offered to buy the first round. Almost as soon as he'd returned with the drinks, Gary started to talk. He took sip after sip on his Coke and told Jimmy about his split with his wife, how he got the sack, and his time in rehab. He explained how, after six months, he was asked back to work at Ritzler. Jimmy sipped on his beer and listened. Occasionally he'd add a comment or question to keep Gary talking. Gary spoke about the work he did, but he didn't mention Harry or Vantiche. When he started to dry up, Jimmy took his chance. He nudged his beer a little closer to Gary.

'So what's this Alex Goad bloke like? He sounds crazy, man.'

'Crazy? He's an absolute arsehole, Jimmy.'

'Yeah. Why's that?'

'You know what he asks me to do?'

'Tell me, man.'

Gary gazed at Jimmy's half-full glass for a few seconds. He looked into Jimmy's eyes. 'You won't tell anyone, will you?'

'Me? No way. Who would I tell?'

Gary stared again at Jimmy's glass. He slid his hand across the table. 'Mind if I have a sip? I feel I need it.'

'You can't, Gary,' Jimmy said. He tried to sound concerned. But he didn't attempt to move his glass away and out of Gary's reach.

'What the hell.' Gary picked up Jimmy's glass and drained it. 'That's better. Let me get you a replacement. What was it?'

~~~

Harry glanced at his house, and then sat back and tried to relax. He was in a taxi. It dawdled down Marlborough Road, turned left into Chiswick High Road, and headed off towards Heathrow airport.

'Which terminal, mate?' the driver asked for a second time.

'Oh, sorry. I was miles away. Em. I don't know. It's Air India.'

'That's Terminal 3, mate. Okay?'

'That's fine. I'm sure you're right. Sorry, I was a bit preoccupied.' Harry had been thinking about Jackie Sentence and her two-worded, text message: **RICHARD MORECOMBE.** He reached over to his bag and pulled out his phone.

'That you, Philip?' he said a couple of minutes later.

'Hello, Harry.' Philip sounded restrained.

'Listen. I know you can't talk or tell me much, but did you know they'd made Jackie Sentence redundant – told her some bollocks about cutting back.'

'I didn't. But why should I? I'm not there anymore.'

'Yeah. Okay. But it's all a load of crap. Look, Jackie was working on the rent-boy investigation.'

'I know that. I put her on it.'

'She found out that Morecombe was using rent boys. That's why they sacked and gagged her.' Harry stopped and waited for Philip's reaction. He heard nothing.

'You still there, Philip?'

'Yes, I'm here. Go on.'

'Your reaction? Surely you've got a view on what I just said?' Harry waited.

'Look, Morecombe – so called pillar of the media, head of a reputed organisation, married to a TV producer ten years his junior, and our ex-boss – pays for sex with young boys. Come on. Surely, you've got an opinion.'

'If that's true, it's shocking. I agree.' Philip's tone remained dispassionate, without a hint of emotion or feeling.

'Can I take it, then, that you knew all about it? That's why you took me off the investigation?'

'That's absolutely ridiculous. Don't be so stupid. You're being precious. Of course I didn't know about it. I took you off because we felt a new journalist might put a different twist on it. Nothing else. Look, I'm out of it now. I can't make much comment. I'm bound by the same gagging order that you are.'

'Not me. I told them where to put their money. Nobody is gagging me.' Harry paused. He looked out of the cab window. He was on the M4, on the flyover at Hammersmith. In the distance, he could make out the illuminated sign on the side of the Ritzler building.

'What's your take on Morecombe's connection with Ritzler?' he said after a few seconds.

'I don't have a view. He's a director of loads of companies. Why? What are you getting at?'

'Nothing, just wondered if you had a view. A girl from Ritzler has been spying on me.'

'What are you on about?'

'Does CCC mean anything to you?' Philip didn't answer.

'Does it, Philip?'

'Nothing. Sorry, I was just thinking. It doesn't mean a thing. Never heard of it.' Philip paused. 'Are you in a car?'

'I'm in a taxi. I'm going to the airport. Why?'

'Where're you going?'

'India, why?' Again, Philip didn't reply immediately.

'Sorry, Harry. I've got to go. Someone at the door. Listen, I don't know what you're doing, but take care. Speak soon. 'Bye.' Philip hung up.

Harry felt bemused. He thought Philip might have told the truth about Morecombe and the rent boys, but his tone and reaction to the questions about the CCC file and Morecombe's involvement with Ritzler were odd. Harry thought back to his brief meeting with Philip in Pimlico, the day after he lost his job. Yet again, he figured Philip was hiding something. Whatever it was, Harry realised Philip wasn't going to tell him at present. His mind moved to other questions and events that needed his attention.

Joe worked for Vantiche on the CCC drug.

Kate Fisher was after the file for Ritzler. They knew Joe was working on a new, world-beating drug, and had to stop him.

'My God.' Ritzler killed Joe. The police know and are hushing it up. Why?

Clare's death – was that Ritzler as well? Maybe she knew too much. Jesus. Ritzler are in it up to their bloody necks.

Morecombe and the rent boys? Where does he fit in? He's a director of Ritzler, so he must be in the know.

And Stacey? What's he up to?

Harry kept searching for answers until the taxi drew up outside Terminal 3 at Heathrow.

~~~

After Jimmy had pressed Harry's doorbell several times and knocked twice with the big, iron doorknocker, he called Harry up. He dialled the home number first, followed by Harry's mobile. Both phones had been switched to a message-taking facility.

'Shit.' Jimmy hoped he wasn't too late and Harry had left for India.

Jimmy sweated. He'd run all the way from Hammersmith to Chiswick. Earlier, once Gary was no longer a 'reformed' alcoholic, he'd told Jimmy about all the special projects he did for Alex Goad. He explained how he hacked into Vantiche's IT system and Harry's e-mails. When Gary had become incapable of speaking, Jimmy paid the bill. He helped him to the door, and pointed him in the direction of his flat, and watched him stagger away before he headed off to find Harry and tell him all he'd heard.

~~~

Jimmy used his key to let himself into Harry's house. He figured, once inside, he'd know if Harry had gone away or not. He'd been right. The fridge lay empty. The main lights were connected to timers that activated at dawn and dusk, and the place looked as though it had been deliberately tidied, with nothing left lying around.

I'm too late. He's gone, Jimmy said to himself. He hurried back down the stairs to the kitchen. He felt worried. Harry faced danger and he had to warn him. He tried to call him again. When he couldn't make contact, he sent him a text, and stood for a while and held onto the back of one of the kitchen stools, and wondered what he should do. Perhaps he'd go to the airport and look for him?

~~~

The front doorbell rang. He rushed to open it, hoping it would be Harry. A short, sturdy-looking man, late twenties or early thirties, stared at him with screwed-up eyes and a sullen expression.

'You Jimmy Ali?'

The man jumped into the house. He stood on the inside doormat.

Jimmy stared back and bristled. He tensed up and prepared for trouble.

'What if I am?'

The stranger stepped further inside, slammed the door and pushed Jimmy to one side.

'Hey, you. Watch it, mate.' Jimmy grabbed the man's shoulder and tried to spin him round.

'Get yer 'ands off me,' the man snapped as he pulled out a long-bladed knife and waved it across Jimmy's waist. 'I'll stick this in your belly and twist it if you try to be clever. Get it?'

Jimmy looked down on the man. He stood at least ten centimetres taller than him, and knew in normal circumstances he'd have no problem in overpowering him. But this wasn't normal or equal. The glistening blade of the stranger's knife was no more than a few centimetres from Jimmy's abdomen. He figured it best to stay put for a while.

'Hey. Cool it, man. Come down to the kitchen. You can tell me what you want.'

The stranger jerked the knife up in a menacing gesture. 'You try anything I'll stick this in your back. Now, lead the way.' He waved the knife again.

'What's your name?' Jimmy asked a few moments later, as they stood and faced each other.

'Me money,' the man said. He'd dropped his hand that held the knife to be level with his side. Its blade pointed forward, at a right angle to his arm, and towards Jimmy's groin.

'What money?' Jimmy's eyes flicked between the menacing blade and the stranger's evil face.

'Yer know. Don't try to be clever with me. The blocks of weed you got from the guy in Stockwell.'

'What, you mean Izzie? I've paid him already.'

The man screwed up his eyes. He raised his hand again and pointed the knife at Jimmy's face. 'No you ain't. He's given me nothing. I want it, now.'

'I gave it to Izzie. I haven't got anymore.' Jimmy shuffled his feet slightly away from the man.

'You Ray?' he asked. He suspected the short-arsed, white guy, who had begun to annoy him, was Izzie's dealer. 'How did you find me here?' Jimmy looked hard at the man, and tried to figure out a plan.

'I followed you, stupid.' The man closed in on Jimmy again, and held the knife up close to Jimmy's neck. It was barely four centimetres away. 'What you mean, you ain't got no more money?' The man stared into Jimmy's eyes. 'One more smart-arsed comment and I'll make yer bleed, big time.'

They both turned their heads. They'd heard the sound of a key turn in the front door. In an instant, the man hid his knife and looked at Jimmy. 'Where's the back entrance?'

They both turned their heads back to the open, kitchen door. A pretty, young woman, who stood about 1.6 metres tall, with shoulder-length, straight, black hair and an Asian complexion, remained still in the doorframe. She stared at them both. Jimmy had never seen someone look so frightened.

It was Amie.

Chapter Eleven

Since 2000, the giant Russian pharmaceutical company, Zeum, and its Chinese rival, Ning, had vied with each other for increasing world dominance. In 2005, both companies set out to acquire large, European businesses. When Zeum fought off Ning's attempt to buy Ritzler and successfully purchased the company themselves, Ning fought back by buying Vantiche in a secret bid that took Zeum by surprise. Ever since, the relationship between Ning and Zeum can only be described as war.

~~~

Located in a small street in the Beliy Gorod district of Moscow is a small, anonymous-looking office. It became the regular meeting place of a female executive from Zeum and a high-ranking, male official from the Russian government. The two people chose the location because of its close proximity to the Kremlin, many restaurants, and the city's nightlife. The meetings took take place at least once a week, almost always at the end of the working day.

At 11:00 p.m. Moscow time on 19 October, as Harry was checked in for his flight to Mumbai, the representative from the Russian government and the smart, well-dressed, forty-year-old, female executive from Zeum were due to meet. It was much later in the day than their normal meeting time. The woman arrived a few minutes before the man. She appeared impatient, and strutted back and forth as she waited for him to turn up. When he did, they were ushered without delay into the heavily guarded building, and escorted to a windowless room. Laid out on a table were bottles of vodka, red and white wine, smoked salmon, slices of ham, some cheese, and dark rye bread. Nobody else followed them into the room. Once they were inside, the one door slammed behind them with a resounding thud.

'Good,' said the man. He looked across the table to the woman as she forked a slice of ham onto her plate. 'What is it that causes us to meet so late?' He smiled in a salacious, leering way. 'However, my dear, I would never turn down an opportunity to meet with you.'

'Boris,' the woman snapped in the manner of a schoolmistress. 'Pay attention. This is serious. There's plenty of time for that at other times.' She stopped and took a sip from her wine, and plonked it down with an authoritative thump. A few drops slopped over the side. 'We have just received some serious news from Alex Goad, the chief executive of Ritzler.'

Boris put down his glass of vodka, leant across the table, and squeezed the woman's hand. He looked up into her eyes. 'Of course, you're right, Natasha. Work is work, and play is play. They shouldn't mix. But...' He started to slide his hand up her arm towards her shoulder. He mouthed a few kisses.

'Boris,' Natasha snapped, 'can't you ever be serious? You're sex mad. I haven't called this meeting to sleep with you. I've something very serious to tell you. Now calm down and get a grip.' Natasha leant over the table and looked into Boris's eyes.

'You may be a good lover, but you're becoming obsessed – unable to function unless you've just had it – it's like a drug with you. You're addicted.' Natasha stood up and looked down at Boris's smirking face.

'I've a good mind to stop sleeping with you. A bit of abstinence will do you good: make you take things seriously.'

Boris sat up. 'Okay, okay. I was just having fun. I'm sorry. What is it that's so important?'

Natasha, who'd paced around, appeared annoyed. She came back to the table and sat opposite Boris. She took a large slurp from her wine glass.

'Now listen. This is serious. Tell your masters that the Englishman, Harry Fingle, who has possession of Vantiche's computer file CCC, is going to India to see Moon Pharmaceuticals. They're the company Alex Goad believes are manufacturing the trial HIV vaccine.'

Boris sat back in his seat. He clasped his hands together and rested them on the table. 'Why would he do that?'

'Because he's a journalist. He's been fired from his newspaper, but is undoubtedly on a personal vendetta to find out what the CCC file is all about. Remember, I told you a few days ago, he was the one who found the file on his brother's computer.'

Boris smiled. 'Oh yes, I do remember. We had just made love. How could I have forgotten? You told me I was the best lover you'd ever had.'

Natasha lunged forward and slapped Boris hard across the face. A big, red mark appeared on his cheek. 'Boris. I warned you. I'm not going to sleep with you again. Concentrate. Get your sex-crazed mind in gear.

'You have to do something. If Fingle discovers Moon are making the drug, he'll publish it and a load of other stuff as well. Things we don't want to get into the public domain. All hell will let loose.'

Boris rubbed his red cheek. 'How can he publish it if he's not employed?'

'The Internet. Don't be so dumb.'

'I see.' Boris looked serious. 'That is important, my dear. I will have to go immediately to the Kremlin and report back to Vladimir Borisenko.'

Natasha stood up and smiled. 'Good. That's better. I've made you see sense.' She had a broad grin as she came around to Boris's side of the table. She took hold of his hands and looked into his eyes. She put one of her hands up to his sore cheek and stroked it gently. Her lips parted.

'My poor, dear Boris. Be quick. Come straight back to my apartment and make love to me, like you did last time.'

~~~

Patrick Tang, the British-educated chief executive of Ning, who spoke English with a BBC accent, looked at his watch. He'd become annoyed. Grigoriy Nabutov had been due to meet him at nine-thirty, and was late. Patrick had flown in earlier that evening from Shanghai especially to meet with Nabutov, and he didn't like being kept waiting. He stayed at Claridge's in the art-deco, Brooke Penthouse suite on the top floor of the hotel. It had been decorated in gentle lilac with light, oak floors. The suite contained a spacious living room, two lavish, double bedrooms and a private rooftop terrace with a panoramic view of London's skyline. Patrick had been too anxious to look or take in the surroundings. He wanted to find out what Nabutov had learnt after his meeting with David Masters, the chief executive of Vantiche. As he went to pour him himself a whisky, his room phone rang. The hotel reception had called to tell him Nabutov had arrived. They wanted to know if it was in order to allow him to come up to Patrick's suite. Patrick asked for him to be sent up at once, and went to check the supply of drinks.

'Come in. Help yourself to a drink and join me,' he said after opening the door to Grigoriy. He walked away, down the hall and towards the living room, with his back to the Russian. Grigoriy dumped his leather jacket on a chair and looked for the bar. A few minutes later, he carried a cut-glass tumbler, filled almost to the brim with ice-cold vodka, to where Patrick sat on a beige and soft-lilac-checked sofa. Grigoriy sat on the large armchair opposite. He took a big slug from his glass, and placed it down on a low, oblong, black-lacquered coffee table.

'So? What news?' Patrick drummed his fingers on his thighs. Earlier he'd worn a suit and tie, but had discarded the jacket while he'd paced up and down the suite waiting for Grigoriy. He loosened his tie, undid the buttons, and turned back the cuffs of his crisp, white shirt. He looked directly at the Russian.

Nabutov narrowed his beady eyes, and touched the scar on his right cheek a few times with his finger. 'We find Fingle. You want him. We see his house.'

'What else?'

Grigoriy rose and walked over to where the bottles and the ice container had been arranged on a marble-topped, serving table. He withdrew the vodka bottle, and filled his glass to the top. He walked back to his seat, took a sip, and looked across to where Patrick sat.

'We follow Fingle to airport. He on flight to Mumbai.' Nabutov pulled back the sleeve of his black, linen shirt and glanced down at his watch. 'It goes now.' Nabutov made a gesture with his right hand to indicate a plane flying through the air.

'Mumbai, I see.' Patrick paused. His moved his head from left to right. His eyes darted around the room in a vague, distant way. He focused on nothing in particular. 'Can you get into his house?'

Grigoriy shot a contemptuous glance at Patrick. 'That insult. What you want us find out?'

~~~

After Grigoriy had left, Patrick poured another large whisky. He walked with his glass to the window and took a large sip. He scanned the view. He didn't like Nabutov. He thought the Russian sneered at him and tried to intimidate and frighten him, but he was glad he'd hired him. He had no doubts about his ability. He would do a good job, and not flinch at whatever Patrick asked of him, even if it was the ultimate solution. Patrick drained his drink, walked back to the bar, refilled his glass, and called up room service.

'Filet steak, rare, a few sauté potatoes, a green salad, and a bottle of Châteauneuf-du-Pape 2004. Make it quick.'

Chapter Twelve

The intruder jumped forward. He grabbed Amie around the neck, and pulled her so close to him that her back was tight against his chest. With his other hand, he pressed the flat side of the knife's blade against her cheek. The sharp edge touched her skin. Amie screamed and then fell silent. She looked terrified.

Jimmy had never met Amie before, but he figured she was something to do with Harry. *She doesn't look like an intruder or burglar, unlike the scum who's threatening her*, he thought, as he tried to work out a way of overcoming the man and setting her free.

'What's yer game, girl?' the intruder said. 'Tell me, or I'll scar yer for life.' He stood with his back to the open door of Harry's kitchen and looked at Jimmy.

'Don't move, you black bastard.' The intruder had seen Jimmy, who had his back against the worktop, try to slide towards him. 'Try any of yer smart stuff and I'll slice her, then yer.'

Jimmy stood still. 'Man, you short-arsed, white-washed honky. When I get to you, I'll pummel you to shit.' He knew he could overpower the man, but wasn't going to try it, not until the right opportunity occurred. The girl would suffer. Jimmy looked at her. He wanted to send a signal that he was on her side, but he couldn't see an immediate way of doing so.

'Listen, you two,' Amie said, taking Jimmy and the intruder by surprise. 'I live here. This is my home. I share it with Harry Fingle. I'm a police officer, and some of my colleagues are about to join me.'

At once the man released Amie. He looked worried, and turned to Jimmy and then back to Amie, who had stepped about a metre away. The knife remained in his right hand. It dangled by his side. He looked at Jimmy. 'She telling the truth?'

Jimmy felt confused. Harry had never mentioned he shared his house with anyone, let alone a policewoman. He guessed it was a bluff. He admired her bravado.

'She sure is,' he said. 'I met her here once before.'

The man turned around as though he was about to make for the front door. Jimmy sprang on him. He grabbed the hood of his fleeced top, and tried to hook his left arm around the man's neck as he started to run down the hall. In an instant, the man swung himself around and thrust the knife towards Jimmy's face. Jimmy jerked his head to one side, but the blade caught his left shoulder, and he yelled and dropped to the floor. The man withdrew the bloodstained knife and disappeared.

~~~

At nine, in the busy waiting room of A&E in Charing Cross Hospital in Fulham Road, Amie and Jimmy started to piece together the thread that connected them both with Harry. Despite Jimmy's objections, Amie had called an ambulance the moment Ray, the intruder, had run out of Harry's house. The ambulance took seven minutes to arrive. Once at the hospital, a doctor and nurse attended to him as soon as the paramedics had carried him into casualty. Thirty minutes later, he'd been sewn up and bandaged, and was able to walk out of the treatment area. Amie had waited for him.

'Thanks,' he said. He looked surprised. 'I didn't expect you still to be here.' He stood and looked down at Amie, who sat on a vinyl-covered bench against the back wall. Next to her on one side was a frail, elderly man, whose face was the colour of his white hair and who seemed to be in some pain. On the other side, a younger man cradled his right hand, wrapped in a bloodied bandage. They both shifted a little to make room for Jimmy.

Amie looked up at him. She could tell he was in pain. 'I thought you might want some help. Here, sit down.'

Jimmy did as she'd told him. He turned his head to face her. He grimaced. 'That's kind of you. But can I ask you who are you? Do you really live in Harry's house; and are you really police?'

'No. That was just bluff. But it worked, didn't it? I'm Amie, an old friend of Harry's. I came to return something.' Amie looked into Jimmy's eyes. 'And who are you? What were you doing there?'

Jimmy winced. 'Oh, I'm Jimmy. I'm helping Harry with something.'

'I see.' Amie nodded and looked hard at Jimmy. She felt a little uneasy, and wondered if she'd done the right thing. Maybe she should have left the hospital as soon as Jimmy had been admitted. He was an impressive-looking man, with sharp facial features and a large, fit-looking physique, but sort of edgy and a little rough. She wouldn't have put Harry and him together. But then, until recently, she hadn't had anything to do with Harry for a year, she told herself.

'What're you helping Harry with?'

Jimmy looked away for a moment. 'Well. I can't really say, like.'

Amie started to gather her things together. She'd become more uneasy, and felt it was probably better to leave. 'Look. I'm really grateful to you. If you weren't there, I'll probably be dead now. But if you're okay to get home, I think I'll be on my way.'

Jimmy held his hand up in the air. 'Hold on a minute. I don't really know much about you, you don't know anything about me, and I get the impression you're bothered about me, but I think we're both concerned about Harry. Am I right?'

Amie nodded again. 'Go on.'

Jimmy screwed up his face. He looked around. People stared at them. They listened in to their conversation. 'Harry's in real danger,' he said. 'We need to contact him somehow.'

'Why? What's happening?'

'Come on.' Jimmy jerked his head to the left. 'Let's get out of here. I'll explain.'

~~~

It was nearly midnight when Alex Goad's mobile phone rang. He sat alone in his luxury apartment that overlooked the Thames at Vauxhall. He'd been finishing off some business papers and had a small whisky by his side. During the week, he lived on his own in London. He joined his wife at the weekends in their large house in Berkshire. On most nights, when he didn't attend a business function, he would return back to the flat around eight, make himself a light supper, and then work until he began to feel tired. Often, he wouldn't reach his bed until one in the morning. He looked at the screen on his phone. The call was from an unknown number.

'Yep. Who is it?'

'You don't need to know…' Alex didn't wait for the caller to finish. He cut off, put his phone to one side, and returned his attention to the document he'd been reading. Thirty seconds later he received a text message. It was from the previous caller.

DAVE TELLS ME YOU ARE THE CLIENT. IF YOU WANT TO LIVE ANY LONGER WE NEED TO TALK. CALL ME.

Alex stared at the chilling message and tried to figure out what it was about. He glanced around his flat, and tried to remember if he'd thrown all his locks. He'd been about to go and find out when he received a second text.

I'M OUTSIDE YOUR DOOR. IF YOU DON'T OPEN IT WHEN I KNOCK, I'LL BREAK IN.

'Holy shit.' Alex rushed to the front door and checked that the three high-security, lever locks were in position, and his alarm had been switched on. Despite his locks being turned and his alarm active, he felt scared. He'd started to sweat. He returned to his desk, and tried to pick up his work from where he'd left off. His hands shook.

After a couple of minutes, all the lights went off in the apartment. It became dark. He couldn't see a single thing. A low-pitched, whining sound came from the alarm box and then stopped, as though it had expired. A silent, eerie stillness descended on the apartment. Alex remained still. The sound of three muffled thuds, one after the other, broke the silence. Alex heard his front door swing open. A thin beam of light broke the blackness. It circled around and focused on him. He remained rigid in his chair. He had never felt so frightened in all his life.

He jolted in his seat as his phone rang. In a flash, a black-gloved hand reached for the handset and held it to Alex's face. He felt what he believed was the barrel of a gun thrust into his ribs.

'Answer it. If you give any clue to what's happened, I'll kill you.'

Alex did as instructed. The caller was a colleague from work. Alex tried hard to sound normal and answer his colleague's questions. A few seconds after he'd ended the call, the lights came back on. An unknown man, dressed in black, with a gun in his hand aimed at Alex's chest, stood still by the front door. The man walked towards him.

~~~

Ed James pulled up a chair. He sat down about a couple of metres from Alex, stared at him, and waved his gun around. He reckoned he'd achieved his aim. Alex trembled and looked terrified.

'Mr Goad. I warned you. You chose to take no notice.' Ed shook his head a few times, and reached forward to pick up a small, black, metal tube that resembled a torch.

'This deactivates all alarms, and cuts the power. And this...' Ed waved a bigger grey, cylindrical, rubber object with blackened ends. 'This will blow all locks. They both worked, didn't they?'

Ed didn't wait for a reply. He turned over his gun with the barrel facing Alex. 'This beauty is a Smith and Wesson M&P-69 pistol, Mr Goad. It's a great little gun. They used it in Iraq to blow the heads off the insurgents.

'See this bit here: it's a silencer. I could pull the trigger now, blow a hole in your stomach, and nobody would hear a thing.' Ed picked the gun up and pushed it into Alex's tummy.

'Some water. I must have some...,' Alex croaked, as he wiped the sweat from his brow with his hands.

'Nope. Not yet.'

'What is it you want? You won't get away with this. I have friends in the police.'

'Snap, Mr Goad. So do I. And they'd love to know you told Dave to hire me to kill Joe and Clare Fingle. Wouldn't they?'

'What do you mean?'

'Come on. You're not going to try to deny it. Dave told me himself a little earlier tonight. How do you think I found where you live, without his help?' Ed stopped and flashed a smile at Alex. 'I had to encourage him a little to tell me. You know: a little prod here, a little push there.'

'Okay, okay, whoever you are. I admit I asked Dave to sort out Joe Fingle, but I was not involved with the woman's death. I know nothing about it.'

'Don't try that.' Ed screwed up his eyes and frowned. He'd become a little confused. Dave had told him, after he'd done the Joe Fingle job, to do the same with Joe's wife, Clare.

'Listen. I shoved her into the Thames at Marlow. You saying that weren't on your instructions?'

Alex shook his head. 'That's right. I had absolutely nothing to do with it.' He sat up in his chair. 'So why are you here?'

Ed stood up. He held the gun by his thigh and walked around the room a few times, and tried to figure out if Alex had lied or not. When he returned to his chair, he turned it around, the back towards Alex, and sat with his legs straddled across the seat.

'If you're telling the truth, why haven't you paid me for the Joe Fingle job?'

'I have. I gave Dave the money before you did the job. He said he had to pay you most of it up front.'

'When?' Ed snapped. 'How much did yer give him?'

'I don't know, about four weeks ago. Sometime in September.'

'How much?' Ed raised the barrel of the gun and pointed it at Alex's head.

'Thirty grand. He said you wanted twenty-five and his commission was five. Why? Hasn't he paid you?'

Ed stood up again and started to pace around. He'd become angry.

If Goad's telling the truth, Dave has done the money. He's sure gonner pay for this, the jerk, he told himself.

Ed returned to his seat and pointed the gun at Alex's middle. 'You lying to me?'

Alex shook his head again. 'No. You ask Dave.'

Ed nodded and smiled. 'I'll do that with no problem.' He waved his gun in front of Alex's face. 'If you're lying, you ain't going to see Christmas. Understand?'

Alex wriggled in his seat and straightened up. He had stopped sweating. He felt some of the colour had returned to his face. He looked straight into Ed's eyes. 'Listen, Mister. I have a proposition for you. It's a big one, a way for you to recoup some of your losses.'

'What's that?' Ed snarled.

'I may want you to do another job.'

'Yer.' Ed looked into Alex's eyes. 'Who?'

'Harry Fingle. He's Joe Fingle's brother. Don't do anything yet, but start sussing him out. You know: homework.'

Ed waved the gun at Alex. 'Don't tell me my business, Mr Goad. I'm the best.' He straightened his arm and pointed the barrel of the gun at Alex's head.

'That'll cost yer. And I want to be paid in full, up front.'

'How much?'

'One hundred grand.'

~~~

Harry sat in the lounge of Terminal 3 at Heathrow, and started to flip through a copy of the *National Geographic*. During the taxi journey to the airport from his home, he'd spent most of the time trying to figure out what lay behind everything that had happened since his brother, Joe, was killed, and he discovered the encrypted file, CCC. He hadn't reached any conclusions, and decided to think no more about it until he landed in Mumbai.

He took a sip from his cappuccino, selected a playlist on his iPod, and started to read an article about the dying coral in the Red Sea. A text message from Amie interrupted him. He didn't read it and tossed his phone back in his bag.

Why doesn't she leave me alone? I've told her it's over. I can't make it any clearer.

He managed to read a few more lines before his phone disturbed him again – this time a call. He guessed it'd be Amie again, and reached into his bag to switch the phone off. He picked it up, and couldn't avoid seeing the screen.

'What's up, Jimmy?'

'We've been trying to call you for ages. You got a minute? It's important.' Jimmy sounded anxious and spoke in short, sharp bursts.

'Who's the "we," Jimmy? What's this all about? You sound panicky.'

'Listen. They know all about you. They're tracking your e-mails. They know you've got the file, and they know Amie helped you. They're after you, Harry. I'm really worried. I spoke to Amie about it. She's worried too. They even know you're going to India. You must be careful. Amie has tried to text you...'

'Stop. Calm down. I don't understand. How do you know all this? You're going too fast – and what's this about Amie? How's she got involved?' Harry paused for a couple of seconds, and gazed up at the departure screen. His flight departure time had blanked out and the space was flashing.

'I'm bloody cross, Jimmy. I told her not to interfere again.'

'Listen, Harry,' Amie shouted. 'I'm here with Jimmy and I'm not interfering. I just care for your life. You're in real danger. Jimmy had a drink with his contact in Ritzler and the guy told all. They are tracking your every movement. They know you're going to India. They're desperate to get hold of the CCC file. From what he's told me, I think they could be behind Joe's death. You said...' The call cut out.

'Jimmy, you there? Can you hear me?' Harry shouted when he called Jimmy back.

'Yeah. I'm here.'

'I'm really confused now. How come you and Amie got mixed up?'

'It's too complicated. I'll tell you later. I was stabbed and Amie helped me out. It's you we're...' The phone cut out again. Harry looked at it. He had no signal. He tried to call both Amic and Jimmy's number but couldn't get a connection.

Shit. Stabbed? What is this? he questioned. He looked up at the departure screen. *Shit, shit, shit.*

His flight had been delayed by an hour and a half.

Chapter Thirteen

Ray followed Amie up the steps of Ealing Common tube station. It was 11:00 p.m. He'd watched Jimmy and her all evening; ever since he'd fled Harry's house after Jimmy and he fought, and he stabbed Jimmy in the shoulder. He'd hid in the unlit porch of an empty house across the road. It had been perfect. It gave him a clear view of Harry's house. He saw the ambulance arrive, looked while Jimmy had been taken out on a stretcher with Amie, and then followed in his car to the hospital. He waited until they both came out, and saw them go into a nearby pub. When they left and went their separate ways, he followed Amie onto the Tube.

She walked across the open common to Grange Road. Ray kept about twenty metres behind. He pulled his jacket close in to shield him from the bitter cold and icy wind that whipped down the street from the trees and directly into his face. At eleven-fifteen he stood behind a van, parked on the other side of the road, and watched as Amie turned the key in the front door of her ground-floor flat and went inside. In the corner of his eye, he caught sight of a man with a dog at the far end of the road. Ray turned and started to walk at a brisk pace in the other direction towards the next corner. He came to a main road, Ealing Green, turned right and then right again into The Grove. After ten minutes he found himself back in Grange Road. The dog walker had disappeared, and the street appeared empty. Ray sneaked up to Amie's flat unobserved. He crept towards the front door, took out a small penlight torch, and started to examine the locks.

They looked too difficult to force. He moved around to the side of the house where a passageway led to the back garden. A wrought-iron gate with a padlock barred his way. He cursed under his breath, and grabbed the lock to inspect it; it sprung open. It hadn't been closed properly. Silently he removed the padlock from the gate and pushed the gate open, bit by bit. He froze. The gate had creaked. He'd also been caught in the glare of a security light, triggered by his movements. He remained still, and listened for any sudden noise from inside the flat. None came; but he was able to make out the sound of water gushing down a drain, and guessed the girl could be taking a shower. The security light went off. He was surrounded by darkness again, and inched his way around to the back of the house.

He came across a patio, illuminated by the lights from the kitchen. He crouched at the edge and in the shadows until he became sure that no one was in it. The top half of a split, stable-style gate had been left slightly open. At the far side of the kitchen, steam poured from the bottom of a closed door. A white towel had been dumped on the tiled floor outside. He'd been right. The girl would be taking a shower. He felt his knife inside his jacket and crept forward. He stood up, opened the top half of the gate, took a couple of paces back, and then ran at the door and leapt over and landed on Amie's kitchen floor.

~~~

When Grigoriy Nabutov had been the boss of one of the most feared Russian organised-crime syndicates, he was powerful and rich but removed from the day-to-day activities, the things he knew he did well when he built up the organization – like extortion and blackmail. So, when he found out Richard Morecombe could be an easy touch, he decided to test his old skills and visit him himself.

He approached Morecombe's office at the top of *The Morning News* building in The Docklands dressed in a navy suit, light-blue shirt and tie, black, polished shoes, and a navy, cashmere overcoat. He'd called the previous day to make the appointment and said he was from the Russian Government. He'd said he wanted to talk to a reputable British newspaper about the murder of a Russian ex-secret-service officer on British soil a few years earlier. The appointment had been booked for 10:00 a.m. on the morning after he'd met with Patrick Tang at Claridge's.

Richard waited at the door to his office to greet him. He stretched out his hand and beamed from ear to ear. 'So good to meet you, Mr Nabutov. Please come in.'

Grigoriy followed Morecombe into the office. He dumped his coat on the arm of one of the squat, cream armchairs around a square, wooden table laid with coffee and tea pots, white cups and saucers, and a plate of pastries. He sat in one of the other empty chairs.

'Some tea or coffee?' Richard asked, as he sat down opposite Grigoriy.

'Black coffee,' Grigoriy replied without looking up, as he pulled out a grey, buff file from his case.

'Help yourself to a croissant or a Danish pastry.'

'Coffee okay.' Grigoriy looked up with a weak smile and focused his dark, beady eyes on Richard.

Richard, who worked on keeping fit and trim, didn't take a cake either, just a cup of Lapsang Souchong tea with no milk. 'So what is it you have for me? I'm not a journalist myself, Mr Nabutov. If you don't mind, I'd like to ask the editor of *The Morning News* and one of his reporters to join us.'

Grigoriy stood up. He held his cup in one of his large hands, and walked to the wide window that overlooked St Katherine's Dock. He swirled his coffee around, drank it down in one gulp, and turned to look at Richard.

'That not necessary, Mr Morecombe.' Grigoriy looked at Richard with a deep, penetrative stare, and screwed up his eyes. 'You see, I come talk to you, only you, about Ritzler. You a director, I understand.'

Richard seemed taken aback. 'What do you mean? Ritzler is nothing to do with the Krauchenko affair. You told me on the phone you wanted to talk to me about it. I don't understand.'

Grigoriy walked back to his seat. He opened the file, and withdrew several large, A4-size photos, and turned them facedown on the table. 'I explain. I need to find out about Ritzler and CCC.' Grigoriy stared at Richard. 'You know?'

'Who are you?' Richard's face had become flushed. He seemed agitated. 'You told me you're from the Russian government. Are you an imposter?'

'I Grigoriy Nabutov, that's all you know. And you answer my question about Ritzler and the CCC file. Yes?'

Richard shot Grigoriy a quick glance before he stood up and reached for his desk phone.

'No, Mr Morecombe. Look.' Grigoriy also stood, and held two of the A4 pictures in each of his hands so Richard could clearly see the images. He watched as Richard's face turned ghostly white.

'Where did you get those?' Richard burbled. Beads of perspiration began to break out on his face. He staggered over to his desk, and placed one of his hands on the desk's edge to support him.

'Okay. Good. You get the message, Mr Morecombe.' Grigoriy paused. His black, beady eyes were fixed on Richard.

'I leave these for you. I have copies. Forty-eight hours these photos go to the offices of *The Daily Journal*. I think they publish them in next edition. Second set go to your wife, at work. She works for television company, yes?' Nabutov picked up his coat and bag and walked to the door. He turned and stared at Richard with a menacing look.

'Ritzler and CCC, please.' Nabutov shrugged his shoulders. 'Or pictures go.

'I let myself out.'

Richard staggered over to the table, and hesitated before he turned over the rest of the photos.

'The bastards.' Each photo, like the other ones Nabutov had shown a few minutes earlier, revealed Richard naked in a compromising position with a different rent boy.

'Jimmy? Is that you?' Harry looked at his watch. It was ten past midnight. 'I've been trying to get you and Amie for ages. What's going on? What's all this about you being stabbed? And how have you and Amie linked up? I don't get any of it.' Harry stretched out his legs and leant back on the hard seat.

'Where are you?' Jimmy whispered in a sleepy voice. 'I was asleep. Look, I've got to crawl out of bed and go into the bathroom or I'll wake up my roommate, and he won't be too happy. I'll call you.'

While Harry waited for Jimmy's call, he scanned the crowded departure lounge. He saw many tired and frustrated travellers. Some of them tried to rest a little, or pacify and entertain a fractious child or two. Others read, listened to music, played a handheld game, or just sat and waited. Harry suspected that, like his, their planes had also been delayed.

'Listen, Harry. I can't talk much and I've got to whisper. I'm in trouble again. I did some drug dealing and a bloke is after me for payment, like. I paid my roommate, Izzie, who I got the stuff from, but I think he's done the money and now the main dealer, like, is chasing me.'

'What's this about being stabbed? And Amie? What's she got to do with it all?'

'She's clean. Nothing to do with her. She disturbed me and the dealer at your place. He came after me to get his money. He followed me.'

'What? She came into my house again? She's insane.'

'She's not. She talks a lot of sense. Did you understand what I told you before, about these Ritzler people listening in on you? Amie and I think they're dangerous and are after you. You've got to be careful.'

Harry didn't reply immediately. He'd been distracted by the sight of the Air India ground staff opening up the gate, and an announcement that the flight was about to board.

'I've got to go. The flight's boarding at last. I'll be okay. Tell Amie I'm getting pissed off with her. I must go now. 'Bye.' Harry switched off before Jimmy said good-bye. There was a scramble for the boarding queue. He dropped his phone into in his bag and joined the line.

Jimmy scratched his head and called Amie.

Amie screamed. The man she'd escaped from earlier at Harry's house stood in front of her, in her kitchen, and brandished his knife. She'd just stepped out of the shower and was naked, apart from a big, white, bath towel that she'd wrapped right around her.

'Take it off, lady. Drop it.'

'What do you mean?' Amie became terrified and felt herself begin to shake and tremble.

'Take the bloody towel off. Do as I say. Drop it on the floor. I want to look at you – in the raw, lady. You lied to me. People don't get away with that.'

Amie started to cry. Tears dribbled down her face. She felt powerless and became sure she would die. The man took a couple of paces closer. He stood less than a metre away. He pointed his knife at her, grabbed the towel, and ripped it away. He threw it on the floor.

On my God, he's going to rape me first, she thought. *And then kill me.*

'Nice,' the man said with an evil, sneering grin as he ran his eyes up and down Amie's body. He moved forward and took hold of one of Amie's nipples. He placed the pointed end of the knife on her bare skin, just above her tummy button, and ran it slowly up towards her breasts.

She felt it drag and scratch and wanted to yell out, but she held back – not wanting to let the man know how terrified she felt. *Please, let it be quick*, she said to herself. She felt sick and light-headed and sure she would soon pass out.

All of a sudden the loud beat of her favourite song blasted around her kitchen. It came from her phone's ringtone, and took them both by surprise. She caught sight of the man's startled expression.

'What's 'at?'

'That'll be my inspector. He's calling to see if I got here okay.'

'What do you mean, lady? Don't try to play that game again!' He lowered the angle of his knife slightly.

'Your choice,' Amie said. She sensed a look of concern on the man's face, and reckoned she had a slim chance. She decided to go for it.

'If I don't answer it, they'll be a police car round here within three minutes.'

'Crap.' The man raised the blade of the knife again. 'Come on, lady. You told me that before at the last house. You said you lived there. What yer bleeding well doing here, then?' He placed the knife up under Amie's left breast, and pushed and twisted it so the point of the blade broke her skin.

She gasped, and took a deep breath.

Her ringtone stopped. She turned and looked at it. 'If you don't believe me, wait three minutes and see; could be less. They'll be on their way now. You see – this is my boyfriend's flat. We rent it, normally, but don't have a tenant. So we use it when...' Amie stopped. The man had taken a pace backwards. His knife no longer touched her body. He looked around the room.

'I warn you, lady.' An evil look shone from his eyes. He waved the knife back and forwards in front of Amie's face, and stabbed it into the air at random. He flashed it close to her cheeks and eyes.

'If you're lying, again, I'll cut you up in tiny pieces, bit by bit.'

~~~

Harry had been asleep for an hour when he felt a light tap on his shoulder. He looked up and saw one of the flight attendants looking down on him.

'Excuse me, sir. Please don't be alarmed, but the captain is about to make an announcement. We've been asked to make sure all passengers are awake.'

Harry rubbed his eyes, shook his head, and sat up.

'Good evening, everybody. I'm Captain Rajiv Patel. Please don't be alarmed; but I regret to inform you we have to return to London. There has been a large explosion in Mumbai, close to the airport, and it's been closed for the time being. All flights bound for Mumbai, within two hours of Heathrow, have been ordered to return. I apologise for this inconvenience, but I'm afraid there is nothing I can do about it. Once on the ground, our staff will do everything possible to update you and make alternative arrangements for your travel. We should be landing at Heathrow at 4:00 a.m. Please relax, and try to get a little rest. We'll talk to you again when we are about to start our descent into London.'

~~~

At five-thirty in the morning, in pouring rain and still dark, Harry's taxi pulled up outside his house. He noticed that his front door was wide open.

What's she doing here now? he thought, as he dumped forty-five pounds in the driver's hand, and grabbed his bag and raced up the small path to the door.

'Amie,' he yelled as he reached the doormat in his porch. He stopped and stared. Bare, splintered wood stuck out in several places from the broken and contorted doorframe. The brass workings of the

106

three locks were mangled and twisted, and the door had large cracks and splits from where a giant hammer or other implement had been used to force it open. Wet leaves had blown in and scattered all over the hall. Wherever he looked he saw dirty footprints.

Harry dropped his bag and ventured in. As he started to call the police, he caught sight of the shambles of his living room. It had been ransacked. The contents of his drawers and cupboards, his books, magazines and CDs, and the cushions from the sofa and chairs were strewn and discarded all over the floor. He dashed from room to room to find similar disorder. Upstairs, his clothes had been rummaged through, the bathroom cabinet emptied, and all his towels and sheets had been pulled from the airing cupboard and dumped at random on the landing floor. He ran back down the stairs and searched for where he'd left his phone.

Odd, he thought as he picked it up. *They've taken my laptop, but left the TV*. He put the phone down on the floor for a second, and picked up the remote to check if the TV still worked. BBC News 24 flashed up with pictures of the bomb blast in Mumbai. Harry couldn't take his eyes off the screen.

'Jesus Christ.'

He put his hands up to his mouth as he watched firemen try to extinguish the last flames from the smouldering remains of a large factory. A female BBC reporter stood in front of the flattened wreckage. He listened as she spoke.

'All that remains of India's largest drug company, Moon Pharmaceuticals, is the burnt-out wreckage behind me. The company was the biggest supplier of medicines to one of the world's largest pharmaceutical giants, Vantiche Pharmaceuticals. Moon employed 5000 people. The nation is in shock and...'

Harry could think of only one person who'd be able to explain both the bomb blast and the break-in to his house.

Chapter Fourteen

MI6, the security service of the United Kingdom, resides at Vauxhall Cross, near Vauxhall Bridge, London, in an impressive, rectangular-stepped building that overlooks the Thames. At 4:00 a.m. on the night Harry tried to fly to Mumbai, Paul Thompson waited there for his opposite number in the CIA, Scott Reynolds, to arrive. Scott was in his early fifties, and had been employed by the Agency since he'd left university. In his time, he'd worked on many high-level assignments, some neutralising severe threats to American national security, and had been praised for his work. On one occasion he received a personal letter of thanks from the president.

He considered his posting to London to be a wind-down before his retirement. Not that he didn't take it seriously: just that he didn't take kindly to being woken at three-thirty in the morning by someone younger and greener, and for something he believed could wait. Paul was the opposite. He was twenty-eight, and had just joined MI6 after a two-year stint at the Foreign Office, and looked to impress.

'Okay, buddy. It'd better be good. I was enjoying a real big, warm sleep, snuggled up to my wife. I don't go much on being called so early in the morning and having to face this god-awful, miserable, British winter. It's so damn cold and wet in this country.' Scott's disapproval showed on his face. He gulped down the black coffee Paul had pulled from the all-night dispenser, and looked across the beech table at him. 'What the hell is so important it can't wait?' he growled.

They sat in one of the small, windowless meeting rooms on the ground floor. Paul had a laptop open in front of him. He smiled and sipped at his black tea. 'Come on, Scott. You're getting soft. You can't tell me you don't get cold winters back in Langley. I saw snow three foot high when I was there.' Paul found Scott difficult and prickly, and looked across at him for a sign that his initial irritability might be passing. Paul had called Scott in because there had been an important development in the joint operation they ran together. He also had to discuss another problem he knew would not be easy or go down well.

'Yeah. Okay. But I'm tired. Get on with it.'

Paul turned his laptop around to face Scott. 'You need to see this?'

Scott looked at the image of the burnt-out wreckage of Moon's factory in Mumbai. He turned to Paul with a puzzled expression. 'So?' He shrugged his shoulders. 'I don't understand. It was an act of terrorism. The ops guys will be on to it already.'

Scott pushed the rolled-up sleeves of his long-sleeved shirt further up his arms, rested his elbows on the table and stared at Paul. 'What the hell's it got to do with CCC? Have you brought me here, at this ungodly hour, just to look at that picture?' Scott jabbed his finger at Paul's laptop. 'I can't believe you'd do that. You're joking, surely?'

Paul stood up. He walked around the table, picked up his phone, and plugged it into the side of his computer. An e-mail flashed up on the screen. 'Read this. It's from one of mine in Mumbai.'

Yellow
Re: EXPLOSION AT THE HINDU TEMPLE AND MOON DRUG FACTORY AT 0130 hrs GMT.
SNAP – 0200 hrs GMT.
Act deliberately made to look like work of fundamentalists. Inside contacts confirm that it was carried out by employees of Moon on the instructions of foreign agency. Origin of agency not positive, yet – but DEFINITELY not Pakistan, Iran or Yemen. Sources suspect Russia. Will confirm shortly.
End. Red

'What's the lowdown then? If it wasn't Ragheads or Hajis, who the hell was it? And what's it got to do with CCC?' Scott's tetchiness remained.

Paul stood up and made to leave the room. He turned to Scott, and put his hand on the back of the chair he'd been using. 'Scott, it's serious. Let's go. We can't talk here. I'll tell you over breakfast what I figure is going on.'

They walked down a long, grey-walled corridor lined with high-tech, metal security doors until they reached a large, open-plan cafeteria at the end. Several severe-faced people passed them on the way. All seemed to be in a hurry, and barely nodded a greeting as they walked by. Paul collected a cooked breakfast for Scott, some muesli and a banana for himself, two glasses of orange juice, and refills of coffee and tea. He carried the tray to the grey, metal, four-seater table that Scott had found at the end of the room. Scott remained silent while Paul distributed the contents.

'Joe Fingle was killed on the orders of the Russian-owned drug company, Ritzler, wasn't he?' Paul said as he sat down. He pushed the empty tray to one side.

'Agreed.' Scott had his head down. He seemed intent on cutting up his bacon and egg.

'But the Russians didn't kill Clare Fingle.' Paul paused and looked directly at the American. 'Did they, Scott?'

'Why you asking me?' Scott mumbled as he ate. 'You're running this. I'm just here for the ride, and to see if we can help.'

'Don't bullshit me, Scott.' Paul waited until Scott looked up. 'Why did your guys kill Clare Fingle? What do you know that you haven't told us? And why do you work behind our backs?'

Scott looked down again. He pushed his fork around a few times, gathered up some bacon and scrambled eggs, and started to eat. He ignored Paul's question.

'Don't be an arsehole. Your guys paid a hit man to blot out Clare Fingle. *Why?*'

Scott dropped his fork. His face had flushed up, and he looked angry. He screwed up his eyes and demanded, 'How the fuck do you know?'

Paul leant back in his chair and took a sip from his tea. He put his mug down on the tabletop with an audible clunk, and faced up to Scott. 'Believe me, or it could get messy. You wouldn't want to know our source.

'Let me tell you something else. You may have a long, distinguished record at the Agency, but you're working on British soil now and we don't like being fucked around. Particularly by people we think of as friends.' Paul glanced down at his laptop and then back at Scott.

'I may be running this op, but you're in it with me. We agreed, together, to run Joe Fingle at Vantiche. You briefed him with me. You can't play the noncombatant now.'

Paul leant forward and looked into Scott's eyes. 'Don't screw us around. You've killed someone in our country. That's against the law. If it were the Russians, we'd be making a lot of noise and kicking out a few of their spooks. But it's not. It's you guys. We're on the same side.'

Paul paused for Scott's reaction. The two of them sat and stared at each other. Scott had his arms crossed, and rested them on the table. His face bore no expression. After a short while, he drummed the fingers from both his hands on his upper arms. The two men stayed in the same positions for about twenty seconds before Paul stuck his neck out. Only five to ten centimetres separated his head from Scott's. Their eyes locked.

'Scott, you're taking the fucking piss.'

Scott leaned back in his chair and gave Paul a withering look. Paul had no doubt that Scott didn't take to being called to order, particularly by someone much younger. Paul prepared himself for Scott's response.

'Hey, smartass. You listen to me. Nobody else knows about the hit on Clare Fingle. If you try to get clever, I'll just deny it. Call you a liar.' Scott smirked. 'That'd screw up your career prospects, wouldn't

110

it?'

Paul remained focused on Scott for a few more moments. A slight grin broke his serious expression. His left hand reached into his trouser pocket and pulled out his phone. He held it up for Scott to see.

'Shame on you. You're getting old. Not keeping up with the new toys. Everything we've said is on here.' He waved his phone a few times in front of Scott. 'I've just sent it to my laptop.'

'You little shit.'

'If you think so.' Paul picked up the phone and put it back in his pocket.

'Okay. Now we have to get down to business. I need you to hang around and meet up with someone, a man called Philip Stacey.'

~~~

At two-fifteen in the morning, about forty-five minutes after Ed James had left Alex Goad, he drew up outside Dave's house in Acton. He turned off the lights and opened the glove compartment. He pulled out his gun, and checked that the ammunition clip was full and the silencer was screwed on properly. He slid it into his jacket pocket and left his car. He found it easier to enter Dave's house than Alex's flat. There was only one lock and, with a low-sounding, muffled plop, he blew it open. He found Dave asleep in his bed beside a woman who he assumed was Dave's wife. He crept round to her side of the bed, covered up her mouth with his hand and shouted out Dave's name.

She woke with a start and looked up. The barrel of Ed's gun pointed at her forehead.

'Wake him.'

'He's in a deep sleep,' Dave's wife said, shaking. 'He takes tablets.'

'Then kick him. Whatever's necessary, but don't try anything clever.'

Dave woke and wiped his eyes 'What's going on?' He turned his head towards his wife. 'Don't hurt her. She hasn't done anything. Please don't…'

'Get dressed. We're taking a walk. If you try to be smart, your wife gets a hole in her head.'

Ten minutes later Dave was back in Ed's car. It was the second time he'd been in it in twenty-four hours. He'd been gagged, and lay on the back seat with his hands and feet tied. Ed drove fast for about an hour through country roads until they parked by a deserted stretch of the Thames in Oxfordshire. He dragged Dave out of the car and propped him up by a tree. He returned and pulled out a large picnic rug from the boot, folded it in two, and placed it on the frozen ground opposite Dave. He walked over to him, removed the gag, and walked back to the rug and sat on it. He pulled out a slim torch from his pocket. He pointed it at Dave's face and turned it on. A thin beam of light sliced through the black night.

'Okay,' Ed said in a sharp, determined tone. He directed the torch's beam in a circle around Dave's face. 'I've two questions and I need answers.' He turned off the torch. The cold of the night, the sound of Dave's irregular breathing, and the burbling of the river made an awful eeriness.

'Why didn't you pay me? Goad told me he gave you the money.' Ed waited for Dave's answer. He didn't give one.

'Second question. Who was the client for the Clare Fingle job?' Dave remained silent. His breathing sounded loud and pronounced.

Ed switched on the torch and flashed it several times around Dave's face. 'So you want to be difficult. Listen to me very carefully.

'I left your wife tied and gagged, and naked in your bath. I filled it with cold water and let the cold tap drip down her face.' Ed chuckled. 'Your choice.'

Dave moaned and whimpered. 'Look. I wanted to pay you, really. I mean it, but I had this other guy who I owed some'ing to who was pestering me. Please, please leave my wife. She hasn't done anything. Please. I'll get the money tomorrow. I've some in the bank.'

'Good, that's better.' Ed turned the torch off again. 'Who was the client for the other job?'

Dave shook and started to sob. 'Promise you'll let the wife and me go if I tell you and promise to pay you tomorrow.'

Ed smiled. Dave couldn't see his smile. 'Of course.'

'It was an American guy. That's all I know. Don't know his name. He called me and said he had a big job. I met him and he paid me...'

Ed jumped up. His gun trailed from his left arm. He raised it and took aim at Dave's head. 'He paid you up front, did he? You twisting bastard.'

A dull plop broke the silence. Dave flopped over to the left and lay still on his side. Blood spouted from his head. Ed moved forward and stood over him, and fired two more shots into his chest, and then dragged his body to the riverbank. He left it for a moment and collected some lead weights from his car. He attached them to Dave's arms and legs, and rolled his body into the Thames. He took a bucket from his boot and, using the light from his headlights, sluiced away the bloodstains from the tree and grass. He then drove at speed to Dave's house and killed his wife. He disposed of her body in the docks near his apartment.

~~~

As the sun rose over the river, Philip Stacey, Scott Reynolds, and Paul Thomson sat around a table that overlooked Vauxhall Bridge. If they'd been inclined, they could have seen the build-up of the morning traffic. But they weren't. Philip had just arrived, and they'd just completed their greetings. They sat around a small, circular table. The mood was strained.

Paul unbuttoned the cuffs of his cream shirt and started to turn back the sleeves. He turned to Scott. 'Philip's been onboard and worked for us ever since he was editor of *The Morning News*.' Paul turned to Philip. 'Tell us about Harry Fingle, Philip.'

Scott looked up and glanced at Philip. He appeared surprised. 'You still there, at *The Morning News*?'

'I'll answer that,' Paul said. 'When Fingle started to close in on Richard Morecombe, the owner of *The Morning News*, and his penchant for young boys, it started to get too hot for Philip, so we had to get him out. We used the excuse of him not being willing to sack Harry: as a friend, you know.'

'Uh-huh,' Scott said. He leaned back in his chair and looked at Philip. 'So is Fingle working for MI6?'

'No, not at all.' Philip straightened his tie. 'He doesn't have a clue what we're doing. Look, he's probably the best investigative journalist around. We're using him to help with CCC. But I'm worried. I think it's getting risky for him. He's not safe. We need to keep him under observation and covered.'

'Why?' Scott asked. He scratched his chin.

'Before Philip answers…,' Paul said. He turned to Scott. 'Brief him about Clare Fingle. He needs to know.'

Scott twisted his seat round to face Philip. He took another sip from his mug. 'Must I?'

'Yes,' Paul snapped. He looked directly at Scott.

'Okay.' Scott frowned with disapproval. 'It goes like this.' He sat back in his chair and glanced for a moment at Paul and Philip.

'We know Joe Fingle was knocked off on orders from the Russian owners of Ritzler, Zeum Pharmaceuticals, and the Russian government. But what you don't know…' Scott, tight-lipped, turned to Paul. 'Clare, Joe Fingle's wife, was working for the Russians. She was their agent. Her job was to get hold of the CCC file from her husband, so Ritzler could sabotage Vantiche's attempt to be the first to bring a successful vaccine for HIV to the market.' Scott stopped and raised an eyebrow quickly at the other two. 'Or so they thought.' He looked again at Philip and grinned.

'We couldn't allow her to find out anything about CCC. She would have blown the whole thing.'

'They took her out,' Paul said. He looked at Philip.

'We did. We had no alternative.'

Paul stared at Philip, who looked shocked.

'You sanctioned *it*?' Philip asked. He frowned and fiddled with his tie.

'No.' Paul glanced at Scott. 'But that's been sorted.'

'What! The CIA is murdering people on our soil and without our knowledge. That's outrageous. If I was still at *The Morning News*, we'd...'

Paul leant forward and looked into Philip's eyes. 'Well, you're not. You've signed the Official Secrets Act and can't do a damn thing. Now, let Scott finish.'

'I'm done,' Scott said with a deadpan expression.

He turned to Philip. 'I thought we're here to listen to this guy brief us about Fingle.'

'Why do you think Fingle is more at risk, Philip? What's changed?' Paul asked.

Philip sat up straight in his seat. He clasped his hands together and rested them on the tabletop. He looked at the other two in turn. 'He was on his way to Mumbai to see Moon. Not coincidentally, it was blown up – and not by fundamentalists. When he got back this morning, he found his house had been ransacked and his laptop was gone.'

Scott looked straight at Philip. He looked concerned. 'Was the CCC file on it?'

'Luckily not,' Philip said. 'He'd deleted it before he left for the airport.'

Scott shifted in his seat and said, 'How do you know all this? And where's the file now?'

'I've had someone on the ground, working close to Harry.' Philip looked down for a moment, and brushed a speck of dirt from his pinstriped trousers before turning back to Scott and Paul. 'Harry called me up at home this morning. I don't think he trusts me, but we go back a long way. He calls me from time to time to try to get information and sound me out. He was pretty distraught, and just wanted to talk it through. He's off to see Kate Fisher. He thinks she'll know what's going on. She works for Goad, the guy who runs Ritzler.'

'Where's the file?' Scott said. He leant forward and placed his hands on the table. He looked concerned.

Philip gave Scott a disparaging look. 'I could hardly ask him that, could I? He doesn't know I have any interest it.'

'I get it,' Scott said. His chin rested in his cupped, right hand and he looked deep in thought. 'You figure if they think he knows too much they'll top him?'

'Look.' Philip looked annoyed and faced Scott. 'Vantiche and Ritzler, spurred on by their Chinese and Russian masters, will do anything to get the CCC file. The Russians have already killed Joe, Harry's brother, and Vantiche have this Russian, Grigoriy Nabutov – ex-Moscow mafia I believe – working for them over here. Surely you can see Harry's in danger?'

Scott looked away and bit on one of his thumbnails. 'Yeah, I see that. But what are you asking us to do? Call the goddamn thing off?'

'Listen,' Philip said. He'd raised his voice. 'Harry is an innocent, British citizen in all of this. I understand the big picture. I agreed to help, and I'm not suggesting for one minute that we should abort. But we must be aware of the risks involved. If Harry cops it, it's on our heads.' Philip turned to face Scott. 'You've already got one life on your hands.'

'Philip, that's a crap comment. She was a Russian spy.'

'Leave it,' Paul said. He turned to Philip. 'You have a man on the ground with Harry, don't you?'

'Yes. But he's not with Harry all the time.'

'Okay. But he's close. This is what we'll do.

'Philip, tell your man to keep close to Harry. We'll set up an armed surveillance team to keep watch as well.'

'Good result.' Scott leant forward and clapped his hands. 'So, who do we think was responsible for the bombing at the Moon factory? Vantiche or Ritzler?'

Chapter Fifteen

Amie leant against the kitchen sink and vomited several times. She turned on the tap, bent her head sideways and gulped in as much cold water as she could swallow. She splashed and rinsed her face, and slowly stood up. The towel the intruder had ripped away from her lay on the floor where he'd dropped it. A thin line of blood ran down her body from below her breast. Not a deep incision, but it needed attention. She tried to take a couple of steps to the bathroom and stopped. Nausea had swept through her body. She felt dizzy: sure she was going to collapse and be sick again. She reached out to the wall for support. A minute or two passed before the queasiness eased and she was able to reach the bathroom. She cleaned the wound and found a plaster, and stumbled back to the kitchen to call the police.

This saved my life, she thought, as she held her phone in her hand and began to dial **999**. As she was about to press the green call-key, the phone sprang into life and vibrated, and her favourite tune rang around her kitchen again. In shock, she dropped it onto the table.

It's him, the intruder, she was sure. He was lurking somewhere outside with his knife. He'd called to scare her.

Please, not again, she prayed. Her eyes closed. She reached out to hold onto the table.

'The police. My only chance. I must call them,' she whispered and stretched down for the phone. Jimmy's name showed on her screen. They'd exchanged numbers in the pub earlier.

'Oh, Jimmy, Jimmy, where are you?' she answered. A surge of relief swept through her.

'What's up?'

'Jimmy,' she sobbed. 'That man, the one with the knife. He…' Amie didn't finish the sentence. She became distraught, unable to speak, and dropped the phone again. She slumped down into one of the chairs. She wept and wept, and cradled her head in her hands on the table.

~~~

Jimmy arrived at her flat at four in the morning. He knocked on the door and pressed the bell several times with no effect. He became worried, concerned he was too late and Amie would be lying unconscious or, worse still, dead. He kept his finger on the bell push and shouted through the letter box, caring little about the noise he made. After five minutes of no response, he became anxious. He feared

116

the worst, and stepped back from the door to look around for a way in. There wasn't an obvious one. He was about to go down the side path when the door opened. Amie stood in the doorframe. She wore only a white bathrobe. She looked devastated.

'I'm sorry,' she said as she let him in. 'I thought it was him again, coming back to finish me off.' She buried her head in Jimmy's large chest. He put his arms around her. 'Oh, Jimmy,' she sobbed. 'I'm so frightened. It was awful.'

'Come on. Let me make you some tea,' Jimmy said.

Amie looked up at him. She wiped the tears from her eyes and smiled. 'Thanks. That would be nice. Come with me. I'll show you where everything is.' She turned and led the way to the kitchen, and switched on the kettle. With one hand on her work surface, she twisted around and faced Jimmy. He stood by the table.

'I feel a bit better now. I guess it's having you here; it's sort of reassuring. Have a seat.' Amie nodded towards a chair. 'I can do the tea.'

'Sure? You look a bit shaky to me.'

'I'm fine.'

'As you like.' Jimmy pulled out a chair and sat down. 'Want to tell me all about it?'

While they drank the tea and munched on some chocolate biscuits that Amie had found, she told Jimmy all about Ray and how he'd fled shortly after her phone had rung.

'I think that was me. I called you sometime after midnight, after Harry hung up on me.'

Amie looked into Jimmy's big, brown eyes. 'You saved my life.' She smiled, stretched her hand across the table to take hold of Jimmy's hand, and squeezed it. 'Thanks.

'I'm scared, Jimmy. I don't know what to do. He'll be out there, waiting for me.'

'What did the police say?' Jimmy sipped his tea.

'I didn't call them.'

'What. Why not?'

'I don't know. After you called, I could hardly move. I just stayed here with my head on the table and wept. I think I eventually passed out. I woke after ten or twenty minutes. I was cold and stiff, and just managed to struggle to my bedroom and pull the duvet over my head. I fell asleep for about an hour, I think, until you knocked just now.'

Amie glanced at Jimmy. 'Should I call them now?'

Jimmy reached across the table and took hold of Amie's other hand. 'You can't, not while I'm here. Look, I've got a police record and I'm on probation. As soon as they come, they'll take one look at me and check me out. They won't believe my story. They'll think I'm something to do with it.' Jimmy tightened his hold on one of Amie's hands. 'I'll look after you.'

'But, Jimmy, I've got to go to work tomorrow. I've got an important lecture to give. I can't let my students down. I'd be scared out of my mind, here alone. I'll never sleep.'

'I'll stay. I can sleep on the sofa. I'll walk you to the Tube, or however you get to work.' Jimmy looked into Amie's eyes.

'Listen. Let me explain. I've done time for drug dealing. I told myself when I came out I'd never do it again. But I had no money, like, and my roommate got hold of some weed and told me if I moved a bit, he'd give me a decent cut.' Jimmy looked away for a few seconds and then back at Amie.

'What I didn't know was that he got it from that scumbag with the knife. I think his name's Ray. I'll kill him if I lay eyes on him.

'You see. If you call the police while I'm here, it'll be a problem. They'll trace me back to him and I'll end up inside.'

Amie picked up their two mugs, and walked over towards the kettle. She filled it, switched it on, and turned to face Jimmy. She leant against the worktop.

'I don't want to do anything that'll get you in trouble.' Amie shook her head. 'I feel safe while you're here; but he'll come back. I'm sure he will. What am I going to do after you've gone? You can't stay here forever. This flat's tiny.'

'I don't know right now, but I'll figure something out. Trust me; I'm not going to let that guy get anywhere near you.'

Amie walked back to the table and around to Jimmy's side. She put her arms around his big, broad shoulders. He turned his head to look up at her. Their eyes met.

'Sleep with me, Jimmy. In my bed.' She took his hand. 'I'd like you too.'

~~~

Ray saw the light go out in Amie's flat. He looked at his watch. It was 5:00 a.m. and he was cold and hungry. He guessed the tall, black guy would stay the night. He became annoyed, and wanted to get back into her flat and finish things off. She'd lied to him again, and he was going to make her pay for it, but he didn't fancy his chances with the big guy around. He looked powerful and more than a match.

I'll be back.

~~~

Twenty-four hours after Richard Morecombe had received the threatening visit from Grigoriy Nabutov, he pushed open Alex Goad's door unannounced. Alex sat at his desk. He had been reading his mail and checking e-mails. He looked up and saw Richard stride towards him. Alex could tell, from the urgency in Richard's pace and the look on his face, he had something on his mind.

'What's the big deal, Richard? Most people either knock or let Lucy know they want to see me. It's polite you know.'

'Bollocks. I can't be doing with all that. I need to talk to you.'

Alex put his pen down on his desk. He took his glasses off and placed them on top of his A4 pad, and stared back at Richard, who sat in the middle chair of the three chairs that faced Alex's desk.

'Listen to me. You may be the biggest thing in the media world, used to snapping your fingers to make things happen, but you're just a nonexecutive director in this company. In case you don't remember, I'm the chief executive. I call the shots, not you. I'm not used to people barging in here and playing big balls with me. Now what's your gripe?' Alex leant back in his big chair. He tilted it backwards and swung it a little from side to side. He stared hard at Richard. He felt angry. He waited for Richard's response.

Richard drew his chair up to Alex's desk. He placed both his hands on the rolled edge and frowned. 'Enough of the *Boys' Own* stuff. Cut the crap and listen to me.

'As a nonexecutive director, I'm legally supposed to be kept informed of everything that goes on in the company.'

'So? You are.'

'Not so. I had a chat yesterday with your assistant, Gary Lester.'

'You what?' Alex snapped. 'You've been talking to my staff, behind my back?' Alex felt furious and concerned.

What's Gary told him? he wondered.

'He told me we're concerned about Vantiche's development of a new drug, codenamed CCC; and it's likely to be a vaccine against HIV. That's important. Why don't I know anything about it? As a director, I insist you tell me all, today.'

Alex fought hard to contain his outrage. He felt like telling Morecombe to get the hell out of his office, but he knew he couldn't. Morecombe was right. He'd deliberately withheld all the CCC information from him, and from one or two of the other non-executives. He didn't want them asking too many questions. He stood up, buttoned

119

up his jacket, walked around to Richard's side of the desk, and sat on the edge, facing him.

'Yep. You're right. We haven't told you. But we will. I can't brief you now as I have a full diary. But I'll get the file and take you through it tomorrow.'

'When tomorrow?' Richard sounded anxious.

'Same time or a little earlier. Say eight-thirty?'

After Richard had left, Alex asked Lucy, his PA, to hold all calls and put back his meetings for half an hour. First, he called the Kremlin: the number for the official in the Russian government he'd been told to ring in an emergency. After an elaborate series of security checks, he was put through.

'This is Boris, Alex. What can I do for you?'

'I was told to contact you if things with the CCC business turned sour.'

'Yes, that's right. But Natasha, from Zeum, has told me that the Fingle man flew to Mumbai to see Moon. We've dealt with that. What else do you want?'

'It's a man called Richard Morecombe. He's a nonexecutive director of Ritzler and he's demanding to know all about CCC.'

'What's wrong with that?'

'He's the owner of *The Morning News*. It's one of the most respected British papers. If he finds out, it'll be…'

'Stop. Don't waste my time. Eliminate him. Understand?'

'Okay. That's what I thought you'd say. It'll be done. That's all.'

'Don't go,' Boris said. 'Listen. How close you are to getting the CCC file? I thought you had it.'

'Not yet. The man Fingle has still got it. But I've got someone good on to it. She'll get it.'

'She?' Boris grunted. 'Do I take that to mean she's using all her powers? If you know what I mean.'

'That's right.'

'Lucky man.'

'Yes,' Alex said, as he remembered with nostalgia his brief, passionate affair with Kate.

'Listen. When you've got the file, eliminate this Fingle man as well.'

The line went dead.

Alex's second call was to Ed James.

~~~

Gary Lester turned up to the meeting late. He sat at the back of the room and listened to June, a woman he'd never seen before, conclude her story. She cried.

'So it was shortly after she died that I went back on the booze,' June sobbed. 'I couldn't stop myself. I felt so low and down and depressed. I thought just one drink would be okay. I poured a glass of wine.' June looked around. She smiled a little.

'It felt great to start with. Made me forget all about Elizabeth. Then I had another and another. Soon, I'd drunk the whole bottle and went out to get more. I bought two bottles of wine and a few mini-bottles of vodka, brought them back home and did them all. Then I must have passed out. I found myself on the floor of my kitchen in the morning.' June stopped and looked around again. She seemed frightened and ashamed, and started to sob again loudly, drawing in deep breaths.

She dropped her head. 'I've let everyone down. I'm so sorry. I really am.'

'Thank you, June. Thank you for being so brave and sharing your experience,' the chairperson said. He looked at Gary. 'Would you like to say something, Gary?

Gary had not expected to speak. He'd come straight from work; uptight about the awful meeting he'd had with Alex. He'd torn into him about telling Richard Morecombe about CCC. The possibility of being asked to stand up and talk had not entered his mind. He was just grateful he'd got to the meeting. His first impulse on leaving the office had been to go the pub and get wasted, but AA had won through. He straightened up his trousers, tidied his shirt around his tight waistband, and stood up.

'I'm Gary Lester and I'm an alcoholic. I didn't have a drink for seven months. Then I went back to work. I hate my job, I hate my boss, and my children never seem to want to see me. A week ago a friend asked me if I would mind going to a pub. I said it didn't bother me. I'd drink Coke. But I didn't. I gave in and drank five pints of beer, went to another pub on the way home – on my own – and downed three large glasses of whisky before I was thrown out. The next morning, I went to the corner shop before work and bought a half-bottle of scotch. I drank half of it before I left the house, and finished the rest at work.' Gary stopped. He'd spoken quickly and fluently without any emotion or pause. His words had rolled out of his mouth, as they'd come into his head.

He looked around the room. Most of the faces were different from when he'd attended the meetings before. But they all looked the same somehow; people with anxieties and problems written all over their faces. They'd be divorcees, emotional cripples, some who'd lost their jobs, or just plain, ordinary folk who couldn't say no. And he was one of them – again.

What have I done? he thought. *I'm right back at square one.*

He felt weak and put one of his knees on the plastic chair he'd sat on. He wiped his sweaty brow. His head spun.

'Are you okay, Gary?' asked the chairperson.

'No, I'm not. I'm shit. I've thrown everything away. I'm so, so sorry. I've let you all down. I really want to stop.' He broke down in tears and dropped down onto his chair.

'Well done, Gary. Good luck. Let's give Gary a round of applause.'

Chapter Sixteen

Harry pulled on his helmet. He mounted his bike and headed off towards Barnes. It was dark. Dawn showed no signs of breaking, and heavy rain pounded the road. He checked his watch. It was 7:00 a.m., but felt like the middle of the night.

To avoid the early morning traffic, he weaved his way through the back roads to Chiswick House. He reckoned he could speed through the grounds and pick up the small pathway that ran along the north side of the Thames. He would cross the river at Barnes Bridge. He cycled fast, dodged in and out of cars, and paid no attention to the many large puddles and the slippery roads awash with surface water. He wore only an old, torn, waxed jacket and jeans, and became soaked before he'd covered a kilometre. It didn't bother him. He thought only of arriving at Kate's house before she left.

Earlier, after he'd discovered the break-in and found someone that would come to fix and secure his front door, he'd called Philip Stacey. He wanted his view on the bombing in Mumbai and the forced entry to his house. But Philip had been vague and unhelpful. Harry became convinced he worked for some covert organisation and politely ended the call. He took a shower, changed, gulped down a shot of espresso and left.

It took him thirty minutes to reach Kate's house. No lights shone. The curtains were drawn. There appeared to be no sign of life. He propped his bike against the railings and looked around. He noticed a big, old door knocker attached to the dark-green front door and took hold of it. He knocked hard several times. When, after one or two minutes, he heard no response, he knocked again with more force and intensity. Nobody and nothing stirred. He noticed a disused-looking doorbell and pressed on it several times as he stared at the two upper windows. The curtains remained closed.

While he figured out his next move, he noticed one or two people leaving the adjacent houses. He guessed they were going to work or to the shops, or whatever was their business. Some looked at him with interest, others passed by without the turn of a head. Maybe he should ask if they knew if Kate was around? But after his third attempt at knocking, louder and harder than the previous two, he heard the sound of keys turning in a lock. He waited. The door opened a touch. He could just make out Kate. She looked bleary-eyed, and peered at him through a small gap with a brass chain across it.

'Harry; what the hell are you doing here? I thought you'd gone away. You'll bring the house down you're making such a racket.' Kate looked down at Harry's sodden jeans and shoes. 'Hold on; I'll open up.

'Jesus, Harry. You look awful.' Kate wore a towelling bathrobe. Her face appeared to be devoid of any makeup. 'You're soaked. *Your feet!*' She pointed down to her doormat. 'You're leaking. You look shattered. What's this about?'

Harry took a step backwards and rubbed his eyes. He felt tired. He guessed his lack of sleep, and the tension and drama of the previous days, must have shown.

'Kate,' he barked and took a step backwards. 'My house was ransacked last night. The factory I'd been due to visit in India has been bombed, razed to the ground. I want some answers, urgently.'

Kate looked aghast. She put her hand up to her mouth. 'Has anyone been killed?'

Harry placed his hands on his hips and stared hard at her. 'Yes. I don't know how many. On the news, they said it could run into several hundred.'

Kate gasped. She covered her mouth and turned away 'Oh my God,' she said with her back to Harry. She turned back to face him. Her hand still covered her mouth. She trembled, and her eyes filled with tears.

'You'd better come in,' she said. Her face looked white, drained of any colour. 'Dump your jacket on the floor.' She met Harry's eyes, and fumbled with the two edges of her robe to pull them closer and up around her neck. She bit on the thumbnail of her other hand.

'You must tell me all about it.' Kate shook as she spoke. 'But I have to go and put something on. You know where the kitchen is. Make yourself a drink. I'll be as quick as I can.' She glanced at Harry's jeans and shoes. 'Why don't you take your shoes and socks off and stand by the radiator.'

'Fine, I'll do that.' Harry watched as she turned and made for her stairs. He felt surprised. She seemed to have been taken aback and upset by what he'd told her. *Surely she would have known about it all,* he thought. Or was she a good actress?

~~~

Kate cried in the shower. She felt certain Ritzler and their Russian masters had organised the bombing of the drug factory. They would have fixed it after she'd told Alex about Harry going there. The responsibility for the death of innocent people lay with her.

How can I live with myself? It's appalling. Those poor people who've been killed, and their relatives. It's wrong. Why did I do it? Why did I let myself be dragged into Alex's evil web and let him control me?

Oh Jack. My dear, dear son. What do you think of me? I've let you down. Please, please forgive me. Jack, I miss you so much.

She sobbed for some time. She splashed water across her face in the hope she'd flush away her wrongdoings.

Could I have done differently? Should I have turned my back on Alex and told him to find someone else to do his dirty work?

But then he would have lied and lied. I would've ended up broke and had to sell this house. Ian would have got it all.

It's no excuse. I knew Alex was evil. Why did I let him blackmail me? I should have gone to the police.

Oh, how I hate that man.

She shook as she dressed. She searched her brain, and asked herself again and again what she could do to right her wrongs.

~~~

Harry looked up. He sat on one of the stools in Kate's kitchen. He'd been flipping through his notes. Kate gave him a slight smile. She wore dark-navy jeans, a V-neck, red T-shirt, and she had nothing on her feet. Her face still bore no signs of makeup. Her blonde, spiky hair looked a little wet. Harry caught a whiff of the perfume she'd worn the previous evening.

'You okay?' she asked, as she came and sat opposite him. 'You look tired. Can I get you something to eat? I could do you egg on toast or something like that.'

'Yeah, okay,' Harry said in a disinterested way. 'I need some answers.'

'Go ahead.' Kate stood up to start preparing the eggs. She had her back to Harry.

Harry stood up and moved closer. 'What's so important with this CCC thing that drove Ritzler to kill my brother, his wife, and innocent people in India? And why ransack my house?'

Harry stared at the side of Kate's face. He waited for her to respond. 'CCC is a cure for HIV, isn't it?'

Kate took the frying pan off the stove. She held it in her hand and turned to face Harry. A tear dribbled down her cheek.

'Listen, Harry. If Ritzler are responsible for the bombing in Mumbai, I'm truly sorry. Yes, I did tell Alex Goad that you were going to India.' She shook her head. 'But I had no idea they'd do this.'

Harry took a pace nearer. He frowned and screwed up his face. 'So it was Ritzler?'

'I don't know. I have no idea.' Kate put a hand up to her face and rubbed away her tears. 'It's terrible, awful. I can't tell you how bad I feel about it.'

'How did you know I was going to India? I didn't tell you.'

Kate put the frying pan down and looked up at Harry. 'I've done wrong, Harry. I snooped on you. I saw a label on your case when you went to get the drinks. But I swear; I wouldn't have told Alex if I thought they'd blow up a factory and kill people.' Kate looked earnestly into Harry's eyes. 'I'm not a murderer.'

Harry glanced at Kate for a couple of seconds. He put one hand on the work surface and leant forward. His face was no more than fifty centimetres from hers. 'Surely you don't think I believe you?' He spoke in a mocking tone, and had an intense look in his eyes. 'You've just admitted you spied on me.'

He looked away for a moment and then glared at Kate. 'Last night, you were trying to get the CCC file off me. What do you take me for?'

Kate bit her bottom lip. Her eyes filled with tears. 'Believe me, Harry. My son, Jack, was murdered last year. It almost wiped me out. I'm hardly going to get involved in mass slaughter, am I?' She stopped and started to cry.

'Harry,' she sobbed. 'I'm really sorry, really I am. I will help you with whatever it is you want. I'm having nothing else to do with Ritzler and Alex Goad. I want out.' She sniffed and wiped her eyes. 'Please, please, let me help you.'

Harry moved away. He rested his hands on the surface behind him and stared at Kate for a few seconds. 'You can start by telling me everything you know.'

They moved to Kate's living room. For about an hour, Harry sat on Kate's sofa with his feet propped up on her coffee table and listened as she told him all she knew about Ritzler and their obsession with the CCC file. She confirmed what he'd figured out. Ritzler believed the CCC drug was a vaccine for HIV. If Vantiche brought it to the market, they'd clean up. Ritzler would be missing out on one of the world's most significant medical breakthroughs.

'Alex Goad told me he feared Ritzler's Russian masters would pull all their money out of Ritzler if Vantiche marketed an HIV vaccine,' Kate said.

'That makes it okay to murder my brother and your sister, does it?' Harry sat up and dropped his feet to the floor.

Kate, who'd become composed and more in control, shook her head slightly for a few seconds. 'I know nothing of that. I'm hardly going to kill my own sister, am I?'

'So what do you think, then? You must have a view.' Harry leant forward and waited for Kate to answer.

'I don't know. I don't want to believe it, but I think you're right. I haven't worked for Ritzler since Jack died. I walked out after his funeral. I couldn't take it anymore.'

'What do you mean?' Harry felt confused. 'You're working for them now, aren't you?'

'No. Really, I'm not. Goad's been blackmailing me. He told my husband's solicitor that I'd been having an affair with him all through my marriage to Ian, and unless I spied on you, he'd give them all the evidence they needed to ensure I'd be screwed. All the money would go to Ian. I'd be left with nothing.'

'Have you?'

'Have I what?'

'Been having an affair with Goad?'

'No way.' Kate jumped to her feet. She turned and stared out of the bottom windows at the Thames and then back at Harry. 'I did, years ago, before I met Ian. I can't stand the guy now. He's a piece of shit.'

Kate took a pace forward. She leant down and picked up Harry's mug. Her right breast brushed against his arm.

'I haven't slept with anyone for eighteen months,' she said. She stood over Harry and looked down at him. 'Want another drink?'

Harry nodded slowly. 'Thanks. I'll come with you. I want to keep talking.'

She led the way. He followed, and noticed her slender waist and trim figure, and smelt her perfume. He wondered if she'd told the truth.

'I never cooked you that egg on toast, did I?' She turned to face him as they entered the kitchen. 'I have a question for you.' She looked around and reached out for the frying pan with the two eggs she put in it earlier.

'Go on,' Harry said. He kept his eyes on Kate as she turned back to face him.

She put the pan down on the worktop and held the eggs in her hand, and looked into his eyes. 'What is your game? I mean, what are you after? Are you wanting justice for your brother, or what?'

Harry shook his head. 'No. Not really. I'm an investigative journalist. I expose the truth, and that's what I want to do with this CCC thing.' He shrugged his shoulders. 'Of course, I also wanted to know who killed Joe and Clare.' He looked away for a moment. 'And now I know,' he said with conviction and paused.

'But it's how it all fits together. Mumbai, the break-in at my house, my sacking from *The Morning News*, Richard Morecombe's games, and all the rest of it.'

Harry glanced at Kate. She had moved away, and stood with her body facing the hob. She twisted her head around to listen.

'What you've told helps, but it isn't the final piece of the jigsaw.'

'What is then?' Kate asked.

'What I asked you before. Was Ritzler behind it all?' He paused. 'I believe they were, but I need confirmation.'

Kate looked down at the pan. She scooped out the eggs, laid one on each piece of toast, and brought the two plates to where she'd placed them both.

'I think I can help you.' She looked into Harry's eyes.

'How?'

'I'm going back to work at Ritzler. I'm going to spy on Goad, and find out what's really going on.' She reached out and touched Harry's hand.

~~~

At twelve – midday – Ed James's patience was rewarded. The front door of Kate's house opened and a man – who Ed knew for certain was Harry – came out, unlocked his bike from the railings, and prepared to ride it. An attractive woman in her early thirties followed him, and talked to him as he fastened the straps of his helmet.

Almost as soon as Alex Goad had alerted Ed to the likely hit job on Harry, Ed had started watching him. He'd followed his movements and tried to identify his patterns of behaviour. After not being paid by Dave, Ed was anxious to complete the job.

Harry pushed his bike forward. He turned to Kate and said a few more words. She put her hand out and touched his shoulder, and leant forward to kiss him on the cheek. He smiled and kissed her lightly on the lips. He swung his leg over the saddle and cycled off, and gave her a quick wave as he disappeared down the street.

'Hmm,' Ed grunted. He smirked. *He'll soon be dead*, he thought.

He followed Harry in his car all the way to the gate that led to the grounds of Chiswick House. Harry swept in; Ed was unable to follow him. No cars were allowed. He cursed and drove off. He'd figured Harry had been on his way home. He decided to go and park up near Harry's house, and watch from there. While he waited in a traffic queue, he thought through his plans. His preferred method revolved around Harry's use of his bike. He had tagged Harry as an aggressive, fast cyclist. One who took chances and paid little attention to the Highway Code, signs, or limits. Ed wasn't complacent, but believed it would be relatively easy to knock Harry off his bike. He'd do it in such a way that Harry would fall under an oncoming lorry or bus, or similar. That way, if the bus didn't kill Harry, the following vehicle undoubtedly would. The lights changed, and Ed drove off. He hoped Alex Goad would give him the go-ahead for the job shortly. He was ready.

~~~

Grigoriy Nabutov gave the two men opposite him a menacing look. They sat in the living room of the luxurious apartment Zeum had rented for Grigoriy in Mayfair. He lived in Shanghai, and he had a small apartment in Moscow. But ever since Joe Fingle's death and the disappearance of the CCC file, he'd taken to living in London to run the operation to recover it.

'You didn't find it, then? Did you search everywhere?' he asked in Russian. He looked at the two men in turn. They were Russians. They were paid employees of the Russian state, and worked for the FSB as secret agents based in London. Grigoriy knew them from his days in Moscow. He called them up and bribed them to work for him on the side. He was well aware they could double-cross him, particularly as the Russian government had an interest in Ritzler.

'No. We didn't. But we took the place apart. There wasn't a single disk or memory stick that we didn't check. We had this with us.' The FSB agent who'd spoken tapped on the side of a small, box-type piece of equipment that Grigoriy recognised. It was one of the powerful, laptop-style devices that the FSB took with them everywhere. They were ideal for instant photographing of papers and fast downloading of data from PCs or laptops.

'What about his computer?' Grigoriy picked up his glass of vodka.

'Nothing on that, either.'

Grigoriy sipped again on his drink. His gaze moved between the two men. He knew they would have done a thorough job. But he wanted to be sure of their loyalty. He reached into the soft, black-leather case sitting next to him on the sofa. He pulled out a large, brown, A4-sized envelope. He placed it out on the table. He kept one of his hands on top. He stared intently into both their eyes.

'Both your families are still in Moscow, aren't they?' he said.

'Why?' one of the men snapped. He had a nervous expression on his face.

Grigoriy smiled and screwed up his beady eyes. 'Because, my friends; I wouldn't want anything to happen to them.' Grigoriy smiled again and turned his head quickly to the left. 'I'm sure you understand. Yes?'

'Yes, we understand. We won't tell.'

Grigoriy, with his hand still on the envelope, turned to the man who hadn't spoken. 'And you?'

'Yes, Grigoriy. I understand.'

'That's good then,' Grigoriy said. He raised his eyebrows and glanced at them both again. 'Remember, I still have friends in Moscow. People who are willing to do as I ask, like pay a visit to your family.' He narrowed his eyes again and repeated his flash of a smile. 'If I told them to.'

He looked down and lifted his hand from the envelope that contained their money. He pushed it across the table towards them. He turned back to the agent who'd first answered his question.

'And, Igor.'

'Yes.'

'Continue keeping an eye on Fingle. Be prepared.

'We may have to take him out. No mess and no trail. Understand?'

The man nodded.

'Good.' Grigoriy finished his drink and showed them out of his apartment.

Chapter Seventeen

Gary walked away from the AA meeting, and stared at the pub across the road. His first reaction was to run over and go inside. *One drink wouldn't hurt*, he thought, and started to cross over. He stopped and turned back. He quickened his pace and looked straight ahead. He needed something to take his mind off the temptation, and thought back to the distant memories he still had of his parents. Both had died in a car crash when he was in his late teens, some twenty-four years ago. He remembered them both as kindly, fun-loving people, who did their best for him and his sister. After they died, he had to leave school and find a job. He never finished his education. His parents had wanted him to go to university, and he knew he would have been offered a place. But, after their deaths, he had no money, and his dream came to a sudden end.

Shortly after his parents' joint funeral, his sister, older than him, went to live with her boyfriend. The two of them had applied for Australian visas, and left to go there shortly before the first Christmas after Gary's parents' death. He'd been left to spend it alone in his tiny bedsit. His sister wrote to him some months later to say she'd become engaged, and would he like to go out to the wedding. He couldn't afford it. He hadn't seen his sister or her husband since. He had never met his niece and nephew.

When he was nineteen, he was offered a job at Ritzler as a junior in the IT department. At first he spent most of his time entering data and doing odd jobs. He worked hard, and found he understood computers and the programming as well as his colleagues with their computer-science degrees. On his thirtieth birthday, the company promoted him to head of the department.

They were good times, he thought. He enjoyed the job. He felt well-respected and remunerated, and had a good social life. Then he met his wife, Bryony. She'd been a programmer in the department. Their relationship started well. They talked a lot, had many friends and enjoyed a good and varied sex life. But after a couple of years things started to go wrong. He worked long hours. Ritzler appreciated and rewarded him: but Bryony didn't. She behaved as though jealous of his success, often criticising him for staying late and not spending enough time with her and the children. They rowed often, and then she took a lover: Gary's best friend. With the help of a clever lawyer, she managed to sue him for divorce, take possession of the family house, obtain custody of the children, and be entitled to the majority of his income. He was forced out of his home, separated from his children, and left with little money. His heavy drinking followed.

What have I become? he asked as he neared his front door. *My children don't want to see me. I live in a tiny, rubbish flat that I don't own. I have an arsehole for a boss, no friends, and I'm a drunk.*

As he pushed open his front door, he thought of Jimmy, and wondered if he could meet up with him. He called him. While he waited for an answer, he caught sight of the three empty wine bottles that lay on their sides on his kitchen table. The dregs from the bottles had dribbled down the table's legs and made dark-red stains on the wood. Next to one of the wine bottles stood a half-empty bottle of whisky.

Jimmy didn't answer his call.

~~~

Harry stopped on Barnes Bridge and stepped down from his bike. He felt the day had become one of those rare occasions in late October when the weather and conditions uplifted the soul. The torrential rain had stopped, dried up, and disappeared without trace. A bright sun shone high in the clear, blue sky. There wasn't a cloud in sight and it felt unseasonably warm. Harry guessed the temperature could be close to 20 degrees. He looked down over the Thames, and watched a riverboat packed with tourists making its way upriver in the direction of Putney Bridge. As the boat moved farther and grew smaller, he reflected on his lack of sleep over the last thirty-six hours. He felt surprised at how bright and upbeat he felt.

He thought back to his time with Kate, and guessed what had taken place had affected his mood. They'd slept together. He felt astonished as to how it happened. A relationship with her of any sort could not have been further from his mind. But it happened, and was good, and he had no regrets. He thought back to how it started.

Kate had become distraught with guilt over her dealings with Alex Goad. She blamed herself for the deaths of the innocent people who'd died in the Moon factory in Mumbai. She said she wanted to prove Ritzler was behind the atrocity, and pleaded with Harry to let her help, even if it meant appeasing Goad a little longer.

Harry smiled. He remembered her standing up. He'd been sitting down. She had moved so close she was almost on top of him.

'You don't believe me, do you?' she'd said, and took a small step nearer. 'I've got to help, Harry. Let me, please.'

He had looked up and caught sight of her naked midriff, and the short, scanty T-shirt that clung to her breasts.

'How?' he'd asked, suddenly aware of her powerful sexuality.

She'd leant forward and kissed him. Without a thought, he'd followed his instincts and stood up and pulled her to him. Then they'd made love. It had seemed so simple and uncomplicated.

He wasn't sure how he felt about it emotionally, but was comfortable about it and glad he'd be seeing her again. He didn't know where it would lead, but felt easy and content to let it take its course.

He mounted his bike. It was time to return to his house. He had much to do: check the new locks, verify the repairs to his front door, and clear up the mess left by the intruders. And there was Jimmy and Amie. He had to find out what they'd been up to. He cycled off at speed.

~~~

Gary went to the men's room and cleaned his teeth. He pulled his mouthwash out of his bag, and sluiced a load around his mouth. He was due to meet up with Alex in ten minutes, and had to be sure the two large slugs of whisky he'd consumed earlier left no trace. He had good news for Alex. He figured, once they'd discussed it and after Alex had thanked him, it would be the appropriate moment to ask for a role change. He reckoned that, if he could stop working directly for Alex and move into a normal line-management position with less pressure, it would help him quit the bottle for good.

'Come in, Gary. Take a seat. What's so urgent?' Alex pointed to one of the armchairs in front of his desk. He sat opposite Gary.

'You need to come round this side, Alex. I've something to show you on my laptop.' Gary lifted the lid and logged in.

'Must I? Can't you just tell me?' Alex seemed irritated.

'It'd be difficult to explain. It's easier if you come and see it.'

Alex stood up and moved to the seat next to Gary. He appeared displeased. Gary reckoned he didn't like sitting next to someone. By sitting opposite, he could appear important, in control, and make others nervous and in awe of him. Gary started to feel jittery. He hoped he wouldn't start shaking or perspiring, a trait that had returned lately since he'd started drinking again. He looked Alex in the face.

'I've broken the CCC file encryption. It's all there, in front of you. The details of the drug, its uses, and the chemical composition.' Gary turned to look at Alex. He expected to see an appreciative expression. Instead, Alex frowned and moved his head close to the screen. He reached forward and picked up the laptop. He placed it on the table in front of him, and paged up and down the screen. He clicked repeatedly on the touchpad in a frenzied manner.

'Shit. Why doesn't it move on?' He appeared frustrated, unable to operate Gary's laptop.

'Here, let me do it.' Gary reached for the computer. 'What do you want to see?'

'There, that.' Alex jabbed his finger a couple of times at the screen. 'Where it lists its uses and benefits.'

With ease, Gary adjusted the screen to the page Alex wanted. Alex grabbed back the laptop, leant back in his seat, and gazed at the mass of dense information that appeared in front of him. He took several minutes to absorb it all. He looked shocked. His face turned pale.

'Fuck.' He snapped the lid closed and passed it back to Gary.

Gary began to feel stressed and agitated. His hands were unsteady and shook a little, and he had begun to perspire.

'What's wrong?' he forced himself to say.

Alex stood up and stared down at Gary. 'Nothing. Well done. Now leave me please. I've work to do.'

Alex started to walk back to his desk.

Gary took a deep breath. He ignored his nerves and said, 'Alex, I was going to ask. Now I've done most of the work on the CCC project, could I move...'

Alex turned and glared at Gary.

'I'm too busy now. Later.' He turned again, and went and sat in his seat behind his desk. He had his head down and made notes on a pad.

'What do you want me to do with the CCC file information?'

Alex didn't look up. 'Oh. Make a copy and put it on my PC: but later. I'm too busy now to be disturbed. Leave now.'

As soon as Gary had left the room Alex picked up the phone. 'That you, Margaret?' he snapped at Margaret Hudson, head of human resources.

'Yes, Alex. What can I do for you?'

'Gary Lester's drinking again. I want him out of the company today.'

~~~

It was 4:00 p.m. when Patrick Tang in Shanghai took the call from Grigoriy Nabutov. It hadn't been a good day for Patrick. The bad news started at eight in the morning when David Masters, the CEO of Vantiche, called. He'd told Patrick about the bombing of Moon Pharmaceuticals, the company that manufactured the CCC drug. At ten, a couple of hours later, Patrick found out his financial director had been caught up in an American financial fraud involving billions of dollars. Patrick had broken off from a meeting discussing the two crises to take the call from Grigoriy in his private office. He hoped Grigoriy had some good news. He sat back in his reclining, leather chair, and put his feet up on his desk.

'What have you got for me?' he asked in fluent Russian, and swivelled back and forth in his seat while he waited for Grigoriy to answer. He knew Grigoriy would be surprised. He'd never spoken to him in Russian before.

'We've been all over Fingle's house, and searched his computer, and can't find the file. I think he has it on a memory stick with him.'

'How can you be certain of that?' Patrick snapped. He lowered his feet from his desk and sat up.

'I told you before. My contacts in the FSB said Clare Fingle had been working for them. She found out, shortly before she died, that Fingle had taken a copy of the file and wiped it off her husband's PC. My people have scoured through Fingle's computer. The file's not there, but there is an empty folder on his computer named *joe chinese file.*'

'So?'

'Look, Patrick. If he uploaded it anywhere, it would have been there. I guess he deleted it before he went to India.'

'And you think he's got it on him?'

'Well, it's not in his house. He could have given it to somebody else, but because of the sensitivity of it, I think that's unlikely. My guess is; it's with him.'

Patrick thought for a few seconds before he replied. He recalled his earlier conversation with David Masters. It would be difficult enough finding another supplier to make the CCC drug. Now, with this guy Fingle wandering around with the file containing all the secret manufacturing details, the problem had a whole different complexion. He came to what he believed was a pragmatic and necessary decision. 'Wait a minute. Don't hang up.'

Patrick stood up from his desk and walked to his office door. He closed it, and then made the inner door secure as well. He returned to his chair and withdrew from his drawer a small gadget, similar to a remote control for a TV or other entertainment equipment. He pressed a key. A small, pinprick-size green and red light shone from the top. With his eyes on both the lights, he made a sweeping motion, pointing it at the walls and ceiling of his office. He moved close to the hanging picture frames and directed it at them one by one. Then he did the same with the ceiling and wall lights. He checked around and underneath his desk. When he was confident there were no listening devices, he sat back in his chair and picked up the phone.

'I'm going to call you from another phone, Grigoriy. Is your line secure?'

~~~

After Alex Goad had spoken to Margaret Hudson, he cancelled all his appointments for the rest of the day. He told his PA not to interrupt him in any circumstances, or put any calls through, and locked his office door. He went to the wardrobe in his room and pulled out a soft, leather bag. He packed a few lightweight clothes, a couple of pairs of shoes, some toiletries, a few books, his iPod, and a spare phone. He placed a change of clothing and a cotton jacket on the sofa by the cupboard. He then moved to the safe, punched in the combination, and withdrew a sealed, brown envelope that he took with him to his desk. He opened it carefully, and laid in front of him three different passports. One was in the name of Edward Williams, and one in the name of John Salter; the third was his real passport. He pushed the real one to the side, and examined the other two in detail. He chose Edward Williams. He spent the next thirty minutes deleting every file on his PC, and shredding his real passport, the other false one, and every piece of paper from his filing cabinet. Using his mobile phone, he booked a one-way flight to Panama City before he changed into the clothing he'd left on the sofa. He left his suit, tie, and shirt hanging in his cupboard. He buzzed his PA and told her he'd had to leave, due to the unexpected death of a relative. Finally, he returned to the safe, took out a large wedge of US dollars and a small revolver, and left.

~~~

Ed James watched Harry cycle past him and up to the gate of his house. He saw him demount from his bike, open and shut the gate, secure the cycle to a fastening on the small brick wall, and go inside. Ed became concerned: not about Harry, but about the black car parked a few cars behind with an unknown man sitting inside it.

Ed had watched in his car mirror as the man stared at Harry while he had locked his bike. Once Harry had gone into his house, the man had pulled out a mobile phone and made a call. Ed didn't like unknowns, and tried to figure out what the man was about. He couldn't risk fouling up on this one. He needed the money.

His thoughts were halted. His phone rang.

136

'That you, Ed?'

'Who's that?' Ed kept looking at Harry's front door and the occupant of the other car.

'Alex Goad here. Have you dealt with Morecombe?'

'Hardly. I'm keeping an eye on Fingle. You've only just agreed it.'

'I told you to do it immediately.'

'Hey. Calm it.' Ed became angry. 'Don't go pushing me around. I call the shots around here. If you start to get arsy with me, mate, I'll add you to the list. Anyway, we haven't agreed on payment terms. I'm not doing anything until then.'

'I'll pay you as soon as the jobs are done. I told you that. Now fix Morecombe…'

'Jobs? What do you mean jobs? You haven't given me the go-ahead on Fingle yet.'

'Well, I am now. I want Morecombe topped first, then Fingle. I want them both done today. Come round to my house tomorrow morning and I'll have the cash.'

'How do I know you'll pay me?'

'I will. Just get them done.'

'Listen, Goad. I'll do them, no problem. But believe me. If you mess with me, you're dead meat. And it won't be pleasant. You'll scream your little head off. A long, slow death. Understand?'

'Just get the jobs done. See you tomorrow.'

~~~

Alex cut the call. He'd been parked alongside the Thames at Hammersmith. He opened his window and flung his mobile phone into the river, and watched it plop into the dirty, brown water before he drove off at speed towards Heathrow airport.

Chapter Eighteen

Normally, Richard Morecombe would never worry about anything. By the time he reached fifty, he had achieved much in his life. He'd made himself rich. He controlled a vast media empire, and sat on the boards of many companies as a nonexecutive director. His talented and well-respected wife, a presenter for one of the nation's favourite morning TV programmes, adored him. Their circle of friends grew by the day. They entertained often, throwing lavish parties and regularly taking over entire restaurants for the evening. But, on his fifty-first birthday, he was troubled, and not himself.

Richard had no doubt he would be ruined if Alex Goad failed to come up with the information that the Russian, Grigoriy Nabutov, had demanded. Nabutov didn't seem like a sympathetic man. Richard knew he would carry out his threat, and make sure the compromising pictures of him having sex with rent boys would fall into the hands of *The Daily Journal*, one of Richard's rival newspapers. They'd be delighted. They'd clean up and become the biggest-selling daily paper for some time. They'd make an initial splash, probably several pages, and then drag and dribble out the story for as long as they could. Richard would be ruined. He would have to resign from his media group. The sales of *The Morning News* would slump and he'd be asked to step down from all the other companies. If he refused, they'd find a way to sack him. What's more, Sam his wife would be annoyed and deeply upset. She had a very public TV role, and might have to resign as well. He feared she'd leave him.

My God, he thought. *This is dire. I have to make sure Alex Goad delivers.*

He picked up his phone. He'd been due to meet Sam for his birthday lunch before they went to look at a new house in Eaton Square, a property they'd admired and sought after for some time, but had not been available. As soon as it came on the market, the agent contacted them to arrange an appointment. He'd said the recession had brought about the new, lower price. The owner, an ex-director of a defunct hedge fund, had been forced to put it on the market for a million pounds less than the price he paid for it. It was a one-off opportunity for Richard and Sam to buy an outstanding and substantial property.

'Hi darling,' he said when Sam answered. 'Look, I know you're going to be cross with me. But I've got to pull out of lunch and seeing the house. Sorry, something's come up that I have to deal with.'

'I've changed my schedules so I can finish early. You can't not come to lunch; James and Angie are coming and they adore you – you know that. Freddy and Marcus said they'd come in for a quick drink. You can't duck out now.'

'I'm sorry. But I have to be here. Please understand. I'll see them all tonight at the party.'

'What's so important that you can't cancel? Come on. You've never missed your birthday lunch before. We're going to Gordon Ramsay's place at Claridge's.'

Richard scratched his forehead. Sam was right. He had always managed to skip or change appointments that clashed with his social life. After all, he owned the business. He would simply change meetings and inconvenience everyone else to fit around his timetable. But this was different. He wasn't in control.

'Look. I can't explain now. Just believe me. I can't be there. Please apologise to the others. I'll see them tonight. I have to go now.'

'Richard,' Sam snapped. 'We are not going to have lunch without you. It's for you – your birthday thing. We do it every year. If you're not coming, I'll cancel it and see you at the house in Eaton Square at three this afternoon.'

Richard took a deep breath. 'I can't do that, either.'

'What's going on? You've never been like this before.'

I've never been blackmailed before, he thought.

'I'm sorry. I can't explain. I'll tell you later. You go and look at it.' He paused and thought for a few seconds. 'If you like it, make an offer.'

'Don't be so stupid and bloody patronising,' Sam yelled into the phone. 'I'm ending this call. It may be your birthday, but you're behaving as though you're insane or something. I've never known you like this. I would never, ever make an offer on a house without you seeing it. You know that. I hope you're over it by tonight. 'Bye.'

Richard was left staring at his phone. Sam had cut off on him. He shuddered and called Alex Goad. There was no reply. He had wanted to tell Alex that he couldn't wait until the morning and would collect the information himself later that afternoon.

~~~

Ed dropped his phone down on the front seat next to him, turned on his car's engine, and drove off in the direction of Richard Morecombe's office in Kensington. He felt cross. Alex Goad had put pressure on him to complete two jobs in one day, something Ed would never normally do. But these were not normal hits. Alex had offered him £150k if he topped Morecombe and Fingle by the following morning.

He didn't like working to a deadline or being hassled. He'd always plan and prepare well in advance, with detailed precision, leaving nothing to chance. No clues, no trail, nothing that the police could pick up on. He had a reputation, and would never do anything that might lessen it's high standing. But in this case he would have to compromise. He had to deliver.

~~~

At a few minutes past eleven, Richard left the main door of his office. Ed watched him from Starbucks across the road. He dropped the paper he'd used to hide behind on the table, and dodged between the traffic to cross. Richard flagged down a taxi. Ed moved up close behind him. When the taxi slowed and drew up, Ed moved in. He raised the barrel of the gun he had hidden under his bulky jacket, and stuck it into Richard's back.

'This is a gun I have in your back. If you don't do as I say, I'll pull the trigger. Now, look straight ahead and don't turn around.' Ed twisted the barrel a little to make his point.

'Get into the taxi. I'm right behind you.' Ed followed Richard into the cab and gave the driver the address of his lockup garage in Stepney. Once they were both seated, Ed closed the sliding-glass window that separated the driver from the two of them. He turned to Richard. His gun lay on the seat.

'One word and I'll blow your brains out. Get it?'

Richard's eyes looked as though they would pop out of his head. His jaw dropped. His mouth opened wide. He looked terrified. He glanced at the back of the driver's head. 'Where are you...?'

'I said shut it. Not a word. Understand?' Ed whispered, his tone menacing.

Richard nodded and stared ahead with a frightened, vacant expression.

The journey took an hour, during which time neither Richard nor Ed spoke. As they turned into the road where Ed had his garage, Ed slid back the glass panel, pushed two fifty-pound notes through to the driver, and told him to stop. He closed the panel and turned to Richard.

'Get out. Walk a few paces away from the cab, and look as though you're waiting for me. Don't think you can get away. You can't.'

Richard did as he'd been instructed and watched the cab pull away. Ed faced him.

'Turn around. Walk a few paces in front of me in that direction, down the road, towards the garage at the end. See it?'

Richard nodded. He looked scared.

'If you try anything, I'll shoot you in the back. It's the most painful way of dying.'

Once they were locked inside the dark and damp garage, Ed plugged in the floodlight and moved close to Richard, so their faces almost touched. He shoved his gun into Richard's stomach and stared into his eyes.

'You've been a bad boy, Mr Morecombe. You've upset someone. I don't know what you've done, but they want you rubbed out.'

Richard shuddered and turned a ghostly shade of white. He perspired heavily.

'Not feeling well?' Ed smirked. 'That's a shame. Now, turn around.'

'Please, what's this all about? We can do a deal. Who put you up to this?' Richard's pleas were almost incoherent. He dribbled. His whole body shook. 'Please don't kill me. Please, please.'

Ed looked at him. 'I said turn around. Do as I say.'

Richard's eyes glazed over. His head started to roll around. He fell to the floor in a crumpled heap. Ed kicked him in the back, but he didn't move. He bent down to look at him. Richard was alive. Ed went to the back of the garage and collected some rope and a dirty towel. He tied Richard to a chair, and gagged and blindfolded him.

He'd have to leave him like that, he thought. He didn't want to kill him and rush off to deal with Harry before he'd disposed of the body properly.

~~~

Harry hadn't seen the Russian man who sat in a parked, black Mercedes about one hundred metres away from his house, nor had he seen Ed James in his BMW a little distance from the Russian. He'd been preoccupied. He wanted to check that the new keys for his house worked, and clear up the chaos left behind by the intruders. He'd called Jimmy from Kate's house, but had been unable to speak to him. He sent a text message asking him to make contact or come around to his house as soon as possible.

His house was as he'd left it. A mess. Drawers and cupboards were wide open, and his belongings strewn all over the place. He stood and stared at it all for a couple of seconds, flipped on the kettle, and started to tidy up. He heard a knock on the door. He went to the open it, guessing it to be Jimmy. A large, foreign-looking man with a stony face glared at him. He wore a knee-length, black-leather coat buttoned up to his neck and dark, navy-coloured jeans. He looked menacing. A frisson of fear ran through Harry's body.

In an instant, the man shoved Harry to one side. He pinned him to the wall and slammed the door closed behind him. Harry felt something hard thrust into his back. He figured it was a gun.

'You Harry Fingle?' The man spoke with a heavy, eastern-European accent. 'Hands up, behind head.'

Harry did as instructed. 'No. That's not me,' he replied. 'You have the wrong person.'

'You lie.' The man took hold of Harry and swung him around. He pointed his gun at Harry's face. 'Keep hands up.'

'If you think I'm lying, why did you ask me if I was...? Who did you say? Somebody called Fingle? That's an odd name.' Harry knew the odds were against him. He had no plan. But he reckoned if he could play for time he might work out a way of overcoming the guy.

'Not your business.' The man started to fumble around in the left pocket of his jacket. He pulled out a photo. Harry caught sight of it: an image of himself. He knew from that moment, he was doomed. His life was probably about to come to an end. He'd just be another of the many statistics in the CCC story.

The man looked down quickly at the photo and held it up to Harry's face. 'You lie. You Harry Fingle. This his photo.' The man raised his gun and held it to Harry's temple.

'That's my photo, alright. But I'm not this Fingle person you mention. You've got the wrong man. My name's Bill Bailey. Who is this Fingle guy you talk of? I've never heard of him. He must have done something mighty bad for you to behave like this.'

The man studied the photo and then looked at Harry and took a pace backwards. He kept his gun trained on Harry's heart. He pulled out a phone from his jacket and called up a number. All the while, he kept his eyes on Harry. After several seconds he started to speak quickly and urgently in a foreign language. Harry recognised it to be Russian and guessed that, since Ritzler was a Russian-owned company, the predicament he found himself in was of their making.

'Okay,' the Russian snapped. He clicked his phone closed and put it back in his pocket. He closed on Harry and put his gun up to his temple. 'You lying shit. I kill.'

Before Harry had a chance to think about his fate, his doorbell buzzed. The man moved his head and took his eye off Harry for a split second. Harry flung his two arms down hard on the man's arm and knocked the gun to the floor. He kicked it away and rushed to the door.

'Watch out, Jimmy! He's got a gun,' he yelled, as Jimmy charged in and the Russian scrabbled towards the pistol and grabbed it. He started to turn around. Jimmy launched at him with a rugby tackle to his thigh, and brought him down. Harry saw that the man still had hold of the gun and had turned it towards Jimmy's neck. Harry lashed out with his foot at the man's hand. The gun went off and made a deafening crack. Harry watched it spiral away from the man's grip, and spin and slide along the wooden floor to stop at the kitchen door. Harry ran and grabbed it. He pointed it at the Russian's head.

'Let him go,' Harry yelled, seeing the man's large hands clasped around Jimmy's neck. He was trying to squeeze the life out of Jimmy. The Russian looked up. Harry lunged forward and pushed the gun up close to his face.

'I said, let him go.' The man stared at Harry. His expression remained stony. His hands were gripped tightly around Jimmy's neck. Harry moved close and pushed the barrel of the gun up one of the man's nostrils.

'I said, release him,' Harry screamed, and twisted the gun further up the man's nose. The man yelled out and released his grip.

'Jimmy,' Harry shouted as he looked down on Jimmy's motionless body.

~~~

Ray returned to Amie's flat in Grange Road at about midday. He walked past it and up and down the road a couple of times. He wanted to make sure nobody had seen him, and that there was no sign of life from inside. Once he was sure that neither Amie nor anyone else occupied the flat, he crept along the side path he'd used the previous night towards the back garden. To his surprise, he found the padlock on the side gate had still not been securely closed and he could gain access to the back garden and patio. But, unlike his last visit, the windows and doors had been well-fastened. An easy, concealed entry into the flat was not obvious. He didn't want to force his way in. It would show. He needed surprise.

She tricked and lied to me, he said to himself. *I warned her. Now she will pay.*

He went back to the tiny, rear garden. He noticed an outside shed, and pulled open the door. It was small, housing a food freezer, and shelves with cans of food and bottles of wine. He considered hiding in it, figuring he could wait there until the girl came to collect something. But he soon gave up on the idea. It would be too cramped. He couldn't conceal himself properly, and she might not go to it for several days. As he made to leave the shed, his foot kicked on something hard. It cracked. He switched on his torch to find he'd trodden on a terra-cotta flowerpot. Amongst the broken pieces lay something shiny and metal. It looked familiar. He reached down to find a small key ring with a Chubb and latch key attached.

Thank you, you silly bitch, he said to himself with a mocking smile as he opened the front door and walked in.

Ray checked around all the rooms before going to Amie's bedroom. He pulled open the door to her wardrobe. It was full of her clothes, but still big enough for him to stand in, he thought. He grabbed the dresses and other hanging items, flung them on the floor, and stepped inside and pulled the door closed. He could stand up and still move around a little.

It'll do fine, he thought and took his jacket off, left it in the cupboard, and stepped out. He looked at his watch. It was 1:00 p.m. and he needed to figure out and rehearse his plan – fast. He knew he couldn't wait and hide in there for too long, and went back to the living room. There was a front window that looked out onto Grange Road. If he acted smart, he could hide close to the window and behind the sofa and watch out for the girl. The moment she turned the corner into the road, he reckoned, he'd have just enough time to return to the wardrobe and hide.

He started to work out his routine. Once the girl came into view, he'd crawl on his hands and knees to the bedroom cupboard and climb inside. After he practised several times, he managed to complete the procedure in less than thirty seconds. He figured it would take the girl almost a minute to reach the door, fumble for her key, and enter.

At 3:50 p.m., Ray sat on the floor of Amie's bedroom. The light outside had started to fade. He reached for one of her blouses and wiped the blade of his knife several times. He placed it on a ledge in the wardrobe, and stuffed the blouse with the rest of Amie's clothes under her bed. He looked around the room one last time, removed his shoes, and padded to the living room. He stood quite still for a few minutes. It had become dark and gloomy, with just a glimmer of light from the street.

Perfect, he thought as he slid behind the sofa and out of view.

Chapter Nineteen

Harry had never handled a firearm in his life. He didn't have any idea what to do with one – how to hold, aim, or fire it. The closest he'd come to a gun was when he failed the aptitude test for the army cadet force at school. Faced with an aggressive Russian who threatened to kill him, he learnt fast. He clasped the gun in his right hand and pointed it directly at the Russian's head. The man seemed to understand. He lay still on his stomach in the hall, his hands stretched out in front of him. Harry watched for the slightest movement.

He heard a groan. 'Is that you, Jimmy? You okay?' he asked as he saw a flicker of movement in the corner of his eye.

'Yeah, boss. I'm fine.' Jimmy had slid away from the Russian and stood up. He brushed himself down, looked at the man, and then back at Harry. 'What the hell, man? I've nearly been topped twice in the last twenty-four hours. Both times in your hall.'

Harry's eyes stayed fixed on the Russian. 'I figured that from what you said on the phone last night. You must tell me about it, but not now. We've got to work out what are we going to do with this guy?' The Russian started to wriggle.

'Don't try it. Stay completely still.' Harry leant forward and moved the gun closer to the man's head. The man did as instructed. His eyes stayed fixed on the gun's barrel, which was no more than thirty centimetres from his head. A second flash of movement flicked in the edge of Harry's eye and he turned his head a little in response. He guessed it was Jimmy and focused back on the Russian, who no longer stared at the gun barrel. Something behind Harry had caught his attention.

Harry's heart started to thump. He became worried. *Has he an accomplice?* he questioned.

'Don't move,' he shouted and tightened his grip on the gun. If you do – I'll blow your friend's head off.'

'Harry; It's me, Jimmy. I'm right behind you.'

Harry felt reassured but remained uneasy. Jimmy could have been prompted, he thought. 'Okay, Jimmy. But move well in front of me, so I can see you.'

Jimmy moved forward, his feet close to the Russian's head and held his hand out for the pistol. 'Here, let me take it.'

Harry kept his eyes fixed on the Russian, with the gun pointed at the man's head, and slowly moved his arm to the right so Jimmy could take hold of it. Once Jimmy had it in his hand, he knelt down and put one of his big knees in the man's back. He pushed the gun into the back of the man's neck, beneath his head.

'Now listen, matey. I don't give a fuck who you are. But if you try anything again, you're finished. Understand?' Jimmy tapped the side of the Russian's face with his other hand. 'Answer me.' The Russian grunted.

'Good.' Jimmy stood up and moved closer to Harry. 'Got any rope and old sheets? We'll tie him up. Then we can work out what we're going to do with him.'

Twenty minutes later, Harry and Jimmy had bound the Russian's feet together, tied his hands behind his back, and gagged and blindfolded him with torn-up towels and sheets. They found a pair of earplugs Harry used for swimming, and stuck them in the man's ears. They dragged him into the kitchen, and left him facedown on the kitchen floor. Harry stood up and reached for the phone.

'What yer doing?' Jimmy said. He grabbed Harry's hand.

'I'm going to call the police.'

'No way. Not while I'm here. They'll bang me up again. We've got to work this out without them, Harry.' Jimmy shook his head. 'I can't have nothing to do with them. They won't believe me.'

Harry put the handset down on the worktop and looked at Jimmy. 'Okay. So what do you think we should do? Look, I get home this morning. My house has been ransacked, a Russian man barges in on me and tells me he's going to kill me, and the factory I was going to visit in Mumbai is blown up. Many people are dead. This is big, Jimmy. Governments and dangerous criminals are behind it, and they'll stop at nothing. It's not something that an out-of-work journalist and an ex-con can handle alone, anymore. We need help.'

The Russian groaned again. Jimmy walked over to him and poked him in the back with his foot. 'Shut it, man. Don't cause me no trouble. I don't want to hear another peep from you.' Jimmy kicked him in the ribs. 'Get it?' The Russian groaned again. Jimmy walked back to where Harry stood.

'Listen, Harry, man. I understand what you're saying, like. But I can't risk it.' Jimmy looked down at his feet and then at Harry's face.

'I've done a little dealing since I came out. A bloke came after me here last night for some money with a knife, like. He was a nasty bit of shit. He was gonna cut me up if Amie hadn't turned up and saved my skin. She gave him some shit about being in the police and he fell for it and scarpered; only trouble was, he followed her home and broke in and attacked her.'

'What!' Harry yelled. 'Where is she now? Is she okay? Why haven't you told me this before?'

'Calm it. Listen. She's a clever girl, that Amie. The bloke jumped on her with a knife when she got out of the shower. She kept her cool and kept to her story, like. When the bloke held the knife against her, her phone rang and she told him it was her police colleagues, checking she was okay. If she didn't answer, they'd be round in a flash. He didn't risk it and scarpered like greased lightning. When I got there, she was in a hell of a state, poor luv.'

'Where is she now? You left her there, alone? She's in real danger. We've got to get to her. I can't believe you left her.' Harry felt bewildered. He didn't fully understand, but he knew Amie was in trouble and needed help.

My God. This is my fault, he thought. *I've been so wrong. I thought she was being intrusive again.*

'Of course I didn't leave her. I stayed the night.'

Harry shot Jimmy a quick glance. 'Where is she now?'

'She's at work. I took her to the Tube.'

Harry looked at his watch and then at the Russian. He lay still and motionless.

'We need to get back over there, to her flat,' Jimmy said in an urgent tone. 'The bloke, I think he's called Ray, might come back. She's not safe.'

Harry frowned, scratched his cheek and took a step backwards. 'I just said that, a few minutes ago.' He looked down at the Russian. 'What are we going to do about him? We can't leave him here.' Jimmy and Harry stared at each other.

'I'm going to call someone who I think can help.' Harry reached for his phone. He saw Jimmy's worried look. 'It's not the police.'

After a few moments, he spoke. 'Listen, Philip. I don't know what you're up to. But you and I go back a long way and I'm in a bit of a spot. I need your help.'

'Go on. What is it you want?'

'A Russian tried to kill me a little while ago.'

'What. Are you crazy? How?'

'I haven't time to tell you. I have the man tied up on my kitchen floor. I want him removed, quickly.'

'You're mad. How do you think…?'

'I don't think. I know. I can either call the police or your people can deal with it.'

'What do you mean? My people?'

'You know what I mean.'

There was a pause in the conversation for several seconds. Harry waited for Philip to respond.

'How long have you known?' Philip asked eventually.

'Not long. But I'm right, aren't I?'

'Yep,' Philip snapped. 'We must talk about it later. Where are you? What are you doing next?'

'I'm at home, but I can't say anymore. I haven't time. I just want this man taken away, fast.'

'Okay.' Philip spoke in a matter-of-fact, efficient way, without any emotion. 'Someone will be round in an hour. We need to talk later.'

'Yes, we do. But not now; I have to go.'

Harry ended the call. He put the phone down on the worktop, and looked at Jimmy, who seemed stunned and speechless.

'Come on. We need to move this guy to the hall, and be ready to get out fast and go to Amie's.'

Jimmy took his hand away from his mouth and glanced at Harry. 'What the hell was that all about, man? Who were you talking to?'

'An old friend of mine. He's a spook: MI6.'

'Crazy.' Jimmy blinked and looked away for a few seconds. 'What's it all about?'

'Search me. But we are about to find out. Come on.' Harry leant down and took hold of one of the Russian's legs.

'Did you know he's a spy?'

'No, not really. But I had a hunch. I thought the whole of this fucking CCC thing was so screwball that only spooks could be behind it. So I went for it. And I was right.' Harry looked up at Jimmy, who'd taken hold of the Russian's other leg. 'Ready?'

~~~

Grigoriy Nabutov sat in his hotel apartment and waited for the call from Igor. He would confirm that Harry Fingle was dead. When the call didn't come at the time he expected it, he started to become worried and poured himself a large slug of Russian Standard vodka, straight from the fridge. He called Igor. No one picked up.

His phone rang an hour and a half later. 'Yes,' he answered in a gruff tone and reached for his glass of vodka.

'Good and bad news,' the caller said.

'Go on.'

'They've got Igor. He failed.'

'The imbecile,' Grigoriy shouted. 'How can he screw up so badly? I take it he didn't complete the job. How do you know they've got him?'

'Can't tell you. But you're right, he didn't complete.'

'And the good news? Can there be any?'

'Before Igor was overcome by Fingle and another man, he managed to place an electronic tracking device on Fingle. At this precise moment, Fingle's cycling along Chiswick High Road.'

Grigoriy jumped up. He rushed to one of the cupboards and withdrew a black case.

'Which direction is he going in?' he snapped, as he flipped open the case and took out a Glock 17 semiautomatic pistol with a bronze handle.

'He's heading west, towards Chiswick roundabout.'

Grigoriy thought for a moment. He tried to think of a convenient place to meet up with Oleg. 'Keep watching him and meet me in the Starbucks, almost at the end of Chiswick High Road, on the north side. Bring all the tracking stuff with you. Hurry. I'm leaving now.' Grigoriy paused. 'And Oleg.' Grigoriy sounded threatening.

'Yes.'

'Don't lose him. Am I making myself clear?'

'Yes.'

Grigoriy turned off his phone and slid it in his pocket. He drank the remainder of his vodka, then poured another one and gulped it down while he checked he had a full clip of ammunition. He raced out of his room and flagged down the first available taxi.

'Here, take this. Get me to the far end of Chiswick High Road in fifteen minutes,' he said, and pushed two fifty-pound notes into the taxi driver's hand. He climbed in, sat back, and closed his eyes.

~~~

Kate became euphoric after Harry left. Ever since her son, Jack, had been stabbed and died, she hadn't given any thought to having an intimate relationship with a man again. It hadn't entered her mind. She didn't believe Harry had intended to sleep with her, or that she had made any moves towards him. He just turned up, wet and tired, and demanded information about Ritzler and the CCC drug. He'd told her about the awful bombing in Mumbai. He seemed so right and moral in what he did, and she'd felt such guilt and responsibility for the lives lost, it sort of seemed right to go to bed with him. She knew she kissed him first, but was sure he would have done the same a minute later. They fell together in a natural bond of mutual need. A tender and sensuous act that left them refreshed and revitalised, determined to bring those involved in the bloodshed and havoc caused by the CCC fiasco to account.

She started to clear up the plates and stuff from the snack Harry and she had eaten. A feeling came over her that she hadn't experienced for some time, a sort of confidence and strength, coupled with a wish and need to confront the past, however painful it was. She left the dishes, and went to her bedroom and knelt down in front of a pine chest at the foot of her bed. She gathered up the clutter of books, magazines and odd letters that covered the top, dumped them on the floor and opened the lid.

One by one, she took out all the mementoes of Jack she'd deposited inside the box immediately after his death, and laid them out on the wooden floor. There was his old phone, some of his CDs, his iPod, a couple of his T-shirts, an old exercise book he'd used at school, and the last birthday card he'd given to her. She picked up the phone and felt it. She sensed Jack's fingers touching the keypad, his ear close to it, and his breath all over it. She turned it over a few times and checked herself.

Yes, it's hard. I hurt. I guess I could easily cry, but I can handle it.

She felt the same as she lingered over his other items. She listened to some of his music. She read his attempts at poetry in his exercise book. She smelt his T-shirts. Finally, she picked up the birthday card with his scrawled writing inside, and stared at it for some time.

Love you, mum. Have a good one. Jack

And then she cried. Not uncontrollable sobbing as she had done in the past, or big splodgy tears, but a little trickle from each eye. She put the card down next to the other things, and dabbed her eyes with a tissue. She'd leave his stuff on the floor, for a while, she decided, and stood up.

Is this because of Harry? Has he given me the ability, at last, to look back and accept things?

At that moment, in her mood similar to intoxication, she felt a craving she'd hadn't experienced for some time. It felt familiar, and was a craving she recognised. She went down to the kitchen, feeling hopeful, and started rooting around at the back of the high kitchen cupboards: the ones she rarely used. She went from one cupboard to the other without finding what she wanted. She began to fear she'd thrown it all away. Then, as she reached right back into the last cupboard, she found the old, oblong tin she'd been after.

It's bound to be a bit old and dry, she told herself, as she climbed down from the stool, and took the tin to her kitchen table and opened it.

'Oh good,' she said out loud and smiled. Inside the tin, she found three ready-rolled spliffs, made with best, Red King Rizla Size paper and some good-quality Afghan grass. She thought they must have been there for nearly a year, and tried to remember when she'd last smoked one. She looked up and to the bottom of her garden, and saw the sun shining on the Thames. *Perfect,* she thought. She picked up the box of matches that lay in a corner in her kitchen, and the three joints, and walked through her studio to the French windows. She pushed them open, dropped into an old canvas chair she used in the garden, and lit up.

~~~

Ed managed to get back outside Harry's house by 4:00 p.m. He felt edgy and not at his best. Ever since Goad had called and said he wanted two jobs done in one day, he'd been under pressure. At first, when Morecombe fell unconscious, he'd welcomed it. But it played on his mind, and he regretted not killing him then and there. It had become an unfinished job.

He stared at Harry's house, to check for signs that he was still inside. The black Mercedes that had been parked outside earlier remained where he'd last seen it, but without a driver. Ed became uneasy. He shook his head. He sensed something had happened, but he was at a loss to know its nature. Fifteen minutes after he'd parked, at four-fifteen, a blacked-out transit van drew up outside the door. Two men, dressed in black tracksuits, climbed out, opened the rear door, and carried into the house a coffin.

'What the hell?' Ed murmured. *Someone's snuffed it*. He stared at Harry's door. After another ten minutes, the door opened. The two men carried out the coffin to the van, and drove off.

This is bizarre, Ed thought. *There's no way they can they pick up a bloody stiff in that time. They have to sort out the body properly before they can take it away. It takes fucking ages. This ain't real.* Ed shuddered. He knew he'd been right. Something underhand had taken place, and he didn't like it.

A couple of minutes after the blacked-out vehicle drove away, the door opened again. Harry came out, followed by a tall, black guy whom Ed had never seen before. Harry locked up, spoke to the black guy, and jumped on a bike and cycled off at speed towards Chiswick High Road. The black guy ran up the road in the same direction.

Ed cleared his mind. Whatever had gone on was of no consequence any longer. The moment he had waited for had arrived. He had a job to do. It was time to concentrate. He started up his car and accelerated to catch up with Harry.

Chapter Twenty

Operation CCC was the first case Paul Thompson had run on his own, and he felt concerned. He became worried about Harry Fingle's safety. He knew if Harry were killed – as Philip Stacey warned – his own career, and possibly his own neck, could be in jeopardy. For that reason, he'd called the other two members of the team back together. They met up in the same, small room they'd used for their meeting earlier in the day.

Paul switched his gaze from Philip Stacey to Scott Reynolds. 'We've got to change things. Pull in Nabutov, and keep a tight watch on Fingle. If we don't, Fingle could go down. We need him alive to tell us everything he's discovered.' Paul took a sip from the plastic mug in front of him, and looked at the other two. 'Do you both agree?'

'No. I don't. Listen,' Philip said. He loosened his tie and undid the top button of his shirt. 'That's too risky. We know the Russians tried to kill him earlier today. They're not going to stop it there. I've deliberately kept my distance with Fingle, and tried to play it cool. But we go back a long time. I think he suspects we're behind it all.' Philip shook his head. 'And I don't know who he's told. If he's killed, I will have lost a friend, but we might not be able to hide our involvement from the media.' Philip took his glasses off and put them on the table. He rubbed a hand across his mouth, and glanced quickly at the other two. 'We've got to bring him in now to protect him, and tell him what it's all about. And by doing that, we stop any leaks.'

Scott put his hands up in the air and held them level with his head, about three-quarters of a metre apart. 'Stop.' He shook his head. 'No, no, no. That's the dumbest idea I've ever heard.' He picked up his pencil and started tapping the table.

'We can't do that. That'll blow the whole thing. We need to keep Fingle out there. Keep an eye on him right up to the last minute, until both parties have played their hands. Surely…' He stopped and glanced quickly at Philip. 'You guys can keep your press under control, can't you?'

'Scott,' Philip barked and looked at the American in a disparaging way. 'Don't you get it? The guy's life is at risk. He's an innocent citizen. If he's killed, the press will give us hell. And just because the Russians screwed up, doesn't mean they won't try again. What about the Chinese? They're going to make a move sometime.'

Paul raised his right hand from the desk. 'Hold on, hold on. You've both missed something. Nabutov, although Russian, is not working for the Russians. Can't you remember?' Paul looked at the other two. Both had puzzled expressions. 'He works for Vantiche's Chinese owners, Ning.'

'Oh yeah,' Scott said in a disinterested manner. He shrugged his shoulders. 'I guess I got a little confused.'

'I don't understand,' Philip said. He looked directly at Paul. He held his coffee in his hand, and rested his elbow on the table. 'It was a Russian we brought in earlier from Fingle's house. You telling me he's not working for the Russians, but the Chinese?'

Paul turned back to Philip. 'The guy we brought in – Igor – was working on the orders of Grigoriy Nabutov.'

'Who is this Nabutov guy?' Philip snapped.

'Nabutov is Head of Security for Ning, the Chinese pharmaceutical giant, Ritzler's rival.' Paul looked down at the sheet of paper in front of him, and then back at Philip. 'Nabutov reports directly to Patrick Tang, who is the boss of Ning and also a deputy of the National People's Congress of China.'

'So this Tang guy is a Chinese government official, then?'

'Correct,' Scott replied as he gazed at the ceiling and swivelled around in his chair.

Paul leant forward and faced Philip. 'Listen. Let me explain. The Chinese government have given him time off to build up Ning to be one of the world's leading pharmaceutical companies.' Paul covered his mouth with his hand and waited.

Philip had listened to Paul with his chin held between the thumb and forefinger of one of his hands. He looked into Paul's eyes for a few seconds. 'I understand. But what is this Igor guy who we picked up from Fingle's doing working for the Chinese? He's a Russian, isn't he?'

'Money.' Paul leant back in his chair. 'He's also a member of the FSB.'

'What?' Philip shook his head. 'This is all so bloody flaky. I can't believe it.'

'I agree. It is,' Paul said. 'Let me explain. Nabutov works for the Chinese. But he's still very powerful in Russia, and a force to be reckoned with. He's got friends there who'll gladly do his dirty work for rubles and protection. He knows these FSB agents are good. By using a combination of money and fear, he gets them to work for him.'

'Against their own country's interests?'

'Sort of. Think of them as double agents,' Scott said and turned away.

'What if they got found out?'

'Oh, they'd be killed, all right. Nabutov doesn't give a shit about that,' Scott replied.

Philip sat up. He looked annoyed. 'How do you know all this?'

Paul swung round in his chair. He clenched his fists, put them together in front of him, and met Philip's concerned expression. 'We've had a tail on Nabutov ever since he arrived in the country. We've listened in to almost all his conversations with the FSB guys.'

Philip sat up with a jolt. 'What!' He banged his hand down on the table. 'You let that Igor guy go to Harry's house and nearly kill him?' He put his glasses back on, gripped the side of the table, and leant forward. He stuck his neck out so his face ended up just over half a metre away from Paul's. 'Why haven't I been told about all of this?'

Paul didn't answer. His phone rang. He picked it up and listened. His face drained of all colour, and he looked grave.

'Okay. Where are they?' He turned to look at Philip while he listened to the caller.

'Oleg is to do whatever is necessary to stop him. Okay?' He ended the call. He put his phone down on the table, and turned to the other two.

'Grigoriy Nabutov is following Harry Fingle up the A406 to Ealing with intent to kill him. He intends to draw up alongside Fingle's bike and shoot him.'

'How the fuck do you know that?' Philip shouted.

'The man, Oleg, who's with Nabutov, is one of ours. Come on, let's go.'

~~~

Ed James turned the air conditioning in his car down to 16 degrees. He needed to concentrate, and had found from experience that he thought better and was at his sharpest when the temperature felt almost chilly. It made him focus on what he had to do. Harry was an experienced cyclist, and had moved fast in front of Ed, changing lanes often, and darting in and out of the traffic. Ed had to work hard to keep him in his sights. When Harry first turned onto the main road, Ed had been held up at Chiswick roundabout and had lost sight of him. Moments later, a gap appeared in the traffic, and he'd seen him peddling at speed in the inside lane.

Gunnersbury Avenue is one of the busiest roads in London, and an inner, circular route around the capital. Ed was pleased Harry chose such a route. The heavy flow of large vehicles – mainly buses, lorries, and trucks transporting waste skips – gave Ed many opportunities. He planned to wait until Harry was in front of one of them, cut in quickly, and knock him over. The vehicle behind would finish him off, and Ed could melt away into the traffic while all attention was on the accident. He'd done hits in a similar way many times. All he needed was to wait for the appropriate moment. He just had to be patient.

It came ten minutes later. Ed stopped in the outside lane at the traffic lights at the intersection with the busy Uxbridge Road. Although he'd lost sight of Harry, he wasn't worried. He'd seen him a few seconds earlier in the inside lane. Ed knew that, when the lights changed, Harry would be the first to pull away, and he'd see him. He looked around and saw a large tipper-truck, laden with two overfilled skips – one perched on top of the other – draw up alongside. He was in luck. Harry had squeezed his bike into the narrow gap between the tipper-truck and Ed's car. He'd stopped close to the white line.

Perfect, Ed thought. He couldn't have had a better opportunity. All he had to do was linger a little, let Harry move into the middle lane, and accelerate. He'd knock him over and let the tipper-truck do the rest. He looked up at the red lights and glanced to his left. Harry sat still on his saddle, waiting to race across the intersection. Ed turned his head. He looked straight ahead.

He felt a surge of adrenaline. In the corner of his eye, he'd seen the driver of the skip drop his paper and take hold of the steering wheel. Ed looked up at the traffic that crossed Gunnersbury Avenue in front of him. It slowed and came to a halt. The lights were about to change. In a minute it would all be over, he thought. The Fingle man would be dead, mangled under a big tipper-truck.

The lights changed. He tensed his leg. His foot touched the accelerator pedal. The vehicles around him started to move. 'This is it.'

The sound of beeping horns from angry motorists exploded in his ears. Their annoyance was directed at him. 'Okay, okay. I can hear you all.' He was forced to move off, cross over to the other side of the intersection, and join the forward-moving traffic.

Harry had not behaved as he'd expected.

~~~

'Where is he?' Grigoriy Nabutov barked as he tumbled out of the taxi. Oleg stood and waited for him outside Starbucks in Chiswick High Road, as they'd agreed.

'Come to my car. I'll show you.' Oleg pointed to the blacked-out Jeep Cherokee, parked in front of the coffee shop on double yellow lines. It took up half the pavement. Grigoriy followed him and jumped into the front passenger seat. He slammed the door closed behind him.

'Look. He's there. About a kilometre away?' Oleg said. He pointed to a laptop that showed Harry as a red spot that moved along Gunnersbury Avenue.

'Catch him up. Do whatever it takes to reach him. Don't worry about anything. Just get there.'

'I'll do my best.' Oleg started up the engine. He put his phone close to him on the ledge in front of the steering wheel.

'Best!' Grigoriy barked. 'Best is not good enough. Just find him.' Grigoriy took out his Glock pistol and started to fiddle with it.

Oleg jumped a set of lights, overtook a slow-moving car, forcing one of the two oncoming vehicles to brake suddenly, and the other to swerve and mount the curb. He raced towards Chiswick roundabout, pushed in on other vehicles, and barged his way around it. Three minutes after they'd set off from Starbucks, he headed up Gunnersbury Avenue in pursuit of Harry.

'What are you going to do to him?'

Grigoriy, who had been attaching the silencer to his gun, gave Oleg a withering look, and returned his attention to the firearm.

'Idiot.' Grigoriy sneered, and rubbed his left hand up and down the barrel of his gun. 'What do you think I'm going to do? Make love to him.'

'I mean, how are you going to do it?'

'I want to you drive right up to him. Then I will shoot him through the head.' Grigoriy looked down at the laptop that rested on his lap. 'How close are we?'

'I'm driving. You've got the laptop. You can see for yourself.' Oleg reached for his phone.

'What're you doing?' Grigoriy frowned as Oleg sent a text with his right hand while holding the wheel with his left.'

'I need to report in. You're not my only paymaster. Remember, I'm paid by the Russian government.' Oleg glanced quickly at his phone again. He'd received a reply from his text.

'We're close.' Grigoriy jerked his head up from the laptop's screen, and looked around to find Harry.

'There he is.' Grigoriy wound down the window, and held the gun just below the opening.

'Listen. This is what you've got to do.' Grigoriy turned to Oleg and then back to Harry, who cycled fast in the inside lane.

'Go right up behind him, and pull out to overtake. Keep as close to him as possible, no more than a metre away. When we are next to him and parallel, slow to his speed.' Grigoriy gave Oleg another quick glance. 'Then I'll shoot. I'll fire twice. I won't miss. Then, get the hell out of here.

'Now. Go for it.'

Oleg worked his way through the traffic so there was just one vehicle between him and Harry. After two minutes, he managed to overtake the car in front to be directly behind Harry.

'Here we go,' Oleg said as he started to draw alongside Harry's bike. Grigoriy lifted his pistol so it was only a few centimetres below the window opening. Oleg brought the car alongside Harry as Grigoriy had instructed. Grigoriy swung round and lifted the pistol. Oleg slowed, and reached with his right hand inside his jacket pocket. Harry's head was no more than one and a half metres from the pistol's barrel.

Oleg plunged the syringe into the back of Grigoriy's neck, and pushed down to inject the fluid. The gun fell from Grigoriy's hand into his lap, and he slumped against the open window. He slid down the side of the door, and ended up in a crumpled heap on the leather seat. He was unconscious. Oleg closed the window, and drove off at speed. He turned off Gunnersbury Avenue and stopped. He pulled out his phone and sent a text message.

FINGLE SAFE. NABUTOV NEUTRALISED. REQUIRE INSTRUCTIONS ON HOW TO PROCEED.

Chapter Twenty-One

At 5:30 p.m. Amie turned the corner into Grange Road and started to walk towards her flat. The light, grey drizzle felt damp on her face. Several of the streetlights didn't work, and made the road feel dark and foreboding. She looked towards her home. She hoped she'd see a light. When Jimmy had dropped her off at the Tube earlier that morning, he said he'd be back before her. She told him she always left a set of keys under a flowerpot in the shed.

The flat's in darkness. He's not there, she thought, as the sound of her own feet squelched on the wet, fallen leaves. It made an eerie kind of noise. She looked around to see if anyone else walked in the road with her. But it was empty. She was on her own, and felt a little anxious, and hoped Jimmy would soon turn up. She reached into her bag for her keys. She held them tight until she reached her flat, and stopped and looked around for few seconds. She wondered if she should wait for Jimmy, but dismissed the idea as being pathetic, and strode up the short path to her front door.

The flat seems normal, she thought, as she slid the key into the lock, turned it, and pushed. The door swung open with a creak. With her other hand, she reached in for the light switch, and then took a step inside. She stood still and gazed around and listened before she stretched down to pick up her mail. It all looked like junk; she left it on a small, hall table with her bag and coat, went down the hall to the kitchen, and turned on the kettle.

An empty glass, not of the kind she used every day, sat on the draining board. She shivered and felt a little uneasy, and reached out to touch the radiator. It felt hot. She leant against it and let the warmth spread through her body. She remembered that Jimmy had asked for a glass of water before they'd left that morning. She closed her eyes. Her thoughts turned to the nightmare she'd endured the previous evening.

He was going to kill me. She shuddered, and took a large slurp from her mug of tea, and carried it into her bedroom. She put it down on the small table next to her wardrobe, took hold of the door and pulled to open it. It wouldn't move. It seemed stuck.

Something's caught. Maybe it's one of my dresses or blouses, she told herself, and gave the handle another tug. When it didn't budge, she gave up and left it for later, and decided to take a shower. She moved away. She stood close to her bed, with her back to the wardrobe, and pulled her jumper over her head. She undid her bra, and dropped it, together with her top, onto the bed. She unzipped her jeans and stepped out of them. She left them, and her knickers, on the floor. Naked, she took one step toward her bathroom, and froze. The wardrobe door had opened behind her.

Oh my God. He's here. It was him who used the glass, she thought.

A gloved hand clasped her mouth, and then an arm grabbed her around the waist and pulled her backwards. She tried to scream. She couldn't.

'See. I said I'd come back. Nice of you to undress for me,' Ray whispered in her ear.

Amie closed her eyes. Her legs felt weak and wobbly, as though they would give way. Her head dropped forward. She knew she was about to be sick.

'Now, girl. Listen to me. Lie on the bed.' Ray pushed her away from him, and waved his shining knife through the air.

Amie retched and threw up on the floor in front of them both.

'Okay. Get it over with, and then do as I say and get on the bed. I want to have a good look at yer before...' He stopped talking and screwed up his eyes. Slowly he turned up the corners of his mouth in a frightening smile.

Amie's legs buckled and she dropped to the floor.

She knew that, this time, she was going to die. But there were no sudden flashes of her past. No regrets or fervent wishes to have lived her life differently – just an overwhelming determination. She was going to fight him to the last.

Oh, Jimmy. Please, please get here quickly, she prayed as she heard Ray step closer.

~~~

Harry didn't know why Amie had come back to his house uninvited for a third time, and become involved in a crazy incident with Jimmy. Or why Jimmy had been there. He didn't care. All he could think about was getting to her flat in time to stop some madman with a knife doing her any harm. He was unaware that a professional hit man was out to kill him, or that a ruthless Russian – once head of the Moscow mafia – pursued him with the same intent. And he gave no thought to his tiredness, or his danger from the many large vehicles that drove along Gunnersbury Avenue with him. He regarded them as no more than an irritation; an obstacle to cycle around and move past so he could continue his dash to Ealing. In the few moments when he waited at traffic lights, or when he couldn't wheedle and wend his way through the stationary vehicles, he thought about what drove him on.

Was it guilt, loyalty, or even love? None of it mattered. He had to get to Amie's, and nothing would to stand in his way. He dodged between slow-moving lorries, sprinted across intersections, and paid no heed to traffic signs. He changed lanes frequently, with no regard to the many cars, buses and lorries capable of mangling him and his bike within seconds. He had used a bike in London for seven or eight years. After no accidents, and having become used to selfish drivers, he reckoned he had nothing to fear.

~~~

Alex Goad parked in the short-term car park at Heathrow at 2:00 p.m., well before his evening flight to Panama City. His small bag, no more than hand luggage, sat on the front passenger seat beside him. He took out his gun and started to dismantle it. Once he'd broken it down and into its various parts, he dropped them all into an old, canvas bag, sealed it up, put the bag inside a Sainsbury's carrier bag, and climbed out of his car. He looked around to check that nobody watched him, and then locked up the car. He added the car keys to the contents of the carrier bag, and dumped it in a waste bin. Taking only his small hand-luggage bag with him, he walked into the terminal, and went through departures and security to airside.

At one of the Internet kiosks, he signed up for three hours' web time, and started to research Panama City. He found, with the $50,000 he had in cash, he could rent an acceptable apartment for a few months, until he was able to get hold of some of the funds he'd transferred to the various individuals who'd agreed to receive money on his behalf. Some months earlier, he discovered a way of anonymously sending large amounts of money to sponsors in foreign countries. Once in Panama, all he had to do was to contact the sponsors. After that, he wouldn't have to worry about money for the rest of his life.

At five he logged off the computer, paid his bill, and went to find a bar. He downed a couple of glasses of champagne, and headed for Gordon Ramsay's Plane Food restaurant. To start with he had cured salmon, green beans, and a sweet mustard dressing, followed by rib-eye steak with red wine and shallots. For his dessert he chose a buttermilk panna cotta with blood oranges and pistachios. To accompany it all, he drank a glass of Chablis and a half bottle of Châteauneuf-du-Pape. While he waited for his bill, he ordered an espresso coffee and a glass of Ardbeg malt whisky. After he'd paid and made ready to leave the restaurant, he heard his flight called.

Perfect, he thought. *Only forty-five minutes before take-off.* He popped a sleeping tablet in his mouth, picked up his bag, and started to walk to the departure gate. He felt content and at ease.

'Mr Goad,' a voice said from behind him. He ignored it and walked straight ahead.

'Mr Goad.' A hand touched his shoulder. He stopped and turned to face a man with a well-chiselled face, slim and tall, and about mid-thirties. He was accompanied by a smartly dressed woman of a similar age, flanked by four armed policemen.

'Yes, can I help you?'

'Excuse me, sir. Are you Alex Goad?' the plainclothes, male police officer asked as he flashed his warrant card.

Alex shook his head. 'Sorry to disappoint you. That's not me. My name's Edward Williams.'

'I'm sorry, sir. There must be some confusion. Would you mind showing me your passport?'

'No problem.' Alex, a touch anxious, reached into his bag and fished out his false passport. The female of the two plainclothes police officers took out a photograph from her bag, and compared it with the passport photo. She passed them both to the male officer and nodded. He looked at them and then at Alex. The armed policemen closed in around him.

'Mr Goad, I'm arresting you for attempting to travel on, and being in possession of, a false passport. Please come this way.'

~~~

Oleg Gavronskii took Grigoriy Nabutov to the address where his contact at MI6 had told him to meet. It was a deserted farm building in Buckinghamshire, just west of Amersham. Oleg and his contact dragged Nabutov, still unconscious, into the large kitchen and dumped him in a big, old, farmhouse chair. Two well-built guards watched on. Once Grigoriy flopped into the chair, they secured him to it with ties and shackles.

'Good, Oleg. Thanks. We'll be in touch,' Oleg's MI6 contact said. He saw Oleg to the door.

Oleg climbed back into his Jeep and headed for Amersham, the nearest town. The day had been tense and he felt in need of a drink. He parked in the car park of The Crown, an old pub in the high street. As he was about to climb out, he noticed a large, brown, buff envelope on the floor in front of where Grigoriy had sat. He picked it up. It was heavy and felt as though it contained a lot of papers or photographs or similar. A printed label had been stuck on the front of the envelope. It'd had been addressed to *The Daily Journal*, Canada Square, Tower

Hamlets, London E14 5AP. Oleg took it into the pub with him.

He ordered a pint of beer and carried it to a quiet corner of the room where no one else sat. After he'd taken a large slug from his drink, he carefully started to prise open the envelope.

'Shit,' he said in Russian in a whisper, as he examined the contents of the envelope. Every photo was of a middle-aged man having sex with several different young men. He didn't recognise the man, but guessed if the package was something to do with Nabutov, the man would likely to be important or famous in some way. The images disgusted him. He sealed up the envelope, dropped it down on the table, and took another large gulp from his beer.

Oleg had joined the FSB after doing his conscription in the Russian army. He liked the work at first, until he was posted to the UK shortly after his wife announced she was expecting their second child. He'd put in a request for his posting to be deferred until at least after the birth of the baby. It wasn't granted and he had to leave Russia when she was six months pregnant. The unsympathetic treatment he received from his superiors in the FSB, and the separation from his family, stirred up feelings of resentment. One morning, when he was feeling particularly down and missing his expectant wife and one-year-old daughter, he saw an advertisement for personnel to join the British security services. He called them up. After an intensive screening process, he was recruited as a double agent. He knew he had taken a risk. He planned to build up enough money in the UK to be able to leave the FSB, work full time for MI6, and bring his wife and family over to live in England permanently.

He finished his beer, picked up the brown envelope, and made for his car. He would deliver the envelope personally to the offices of *The Daily Journal*. When he arrived, he asked to see a senior reporter. He'd said he had something to show that would be of interest. After waiting ten minutes, a woman – who he guessed was about thirty – strode from the lift and came towards him. She wore a faintly striped shirt, a smart, black skirt, and had drawn her long, black hair off her face and tied it behind her head. She held out her hand.

'Hello, I'm Jill Fellows. I understand, Mr....'

'Mr Glazov,' Oleg volunteered, and gave her a business card that showed him as *Yuri Glazov*, a manager with a Russian energy company.

Jill Fellows examined the card and looked up at Oleg. 'I understand, Mr Glazov, that you have something for us.'

'I have something that may interest you. Can we go somewhere private?'

Jill led the way to a small office on the ground floor, away from the main entrance area. It contained a small, round, polished, wooden table, four chairs and a couple of abstract pictures on the white walls. Jill pulled out a seat for Oleg and sat down in one opposite him.

'Can I get you a drink?' she asked, turning to a tea and coffee dispenser that stood on a side table.

'I'm fine. I don't have much time.' Oleg put the envelope down on the table in front of him. 'I have some pictures here that I think you'll find interesting. I have to warn you, they're disturbing.' He slid the package over towards Jill. She started to take them out, one by one. After viewing about ten, she put the envelope down on the table and looked up at Oleg.

'Are the rest the same?' Jill's face showed no expression of disdain or shock or emotion. She seemed unruffled by what she'd seen.

'They are. Pretty shocking, aren't they?'

'Do you know who this man is?' she said.

'Never seen him before in my life. I take it you recognise him. Who is he?'

Jill put all the photos back in the envelope and closed it up. Holding it in her hand, she started to stand up. 'I need to show them to someone else. Will you be okay here for a few minutes?'

Oleg shook his head, and jumped up and blocked Jill's way. He reached forward and grabbed the envelope back from her.

'No way. These are my property until we do a deal. They are obviously of interest to you.' He looked into Jill's eyes.

'My terms are simple. Tell me who he is, agree a sum, and pay me. Once I have the money, the pictures are yours. Okay?'

Jill stared at Oleg for a few seconds. 'Where did you get them from? I need to know.'

Oleg put the envelope in the inside pocket of his leather jacket and started to button it up. 'No. A cheque and the name of the man, or I go to another paper. No questions. It's your choice.'

He left twenty minutes later with a banker's draft for £200,000 and the knowledge that Richard Morecombe, the head of one of the biggest international media companies, would wake up in the morning and find his life had fallen apart. Oleg was ecstatic. He didn't care a toss about Morecombe – he was just a pervert getting his due – but Oleg had made enough money in a short space of time to bring his wife and family over immediately from Russia, and pack in his job with the FSB. He stopped at the first bank and paid in the draft.

~~~

163

Ed James tried hard to control his ill-tempered state of mind brought about by his failure to kill Harry. When he drove away from the garage where he'd left Richard Morecombe, he'd thought it would be easy to knock Harry off his bike and under an oncoming vehicle. But it had proved difficult and that made him feel uneasy. Time had begun to run out.

Harry slowed a little. He turned the corner and cycled into Grange Road. Ed sensed he was near his destination, and reached over to the nearside front seat to nudge his Smith and Wesson pistol a little closer. After screwing up the two earlier attempts on Harry's life, he knew this was his last chance, and he'd become determined to succeed. He gripped the steering wheel, concentrated hard, and kept his eyes fixed on Harry. He tensed his right leg to be ready to push down and accelerate. Harry slowed further and stopped. He swung his leg over the saddle and stood up. He looked around and pulled out his phone and started to make a call. Ed's car whooshed forward and came to a halt close to where Harry stood. He pushed the door open, grabbed his gun and leapt out. He ran towards Harry with his pistol in his left hand, dangling by his hip.

'Jimmy, where the hell are you?' Harry yelled into his phone. He was unaware of Ed, barely four metres away. 'The lights are on. There's someone inside. I'm going in to check she's okay. Get here quickly and follow me in.'

~~~

'Fingle is off his bike, speaking on his phone, and looks as though he is about to enter a house,' the police officer in charge of the Armed Response Unit said into his mouthpiece. He'd watched Harry's movements from a vehicle parked across the road, and had reported back to his supervising officer, who sat in an unmarked police car in a nearby street. In the back of the Armed Response Unit vehicle, two armed policemen, who listened in to the conversation on their headphones, had their Heckler and Koch MP5 carbines trained on Ed James.

The officer in charge grabbed his mouthpiece again. 'Suspicious unknown suspect approaching Fingle fast. Permission to take him out.' The officer glanced back at his two colleagues. He looked worried.

'I repeat. Suspicious unknown suspect almost on Fingle. Request immediate permission to take him out.'

Ed was no more than two and a half metres and two seconds away from Harry.

~~~

Out of nowhere, a man rushed towards Harry and pointed a pistol at his head. He froze. He was scared - sure he was about to die. A deafening crescendo of gunshots rang out. The man with the gun slumped to the ground in a pool of blood. Harry felt stunned. *Why am I still alive and unhurt*? he wondered, as he heard the sound of running feet. He turned to see a posse of armed police race from a vehicle, and towards him and the fallen man. Some plainclothes officers followed on behind.

'Harry. Don't move. Stay absolutely still. You'll be okay,' shouted a recognisable voice.

'My God. It's Philip,' Harry mouthed. *What the hell is this about?*

Harry heard an ambulance siren. The uniformed police officers poured over the man who lay still at Harry's feet. One of them shook his head.

'You okay, Harry?' Philip said as he came close. 'This is Paul and Scott, they're from…'

'I couldn't give a shit if they're from the moon.' Harry pointed to the door of Amie's flat. 'Listen. Amie's in that flat. She's in serious danger from a man with a knife who's in there with her. Get your smart-shooting buddies to help her. Come on.'

'What're you on about? This guy was going to kill you.' Philip looked down and pointed at Ed's still and bloodied body. 'We don't know anything about Amie and a man with a knife.'

Harry raced towards the door of Amie's flat. He turned as he ran. 'You bloody well do now. Are you going to help or do I have to do it myself?'

'Come on. If there's a girl in trouble, we're going in,' said the armed policeman who'd examined Ed's body. An anguished scream rang out from the flat. Harry started battering the front door with his shoulder.

'Go,' yelled one of the police officers as he grabbed his gun and ran towards Harry, who kicked and thumped the door hard with his outstretched leg and foot. An officer headed for the back of the house to the patio as two other officers charged up the path with a large, metal battering ram and smashed it into the door.

'Stay back, sir,' one of them yelled to Harry as the door swung open. 'Let us handle this.' They charged in with their guns at the ready. A gunshot rang out from the rear of the house. Harry followed them in.

They found Amie naked on the floor and covered in blood. Harry rushed to her. She seemed unconscious, but she breathed. A knife wound bled from above her left breast. He cradled her in his arms. She opened her eyes for a second and seemed to recognise him and then fell back into unconsciousness.

'An ambulance. Get an ambulance,' he yelled.

'There's one here. It was for the bloke we shot. He's dead, so they can look after the girl,' said the policemen who'd bent down with Harry to try to help Amie.

'Paramedics to the bedroom, immediately,' the policeman yelled into his mouthpiece.

Two paramedics appeared at the door, looked towards Amie, and rushed to her. 'Move out of the way,' one of the paramedics said to Harry. 'We need to get to her.'

Harry slowly stood up. He turned, and put his hand up to his mouth and gasped. 'Jesus.' Lying a few feet away from Amie was a man Harry had never seen before. His body had been mutilated. He had many stab wounds around his groin and to his stomach. He was quite dead. The policeman who'd blown his way in through the kitchen door came over and looked down at the man's body.

'She made a good job of him,' he said, and walked away.

Harry felt a firm hand rest on his shoulder. 'You'll have to leave us now, sir,' said the police officer in charge. 'We've much to do.'

Harry looked at Amie again. The two paramedics had lifted her onto a stretcher and had put up drips and an oxygen mask. He felt sick and weak, and was only just able to stumble out of the flat to the road. He walked into an alarming scene. The road was blocked off. Several police cars were stationed at both ends. The area directly outside Amie's flat, and including several houses either side, was sealed off by police tape. Male and female police officers stopped and checked anyone who wanted to gain access. The crew from a second ambulance covered up Ed's body. Two large, white tents had been erected in the street and several crime-scene investigators, in white overalls, assembled their equipment. The whole area teemed with police and plainclothes personnel.

'Harry, can we talk to you?' Philip Stacey asked, as Harry stumbled into him. Harry stared past him and over his shoulder. He'd caught sight of Jimmy, who stood at one of the police barriers and tried to attract Harry's attention. Harry ignored Philip and walked over to Jimmy.

'Where the hell have you been?' he asked as he approached him.

'I got held up on the Tube. I'm sorry. What's happened? Is Amie okay?'

Harry shook his head. 'I don't know. She looks in a bad way.

166

They…' Harry stopped. He turned and looked to where Jimmy stared. The paramedics carried Amie out of the flat on a stretcher, and to the ambulance.

'Is that her?' Jimmy asked.

Harry nodded.

'Will she be okay?'

'I don't know.' Harry shook his head a little. 'She's been stabbed. She was breathing and looked at me for a second, and then passed out. I just hope she'll be alright.' Harry looked into Jimmy's eyes. They seemed moist. He put a hand on Jimmy's shoulder.

'I guess we were too late.'

Jimmy put his hand up to his mouth. Both his lips were clenched closed. 'Let's pray for her.'

'Yeah, let's do that.' Harry turned to see who had walked towards him. Philip Stacey, accompanied by the two men Philip had tried to introduce earlier, stood about a metre and a half away.

'We need to talk, Harry.'

'I'll be getting on then, Harry. Be in touch,' Jimmy said. He turned and walked away.

Duplicity

Chapter Twenty-Two

The Morning News, The Daily Journal, The Liberation, The Truth, The Post *and* The Voice.

My name is Harry Fingle. I'm an investigative journalist. I used to work for The Morning News *until I was sacked, for no reason, on 14 October, the same day as the editor, Philip Stacey, left without any explanation.*

In late September I found an encrypted computer file, named ccc.doc, on my late brother's PC. My brother, Joe Fingle, who was killed in a road accident under suspicious circumstances, had worked on the CCC file for Vantiche Pharmaceuticals. My brother's wife, Clare Fingle, died two weeks later in a strange drowning at Marlow. Also, I found a supporting document to the CCC file written in Chinese, but not encrypted. I had it translated. It indicated that CCC was the codename for a new vaccine to prevent HIV, and was currently being trialled successfully in parts of Africa.

After I was sacked, I made it my business to investigate my brother's and his wife's unexplained deaths. A source working for Ritzler Pharmaceuticals, Vantiche's greatest rival for world domination in the pharmaceutical industry, has confirmed that Ritzler ordered the death of my brother, and were behind the recent bombing of Moon Pharmaceuticals' factory in Mumbai, where over two hundred people died. Ritzler's motivation was to stop Vantiche bringing to market a drug that would become the biggest medical breakthrough since penicillin. I have no evidence to suggest that they were behind the death of my brother's wife, Clare, but I find her death, so soon after her husband's death, too coincidental not to be deeply suspicious.

I have evidence that Ritzler, whose chief executive is Alex Goad, have tried to obtain my copy of the CCC file by various illegal and life-threatening means. Yesterday morning I returned from Heathrow airport, where I had been trying to fly to India to visit the Moon factory, to find my house ransacked and my laptop stolen. Later in the day, a Russian hit man burst into my home and tried to kill me. He failed. But at 6:00 p.m., when I tried to rescue an ex-girlfriend from a crazed man holding her in her house with a knife, another hit man jumped out of a car and shoved a gun in my face. Luckily for me, he was killed by a police Armed Response Unit, who'd been lying in wait.

My friend was not so fortunate. She's fighting for her life in hospital.

You may find this all crazy and unbelievable. I have all necessary supporting evidence, and you will read all about it in news items in this and all other national papers.

This is about a war, between two of the world's largest pharmaceutical companies, for world domination. However, the British secret service and, by default, the government are complicit in their actions. How else could a police Armed Response Unit and three MI6 officers have been in wait for my assassin?

Harry Fingle.

Harry read the draft through, rubbed his eyes and closed the lid of the laptop. *That's enough for the moment*, he thought. He knew what he'd written would be explosive. He needed to check it thoroughly with Kate, and make sure his claim of having all the supporting evidence was correct. He'd do that in the morning, he thought, and looked at his watch. He had to make a call: one that he dreaded.

~~~

Earlier, at Ealing hospital, where the ambulance took Amie, he'd been unable to see her. He'd been told she was in intensive care and remained unconscious.

'Is she going to make it?' he'd asked the A&E staff at the hospital. The man on the reception desk looked up and studied him with a vacant expression.

'Are you her next of kin?'

'No, but I've been a friend of hers for many years.'

The man shook his head. 'I can only divulge information to next of kin.' He returned to his computer screen.

'Thanks for your help, mate.' Harry headed outside to where he'd left his bike. He guessed the man had been correct and just doing his job, but his cold and uncooperative manner did nothing to ease Harry's concern for Amie's condition. He feared the worst.

After the incident at Amie's flat, and once the ambulance took her away, he'd been asked by the police to stay and answer some questions, and give a statement. He agreed, suspecting he had no choice in the matter. For the next hour, he sat in the back of a police car. Eventually his statement was produced. He read it, signed on the bottom, and asked if he was free to go. As he stepped out of the car, Philip Stacey turned up. He wanted Harry to talk to him and the two men with him. Harry declined. He said he felt tired and wanted to go to the hospital to find

169

out about Amie. Philip said he'd call in the morning.

When he returned from the hospital, he dropped his bike in the porch of his house and pushed open the door. He didn't lock the bike or take off the expensive pump and front light as he usually did. He just left it on its side where he'd dismounted and rushed inside. Using one of his feet as a broom, he swept his mail to one side, ignored the chaos left by the intruders, and made for his hand luggage, which still stood in his hall where he'd left it earlier. He pulled out his iPad, tucked it under his arm, and took it to the kitchen. He logged on and started typing a letter to all the national newspapers.

~~~

'Is that you, Jiang? It's Harry, Harry Fingle.' Harry checked the time. It was midnight. It would be eight in the morning in Hong Kong. He knew Jiang Lau, Amie's father, would normally be up by then.

'Harry?' Jiang replied. He sounded startled and half asleep 'What you want? It early?'

Harry hoped he wasn't wrong about the time difference. He'd deliberately waited, not wanting to disturb Amie's parents with such bad news in the middle of the night. He took a deep breath. He'd always had a good relationship with them in the past. But when he split with Amie after his trial, both her mother and father, independently, sent him long letters telling him they thought he was a big shit. They said he was selfish and didn't care about their daughter's feelings. They were elderly, and although they spoke and understood English, sometimes their accents made it difficult to follow what they said. He didn't expect the call to be easy.

'I'm sorry to tell you that Amie's in hospital.'

'Hospital? What wrong with her?'

'Jiang, this isn't going to be easy, but she's been stabbed.'

'Stab! My God. No. What you mean, stab?'

'Lan.' Harry heard Jiang shout to his wife. He spoke in Cantonese, and Harry guessed Jiang had asked his wife to come to the phone.'

The line went quiet. 'Noh, noh. Ah, noh,' a voice cried out in the background. Harry thought it was Amie's mother. He waited for her to speak.

'Harry. What go on? Jiang, head in his hands, won't talk. What it all about?'

Harry told Amie's mother what had happened. She reacted at first in a similar shocked and disbelieving way as Amie's father, but soon became rational and able to talk. She wanted to know all the details.

170

After Harry had told her as much as he knew, she said Jiang and she would book the first available flight to London that day. Harry offered to hire a car and meet them at the airport.

Harry said good-bye, put his phone down on the worktop, and clasped his hands together. He pursed his lips and stared straight ahead for a few minutes.

Today is hell, he said to himself, and closed his eyes. *I hope and pray they arrive in time.*

Waves of tiredness started to disable him. It felt as though heavy weights pushed down on his shoulders and moved into every part of his body. He forced himself to stand. His legs became leaden and his body ached. He was exhausted, and stumbled off to his bed.

~~~

After smoking two of the old joints, Kate returned to her bedroom. She picked up Jack's iPod and scrolled to a song they both had liked. She started again to sift through his things, and touched items and turned them over. Happy memories filled her thoughts. She felt no pain or sense of loss. The guilt and remorse she'd felt earlier over the bombing in Mumbai had evaporated. She'd been left only with a euphoric sense of peace with the world and all about her: total release.

'God, he was a lovely boy,' she said, as she looked at his picture and read for a second time one of his poems. 'I was so lucky knowing him, even if my time with him was short. Oh, my beautiful Jack.' She started to sing along with the music coming from the headphones as she danced and wandered around her bedroom with Jack's *Stop the War* T-shirt clutched to her breast. She reached down and picked up his Arsenal woolly hat. 'Such lovely, vivid colours.' She pulled it down over her head.

'I feel great.' She fell back onto her bed. It was still unmade from when she'd made love to Harry. She rolled around and giggled for some time, until she felt hungry and wandered down to her kitchen with Jack's iPod still plugged into her ears.

'What a wonderful day,' she sang as she looked out of her window at the Thames and munched on a banana and a chocolate biscuit.

'I think I'll go for a drive.'

~~~

Many drivers flashed her as she headed off down the A3 towards Richmond Park. She wore Jack's T-shirt and woolly hat. Countless cars honked their horns. She took no notice, and continued to weave her way along the fast-moving dual carriageway. Her car veered so close to other vehicles that their drivers braked, or changed lanes, or swerved to get out of her way.

I think I have to stop, she figured, as the cars in front of her slowed to halt at a set of traffic lights. A man in the next car shook his fists at her. *I wonder what he wants?* She opened her window.

'Lady, should you be driving? You're weaving all over the road,' the man said, his tone concerned. 'You'll cause an accident in a minute.'

Kate nodded a few times, with slow movements of her head. She smiled and stared at him. 'What? I'm fine,' she drawled. 'What're you on about? I didn't see any accident. Are you having a good day? I am.' Kate smiled again at the man, and touched the button to slide her window back up. The lights changed. Several drivers beeped on their horns, and Kate slowly pulled away.

'Nutter,' yelled the driver who'd spoken to her, and then he accelerated and disappeared.

'This is nice. So beautiful; I can see some deer,' Kate murmured as she swung her car off the A3 and into Richmond Park. She accelerated hard towards the deer. A couple walking along the side of the narrow park road moved away at speed. They stared at her car in frightened amazement as she raced past. A cyclist pulled in and jumped off his bike to safety. A woman with a buggy pushed it as fast as she could to the centre of the lawn, and as far away from the road as possible. Kate didn't notice any of them. Nor was she aware that a police car, with its blue light flashing, tried to catch up with her. She focused only on the herd of deer in the distance. She rammed her foot down on the accelerator until it touched the floor. She sang John Lennon's Beautiful Boy, substituting 'darling Jack' for 'darling Sean.'

'Oh, you magnificent deer – such lovely creatures: I want to cuddle you all,' she yelled, just before her car veered off the road, turned over in midair, and hurtled towards a three-hundred-year-old oak tree. The car crashed into the tree with a sickening thud. The air became filled with the tinkling sound of broken glass and clanging metal. The few people in the park turned and stared. The deer fled. An unnatural silence followed.

Kate had been driving at nearly 100 mph. She'd misjudged a bend in the road and slewed off onto the grass. One of her front wheels had struck a large mound in the ground. Her small car had spun over, towards the tree. The police car pulled up a few seconds later. The male driver was the first out. He ran towards Kate's upturned and buckled car. The female officer followed.

'Oh my God,' he said as he steadied himself by holding onto the car's roof. He'd caught sight of Kate's torn and twisted body wrapped around the steering wheel. Her head had become embedded in the dashboard. Her bloodied face was peppered and torn by shards and splinters of glass.

'She hadn't worn a seat belt,' the female officer said. She turned her head to speak into her mouthpiece to request an ambulance.

~~~

At the AA meeting on the day Gary Lester had been suspended from his job, he asked to speak. The chairperson said she'd call him as soon as possible. Several other people had asked to tell their stories that night. She told Gary she didn't know how long he'd have to wait. He sat at the back, and listened to all the pathetic, dysfunctional tales. Most were similar to his. He questioned his willingness to stay and hear it all out. He didn't doubt he was one of them. After staying sober for nearly seven months, he'd allowed himself to slip back into alcoholism with little resistance. He felt he didn't want to listen. It would only remind him of his weakness, the self-permitting destruction of his life. All he wanted to do was to leave the room and cross the road to the pub, and get wasted. But he held back. He thought about the talk he'd had with Margaret Hudson a few hours earlier. She'd asked him, straight up, if he'd been drinking again.

He had sat back and looked her in the eye. 'Yes.'

'Have you bought any into the office?'

'I can't lie to you. I have, almost on a daily basis.'

'Thanks for being honest. I appreciate it.' She stared into his face. 'You must know that's a dismissible offence. By telling the truth, you've put your job on the line.'

'I know. But I can't lie about it anymore, can I? Not if I'm ever going to do something about it, for good. When do you want me to go?'

It was then that Margaret offered him a lifeline. She said that she wasn't going to sack him if he promised to go straight to the next meeting of AA, and own up and start again. He would be suspended and wouldn't receive any pay. If he kept off the booze for three months, she'd give him one last chance and find him a job somewhere in the organisation.

'What about Alex? He won't have me back.'

'I'll deal with him. Don't worry; you won't be working for him.'

~~~

'Gary; would you like to talk to us now?' the chairperson said, as she looked to the back of the room to find him.

Gary shook as he rose to his feet. Heads turned and chairs shuffled. Those he'd heard earlier, who'd told of their distressing lives, stared at him. He knew he'd started to perspire. He always did. He could feel his legs tremble, and could see his hands shake. He gripped hard on the back of the empty chair in front of him. He hoped a hole in the ground would open up, and he could drop through it and disappear forever.

This is all wrong. I shouldn't be here, he told himself, and loosened his grip on the chair and started to turn around. He wanted to run out of the room.

'Are you okay, Gary?' the chairperson asked.

He coughed to clear his throat and placed his hand, wet from his perspiration, back on the chair.

'I'm Gary Lester, and I was suspended from my job today for continuing to allow myself to be an alcoholic. I thought I was going to get the sack, but I didn't. They've given me another chance. I didn't want to come tonight. I would have preferred to go and drink myself stupid. I didn't want to hear you all saying all the things you've said. The weak, pathetic way you give in at a moment's stress, not able to control your lives when the going gets tough, unable to see what you're doing to yourselves. I didn't want to hear it.'

'Get out, go. If you haven't got anything helpful to say, piss off,' somebody shouted.

'Agree,' somebody else said, amid boos and hissing.

'Yeah, I agree. Get lost.'

'Who do you think you bloody well are? You're just the same as us all, a bloody drunk, mate. Own up to it.'

'Let Gary finish. Try and listen. Please,' the chairperson said, attempting to damp down the yells and comments of discontent. 'Do you want to go on, Gary?'

Gary nodded. 'You are all correct. I'm exactly the same. A waster who's too bloody weak to do anything about it. I didn't come with any prepared speech, or particular things in my mind that I wanted to say. I just wanted to come, talk, and try to start again. I don't know how I'm going to do it, but at least I'm here.

'Earlier I wanted to run out and go to the pub. But I didn't. I stayed and listened and realised how I'd screwed up my life. Only I'm to blame. I don't know how I'm going to kick it, but I will. I haven't had a drink for about six hours. I hope I can stay off it for the rest of the day.'

Gary straightened himself up.

'I didn't mean to be rude or offend. You're all lovely people and I'm one of you.

'I was just so very, very cross with myself. I realised I was right back at the very beginning. This time I'm going to beat it. I mean it. Thank you for listening.'

Gary sat down to a round of applause.

The meeting broke up soon after Gary's talk. He didn't say good-bye to anyone. He walked directly out and into the night air. His route home took him past several pubs and various venues selling alcohol. He didn't go in. When he was close to his flat, he thought again about calling up Jimmy. Maybe they could meet up for something to eat and have a chat?

He couldn't raise Jimmy. A message said the number was no longer in use.

Chapter Twenty-Three

Harry woke with a start. Someone had rung his doorbell, and had kept their finger on the button. He looked at the alarm clock next to him and saw it was only five in the morning. He'd been asleep for only a few hours. *Christ, who the hell wants me at this time?* he thought, as he swung his legs to the floor, and went to the window and looked down. In the gloom, he could make out two men of the same height, standing back from his door and looking up. Both were wearing similar jackets. He looked to the end of his path, and saw a black, saloon car parked in the road. He thought it was a Mercedes. He slid open the window and leant out.

'What is this? Who the hell are you?'

One of the two men reached into his pocket and brought out a badge. He shone a torch onto it. 'We're police, Mr Fingle. We'd like to come in and have a word with you.'

~~~

Forty-five minutes later, Paul Adams slid the door closed behind Harry and turned to face him. He put out his hand. 'Glad to meet you, Mr Fingle. Good of you to come in and see us so early. Take a seat.'

Harry kept his hands by his side. He remained standing. He looked Paul up and down. He remembered him from the previous evening, outside Amie's flat. He'd been one of the two people with Philip Stacey. He looked slim, and wore a pair of navy, casual trousers and a light-blue shirt with his sleeves slightly rolled up. Harry guessed he was about thirty.

'According to the two policemen who came to collect me, I didn't have a choice. If I hadn't agreed to come, they would've arrested me.' Harry looked into Paul's eyes. 'So what's this about? What's your game, Mr Adams? Whatever it is, I don't like it.' With his attention fixed on Paul, he slid his fingers under his belt and said, 'I want some answers.' He stood and faced Paul. They stood about a metre apart. Harry was seven or eight centimetres taller than Paul.

'You'll get them,' Paul said in a calm and controlled manner. He looked away for a few seconds. 'But first, please sit down?'

Harry looked around the sparse surroundings. He knew he'd been taken to the MI6 building at Vauxhall Cross. They were in a small room on the ground floor with a grey, metal, round table and four padded, grey chairs with matte-chrome frames. A tea and coffee machine sat on a small table in the corner. There were no windows.

Harry, who wore jeans and a long-sleeved T-shirt that he'd hastily pulled on before he'd opened the door to the police, took hold of one of the chairs and plonked it down at a forty-five degree angle to the table. He sat on it, stretched his legs out straight in front of him, and crossed them over at his ankles. He pointed to the coffee machine. 'Is that working?'

Paul nodded and took a couple of steps towards it. 'Tea or coffee?'

'Coffee. No milk.'

Harry watched Paul move towards the drinks dispenser. While in the police car, he'd figured MI6 wanted to talk to him about the CCC file and Philip Stacey's involvement – the conversation he'd put off the previous evening. But why so early in the morning and with such urgency, he had no idea. He knew he should be careful and cautious, and avoid saying anything that might jeopardise the letter he'd drafted to all the major newspapers.

'Why am I here?' he asked as Paul returned with the drinks.

Paul sat down opposite, and pushed a polystyrene mug of black coffee across the table to Harry. He'd chosen the same. He took a sip and looked up. 'I guess you've had a bit of a rough time lately, Mr Fingle: or can I call you Harry?'

'You can call me what you like. Just tell me what this is all about before I lose patience. If we can't get this sorted soon, I'm going. I've things to do.'

'I wouldn't do that. It would only complicate matters.'

Who is this guy? Surely he can't behave like this? Harry put his mug down on the tabletop. He leant forward so his face was close to Paul's face. Their eyes met. 'Are you threatening me, Mr Adams?'

Paul slowly pushed back the rolled-up cuffs of his shirt, one by one. 'No,' he said in a tone that seemed almost flippant. He looked up at Harry. 'But I'd like you to tell me everything you know about the computer file – ccc.doc – that you found on your brother's PC.' Paul paused. 'And all you know about the two pharmaceutical companies, Ritzler and Vantiche.'

Harry glowered and rose from his seat and stood behind it. He gripped the frame and looked down at Paul. He felt astonished. He wanted to shout out, but knew it would do no good. He had to keep his feelings and frustration under control.

'Listen, Mr Adams. It's you, not me, who needs to do the explaining.

'A bomb went off in Mumbai less than forty-eight hours ago, and my flight had to turn around. Hundreds were killed. Somebody broke into my house the night before last and ransacked it, and stole my laptop. Then a Russian hit man tried to kill me yesterday morning.

'I call Philip Stacey, and your crew come round and whisk him away. I rush off to try and stop some crazed madman from knifing my ex-girlfriend, and another weirdo leaps out of a car and pops a gun in my face. He's about to pull the trigger when your boys take him out. Meanwhile, the knife man stabs my ex-girlfriend.

'It's all madness, unbelievable – if it wasn't true. What the hell is going on? I need answers.' Harry, unable to contain himself any longer, banged his hand down hard on the table. 'Now.'

Paul looked up at him. He appeared unruffled. 'Actually, it wasn't us who killed the man, Ed James. It was a police Armed Response Unit.'

'Don't play games with me,' Harry said with a sardonic gesture and started to pace around the room. 'You told them to be there. Didn't you? You don't expect me to believe a team of heavily armed, highly trained police just happened to be in the area. Don't patronise me.' Harry took a couple of paces to where Paul still sat and stared at him.

'I want to know what this is all about. If you can't explain, I'm going.'

Paul put his hand over his mouth and rubbed his chin. 'You can't. They won't let you out.'

'What do you mean? That's outrageous. You can't do that. You can't hold me against my will.'

Paul looked up and caught Harry's gaze. 'We could arrest you.'

Harry shook his head. 'No. You can't do that. You're crazy. On what charge?'

'Being in possession of information that could jeopardise the security of the nation.'

'Bollocks. That's bullshit.'

'Sit down and listen to me.'

Harry became incensed. He wanted to ramp and rage and give vent to his anger. He looked down again, and glared at Paul for about ten seconds. Paul remained unmoved. With reluctance, Harry pulled out the chair and sat down opposite. 'Go on,' he said.

'Firstly, how's your girlfriend?'

'She's not my girlfriend. She's my ex-girlfriend.'

'Okay: ex-girlfriend. How is she?'

Harry glanced down at the table, clasped his hands together in his lap and thought for a moment about his answer. 'I don't know. When I got to the hospital last night, she was still unconscious. They wouldn't give me any information as I'm not her next of kin.' He stopped and looked at his watch. 'Look, I've got to get out of here soon. I'm meeting her parents at Heathrow later this morning. They're flying in from Hong Kong.'

'What's her name?' Paul asked, and picked up the pencil that lay next to his notepad.

'Why do you want to know?'

'I'm just trying to help, Harry. If you give me her name, we can use our influence to obtain an update on her condition.'

Harry stared hard at Paul, stroked his stubbly face, and considered Paul's offer. He didn't much like the situation in which he found himself, and had no way of telling if Paul had bluffed just to soften him up. But he knew of no other way of finding out about Amie's condition, and decided to take a chance.

'It's Amie Lau,' he said, holding his right hand up to his chin.

Paul jotted down Amie's name, and picked up a phone. 'Can you come in for a moment,' he said, and looked straight at Harry until a guy in his mid-twenties came through the door a few seconds later. Paul gave him the piece of paper with Amie's name. 'She's in Ealing Hospital. Get an update on her condition and prognosis. Come back as soon as you have it. Thanks.' He waited until the man had left. He turned to face Harry.

'Listen, Harry. You're lucky to be alive. There was a third attempt on your life yesterday, which you didn't know about. We stopped it just in time.'

'When?' Harry snapped. He looked at Paul with an expression of disbelief.

'When you cycled up Gunnersbury Avenue, Grigoriy Nabutov – a Russian who works for the Chinese owners of Vantiche Pharmaceuticals and who's the boss of the person who'd tried to kill you earlier – decided to take you out himself. He drew up alongside you in a car and was about to shoot you.'

'You're kidding. You're taking the piss.'

'No. I'm not,' Paul said with conviction. 'You were within seconds of death.'

Harry clasped his hands together and rested them on the tabletop. He stared into Paul's eyes. If Paul had told the truth he had to find out more, however shocking and scary. He pulled his chair closer to the table, and turned and faced Paul.

'Go on. Tell me what happened?'

'We stopped him.'

'What? Shot him?'

'No, no. Far too messy. We just dumped a fast-acting syringe into his neck and neutralised him. The driver of his car works for us. He was the one handy with the needle. After the incident, he brought Nabutov in to one of our centres in the country. He's currently being debriefed.'

Harry shot Paul a quick glance. 'Debriefed. You mean tortured?'

'No I don't,' Paul replied in a defensive tone. He screwed up his eyes and tilted his head to one side. 'We don't torture.'

Harry tried to remain expressionless. As a journalist, he knew much about the methods of interrogation used by British intelligence. He'd written several articles about it in *The Morning News*. But he guessed the time was not right to pick a fight. He needed to find out more.

Was this third attempt on my life and the CCC file connected? he asked himself as he turned his head slightly to catch Paul's eyes. 'If that's so, I guess I owe you guys.'

Paul sat up. 'Maybe. But we need your cooperation.'

'Go on.' Harry nodded.

'You agree to help us, then?'

'I don't know what you want.' Harry looked at his watch. 'Look, I've got to be at Heathrow by ten. Will we be through by then?'

'Can't say. But if we're not, we'll send a car to pick them up.' Paul placed his right hand over his left wrist. He gripped the edge of the table and leant forward so he was close to Harry. 'Okay?'

Harry nodded again.

'I need to tell you one thing before we get going.'

'What's that?'

'We don't know anything about the man who broke into your friend's flat. That wasn't on our radar. We were there to protect you. It was just a coincidence.'

'Who was he then?' Harry said as the door opened. The guy who'd taken the details about Amie came in and waited. Harry looked at him. He didn't look back at Harry. The guy waited for Paul to speak. Harry took a deep breath. He feared the worst.

'Yes, Mathew? Any news?' Paul asked.

Mathew, his face expressionless, turned to Harry and then back to Paul. 'She's conscious,' Mathew said and looked at Harry.

Harry felt his heart miss a beat. He looked at Mathew's expression for some indication of what he would say next.

'She has a stab wound above her left breast.'

Harry bit down on his lower lip. He covered his mouth with his left hand. He prepared himself for the next information. It would be bad, he knew.

'No major organs have been damaged.' A tiny smile cracked Mathew's stony expression. 'She's doing okay,' he said with a nod. 'The hospital reckon she should make a good recovery.' He turned back to Harry. 'A bit sore for a while.'

Harry closed his eyes, and buried his head in his hands. Feelings of relief and elation surged through his body. He felt light-headed, as though he'd drunk a shot of whisky in one gulp. He became unsteady and emotional, almost tearful, and asked for some time on his own.

~~~

At nearly three in the morning, two police cars and an ambulance raced down the road that led to Ed James's lockup garage in Stepney. Early in his interrogation by MI6, Alex Goad had told them about Ed and the two jobs he'd given to him – Richard Morecombe and Harry Fingle. It had taken the police several hours to locate Ed's lockup. Eventually, they traced the address through the pub Ed owned around the corner. Richard was unconscious when they found him. His head hung forward on his chest. He remained tied to the chair where Ed had left him thirteen hours earlier. Once the paramedics released him, he started to regain consciousness and became lucid and able to give the police a full account of what had happened. They took him to The Royal London Hospital in Whitechapel.

At nine the following morning, the hospital discharged him. The police waited. They said they wanted to debrief him, and took him to a nearby police station. They led him into a small, grubby interview room with a long, vinyl-topped table in the middle and two stained, plastic chairs on either side. A tall, male detective and a shorter female detective met him. Both looked Richard up and down with similar disapproving expressions.

'Take a seat, Mr Morecombe,' the female detective said, in a cold manner. She indicated the far side of the table. She sat opposite him. Her colleague stood and leant against a wall. His left hand rested on a shelf. One of his fingers touched the controls of a tape recorder. The female detective had a newspaper in front of her. It was *The Daily Journal*. She'd placed it facedown on the table with the sports page uppermost.

'Know anything about this?' she asked. She flipped the paper over and pushed the front page in front of Richard.

MEDIA TYCOON EXPOSED AS A PAEDOPHILE

Richard Morecombe, the owner of The Morning News Newspaper Group and with many other media interests, has been pictured having illicit sex with underage boys...

181

Chapter Twenty-Four

After Harry had been told the news about Amie, they left him alone. Paul had said he'd be back after about thirty minutes to take Harry to another room, where all his questions would be answered. He arranged for someone to fetch Harry some breakfast. Harry felt hungry and grateful, but he remained uneasy and apprehensive. Why was he being held like a prisoner, locked in a small room, and having to call someone if he needed anything or simply wanted to relieve himself? Why had Paul said they had to go to another room? Where was it all leading? These and other questions occupied his thoughts while he ate. He didn't linger over the meal, pushing the tray to one side after about five to six minutes. He stood up, poured another coffee, and started to pace around the room with his cup in his hand.

'Breakfast okay?' Paul asked in a chirpy tone as he entered the room after exactly thirty minutes.

Harry remained seated and looked up from the newspaper he'd been reading. 'I have a question. Why do I have to go to another room to get the answers I want?'

Paul stopped and frowned at Harry. 'We need to brief you properly. The room's bigger, and there's some other people you need to meet.'

'What do you mean, "brief me?" I just want you to tell me why I'm being held here against my will. I don't need to meet anyone else.'

'Come on.' Paul gestured with his hand and arm for Harry to stand up and go to wherever he wanted to take him. 'We need to move.'

Harry folded up the paper into an uneven shape, dumped it on the table, and stood up. 'We? I don't need to go anywhere, apart from out of this building. You just don't want to be late, do you?' Harry shot Paul a sarcastic grin, and joined him outside the room. They walked off, side by side and in silence, down the corridor and entered a room about ten metres by six. It had a long, grey table, in the style of the one in the room Harry had been in earlier, which ran down the middle. Along each side were six chairs. At the far end, Harry could see a large screen and the equipment for a Power Point or similar presentation. Standing nearby, a tall man dressed in navy chinos and a pale-blue shirt rested his backside against one of the chairs and talked to a grey-haired, middle-aged woman. She wore a black, linen suit and a white blouse and was of medium height, trim, with a pinched-up face, and a tenacious expression. As Harry and Paul closed in on her, she stopped talking and looked Harry up and down in a way he found disconcerting. The tall man with her turned around and raised a hand.

'Hi, Harry. How you doing?' He spoke with a US accent.

'Hello,' Harry replied curtly. He recognised the man from the previous evening. He'd been with Paul and Philip Stacey outside Amie's flat. Harry didn't think they'd been introduced. In the far corner he could see Philip. He poured coffee into white cups. For once he didn't wear his standard, pinstripe suit. He wore jeans and a white shirt with blue stripes. He didn't acknowledge Harry. Paul guided Harry around the front of the table to where the man and the middle-aged woman stood. They both looked as Paul and Harry approached. The woman placed the half-framed glasses, which dangled on a lanyard around her neck, onto the end of her nose and held out her hand.

'Pleased to meet you, Mr Fingle. My name's Sheila Robinson. I'm head of section here.' Her face seemed stern. Her stare was fixed. 'You have been through quite a lot. We want to explain things to you. Please take a seat.' She motioned towards a chair towards the front of the table, close to where they stood. Paul sat next to Harry on one side. The tall man took a seat on the other side. Sheila sat down opposite Harry. Once they were seated, Philip joined them with a tray of coffee.

'Morning, Harry,' Philip said, without so much as a glance. He sat next to Sheila.

'Does everyone know each other?' Sheila asked as she looked around the table, while Philip passed cups of coffee, and milk and sugar around.

'Nope,' Harry said and shook his head.

This is the screwiest and most bizarre situation I've been in, he thought. *I've known Philip for years. I'm the godfather to one of his children, but he doesn't acknowledge me. The American guy pretends we've met, and this Sheila person – she's clearly something else.*

'I don't know – *you*,' Harry said, turning to Scott.

'Sorry, Harry. I thought we met last night. I'm Scott Reynolds from the CIA. Pleased to meet you.' He held his hand out to Harry.

'Hi.' Harry shook Scott's hand for barely a second. In the corner of his eye, he caught sight of Sheila leaning forward. He turned to face her.

She rested both her forearms on the table and clasped her elbows. She flicked her gaze between Harry and the other two opposite her. 'Good. Let's start.' She opened the folder in front of her, and took out a typed, official-looking sheet of paper. She directed her gaze at Harry.

'Mr Fingle.' She held the paper up in her hand. 'This is just a formality. It's a short document that we ask all our....' She stopped and looked at Harry. 'I was going to say *informers*, but in your case it's *collaborators*. We ask them all to sign it.'

She raised one of her arms to rest her chin in her hand and continued to look across the table. 'By signing it, you agree that none of what you hear in this room will go beyond these walls.' She raised an eyebrow for a moment. 'It's an abbreviated version of the Official Secrets Act.'

Harry returned her stare. *What the hell. I can't do that*, he told himself, as he raced to gather his thoughts. If he signed, he'd be stitched up, unable to go public on anything he knew about the CCC file and all he'd learnt. 'And if I don't sign?'

'Harry,' Philip Stacey said, as he leant across the table and engaged with Harry for the first time. He had tilted his head to the right. His cheek rested in the palm of his right hand with his elbow on the table. He massaged his chin with his thumb.

'That wouldn't be a very wise thing to do. You've escaped three attempts on your life. Okay, one of the assassins is dead, and the other two are in our custody, but, as you'll find out, we're dealing with ruthless and determined people. By simply signing this, you can be fully briefed.' He glanced down at the table for a second and then back at Harry. 'And then we can give you the protection you need.'

'I don't get it.' Harry stopped and shot a glance at Scott and Paul in turn. Paul looked ahead with a deadpan expression. His hands were clasped together on the table in front of him. Scott stared at the walls and ceiling. Harry looked across at Sheila and Philip. Both gazed directly at him.

'What don't you get, Mr Fingle?' Sheila asked as she sat back in her seat. She took off her glasses, and let them hang on the lanyard so they touched the knobbly bones at the end of her collarbone, at the bottom of her neck. 'Tell me.' She gave Harry a withering look.

Harry put his right hand on the table and drummed a few times with his fingers. He looked across at Sheila. 'I don't get what this is all about. You've asked me to cooperate with you and tell you what I know about the CCC file.' He paused, looked down and drummed his fingers on his thighs.

'I decided earlier; in return for you saving my life and getting information on my friend, Amie, I'd help. Now you want me to sign the Official Secrets Act.' He shook his head. 'I thought I was doing the telling, not you?'

Sheila glanced at Philip, and then turned back to face Harry. She touched her glasses again. They seemed to irritate her.

'You've been caught up in something big, Mr Fingle. It's only right of us to explain. Of course we want your cooperation, and are interested in what you know. But you'll want to ask questions, and we're obliged to give you answers. If you don't sign the act, we can't tell you anything.' She put her glasses back on, fiddled with them for a bit, and looked down at her notes.

'National security is at stake here,' she said and gave Harry a fleeting, weak smile. 'If you don't sign…' She looked away for a moment, and then back at Harry. Her expression remained resolute. 'We'll charge you with withholding information.

'What do you want? The easy way, or the hard way.'

Harry felt his heartbeat quicken. His throat became dry. Adrenaline rushed around his body. He felt furious. Paul had threatened to charge him earlier. It was a stitch-up, and he wanted to jump up and tell the lot of them where to put themselves, and then get the hell out of the place. He turned to look at Philip, in the vague hope he might get some encouragement or support from his old friend. But Philip looked away. Harry knew he was trapped.

My God. Is this how the British secret services behave? he asked himself. He had no choice, no other option or route out of his predicament. *These people mean business; they're not here for the fun of it. They're not bluffing. He took a deep breath, reached forward and signed the document.*

'Good,' said Sheila. She stretched across the table to retrieve it. She put it in her folder, snapped the stud on the front closed, and looked across at Paul. 'Let's get started.' Paul stood up, and went to the door and opened it. A casually dressed young woman came in and switched on a projector. The lights dimmed. A document flashed up onto the screen.

'I think you'll find this helpful, Mr Fingle,' Sheila said. Harry looked up and started to read.

~~~

RUSSIAN/CHINESE INTELLIGENCE ACTIVITY

Background

Russian

107+ intelligence operatives currently operate in the UK – highest since the cold war. In 2007 there were 30 tagged operatives

Targets – military hardware, scientific establishments, technology, Westminster politics, businessman with access to sensitive information and Russian dissidents.

Once targets are compromised, they're run in the known case-officer and agent manner.

Activity doubled after the murder of Alexander Sidorov.

Chinese

Current Western political attitudes hide specific operative numbers.

European intelligence agencies tag hundreds of Chinese agents working within European industry.

Chinese government pressures young business trainees to gather technological and commercial intelligence in major Western companies.

Chen Yong, Chinese diplomatic defector to Australia, reported Beijing had 1,000+ agents operating in Australia.

China denies espionage as Western fabrication, stating narrow-minded West fears legitimate commercial and industrial competition.

Pharmaceutical Industry Backdrop

The global pharmaceutical market will double in value to $1.3 trillion by 2020. China and Russia are both aiming to be major operators in this market.

In 2007 China was the ninth world drug market. By 2008, it was the eighth; by 2010 it will be the fifth. By 2050, it's forecast to be the No. 1 drug producer in the world. All Chinese pharmaceutical companies are wholly or partly funded by the Chinese government.

Chinese pharmaceutical companies are regarded by the World Health Organization as robust, and best practice operators capable of meeting the rapidly growing world pharmaceutical industry demands.

The Russian pharmaceutical industry, although equally determined to compete with China and the rest of the world, is different. Historically controlled by the Russian mafia, the Russian government recognises that to make it both able to compete and overtake its competitors and to receive a seal of approval from the World Health Organization, it needs to clean up its act and rid itself of the criminal influence. Consequently, the Russian government has bought into most of the drug-producing companies.

Inside the Kremlin, the pharmaceutical industry department is autonomous, reporting directly to the president.

Zeum, the leading Russian drug company who owns Ritzler Pharmaceuticals, adopted KGB practices in pursuit of its commercial policies.

Conclusion

The determination and aggressive approach of the Chinese and Russian drug companies provides us with an excellent opportunity to observe the methods and means of both Russian and Chinese intelligence operations in the UK.

~~~

The lights went on. Harry stifled a yawn. He looked around the room.

'So what's the big deal? Apart from your vague reference to Ritzler at the end, and spooks' jargon about an opportunity for you boys and girls to play spy games, none of that's new. You can find it all on the Internet. It's hardly a state secret.'

Paul straightened in his seat and turned to face Harry. 'Background information, Harry. What we have to tell you next is the sensitive bit.'

Harry stared at Paul for a few seconds. 'Can't wait.'

Sheila leaned across the table. She had her glasses perched on the edge of her nose and looked intently at Harry.

'First.' She paused. 'I want you to tell us everything you know about the CCC file, and Ritzler and Vantiche.'

Scott stood up and made for the coffee machine. He stopped, and turned and gazed at Harry. 'Make it interesting. I've been up since five this morning. These guys said you were coming in and it'd be entertaining. So far, it's bored my nuts off.' He glanced at Sheila. 'Shall I make some more?' She nodded.

'You see, Harry. I come from across the pond. We do things a bit differently there, and have none of this crap stuff at the beginning. Please, get on with your story. Otherwise I might fall asleep – and I warn you, I snore loudly.'

'Scott.' Sheila shot him a contemptuous look. 'You may be paid by the CIA, but while you're in our building, show some respect.'

'Yes, ma'am,' Scott said as he jumped up. He clicked his feet together and gave Sheila a mock salute. 'As you say, ma'am.'

Sheila ignored him. 'Go on, Mr Fingle. We're waiting.' She still leant forward, with her attention firmly on Harry.

Harry pushed his chair back a little. He filled up his cup from the fresh coffee Scott had made, and took a sip. They had him cornered. He wanted to quit and walk away, but he knew couldn't. There was no way out.

'I guess it all started at my trial. Just over a year ago. Richard Morecombe...'

Philip put his hand up. 'Forget Morecombe, Harry. He's not an issue. Besides, he's washed up. He's just been charged with engaging in acts of sexual intercourse with minors, young boys. He's finished. It's all in today's *Daily Journal.*'

Harry stared at Philip and held his chin between his thumb and forefinger.

'You knew all the time?' Harry gave Philip an accusing look.

'Come off it. That's crap. I knew no more than you. I...'

Sheila tapped the table with her knuckles and looked across to Harry and Philip. She picked up a pen, and pointed and wagged it at Harry. 'That's irrelevant, Mr Fingle. Tell us about Ritzler, Vantiche and the CCC file.' She stopped, moved her glasses further down her nose, and gave Harry another of her penetrating looks. 'Move on, please.'

My God, you lot are unbelievable, Harry thought, and pushed back in his chair so he sat at little distance from the table, and could see Scott and Paul without having to keep turning his head.

He told them everything he knew. He started with his discovery of the file on his brother's computer, and continued right up to his attempt to fly to India two days previously. He went on to describe the attempt on his life at his house earlier, and his last meeting with Kate. As he spoke, Sheila, Paul and Philip listened intently, their eyes fixed on him. Sheila's glasses remained perched on the end of her nose. Her arms were folded in front of her, and rested on the table. Paul remained motionless, with his lips firmly closed, his expression serious, and his hands under the table. Philip frowned and stroked his chin a few times.

When Harry finished, Scott, who had seemed bored by Harry's testimony and who'd spent most of the time staring at the ceiling, spoke first. 'Hey, how come this Kate chick suddenly comes onboard, on your side? That was a bit of a turn around, wasn't it? Have you two got something going on?' Scott smirked as he finished speaking.

Before Harry had a chance to respond, Paul, with his right elbow on the table, leant forward and turned to face Harry. 'You think the CCC drug was a vaccine against HIV?' Paul moved his head forward and looked into Harry's eyes. 'Yes?'

Harry looked away from Paul, and glanced at Sheila and Philip. They looked expectant, waiting for his answer. 'Yeah. From what I've told you, it's pretty obvious, isn't it? Why, have I missed something?'

Sheila took her glasses off, and put them down on the table in front of her. She sat back in her chair and fiddled with the lapels of her suit jacket. Harry thought that, for the first time, she seemed anxious and slightly off guard. He guessed something he'd just said concerned her. He waited for her to speak.

'Harry.' She stopped to clear her croaky voice. 'Kate Fisher was killed in a car accident yesterday afternoon in Richmond Park. She'd been driving erratically at speed through the park and lost control. Her car overturned and hurtled into a large oak tree. Nobody else was involved. She was dead when the police arrived, minutes later. They'd followed her after other cars had reported her driving dangerously. A blood sample indicated she'd recently taken drugs.'

'Jesus.' Harry dropped his head into his hands. 'That's awful. How do you know all this?'

Paul looked at Sheila. She nodded. 'She was a senior employee of Ritzler. We've had her under surveillance,' Paul replied.

Harry raised his eyebrows, and looked at them all in turn. He felt a hand on his shoulder.

'Sorry, Harry,' Scott said. He looked shocked and sad. 'I didn't know.'

Chapter Twenty-Five

The journey to Heathrow took forty-five minutes. Harry sat in the back seat of a black, official car next to Jane, the young woman from MI6 who had given the presentation earlier. They were going to meet Amie's parents off their flight from Hong Kong, due to land at 10:00 a.m. After Harry had been told about Kate's death, he'd asked for a break, and permission to go to the airport. Sheila had dismissed the idea outright. She said she'd send a car to collect Amie's parents and take them directly to the hospital.

'That's plain stupid, and bound to make them panic,' Harry had snapped in reply. 'Look. They don't know she's going to be okay. They've been sat on an aircraft for about twelve hours, worried sick about their daughter and if they would get to see her alive. Instead of me being there, as they expect, they're met by some unknown stony-faced MI6 operative who they'll immediately think is the bearer of bad news.'

Harry moved his head a little to meet Sheila's gaze. 'I have to go. I insist.'

~~~

After they'd turned off the motorway, and before they entered the tunnel, Jane made a call. 'Five minutes,' she said to whoever she'd called, and then leant forward and tapped the driver on the shoulder. 'You know the way?' The driver nodded.

She turned to Harry. 'We're going right up to the plane. It'll save time. An immigration official will meet us and check their passports, and then we can go straight to the hospital.'

'You're kidding?' Harry felt astonished and unaware that such action was possible. 'Why are you doing this?'

'To make it easier. It's quite normal when we meet people. VIPs do it all the time.'

Harry glanced at Jane and then looked out of the car window. During the journey to the airport, they'd chatted about movies and restaurants and gigs. Harry found her pleasant and normal. But he was wary. He knew MI6 were able to bypass the normal procedures. To do it for two people from Hong Kong, who were completely nonpolitical, and no use to the security services in any way, seemed odd, and suggested some other, more sinister, motive.

'Amie's parents?' Harry turned back to face Jane. 'How're they going to know what's going on? If their names are called out on the plane, they'll panic and fear the worst.'

Jane sat back in the seat and hitched one of her legs up over her knee, grabbed hold of her ankle, and turned to Harry. 'We've got that covered. We've arranged for you to go onto the plane first. okay?' She looked away and out of the window. They approached a Cathay Pacific Boeing 747 that had just come to a halt. The car stopped close to the front cabin door. Harry watched as the steps were locked into position. A member of the cabin staff came to the door and signalled to their car. Jane turned to Harry. She pointed and said, 'Okay. You can go onboard. Good luck.'

~~~

At eleven-thirty, Harry and Jane drove back inside the MI6 building after they'd dropped Amie's parents at the hospital in Ealing. The luggage had been taken separately to their hotel. On the way back from the airport, Harry had told them as much as he could about the incident. He tried to assure them that Amie would be okay. He didn't go into the hospital with them, thinking it best if he left them on their own with her. He asked them to tell her he'd be in later.

Jane took him straight up to Sheila's own private office on the top floor, a spacious room decorated in a restful, contemporary style with dimmed lighting. It felt unlike the two other offices he'd visited earlier in the day. At the far end, a large sheet of smoked glass stretched from one wall to the other, and presented a stunning view of the Thames. A few modern paintings hung here and there. Small bronze replicas of Buddha and miniature wooden elephants had been dotted around the shelves and on the tops of the furniture. Sheila's desk sat in an alcove off to one side and was not obvious. Two large, tanned-leather sofas faced each other in the main part of the room, separated by a long, rustic coffee table. In one corner, Harry noticed a leather-bound photo frame with a picture of a well-dressed, distinguished woman of a similar age to Sheila.

'Thanks, Jane.' Sheila rose from her desk and closed the door after Jane had left. She turned to Harry.

'Everything go okay?'

'Fine, thanks,' Harry said as they stood and faced each other. They were close to the two sofas. 'Thanks for the help. It was much appreciated.'

'No problem.' Sheila gestured to the seats. 'Come and sit down. Paul is going to join us in minute. I've arranged for some coffee.'

A few minutes later, a waiter brought in a tray of fresh coffee and some biscuits. Paul followed him in. He stood and waited until the man had left, and then he joined Sheila and Harry, who sat and faced each other on opposite sofas. Sheila was in the midst of explaining to Harry about the various Buddhas. Paul filled up the cups, and sat down next to Harry. Sheila clunked the small Buddha she held down on the table, and looked up and across at Harry and Paul.

'Right. Down to business,' Sheila said. 'I think it best if you let me talk. I'm more than happy to answer your questions, but if you could hold them until an appropriate moment, it would help enormously.'

Harry reached forward and picked up his cup. He left the saucer on the table. He took one of the digestive biscuits, broke a piece off against the side of the plate, sipped on his coffee, and sat back and waited for Sheila to start. He was grateful for the help she'd organised for Amie's parents, but remained sceptical: wary that another trap could come at any time.

Sheila took off her glasses. She put them down on the table, and focused on Harry in a way he'd become used too.

'You're familiar with the Alexander Sidorov affair?'

Harry nodded.

'Ever since he was murdered on British soil, we've been concerned about the Russians. If they were capable of killing him and getting away with it, what else could they do? We needed to test them. Equally important are the Chinese. We know they have people everywhere, and could possibly be just as ruthless.' Sheila stopped and drank a little of her coffee. She checked she had Harry's full attention. He sat back and listened. He suspected he would be subjected to another bout of what he called *spook talk*.

'We know there are many of them, all over the place. They're in restaurants, factories, call centres, banks, and many other establishments.'

'Who're you talking about?' Harry asked in a brusque way.

'The Chinese.' Sheila glowered at Harry as though he hadn't paid attention. 'We decided to create a situation in which we could test them. See how they'd operate when we dangled a juicy carrot in front of them. We had to set them up.'

'What?' Harry interrupted. 'What do you mean, set them up?' He turned to look at Paul, who sat back with his hands clasped together in his lap, looking attentive and listening to Sheila.

'The CCC file was a hook, a means of getting them to confront each other. We wanted to create something big that would put the largest drug companies of Russia and China against each other, competing under our noses.'

Harry jumped up. 'Ah, come on. Do me a favour. You're not expecting me to believe that.'

Sheila appeared unmoved. She stared at Harry with a serious expression, and with her glasses perched back on the end of her nose. 'We wanted to check out our surveillance techniques on them. See how they'd operate if they thought the other was onto something big. That's why we gave you all the background earlier.' She paused. She looked down and then, almost immediately, lifted her head, touched her glasses and stared at Harry.

'We set you up.'

Harry, who still stood, looked down at Sheila. He turned to Paul and met his eyes: impassive and unmoved. Harry stroked his chin, and gazed out of the large window. He felt stunned. *Surely this wasn't true*, he thought. If he'd understood correctly, they'd made a complete fool of him. He took a pace backwards, towards the sofa and sat down. He raised his head. Sheila's gaze remained fixed on him.

'We used you and the CCC file as the bait,' she said coldly.

Harry shook his head from side to side. 'I can't believe this. It's shocking. I'm in the office of a senior official from the British intelligence service who tells me, in a casual manner, that I've been used as bait.'

'Correct,' Sheila said. Her expression remained steadfast and devoid of any emotion.

Harry could feel himself about to explode. He'd become angrier than he'd been all day. He glanced again at Paul, and then at Sheila. Both stared at him with the same fixed, stern faces.

Contemptuous shit, he thought. He guessed his feelings showed, but he didn't care and stood up again. He turned back to face Sheila. He looked down at her.

'You mean you were responsible for putting my life at risk so you could play out one of your games. Your behaviour is unbelievable, scandalous, disgraceful.' Harry shook his head and took a few paces around the room, and then came back to stand in the middle of the two sofas, close to where Sheila and Paul sat. 'You're not getting away with this.

'To hell with your bloody Official Secrets Act. I'm publishing this on the web. The whole world will see what you've been up too.

'You lot...' Harry switched his gaze between Paul and Sheila. 'You lot are unbelievable. Fuck you all.' He stared at the wall above Sheila's head. He had become so angry he could feel himself shake. He decided to leave, whatever the consequences, and turned towards the door.

'I apologise, Harry,' Sheila said before he'd moved. 'I understand how cross you must be. I can offer little in recompense. Just that we are grateful. You have helped us enormously.'

'Helped you?' Harry turned to face them. 'All you've done is played some giant spy game with me that has caused the loss of lives. Now I see why you were so helpful with Amie's parents. You wanted to soften me up before you told me the truth.' He took a pace nearer to them and stood very still. He stretched out his arm and pointed his finger at Sheila.

'You knew I was onto this – that I would expose you all. So you brought me in, threatened me and got me to sign the Official Secrets Act to stitch me up and keep your illegal and immoral practices undetected.'

Harry bit on his lip and looked away. 'Well, you've failed.'

Sheila shook her head. 'That's not true. Let me continue. You'll find it'll all make sense to you.'

'Make sense? Impossible! The whole thing is nonsensical bollocks. You lot should be shot.'

Sheila remained unruffled. 'Joe, your brother, worked for us,' she said in a raised voice. 'He'd been a sleeper agent for MI6 for some time.'

Harry narrowed his eyes and stared at Sheila. He scratched his head. He covered his mouth with his hand.

'We put him into Vantiche. He set up the CCC drug, and then was killed by the Russians. Alex Goad, the CEO of Ritzler, got a hit man – Ed James, the one who tried to kill you – to take your brother out.'

'My… God. You were responsible for his death, and you calmly admit it as though it was just an inconvenience.

'What about Clare, his wife?' Harry snapped. 'I suppose you have her blood on your hands, as well.'

'No. That wasn't Ritzler or the Russians.'

Harry sat down at the far end of the sofa next to where Paul sat, and turned to face them. 'Who was it then?'

'The CIA.'

Harry opened his mouth, and stared for a few moments at them both in turn.

Am I going mad? He looked at Sheila and shook his head again.

'You don't really expect me to believe all this. Are you taking the piss? Is this all some giant game to see how much of your Mickey Mouse shit I believe?'

Sheila continued. 'Clare was a Russian spy. The CIA became worried that she would get hold of the CCC file and give it to the Russians, and then all would've been lost.'

'Clare! Worked for the Russians? Now you really are talking horse shit.'

Paul nodded. 'I'm afraid she was. Had been on their payroll for some time.'

Harry kept his gaze fixed on Paul. 'So the Americans took it upon themselves to murder her,' Harry said after several seconds. 'What about the Mumbai bombing? Did they do that as well?'

Paul leant forward and filled up his cup with more coffee. He twisted his head around to face Harry. He held the cafetière over Harry's cup. Harry shook his head.

'No. That was the Russians,' Paul said. 'They were tipped off by Alex Goad, who'd been told by Kate Fisher that you were going to India. They figured you were on to Moon Pharmaceuticals, who Ritzler believed were manufacturing the CCC drug.'

Harry bit on his right thumbnail. He kept his gaze focused on Paul. His mind was like a cauldron. It bubbled and boiled over with anger and fury. His stomach churned, his head throbbed, and he felt light-headed. He hoped he could keep his emotions and feelings under control for a little longer. He decided that, whatever the consequences, he was going to post everything he'd been told on the Internet. It was a scandal of national importance and the world needed to know.

'How do you know all this?' he asked.

'We have Alex Goad and Grigoriy Nabutov in custody. They're being very cooperative.'

'I bet they are. Surprising what a bit of torture can do.'

Sheila looked up and gave Harry another of her looks. 'Jimmy Ali. I think you know him, don't you?'

'Jimmy? What's he got to do with this?'

'He's one of us,' Paul said, as he shrugged his shoulders.

'What the hell do you mean by that?'

'He's a paid informer. We got him to spy on Ritzler and, by luck; he was also working for you. So he could snoop on Ritzler and Alex Goad and, at the same time, keep an eye on you.'

Harry scratched his forehead. He shook his head in disbelief. 'I see... So everyone knew what was going on except me.

'This is a bloody debacle, a national catastrophe. Two people have been murdered, a factory's been blown up and two hundred people killed, and my life has been put at risk.'

Harry stood up and pointed at Sheila again. 'You should be ashamed. You're not getting away with this.' He stared at Sheila for ten or more seconds. She seemed unmoved.

'Basically, you're murderers with blood on your hands.' Harry switched his gaze between Sheila and Paul. 'What have you achieved from it all?'

Sheila leant forward. 'We've found out how ruthless the Chinese and Russian governments can be to achieve their aims. They'll kill people, on our soil, with no compassion or remorse.' Her piercing eyes locked onto Harry. 'We regret the loss of life. We didn't do it. They did. But we've proved we can infiltrate their operations. And that's important.'

Harry looked at his watch. It was nearly one. He'd had enough, and wanted to get out. 'When can I leave this shithole?'

'Whenever you like. You've been very helpful. We'll have a minder watch out for you for a few weeks, until we are sure you are out of danger and there are no other agents on your trail.' Sheila straightened up and sat back. She took her glasses off. 'There's one more thing you should to know.'

Harry, who'd turned, ready to leave, looked back at Sheila. 'Go on?'

'The CCC drug. You haven't asked what it is.'

'We discussed that earlier. It's a vaccine for HIV, isn't it?' Harry turned again to walk out of the room.

Sheila stood up. She took a couple of paces towards Harry, and placed her glasses on the end of her nose. 'No it isn't, Harry,' she said as he approached the door. She waited until he had turned around. She shook her head.

'Joe made CCC look like a vaccine for HIV to deceive Vantiche and Ritzler. Once he'd been killed, and you became involved and took the file, we watched and waited to see what the Russians and Chinese would do.'

'So you could have stopped this there and then?'

Sheila took her glasses off, folded them up, and put them in the breast pocket of her jacket. 'Ritzler and the Russians took the bait. They told Ed James to kill you to stop you doing anything with the CCC file.' Sheila stopped and shot a glance at Paul, and turned back to face Harry.

'The Chinese acted in a similar manner. Once they knew you had the file, they raided your house to try to retrieve it. They were unsuccessful, as you know, but decided you posed too much of a risk and ordered Grigoriy Nabutov to take you out.' Sheila smiled for the first time. 'As you're aware – we stopped him.'

Cow, Harry thought, and took a step back and nearer the door to her office. He noticed Paul move towards him. 'So you were completely in control all the time?' He made no attempt to hide his contempt.

'Correct,' Sheila said and smiled. 'Jimmy Ali had been watching your house when the Russian broke in and tried to kill you. That's why he turned up at such an appropriate time.' She smiled again. 'See. We were looking out for you.'

Harry shook his head and turned towards the door. Paul moved in front of him and took hold of the door handle. 'I thought I was free to go?'

'You are, but I have to see you off the building.'

Harry stopped and stared at him. 'If the CCC drug isn't a vaccine for HIV, what is it, then?'

'Nothing. It's a fake,' Sheila replied. She stepped forward to be little closer to Harry. 'CCC stands for common cold cure. It's routinely used within the pharmaceutical industry as a cover for the development of an important drug. Your brother, Joe, was sadly one of the best pharmaceutical scientists in the world. He was able to create a formula so complex that, not only did Ritzler believe it was a vaccine for HIV, so did his fellow scientists at Vantiche.'

Harry glanced at Paul and then back at Sheila.

'The encrypted ccc.doc file that you copied from your brother's PC was unique. If anyone were able to open it, they would have found out that CCC was just a hoax. That's why Alex Goad tried to leave the country on a false passport.'

Harry looked at Sheila with a puzzled expression. 'Explain,' he said.

'Only Joe had the code for the CCC file. Nobody else should have been able to break it. But Alex Goad employed a brilliant computer hacker who did manage to break it. When Goad found out CCC was a load of rubbish and not a vaccine for HIV, he flipped. He realised he was finished. Ritzler's owners would hang him out to dry. We'd been watching him for a while. We picked him up at the airport after he'd made an airline booking using a false name.

'You see, Harry. We had it all covered,' Sheila said. She smiled again as Harry reached for the door.

He turned and looked at them both. They stood and stared at him like stone statues, with fixed emotionless expressions.

Urr, they make me sick.

Chapter Twenty-Six

Harry arrived back at his house at 2:00 p.m., barely an hour after he'd walked out of the offices of MI6. He ignored the mess left by the intruders and the disruption caused by the fight with the Russian the day before, and rushed straight to the kitchen, where he'd left his slow, backup laptop. He opened up the letter he'd drafted to all the national newspapers and read it through.

'Well, well, well,' he muttered. He deleted all but the first paragraph and started to type with a vengeance.

Today I spent eight hours in the custody of MI6 for no reason, other than that they wanted to tell me that they had played a game with me, and risked my life to allow them to observe the Russian and Chinese secret services at play. Their actions put me within a centimetre of death three times. Sheila Robinson, the senior MI6 officer present, told me they'd deliberately set me up, and that the CIA were responsible for the death of my sister-in-law. This joint operation by British intelligence and the CIA, code-named Operation CCC, caused the recent bombing of the Moon pharmaceutical factory in Mumbai, where two hundred lives were lost. What follows is a true and accurate account of these events, and the involvement of MI6 and the CIA...

Harry typed for two hours. He changed and altered the letter several times. But he left nothing out, and laid the blame for the death of his brother, his sister-in-law, and the workers of the factory in India squarely on the British and American security services. At four o'clock he stopped. He felt tired, and knew he had begun to make mistakes. He stood up, saved what he'd written, and flicked on his kettle. He made himself a mug of Earl Grey tea, popped a slice of bread in the toaster, and rummaged around his kitchen for his pot of Marmite. With his toast buttered and spread, and his tea next to his laptop, he started to read through his letter again.

After he changed and fiddled around with the wording, and deleted and added bits here and there, his doorbell rang. He felt uneasy, unsure if he should open the door. Twenty-four hours earlier, a big Russian man had burst into his house, intent on killing him. Earlier that day he'd been whisked away to face MI6. He decided to ignore it in the hope that the caller would think he wasn't in and go away. The bell sounded again; the chime longer and more insistent. Harry stood up, closed his kitchen door, and returned to the letter. Minutes later his phone rang. The screen showed an unknown number.

'Yes.'

'Harry. Are you going to let me in? It's me, Philip. I know you're inside.'

'You can't be serious. Do you really think I'm going to let you in, after what your lot have done to me today? I don't ever want to see you again, Philip. Now, leave me in peace.' Harry ended the call and went back to the letter. He was incensed and couldn't concentrate. He stood up and started to pace around his kitchen.

What do these people want? Haven't they done enough? What do I have to do to be rid of them? Philip must be out of his mind. Does he think he can behave like he has and then just turn up as though nothing ever happened? He's lost it.

Harry's thoughts were interrupted by a text message. He guessed it was from Philip and went to delete it. He hesitated. He was curious and wondered how Philip could possibly explain his behaviour.

Harry.

I understand what you must think of me, but we have to talk. I'm worried about you doing something silly. If you go public on anything about today, you'll go to prison for a long time. If you let me in, I can explain my actions. Philip.

~~~

'You've got five minutes. I'm tired, hungry and I have a lot to do. I've let you in because I want to hear what you have to say. I thought you were a friend. I'm the godfather to one of your children. I want you to explain your unbelievable and contemptible behaviour.'

They sat in Harry's living room: Harry on the sofa, Philip on one of the old, restored chairs. A large bottle of unopened Ardbeg malt whisky stood on the coffee table.

Harry waved his arm around the room. 'You can see I haven't had anytime to clear up the mess made by the intruder and the Russian. So please get on with it.' Harry took a sip from his tea. He hadn't offered Philip a drink. Philip had brought the whisky, but Harry had declined to open it.

Harry listened. Philip told him how he was recruited into MI6. He then moved on to explain the rationale behind Operation CCC, and what the security services believed they had achieved.

When Philip paused, Harry looked at him. 'I got the gist of all that this morning. Okay. Your reason for joining a bunch of loonies is your problem.' Harry shook his head. 'I'm not really interested.'

He rubbed his left arm and looked at Philip. 'So what's so important you have to rush over here to see me?' He waited a second or two until he was sure he had Philip's full attention. 'Make it quick, and make it good, otherwise you're out of the door.' Harry pointed to the bottle of whisky. 'You can take that away with you.'

Philip sat back in the chair. He had his head down. He stroked his thighs. 'We go back a long way, Harry.'

Harry nodded. 'I know we do. Been good friends for some time, but it doesn't seem to mean anything.' He looked away for a second and then turned back to Philip.

'Cut the sentimental crap and come to the point.'

Philip shrugged his shoulders. 'Okay. If you want it like that.' He glanced for a moment at a photo on a side table of his daughter, Harry's goddaughter, and then looked at Harry.

'You're angry. I understand. But getting your retribution by going public on today's events isn't going to solve anything. It'll make things worse, and get you into serious trouble.'

'Philip.' Harry had twisted around so he could face Philip. He leant forward and stuck his neck out. 'I've had enough of you lot telling me what to do. This is my house. I invited you in against my better judgement. Tell me what you've come to tell me. Then get the hell out of here.'

Philip shifted in his chair and pushed down on both edges of the seat with his hands. 'I just wanted to try and stop you doing anything silly. If you do...' He raised an eyebrow and looked at Harry sideways. 'You'll go to prison.' He stopped again for a few seconds and turned away. 'It'll be for a long time, Harry.'

Harry put his right hand up to his face, and started to scratch his cheek with his finger. He felt cross. He'd let Philip in, believing he might say something different and put a fairer perspective on the day, but he hadn't. He just repeated the same stuff Harry had heard all day. Harry reckoned the warning on going public was to stop a media onslaught. He stood up and looked at Philip. At that moment, he realised he'd lost a friend.

'If that's all you have to say, you can leave now.' Harry paused. 'I don't want to see you again – ever.' Philip looked up at Harry for a few seconds. He pursed his lips. He looked resigned to Harry's intransigence. They both walked to Harry's front door in silence. Neither shook hands. Harry closed the door on Philip, and went back to his living room and poured himself a large whisky.

'Shit.' He looked at his watch. He'd promised to see Amie at the hospital in ten minutes' time. He left his drink untouched, and ran out of his front door and jumped on his bike.

~~~

When Harry returned from the hospital, a black car sat outside his house, similar to the one he'd travelled in to the airport earlier. Sitting in the front two seats were two men. They appeared to be reading. As he walked up the small path to his front door, they opened both doors and stepped out. He was aware they followed him. He turned. One of the men held out a police identity card.

'Mr Fingle. We've been sent by MI6. We need to talk to you.'

'What about?' Harry snapped. He continued to push his bike up the path to the door.

'Can we talk about that inside, Mr Fingle?' Both policemen stood close to Harry. They left him little room to manoeuvre his bike while he turned his keys in the lock.

'It looks as though I have no choice, do I?' Harry pushed open his door. He brought his bike inside, and stood holding it until the two officers had come in and he'd closed the door.

'In there.' He pointed to his living room. He leant his bike against the wall, and bent down to pick up a few of the items strewn around the hall. After a couple of minutes, he joined the two policemen.

'Yeah, I'm a messy pup.' Harry made a sarcastic grin. The two policemen were looking around at the chaos. 'I like throwing things around from time to time. Helps me let off steam after spending a day with the likes of you people.'

'What is it you want?'

Both policemen were big, broad, and looked strong. They were dressed in a similar manner. One wore dark-navy jeans, the other navy chinos. One had a grey, long-sleeved shirt on, the other a cream one. Both wore black, leather jackets. The one who'd shown his ID card brought out an official-looking form. He handed it to Harry.

'This isn't very easy, Mr Fingle. We've come to collect your computers and mobile phones. We have instructions to take them away to permanently delete all information or data that might contravene the Official Secrets Act. The piece of paper I gave you is an official court order. It's signed by a magistrate authorising us to take temporary possession of the items I mentioned.' The policeman who'd talked turned his head to catch Harry's eyes.

'Mr Fingle, I have to warn you. If you won't give them to us voluntarily, we can arrest you for contempt of court.' The officer put his hand inside his jacket and withdrew a sealed envelope. 'In this letter is an official caution. I suggest, Mr Fingle, you read it carefully and take notice.' The policeman held the letter out for Harry to take.

Harry took the envelope. He tore it open and pulled out the letter. It took him a few seconds to scan it. He looked up at the two policemen. They were sat opposite and stared at him.

'What the fuck?'

~~~

After the two policemen left with Harry's laptop and mobile phone, he grabbed a bottle of whisky and a glass from the kitchen and returned to his living room. He poured out a large measure. With the drink in his hand, he stood still for some time and read the letter several times. After a few minutes, he dropped it down onto the sofa and refilled his glass. The bottle from Philip stood unopened next to his own.

I'm well and truly screwed. They've stitched me up like a kipper, he told himself as he stared out of the window. He drained his glass, and picked up the letter and started to read it again. It was from a Commander Michael Walsh and written on headed Metropolitan Police paper. Harry had never met or heard of the man.

Dear Mr Fingle

Further to your meeting today with two officers from the Secret Intelligence Service, MI6, one Sheila Robinson and one Paul Thompson, it is my duty to officially caution you.

You have voluntarily signed the Official Secrets Act. You are therefore bound by law not to divulge to any person the substance of the matter or matters discussed with the aforementioned officers and anything related, linked, or in any way associated to the matter or matters. This includes information you were given or gave freely by yourself to the officers. You must not enter in any form of written communication, publication, or other forms of promulgation that could inform others of the nature of your meeting. This includes information you may have personally gathered about the matter discussed prior to meeting with the officers.

I must also inform you that a D Notice has been served on all outlets of the British media that restricts any publication or promulgation of any item relating to the aforementioned matter.

Contravention of the Official Secrets Act is a serious matter punishable by imprisonment. Any person found guilty of such will have jeopardised the national security.

All information storage and communication equipment such as PCs, laptops, and mobile phones in your possession must be

surrendered for screening. Once that process has been completed, the equipment will be returned to you.

You would be well advised to take heed of this caution and adhere to the aforementioned stipulations.

Yours sincerely

Harry looked at the illegible signature with the name Commander Michael Walsh typed underneath it for a few seconds, and then dropped the letter onto the floor. He leant forward, filled up his glass and flopped onto his sofa.

'You can all screw yourself.' He drained his whisky, dragged himself to his feet, and weaved his way off to bed.

Inequity

Chapter Twenty-Seven

Fourteen days after Amie had been stabbed, and while she was still in hospital, she called up Detective Inspector Katherine Ford, the policewoman who handled the incident, and said she wanted to meet her at Ealing police station. Amie wanted to read through the statement she'd made a few days after the stabbing. She felt under no illusions. She'd killed a man and knew there would be a thorough investigation.

~~~

DI Ford met her at the reception. 'Thanks for coming in, Ms Lau. Are you sure you're up to it?' The detective shook Amie's hand. Katherine Ford was not in the image of the female detectives portrayed by the movies and TV dramas. She was short, a bit overweight, and never wore makeup. She always wore jeans and a polo shirt. The day Amie went to see her, DI Ford had draped a navy, canvas jacket around her shoulders.

'I'm fine. I just want to check my statement,' Amie replied. She smiled to hide any sign of the spasm of pain that had darted through and around her stab wound. Her stitches had been removed a few days earlier, and she had to be careful how she moved about. She turned to the nurse who accompanied her.

'This is Nurse Jill Williams. She'll make sure I don't come to any harm.'

'Hi,' Jill Williams said and grinned.

DI Ford showed Amie into an interview room where a male detective waited. Nurse Williams remained outside. 'This is Detective Sergeant Watson. He's assisting me.'

'Hi,' he said. He looked up for a split second. He made no attempt to shake Amie's outstretched hand.

'Please take a seat,' DI Ford said. She indicated a single chair on the opposite side of the table from where the two detectives stood.

Amie pulled out the seat, sat down, and looked around. The room looked sparse, with a faint odour and grubby, grey walls. On the lower half of the door, deep gouges could be seen in the woodwork. Amie guessed it indicated some sort of physical confrontation. A wired glass section had been cut into the upper part of the door to allow two-way vision. The door's metal handle, positioned about a quarter of the way from the top and just above a large keyhole, looked scratched and worn. There were no windows. The air felt stuffy. The room had a functional, almost confrontational feel to it. It made Amie feel on edge and a little anxious. She remembered Jimmy had said she should take a lawyer with her.

'Why should I do that?' she'd asked him. 'I'm the victim. I'm just going along to help them close their file.'

He'd shrugged his shoulders and said, 'Okay. Up to you. I never trust the fuzz.'

DI Ford and Sergeant Watson sat down opposite Amie. Amie thought Watson had his hand on what looked like a tape recorder.

'This is the brief statement you gave us shortly after the incident. Would you like to read it through?' Ford said, and pushed a large, A4, typed sheet over to Amie.

I was at Harry Fingle's house. A man, who I now understand to be Ray Faulks, broke in and grabbed me and held a knife to my throat. I told him I was a policewoman and that my colleagues would be around shortly. He believed me and ran out of the back door, but followed me later to my flat where he broke in again and attacked me with a knife when I came out of the shower. Somehow, I convinced him again that I was a policewoman and he fled.

Then he came back the next night and hid in my cupboard until I came home. He jumped on me with a knife as I undressed. I was naked and threw up. He told me he was going to rape and kill me. I became terrified. He got me on the bed and tried to forcibly have sex with me, but I resisted so much he couldn't do it and he grabbed his knife and lunged out at me and stabbed me, but he dropped the knife. I was in agony, but managed to raise my knee and kick him hard in the crotch. He yelled out and I grabbed his knife. I didn't know what I was doing, but just lashed out and stabbed him all over until he fell off the bed. I guess I'd killed him.

Amie looked up and into the blank faces of the two detectives. They stared at her. 'Yeah, that's it. It's all there,' she said.

DI Ford covered her mouth with her right hand and rested her elbow on the table. She turned and looked at Sergeant Watson and nodded.

'Okay, Amie. If I may call you that?' Sergeant Watson said. 'We need to ask you a few questions. I'm going to turn this tape recorder on. It's normal practice.' He touched a switch and announced he was starting an interview, and looked up at Amie.

'What were you doing at Harry Fingle's house when Ray Faulks broke in, and how did you get in?'

Amie glanced at DI Ford and then at Sergeant Watson. She felt her heartbeat increase. Both of them looked at her with similar, impassive expressions. They waited for her answer. Pain from her wound throbbed. It felt so intense she thought she would shout out. She tensed all her muscles, bit on her bottom lip, and squeezed the edge of the table.

'Harry and I used to be lovers. I'd gone to collect some of my things.'

'So how did you get in? I understand he was away,' DI Ford asked.

'I used to live there. I've still got a set of keys. I need to return them to him.'

'There was somebody else there, wasn't there?' Watson said.

'What do you mean?'

DI Ford leant forward and stared into Amie's eyes.

'Jimmy Ali. You haven't mentioned him. Harry Fingle told us he was there.' DI Ford turned to Sergeant Watson.

'Why's that, Amie? Why didn't you tell us about him,' the sergeant asked.

Amie felt sick. The hurt and pain from her wound raged mercilessly. Her heart thumped against her ribcage, almost as though it was about to burst from her. She became worried and confused. She'd deliberately left Jimmy out of her statement for his protection. Now she would have to explain.

'I didn't think it mattered. He was there when I got there. I didn't know him.'

'But he overpowered Faulks and was stabbed in the process, wasn't he? Didn't you think that was important?' DI Ford asked. She leant forward and stared intently at Amie.

Amie felt her hands tremble. She moved them from the tabletop to her lap. She felt frightened and worried and had no idea where the line of questioning would lead.

'Yeah, he did.'

'Why didn't you tell us about that?' Sergeant Watson asked.

'Look, I had only just regained consciousness when I made that statement. I put down everything that came into my mind. I can't say I forgot, just didn't think it was important.'

DI Ford leant forward again, and gave Amie another penetrating stare. 'Do you know why Ray Faulks had gone to Harry's house?'

Amie didn't answer.

'Did he go to get money from Jimmy Ali for drugs?'

'I believe so.'

'Only believe? Surely Jimmy told you?' DI Ford said with a sneer. 'You went to hospital with him, didn't you? And then he came to your flat after Ray had broken in. He stayed the night, didn't he? Didn't you think that was important?'

Amie felt shocked. *Harry must have told the police about Jimmy*, she thought. Now, as a consequence, Jimmy would be brought in, interviewed, and probably charged with possession of drugs.

'Did Harry Fingle tell you all this?'

DI Ford stood up. She looked down at Amie. 'No, Jimmy Ali did. After Harry told us Jimmy had been at his house, we pulled him in. He told us everything.'

Amie felt astonished. Jimmy had visited her almost every day. Not once had he mentioned the police had interviewed him.

DI Ford turned to Sergeant Watson. 'Turn off the recorder.' She turned back and looked down at Amie. 'Look. You killed a man. I suggest you rewrite your statement, leaving nothing out this time.' She turned again to Sergeant Watson. 'Leave her a statement pad. Call me when it's done.' She walked out of the room.

~~~

As soon as Amie returned to hospital, she called Jimmy. 'Hey, Jimmy, listen. You didn't tell me you'd told the police you were at Harry's house and all about Ray being after you for drug money. I'd deliberately kept you out of it. The police were shits to me. Made me look as though I was lying, holding things back.

'Jimmy.' Amie sounded worried. 'I'm scared.'

Jimmy didn't reply immediately. Amie had to ask him if he was still there.

'Yeah, I'm here. I'm thinking, like. Look, I told them everything 'cause I figured they'd find out someway and it would make it difficult for you, like. That Ray bloke was real vermin. I wanted them to know he was definitely out to kill you. Anyway, I figured you would have told them. How've they left things?'

'I don't know. They asked me to rewrite my statement, which I did, adding in all the bits about you being there and then you coming back to my flat. Then they said I could go. They'd be in touch.' Amie brushed her hair away from her face.

'What do you think? Have they said anymore to you?'

'Not a peep. They said they'd pass my statement to my probation officer for him to decide if I'd broken the terms of my probation. But I haven't heard a word.'

'Does that mean you might go back to prison?'

'Anyone's guess with that lot.' Jimmy paused. 'But I'm worried about you. I think you'd better see a lawyer. I'll get the name of a good one and give it to you tonight.'

~~~

When Jimmy didn't turn up that night as expected, Amie started to worry. Had she said too much to the police, or had they been using her to get to him? Either way, she became concerned, and sure the police had picked him up, and she was to blame. As the days increased and Jimmy made no contact, she became distressed and unstable, and blamed herself for Jimmy's disappearance. After a while, her recovery started to slip. The doctors and nursing team became worried about her deteriorating physical and mental condition, and called in a trauma specialist. Amie felt reluctant to talk to him, fearing anything more she said would make Jimmy's situation worse.

~~~

'What's up?' Harry asked, after not seeing her for a few days. He'd lessened the frequency of his visits to give more time to Amie's parents. He felt shocked to find she looked limp and grey, and lay on her back. Her usual brightness had gone, and she could only manage a small, strained smile.

She turned her head slowly on the pillow to face him. 'I don't know, Harry. I just feel depressed and very, very tired. I don't seem to have the will to go on.'

'Have you told the doctors and nurses?' Harry asked. He became worried.

'They want me to speak to a therapist.'

'Have you?' Harry sat down beside her.

Amie turned her head a little more towards him. She tried to force a bigger smile. 'It's Jimmy. I'm really worried about him.'

'Why, what's happened?'

Amie looked at Harry for a moment. 'He's suddenly vanished. He was supposed to be here six or seven nights ago and didn't turn up, and I can't raise him.'

Harry looked around the ward. He had to be careful that no one was in hearing distance. He leant forward so he was close to Amie.

'Amie,' he whispered. 'Jimmy worked for MI6.'

'What! No way?'

As luck had it, Harry had been the only visitor that evening, and told Amie all that had happened to him and everything he'd been told while in the clutches of MI6. Amie sat up and stared at him, and looked amazed.

'You mean Jimmy knew what was going on, all along.'

'Yep,' Harry replied. He noticed some colour return to Amie's face.

'But he said he didn't want to talk to the police because of his drug conviction. He never told me a thing about all of this,' Amie said. She looked astonished.

'Oh, the drug thing is real. He was dealing again and would have got into trouble if the police caught up with him.'

'But he must have known you were in danger? You were paying him, but he didn't do or say anything to protect you.'

'You're right.' Harry nodded. 'But it's not quite as simple as that.' Harry filled in on some of the details he'd missed out earlier – signing The Official Secrets Act, the police confiscating his laptop and mobile phone, the threat from Philip.

'Wow. I don't like that. It's outrageous – and Jimmy was part of it.' Amie pulled herself higher up the bed and sat bolt upright. She stared straight ahead.

Harry looked at her. He was stunned. In less than thirty minutes, a remarkable turnaround in her condition had taken place. No longer was she saying she felt depressed, nor did she look ill and grey, without any spark. Instead, her face had brightened, and she appeared revitalised and much as he'd found her on his last visit. He reached for her hand.

'Don't tell anyone,' he said. 'I'll go to prison.' He squeezed on her hand. She did the same.

She turned back and looked at him and smiled. 'Thanks. I feel a whole lot better now.'

~~~

Amie never thought much more about Jimmy. Almost as soon as Harry had told her about Jimmy's connection with MI6, her feelings towards him changed. She thought the treatment of Harry by the security services was contemptible, and Jimmy's behaviour had compounded it. Her opinion altered. No longer did she think of Jimmy as someone kind and caring. He became, in her mind, a deceitful individual, worried primarily about himself.

Harry reverted back to seeing her every day. Then, one day, when he was sure she would recover fully and be unlikely to have any more relapses, he called her. 'Look, Amie. I guess you're pretty well on the mend now, and what with your parents being around, you don't need me.'

'I always like to see you, you know that.' Amie held her breath. She knew he was about to make one of his announcements.

'Thanks, but now I know you're really getting better, I'm taking a break. I don't want to go over it again. But after all the shit with the CCC file thing, I feel I need to clear my mind. I'm heading off on my own somewhere. I'm going tomorrow.'

'That quick? I'll miss you popping in. But I am okay and I do understand. Thanks for all you've done. Take care and look after yourself. 'Bye for now.'

'See you then, 'bye. Oh, give my regards to your parents and don't forget – not a word about what I told you. Okay?'

'Don't worry. I won't tell a soul. Have fun. 'Bye.'

Amie looked around the small ward. The three other women, who all were recovering from minor surgery, watched TV. None had taken any notice of her conversation with Harry.

I've changed, she thought. *Before I was stabbed, a conversation like that with Harry would have thrown me. I would have been in tears by now. But I feel different. I know he saved my life, and I will always be grateful to him, but the emotional power that took over my mind and controlled my actions and made me do irrational things has gone. Now I can meet him, talk to him, think about him, and not feel that he has to be a major part of my life anymore.*

My God. It was that uncontrollable power that drove me to go to his place so often, uninvited. And because of it, I ended up meeting up with Jimmy, and being stabbed and nearly killed.

Amie shook her head. *I hope, this time, we can stay real friends. Not a one-sided relationship where I chase and behave in an insane way that drives him mad. Wherever he's going, I hope he has fun. He deserves it.* She dropped back onto her pillow and fell asleep.

~~~

A little over a month after Amie had been stabbed, she left the hospital. Her parents took her home in a taxi and stayed with her for three weeks, until after Christmas. On the night before they were due to fly back to Hong Kong, she took them out for a meal to thank them for all they'd done, and their kindness. She went to the airport with them. All three of them cried as they said good-bye. They made her promise to call them every day.

Over the following four weeks, Amie made a complete recovery. She went back to work a week after she left hospital. She asked to be given a full schedule of lectures and other activities, and not treated as an invalid and someone unable to do her job to the maximum. Her gym visits increased in frequency and intensity. Her fitness returned to the level she'd achieved before the attack. Colleagues went out of their way to ask her to many social activities. She joined an amateur dramatic group, an art group, and a film club, where she met Simon, a new lecturer. After they'd watched a couple of movies together, he asked her out for dinner. He was her age, single with thick, black hair, tall and fit from playing county squash, and she found him easy to talk to. She liked him, and they started dating. Amie felt good about herself and her life. She put the horrific stabbing incident behind her.

Seven weeks after she'd left hospital, Simon booked to see *La Bohème* at the Royal Opera House and dinner afterwards. It had been to celebrate their first month together. It fell on a Friday night, and he said he'd be around to pick her up at seven. Amie felt excited. She looked forward to the evening, and had bought a sleeveless black, jersey dress with a plunging neckline for the occasion. At six forty-five she was waiting for Simon in her sitting room when her doorbell rang. She looked at her watch.

He's early, she thought. She went to the door and opened it. DI Ford, Detective Sergeant Watson, and a couple of other uniformed policewomen stood on the doormat. DI Ford took a pace forward. She held a document in her hand.

'Ms Lau, I have a warrant for your arrest in connection with the murder of Ray Faulks. We'd like you to accompany us to Ealing police station.'

Later that day, the police charged Amie with murder.

Chapter Twenty-Eight

Harry dumped his rucksack in his hall, and made for the kitchen. He scooped up the pile of letters and circulars that lay all over the floor, and placed them on the worktop. For eight weeks, he'd travelled alone in South America, backpacking through Peru, Chile, Argentina, Paraguay, and Bolivia. All the time he'd been away, he hadn't read a newspaper, used his mobile phone, or been on the Internet. He felt fresh and invigorated, and ready to start a new challenge. He'd decided to write a book. Not about the CCC fiasco, but a novel. He reached the decision while he walked along the Inca Trail in Peru.

He pulled open the fridge in the hope that his neighbour had left him a few essentials. He usually did when Harry had been away. 'Ah, good,' Harry said as he reached in for a bottle of wine. He unscrewed the top and pulled down a glass. He had his mobile phone clamped to his right ear.

'Hi Amie, Harry here. I've just got back from South America. I had a really good trip. Hope you're fine. I'll catch you tomorrow.' He looked at his watch, 11:00 p.m.

She's better, he thought, *if she's out this late*. He picked up his wine and headed for the shower.

~~~

Once refreshed and feeling clean, he pulled on a pair of old jeans and a T-shirt, and returned to his kitchen. He felt hungry. The few tins in his cupboard didn't excite him, nor did the months-old food in the freezer. He ordered a pizza, poured a glass of Ardbeg malt whisky, and took it to his living room and turned on his TV.

'What the hell,' he said aloud. He'd caught the beginning of a news bulletin. Pictures of Amie filled the screen. She'd been committed to trial at the Old Bailey for the murder of Ray Faulks.

'He was the nutcase who tried to rape and kill her. What the hell is going on?' he said as his doorbell rang. His pizza had arrived. He gave the man a £20 note and told him to keep the change, and dumped the cardboard container on the floor in the hall.

The unopened pizza box remained in the same place in the morning. Harry had spent the night trawling the Internet and watching news bulletins in an effort to find out as much as he could about the case against Amie. By 5:00 a.m., he'd deduced that the Crown Prosecution Service believed Amie had deliberately murdered Faulks. She'd been taken to Holloway prison, where she was held on remand. He planned to visit her later that day. He felt deeply shocked, and vowed not to rest until she was free.

~~~

Harry arrived at Holloway at 2:00 p.m. He'd spent an hour on the phone in the morning trying to arrange his visit. He'd thought that prisoners on remand were allowed to receive visits almost without restrictions. His first call of the morning proved otherwise. The prison office said he had to book his visit in advance, and only at a convenient time. He'd been left with the impression that a request to see Amie that day would not be approved. He'd put the phone down, stomped and fumed around his living room for a bit, and then called a contact he knew in the Home Office. By 10:00 a.m. the matter was resolved. He could see Amie that afternoon, as he'd wanted.

He had never been inside a prison before. He found the security procedures, form-filling, and the searches of his person and belongings repellent and degrading. But he kept his feelings to himself and stayed focused. As the prison officer escorted him to Amie's cell, he wondered how he'd find her. Would she blame him?

'Harry,' Amie said as she looked up from a book with a surprised expression. She wore her own clothes, but had no makeup on and looked tired and strained. Her hair appeared dull and lifeless, as though it hadn't been washed for days. 'What're you doing here? I thought you were away.'

'I got back last night. I didn't know anything about this until I turned on the television.' Harry had sat on the one chair. Amie remained on the bed. 'What's it all about?'

Amie put the book down on the bed next to her. She ran a hand through her long, black hair, and looked at Harry and narrowed her eyes. He sensed a sort of toughness in her expression. 'They think I murdered Ray Faulks. They're going to put me away for a long time.'

Harry felt at a loss for words. *She's innocent*, he thought. How could things have reached this far?

'No, Amie.' He shook his head. 'That's not true. You're innocent. You know that. He attacked you and would have killed you.'

'But I killed him. You came in and found us. It's all stacked against me.' Amie shook her head. 'I've just got to get used to being in a place like this.'

'You didn't murder him. You acted in self-defence. He had a knife and tried to rape you. He was a scumbag. We know that. Jimmy can vouch for it.'

'Jimmy wasn't there. No one was. It was just he and I. He had multiple stab wounds, and is dead. I just had one wound, and I'm alive. Besides, as you know, Jimmy's disappeared.'

'He hasn't shown up, then?'

'Nope. I haven't heard a thing. Last time I saw him was in the hospital, before you told me about him working for MI6.' Amie shot Harry a steely look. 'Anyway, he's not that reliable, and I don't trust him anymore.'

Harry shrugged his shoulders. 'I understand, but he could be a good witness.'

'I doubt it,' Amie replied with a hint of resignation in her voice. 'I know I didn't murder Faulks, but I certainly killed him. They're going to find me guilty, Harry.'

'But he jumped on you. He was about to rape you.'

Amie pursed her lips together. 'I know that. That's why I lashed out. I wanted to kill him. Otherwise he would have killed me.' She closed her eyes, put a hand to her forehead, and rubbed her brow. She looked up at Harry. 'But nobody believes me.'

~~~

Harry left Holloway confused. He felt unsure as to how he could help. Although Amie's resilience and toughness impressed him, he'd become concerned. She seemed resigned to her fate, and appeared to have given up all hope of being found innocent. She hadn't attempted to contact her parents, the only solicitor she saw had been put forward by the police, and the facts of the case, as she'd told them, seemed stacked against her. With no witnesses, it looked bad. He knew she was innocent. Somehow he had to find a way of proving it.

It was nearly five when he walked back into his house. He went straight to the kitchen and poured himself a large glass of water. He pulled an apple from the unwrapped bag of fruit he'd left on his worktop earlier, and made for his living room. He slumped into his leather chair and started to think.

There was only one person who could help, he thought. And he didn't care much about contacting him. He bit and munched on the apple until only a tiny piece of core was left. He took a large gulp of water and picked up his phone. He dialled Philip's mobile number, left a message, and called his home number.

'Hello, Penny. It's Harry. How you're doing?'

'Harry,' Penny said in a loud, animated voice. She sounded pleased to speak to him. 'I'm fine. How're you? We haven't seen you for ages.'

'I'm good, thanks.

'Look, don't think me rude, but is Philip there?'

'I'm sorry he isn't.' Penny paused. 'I don't really know when he'll be home. Shall I get him to call you?'

'That'll be good. Say it's important.'

'I'll do that. We must meet up soon.'

'Yes we must. Thanks, Penny. 'Bye for now.'

Harry waited for Penny to say good-bye. He tossed his phone back on the sofa, and thought back to the last time he'd seen Philip. He'd kicked him out of the house: told him he never wanted to see him again. He shook his head. Philip wouldn't call back.

Harry moved to the kitchen and poured a large glass of whisky. He picked up his iPod and scrolled down until he found an album of rap music.

~~~

When he woke at nine-thirty the next morning, he was surprised he'd slept so well. He didn't know what time he'd gone to bed, only that he'd woken tired, cold, and sat in his leather chair in pitch darkness with his music playing loudly. He could remember he'd stumbled into bed, and thought about Amie and what he could do to help.

I must have blanked out and fallen asleep.

After he'd taken a shower and pulled on his jeans and a black T-shirt, he went to his kitchen to fix some breakfast and make a large cafetière of coffee. *Jesus*, he thought as he looked around at the cleaning that needed doing: his unpacked rucksack, the pile of unopened mail, and the previous night's pizza box, rotting in the hall where he'd left it. *It'll all wait*, he told himself, and flicked through the envelopes to see if there was anything important or interesting. His phone rang. He pushed the letters to one side to answer it. The number showed as an unknown caller.

'Hello.'

'Harry, it's Philip. I guess you want to talk about Amie.'

~~~

At eleven-thirty Harry sat in a quiet alcove of Monteverde's, a Costa Rican coffee shop in Pimlico where Philip and he had agreed to meet. It was close to Philip's house. Harry had just arrived, and looked at his watch. He felt apprehensive. His opinion of Philip and his behaviour hadn't changed. Philip had been disloyal. He'd been complicit in the outrageous conspiracy MI6 set up to use Harry as bait in one of their spy games.

But he had called Harry back that morning, and they'd agreed to meet. Harry believed Philip's position in the security service, his contacts in the media, and his time as editor of *The Morning News* could be useful. He decided to keep the CCC thing out of their conversation, and seek whatever advice and help he could.

'Hello, Harry,' Philip said, as he poked his head around the small wall that separated the table Harry had chosen from the rest of the coffee shop. Harry looked up. Philip wore jeans and a blue shirt. He looked down at Harry. 'Can I get you a coffee?'

Harry stood up and looked into Philip's eyes. He took his outstretched hand. 'Thanks, I'll have a double espresso.'

'Okay.' Philip made a quick smile before turning back to the counter.

As Philip walked away, Harry thought about how he'd handle the meeting. He'd first listen to Philip and see what he suggested, and hear any offers of help he might make. There were things Harry wanted Philip to do, and he needed his agreement. He sensed Philip was nervous, maybe a touch embarrassed. Harry looked up and saw Philip returning with their drinks.

'How do you think I can help?' Philip said, as he spooned some of the froth from his cappuccino into his mouth. He looked at Harry in between spoonfuls.

Harry sipped his espresso. He put the cup down and focused on Philip. 'Amie is not a murderer, Philip. She killed Faulks, but in self-defence. You know that. I've come to you for several reasons. You know Amie. You have a lot of contacts, you're experienced, and I have no doubt you can offer some help and suggestions.'

Philip pulled out his Blackberry from his pocket. 'Has she got a good lawyer?'

He started to scroll through his contacts. He stopped, reached out for one of the white napkins in the dispenser on the table and scribbled down a couple of names, and pushed the napkin across the table to Harry. 'Here, try John Julius and Miriam Rodriguez. They both work for the same practice, and are probably the best criminal defence lawyers in this country.'

'Thanks,' Harry said. He folded the napkin up, and pushed it into the back pocket of his jeans. 'She hasn't got one yet. Well, only a local solicitor the police put her in touch with.' Harry took another sip from his coffee.

'She's in good spirits, but has almost given up. Thinks, because she lashed out and killed Faulks, she's guilty and will go down.'

'I see,' Philip said. He stroked his grey hair.

'I don't understand why they've charged her,' Harry said. 'It was quite clearly self-defence. Faulks broke into her house, hid and waited in a wardrobe, and jumped out on her when she undressed. He would have raped and killed her.'

'I agree,' Philip said, as he stirred the last dregs of his coffee.

'Come on. Tell me. What's the talk about it from those in the know?'

Philip looked down again. He held his hands around his cup. After a few seconds he raised his head and looked at Harry.

'Not much. The security services don't normally get involved or are told much about domestic cases, but because there is a bit of a crossover with the CCC thing we get told a bit. All of us on CCC think much the same as me. Amie's innocent and we can't understand why she's been charged.'

'And...?' Harry said, waving a hand. 'Come on. They must have an opinion?'

Philip fidgeted. He looked around the café, and leant forward so he was closer to Harry. 'It could be something to do with Amie's relationship with Jimmy.'

'What do you mean?'

'You know Jimmy dealt in drugs?'

'Yes, but what's that got to do with it?'

'Look at it this way. Jimmy and Amie were close.' Philip looked away and then back at Harry. 'I think they'd slept together.

'Ray Faulks comes after Jimmy for payment of a drug bill,' Philip said after a pause. 'Jimmy and Amie fight him off. Jimmy tells Amie he's a scumbag and out to get him. They plan to ambush him, and for Amie to kill him. Then they make it look as though he'd attacked her. Perfect.'

'Philip, that's bollocks. You know that. Faulks had broken into Amie's flat and waited for her to get home.'

'How do you know that?'

'Amie told me, shortly after she regained consciousness.'

'Exactly. Think about it. It's only her word. Faulks was the one with multiple stab wounds, not Amie. He's dead: she's alive, and was stabbed only once.'

Harry pushed back in his seat. He felt astounded and at a loss for words. He looked at Philip and then out of the window.

'Come on. You don't believe that do you?'

'Of course not. That's why I'm here. I know and like Amie, and will do anything I can to help, but look at it from the point of view of those that don't know her.'

Harry took a deep breath and stared at Philip for a moment. He drained the remains of his coffee. Philip did the same.

Harry sat up. 'Okay, but listen. Jimmy Ali is key here.

'I called the detective in charge of the case yesterday. I said I wanted to alter my statement. Surprisingly, she sounded pleased, and made an appointment to see me later today. Before I rang off, I asked her directly why they'd charged Amie. She said she couldn't tell me, just that they'd passed the file to the CPS, who'd said there was sufficient evidence to press charges. I may be wrong, but I got the impression it was out of her hands.' Harry stopped and looked directly at Philip. 'What she did say, however, was that Jimmy Ali has gone to ground. They can't raise him, and want to see him again about his statement.' Harry stopped again and gazed at Philip.

'Where is he? He's one of yours, isn't he?'

Philip pushed his empty cup to one side, and placed both his hands on the table. He looked at Harry and pursed his lips. 'Don't know. He hasn't answered any of our calls.' Philip looked away again, and then returned his gaze to Harry. 'He's disappeared. Went to ground straight after Amie was stabbed. We wanted to debrief him on CCC, but haven't heard a thing. I guess it's his drug-dealing past that has spooked him. He probably thinks, if he has to talk to the police, he'll get sent back to prison.'

'Haven't you tried to find him? He had been visiting Amie in hospital quite regularly when I was there.'

'Look.' Philip made a flapping gesture with his left hand. 'With informers and temporary agents like Jimmy, they come and go. They're not on the payroll permanently. We use them now and again. So if they drop out, we tend to let them go. That way, it doesn't make us seem to be too much in control of their lives.'

Harry sat back and looked up at the ceiling. *That's a bit rich*, he thought. They hadn't cared a shit about controlling his life. They'd just about screwed it up completely.

But that's the past, he told himself, and returned his attention to Philip.

'Come on. Surely, you're not trying to tell me that your guys couldn't raise him if you tried hard, are you?' Harry looked at Philip with a raised eyebrow.

'Yer, okay,' Philip replied. He waved his hand in a dismissive gesture.

'Listen,' Harry said and leant forward. 'You said earlier you'll do anything you can to help Amie. Well, there are two things you can do.

'First. Get your boys to pull their fingers out and find Jimmy and get him to make a good, strong statement that fits in with Amie's statement.'

Philip nodded. 'We'll try.' His chin rested in both his cupped hands. He had placed his elbows about thirty centimetres apart on the table. 'And the second?'

Harry sat up and looked into Philip's eyes. 'You're not going to like this, but it's vital.'

'Go on.'

'I want you testify at Amie's trial. You're someone of repute.' Harry crossed his arms. He tilted his head a little to one side, and looked into Philip's eyes. 'Especially now you're whatever you are at MI6.' Harry stopped. Philip had shaken his head.

'I can't. I'm not allowed…'

Harry sat back. He uncrossed his arms, and placed both his hands on the edge of the table and gripped it. He gave Philip a stern, resolute look.

'Listen. I hadn't intended to go back over the CCC thing. Today is about Amie. Getting her free.' Harry noticed Philip fidget again. He'd begun to look uncomfortable.

'But you guys screwed me, and I'm calling in a favour. You have to do it. Whatever it takes. Amie needs all the help she can get.'

Harry leant forward and gazed into Philip's eyes. 'Three things could help, Philip.

'Number one. I'll make sure my statement is beefed up.

'Number two. You find Jimmy and we get him to do the same.

'And thirdly, and the most important. You stand up in court and give Amie the best character reference you've ever made.' Harry clasped his hands together and rested them on the table, and made sure he had Philip's attention. 'Then she might stand a chance.'

He turned his wrist over and checked the time. He stood up. 'I've got to go now. Thanks for the coffee. I'll be in touch when I've spoken to the lawyers. I'll give them your name.'

Harry shook Philip's hand, and turned and walked out. He'd given it his best shot, but he held out little hope. No longer could he rely on Philip.

Chapter Twenty-Nine

Flood Taylor Burrows, the criminal lawyers Philip recommended, had their offices in Artillery Lane, a tiny, narrow street in the City, just off Bishopsgate, and next door to a popular pub where customers flowed in and out throughout the day and early evening. Harry turned up at one-thirty, and was greeted at the door by Miriam Rodriguez, one of the two names given by Philip. She stood about 1.7 metres tall, he thought, with shoulder-length, black hair and a striking, Latin appearance. She looked slim and wore a black, linen suit and a white blouse. A thin, gold chain hung around her neck. Harry felt underdressed in his jeans, T-shirt, and leather jacket. He'd gone to meet her immediately after he'd left Philip in Pimlico. She'd rearranged her day to see him.

'Come in, Mr Fingle.' Miriam shook Harry's hand. She gazed up and down the street. 'It looks cold out there.'

'Certainly feels it after where I've been. I was deep in the rain forests of Bolivia three days ago,' Harry replied, and followed Miriam down the hall to an open door.

'Yeah?' Miriam turned to look at Harry. A broad, friendly smile spread across her face. 'What were you doing there?'

She ushered him into a large room with tall ceilings and a stained, wooden floor, where the long windows, at either end, still had the original shutters attached to the frame. An old, leather-topped desk and three wooden, straight-back chairs sat to one side. At the far end of the room a couple of antique, leather sofas faced each other, and were separated by a low table.

'Take a seat,' she said and gestured to the two sofas.

'Thanks,' Harry replied as he sat down. He looked around and noticed a couple of oil paintings that hung above each other on one of the walls. *This is going to be expensive*, he thought. Miriam sat down opposite him, and picked up an A4 pad and a pencil from the table and looked up.

'I'm sorry. I didn't answer your question. I've been travelling around South America. It's good of you to see me at short notice.'

'No problem. Can I call you Harry?'

Harry nodded. 'That's fine. Shall I start?'

'Go ahead.' Miriam leant forward to a tray with coffee cups, a cafetière, and a jug of milk. 'Some coffee?'

'Thanks, black please,' Harry replied and then started to tell Miriam all about Amie's stabbing incident. He carried on for about ten minutes, taking only one sip from his coffee. He stressed Jimmy's connection with Ray Faulks, and that Amie had never met Jimmy before until the moment she walked into the house in Chiswick.

'So. What do you think?' he asked when he'd finished.

Miriam looked up from her pad. She put it and the pencil down on the table and looked Harry in the eye. She clasped her hands together and placed them in her lap.

'From what you've told me, I have no doubt that Amie didn't murder Ray Faulks and acted in self-defence. Knowing he tried to rape and murder her the previous evening, she would be entitled to use whatever force was necessary to protect herself.' Miriam paused. She reached forward and touched the cafetière.

'Sorry, it's cold.' She turned sideways to Harry. 'Would you like some more?'

'Thanks. If it's not too much trouble.' Harry felt optimistic. Miriam seemed pleasant and straight-forward, and had gone out of her way to see him at short notice.

Perhaps it's a going to be okay, he thought, as she ordered some more coffee.

'However,' she said as she put down the phone, sat back on the sofa, and looked at Harry. 'It won't be easy. The odds are stacked against her. But we'll do our best. We have a high success rate.' She paused and straightened her skirt.

'It's all about belief. The defence witnesses need to be consistent under cross-examination. Amie must come across with real conviction, and we have to get a few strong, respected character references. Then we'll win.' Miriam stopped. There was a knock on the door.

'Come in.' She waited while a young man carried in a fresh tray of coffee and took away the first one. 'Thanks, Ben.'

'I need to ask you a few questions.'

Harry nodded. 'Go ahead.'

'Why did Amie go to your house when you weren't there?'

Harry smiled. 'Sorry, I should have told you. We used to be lovers – had been for seven years. Why she actually went that night, I can't say without asking her. But she'd done it twice before. On one occasion she brought me a meal unannounced. Another time, without my knowledge, she went to my house and put out all the photos of her I'd put away. She played my CDs, got into my bed, took a shower, and then left with the water still running.' Harry looked across to Miriam to see her reaction. She seemed bemused and scratched her head.

'How did she get in?'

'She still had a key. She hadn't returned it. Look, I know it sounds as though she was nuts, but...' Harry stopped and blushed a bit. 'It's a long story, but about eighteen months ago I was charged with...'

221

'I know. I know all about it – the trumped-up case against you. You don't need to go over it, if you don't want to.'

'Thanks. Well, after I was acquitted, I told Amie in a not very kind or sympathetic way that I wanted to split with her. That was after she'd helped and supported me through a long trial.' Harry looked across at Miriam. She looked at him and waited.

'Well, I upset her. I was a shit. When I went back to see her a year later for a favour, I must have triggered something in her, and she started these unannounced visits to my house.' He stopped and looked again at Miriam.

'I see.' Miriam stood up and filled up their cups. 'That's significant. Would you be willing to repeat it all in court? It's a strong motive for Amie's visit to your house that night. It will counter any prosecution attempts to say that Amie and Jimmy were linked in some way.'

'Sure,' Harry said with conviction. 'But they can't prove that. Amie and Jimmy hadn't met until the night at my house.'

Miriam dropped back into her seat and picked up her pad. 'I don't know. I've only just been told about the case. But the prosecution will have to come up with a motive for Amie murdering Faulks – collusion with Jimmy would be the obvious one they'd try.'

Miriam made a few hurried notes on the pad, and looked at her watch and then up at Harry. 'Okay. There's much to do. I need to get down to Holloway to see Amie. She'll have to instruct us, even if you or someone else is picking up the tab. We need to speak to Jimmy Ali. You and he will be our major defence witnesses. Can you get hold of him and get him to get in touch? And you and Amie need to think of some important people who can be cross-examined to give a strong character reference. Anyone spring to mind?'

Harry scratched his head. 'I could ask at her college – some of her fellow lecturers.' He raised a finger. 'There's someone I've asked already.' He shook his head. 'But I'm not sure he'll do it.'

'Who's that?'

'Philip Stacey, the ex-editor of *The Morning News* and now…'

'Okay, Harry. You don't need to tell me. I know what he does. It'd be an ace card if you could get him. Will he do it?

'I don't know. I only asked him this morning.'

'And?'

'He said not, but I'm working on him.'

'Do so, Harry. Work on him hard. We need somebody of his standing. I can't stress enough how we need really good character references.' Miriam looked at her watch again. 'I'm sorry. I have to go now.' She reached into her bag that she'd put on the arm of the sofa.

'Here's my card. I'll call you tonight after I've seen Amie.' She stood up and started to walk towards the door. Harry followed.

'Thanks again, Miriam.' Harry held his hand out to shake hers.

'No problem. Stay positive. I'll do my best. Oh, one last question that I forgot. Why didn't Amie call the police when Faulks broke into her flat the first time?'

Harry shook his head. 'Oh dear, yes. That's what I asked her. Apparently Jimmy didn't want her to call them. He'd been worried they'd find out about his recent drug dealing and report him to his probation officer. He reckoned he'd go back inside.'

Harry didn't wait for Miriam's response. The expression on her face gave it away.

~~~

Harry left the offices of Flood Taylor Burrows at two-fifteen and called a cab. He needed to be at Ealing police station by three-thirty to see DI Ford. He hadn't met her before. After Amie had been stabbed, a male detective with a strong Scottish accent had taken Harry's statement. Harry couldn't remember the detective's name. But he did recall that the policeman had never questioned Amie's innocence.

DI Ford would be new to the case, he thought as the taxi pulled away and started to weave through the traffic. As the Houses of Parliament and Westminster Abbey appeared on the left Harry thought back to the meeting with Miriam. She seemed impressive. He believed if anybody could get Amie acquitted, she would. But she left him concerned. He felt worried he hadn't given a satisfactory answer to her question – why Amie hadn't called the police after Faulks had broken into her flat?

He arrived at Ealing police station with a minute to spare. DI Ford met him and took him to an interview room.

'What can I do for you, Mr Fingle?' the detective said once they'd both sat down on opposite sides of a grubby, vinyl-topped table. She was alone.

'As I said when I called, I would like to read through my statement. The one I gave the night Amie Lau had been stabbed.'

DI Ford put her hands on the table. Harry couldn't fail to notice her chubby fingers and badly bitten nails. He looked up at her face, and noted she didn't wear any makeup. Her hair appeared lank and unwashed.

'Did you know Amie Lau has been charged with the murder of Ray Faulks?' she asked Harry.

'Yes, I did,' Harry replied and stared at DI Ford. She appeared butch, and seemed to have an almost confrontational manner.

'It's not standard practice to release witness's statements after we've made a charge.'

'Really?' Harry raised his head and stared at DI Ford. 'What if I want to change it? You saying I can't?'

DI Ford leant back and stared at Harry. She looked hostile. 'It would have to be a new statement. We can't change the original.'

Harry didn't know if DI Ford had told the truth. He'd taken a dislike to her, and thought she'd tried it on and attempted to rile him. 'Call it what you like,' he said as he pulled out a crumpled square of several sheets of paper from his back pocket and unfolded them. 'I have a copy of my statement here. I'll run through it and make amendments and sign them if you'd prefer.'

'Why do you want to change it?' Ford snapped.

'I didn't say I want to change anything. I said I'd like to look at it again – in your presence. I just want to check if I've missed anything out.'

'Why?'

Harry became convinced she'd been trying to make him angry. She seemed to be looking for an opportunity to kick him out or charge him with some trivial offence. He sat back in his seat and looked directly into her eyes.

'Because, DI Ford, I made it straight after Amie had been stabbed. I'd been in a state of heightened emotion and concern. I've been away for two months, and I've had time to think about it and talk to Amie. I want to make sure I haven't missed anything out.'

'I presume you think you have missed things out, or you wouldn't be here. You've read your statement and decided to come along and change it so it reads better for Amie?' DI Ford twisted her head a few centimetres so their eyes met.

'I'm right. Aren't I, Mr Fingle?'

Harry clasped his hands together on the table. He took a deep breath. 'You couldn't be more wrong.' He leant forward.

'I got back from South America the night before last, and haven't stopped since. I've hardly had time to eat or drink, let alone find time to read it.' Harry looked away for a moment, and then turned back to look at the detective.

'I didn't have a clue where it was. I thought I'd lost it. I looked for it, and found it amongst a pile of papers this morning after I'd arranged to see you. I stuffed it in my back pocket and ran out of my house.' Harry turned his head away to the right and then back to DI Ford.

'Now, Detective Inspector Ford, what do you want me to do?

'I can scribble on the back of this in your presence. I can write what I want to say on a new sheet of paper, or I can go away and write a completely new statement and pop it in the post?

'Your choice?'

DI Ford stood up. Harry noticed her faded jeans stretched across her broad thighs, and her old-looking, navy polo shirt. He wondered if she could be a lesbian. He didn't care. But her aggressive and unhelpful manner riled him.

'I'll send someone in with a new statement pad,' she said, and left.

Harry read through his original statement. There were several gaps. He'd written it in the back of a police car immediately after Amie was stabbed. When he saw her later in hospital, after she'd regained consciousness, she told him how Faulks broke into her flat and attempted to rape and kill her. He'd missed all that out.

He hadn't said anything about their past relationship and her motives for going to his house unannounced on two previous occasions. And, of most importance, he'd omitted the description Amie gave him of Faulks jumping out on her from her cupboard, and how he tried to rape and kill her for a second time.

He rewrote it all on a new statement sheet. He didn't miss anything out. He signed it, and gave it to the uniformed police officer who'd remained in the room with him.

'Thank you, sir. DI Ford asked that you stay a moment so she can read it. If you don't mind, I'll just go and get her.'

DI Ford came back in the room five minutes later with Harry's new statement in her hands. She handed him a copy. 'Your copy.

'Just one question.

'When Ray Faulks broke in on Amie's flat the first time and then fled, do you know why Amie didn't call the police?'

'I don't.' Harry stared into Ford's eyes. 'You said he broke in? Do you know what his motive was?'

'You can go now, Mr Fingle.' DI Ford opened the door and walked away.

~~~

When Harry arrived home after meeting with the policewoman, he again ignored his rucksack in his hall. It was where he'd left it two nights earlier when he returned from South America. He made a mug of tea, took it to his living room, turned on the TV, and sank into the leather chair. He put his feet up on his small table. He didn't try to change channels. He wasn't bothered what programme showed. He wanted only a distraction while he tried to piece together the day.

One thought dominated his mind. Both Miriam Rodriguez and DI Ford had focused on why Amie hadn't called the police. He knew the answer. She hadn't wanted to incriminate Jimmy. They didn't know that, and it looked bad. The prosecution would portray it as collusion. He took a sip from his tea, and stood up and started to pace around his living room with his mug in his hand.

What else can I do, he questioned?

After less than a minute, he stopped in the middle of the room and stood still. He put a hand up to his chin and covered his mouth. Only Jimmy and Philip could swing this for Amie, he thought. He had to do whatever he could to make certain of their cooperation. He reached into his pocket for his phone.

Philip

I spoke with Miriam Rodriguez today. She's good – thank you – and will do her utmost for Amie. Miriam insists you are to be witness. Call her and me ASAP.

Philip. You and I know Amie's innocent. You've screwed up my life. Don't do the same to her.

Harry.

After he'd sent Philip the message, Harry turned his mind to Jimmy. He found two numbers for him on his phone. Neither responded. Philip had said he hadn't heard from him for some time. Harry scratched his head. He took another couple of paces around the room and stopped again. He thought of Ritzler, Jimmy's employers, and that he might still work for them. They would have his address, he told himself. He'd call them in the morning, and then go to Jimmy's home and talk to him. He made for his kitchen. He wanted a drink.

Next to his fridge sat the pile of unopened letters he'd dumped on his worktop forty-eight hours earlier. He'd glanced through the envelopes once, but thought he should look at them again in case he'd missed something important. One envelope, with familiar, scrawly handwriting, stood out. He slid it open with his thumb. He pulled out a lined sheet of A5 paper that had been torn from a notepad.

Dear Harry

Sorry I ain't been in touch, like, but I'm in a spot of bother. I thought I's doing right for Amie by telling about Ray and the stuff, but the police came for me. I'm back inside. Sorry, Harry.

Jimmy.

Harry examined the note closely. It wasn't dated. He couldn't see an address. The postmark was faint and undistinguishable. He tossed both the envelope and letter on the worktop, and took two paces to the left. He reached up to the cupboard by his head and opened it. He pulled out a glass and a bottle of whisky.

Chapter Thirty

While Harry had trekked alone around South America he'd thought about Amie almost every day. Then, one day, he came to a candid conclusion. They'd been lovers and best friends for seven years. They shared everything – each becoming almost the other's oxygen. Often they'd said how much they loved each other and wanted to spend the rest of their lives together.

He'd found his past actions inexcusable.

To split with her, in such a way, had been thoughtless and uncaring. He couldn't excuse himself, and considered his behaviour cruel and unkind. He felt ashamed. He'd treated Amie deplorably and became determined, in some way, to put matters right. Directly after his trial, his own mental state had been unstable and weak, but to walk out on her the way he did was wrong. There was no other way about it.

He hadn't come up with a particular way of saying sorry, or some special act of atonement. He would apologise face to face in as a sincere manner as he could. No flowers or gifts, no surprise dinners, no gestures, just the word: *sorry*. He had no idea how Amie would react. She was entitled to do whatever she wanted. He'd hoped she'd accept his apology as genuine and they'd stay friends. He was almost sure they'd never be lovers again, but he couldn't be certain, and knew, deep down, he'd hoped they could be.

~~~

After he read Jimmy's note, Harry began to fall apart. He knew Miriam Rodriguez wanted to call Jimmy and Philip as her two main defence witnesses. But it wouldn't happen. Jimmy had been banged up in a prison somewhere. Philip wasn't returning any of Harry's calls or texts. It looked bleak. Harry envisaged Amie being found guilty. She'd be sentenced to at least ten years in prison. He blamed himself.

He felt tired and despondent. Since he'd returned from South America, he had eaten little and had slept badly. He knew he should make himself something to eat, try to come up with other witnesses, and think of ways of getting to Philip. But he didn't. Instead, he took the bottle of whisky and his glass to his living room. He filled it up and slumped into his chair. He tried playing some music, but found anything he selected reminded him of Amie. He pulled down a couple of books from his shelves, opened them and read the first few lines of both, and gave up. He couldn't concentrate.

How could he live with himself, he asked? Amie would rot away in some depressing women's prison, and it was his fault. How could he have been so thoughtless? He didn't try to consider anything practical or positive that might help her case. He gave up and fell into a morass of depression and despair. The whisky didn't help.

At eight, he lay in a heap in his chair. The almost-empty bottle stood on the wooden floor by his right foot. All of a sudden his mobile phone rang. It startled him. He jumped up and started to rush around to find where he'd last put it.

'Yes,' he mumbled.

'Hello, is that you Harry?' The caller paused. 'You Okay? You sound a bit rough.'

'Whose that?' he asked. He was dazed and confused, and out of breath.

'Harry. It's Miriam Rodriguez. Have I woken you?'

'No, I'm okay. Just a bit tired. I was dozing, I think.' He saw the whisky bottle, and tried hard to sound normal. He guessed he must have sounded strange. Miriam would have just returned from seeing Amie, he thought. She would have called to tell him how the visit had gone. He feared she'd ask him if he'd got hold of Jimmy and spoken to Philip.

'How did the visit go?' he said. He felt ashamed of his failure.

'I didn't see her. She's free. The CPS have dropped all charges.'

'My God,' Harry yelled down the phone. He felt as though an electric shot had run through his body. 'What? How did that happen?'

'I don't know. I've been trying to find out ever since I got back from Holloway. I can't seem to get any sense from anybody. That's why I haven't called you before.'

'That's wonderful news. When did it happen? Where is she?'

'She's at home. She was released just before I got to Holloway at 5:00 p.m.

'Listen.'

Harry sensed a note of caution in Miriam's voice.

'I've spoken to her just to make sure all is in order. She asked me who I was. I told her and said you had been to see me.'

'I'll call her,' Harry said. He felt elated, as though he was floating on a cloud. 'Maybe I'll go round and see her.'

'Harry, wait. Listen, I haven't finished. She told me all about you going to see her. She was very grateful. Your visit gave her a big lift. She said she had given up and was sure she'd stay in prison for a long time.'

'Yeah, I know that. So, what are you trying to tell me?'

'Nothing. She said she wants to see you, and will probably call you, but...'

'But what?'

'But nothing. It was of no consequence. I'm sorry. Call her. She'll like that.'

They said good-bye and ended the call. Harry felt a touch deflated. He felt sure Miriam was going to say something to him about Amie, but held back. He became puzzled and concerned, and hoped Miriam hadn't hid something from him. He decided to go and see Amie.

It took him twenty minutes to cycle from Chiswick to Ealing. He almost froze, but had sobered up by the time he arrived. The air temperature, several degrees below freezing point, felt colder due to the biting-cold north wind that blew into his face all the way. As he wheeled his bike up to the porch of Amie's flat, his skin felt raw. He couldn't think of a time when he'd been as cold. He stopped and held the numb fingers of his hand up to his mouth, and blew on them to ease their stiffness.

My God, he thought. The last time he'd been at Amie's flat had been the night she'd been stabbed. He felt odd and shaky, and reached out to press the doorbell. He shivered as he waited.

A man with thick, wavy, dark hair and a craggy, handsome face about Harry's age opened the front door.

'Hello,' he said. He stood in the small opening he'd made. His hand held onto the door and barred Harry's entry. 'Who do you want?'

Harry looked him up and down. He'd never seen him before. He wondered for a moment if Amie had moved out or taken a lodger and hadn't told him. 'Amie Lau. She still lives here, doesn't she?'

The man nodded. 'Yes, she's here, but she's in bed, asleep. Can I tell her who called?'

Harry examined the stranger again. *Perhaps he was from social services or suchlike?* he thought. 'Oh, yes. Tell her Harry called. I'll call her in the morning. Emm. Is she okay?'

The man smiled and stretched out his hand. 'Pleased to meet you, Harry. She's told me all about you. I'll tell her you called: and yes, she's fine. Just a bit tired, but elated at being free and home.'

'Oh, thanks,' Harry said. He shook the man's hand. 'Well, I'd better be getting along then. Give her my best wishes.

'And your name?' Harry asked as he turned to leave.

'Oh, I'm Simon, a friend. I'm staying the night to make sure she's okay.' He smiled again. 'Don't worry. I'll make sure she'll get your message. She'll call you tomorrow. 'Bye.'

''Bye.' Harry turned and walked his bike back down to the road.

He arrived home at nine-thirty. He felt so cold he thought his fingers and toes had frozen. He filled up his glass with the remains of the whisky, and dragged himself off to bed.

Chapter Thirty-One

Harry placed a small, white cup under his espresso maker. He dropped a couple of slices of bacon into his griddle pan, moved them around a bit, and walked down his hall to his front door to pick up the day's paper. It was seven in the morning. He'd woken early after a disturbed night, full of thoughts of Amie. He'd been overjoyed at the news of her release, but he'd been thrown by meeting Simon. He had no doubt he'd become her lover. The realisation came as a shock. It had stirred an emotion he hadn't expected.

Was he jealous? He'd asked himself as he'd tossed and turned in his bed. Surely not? He couldn't expect her not to meet someone else; not after all he'd put her through. But deep down, like when he was in South America, had he harboured the faint hope for some sort of full-blown reconciliation? When he wasn't questioning his emotions, he'd thought about Amie's release and the way it had come about. It was so sudden and unexpected. He remembered his mood, minutes before Miriam had called and told him the news. It was dire. He had expected the worst.

With his mind full of questions, he slid his bacon onto a plate, scooped a poached egg from a pan onto a slice of buttered, wholemeal toast, and took the meal to one of the stools around his breakfast bar. He poured some black coffee and pulled the newspaper closer. He thumbed to an article that caught his attention. His phone rang.

'Hello,' he said, anxiously. He waited for Amie to speak.

'Have I woken you?'

'No. I was up.'

'I'm sorry I didn't see you last night. I was out for the count. I collapsed almost as soon as we got home.'

'No problem,' Harry said as he thought about Amie's words, 'we got home.'

'I meant to call you, but I was so tired I could hardly get to bed. How did you find out?'

'Miriam Rodriguez told me last night. I'd planned to call you later this morning, but you've beaten me to it.

'Amie, I can't tell you how pleased I am for you. It must have been awful. I can't imagine what you've been through.'

'Thanks. I have much to be grateful to you for; and I have a lot to tell you about. Can I come round later to see you?'

'Of course. What time?' Harry felt thrown. He knew he'd be delighted to see Amie free, out of Holloway and its depressing environment. But felt unsure how he would he react. She'd be bound to talk about her new lover.

'Oh, sometime late afternoon. I'll bring some wine,' Amie replied.

'That'd be good.' Harry decided to leave any questions about her release until they met. 'I'll look forward to it. See you then.'

By the time he'd returned to his breakfast, it had gone cold. He threw it away. He put a couple of pieces of bread in the toaster, and made a fresh espresso. He spent the next three hours tidying up his house and unpacking. For much of the time, he thought about Amie and how their meeting would go. He looked forward to seeing her, but continued to question his emotions and how he'd deal with her explanation about Simon. Occasionally, he'd think of the book he would write. He'd sketched out the plot while in South America, and planned to talk it through with a couple of literary agents he knew to get their feedback. But as much as he tried to concentrate on his future, his mind returned often to Amie.

~~~

At ten-thirty, as Harry dried himself after a shower, he heard a knock on his front door. It would be his neighbour with a parcel, he thought, and shouted out of his window. He grabbed his jeans and a clean shirt, pulled them on, and raced down the stairs. He opened the door to find Philip Stacey stood on his doormat. He wore a suit and a navy overcoat, and held a bag of croissants in his hand.

'Forgive me. Coming round like this, unannounced.' Philip looked down and pointed at the bag of croissants. 'I passed a French patisserie on the way here, and thought you might appreciate a nibble or two.' He looked Harry in the eye. 'I've come to explain about Amie.'

'What do you mean?' Harry stood in the doorway with one hand held onto the side of his door.

'She's free. You know that, don't you?' Philip kept his gaze fixed on Harry's face. Harry nodded.

'Yes, I do. Miriam Rodriguez told me last night and I spoke to Amie this morning.' He shot Philip an inquisitive look. 'What's it got to do with you? You didn't even bother to reply to the messages I sent you last night.'

'It's a lot to do with me. If you let me in, I'll explain. But I can't tell you here.'

Harry moved away from the door. He stood aside and ushered Philip in. He figured Philip wouldn't have taken time off work and come over to see him unless he had something important to say. 'Let's go down to the kitchen. I'll make some coffee while you're talking.'

Philip followed Harry down the hall, and sat at one of the stools around the breakfast bar opposite where Harry prepared their drinks. Harry had his back to him.

'Happy for me to start?'

'Go ahead,' Harry replied as he measured the spoonfuls of coffee into his cafetière.

'You may find this difficult to believe, but when you asked me to be a witness at Amie's trial I knew there'd be a problem.'

Harry turned and faced Philip. He brought the cafetière and two mugs to the kitchen bar. 'Yeah, what was that?' he said. He kept his head down as he poured the coffee.

'Since Operation CCC finished, I've been promoted. Sheila Robinson's moved on and I've taken her position.'

'Where's she gone?' Harry pushed a mug of coffee towards Philip.

'She's left the service.'

Harry sat down and picked at one of the croissants. He looked up and directly at Philip. 'Why's that? I didn't take to her, but she struck me as a solid sort, a traditionalist.'

Philip pursed his lips and clasped his hands together on the worktop.

'Let's just say we screwed up a bit with Operation CCC. Heads had to roll.'

Harry dropped the hand that supported his chin. He raised his head a little and stared at Philip in astonishment. Philip, who he presumed had become a senior officer in MI6, had just admitted that the security services had 'screwed up a bit.' He felt stunned.

'Why are you telling me this? Surely it's not my place to know anything about it. You know – all that Official Secrets Act shit you lot gave me.'

'Because, Harry. It's all to do with Amie. As Head of Section at MI6, there was no way I could testify in an open court. I'm a secret service officer of the crown, and couldn't be a witness for the defence in a murder case. It's just not possible.'

'So what happened?' Harry hadn't been surprised by Philip's comment. His day in the company of MI6, and their attempts to explain the illegal and disreputable way they operated, left him with the impression that anything was possible.

'After we met yesterday and I realised I couldn't do what you wanted for Amie, I thought hard about how I could help her.'

'Go on,' Harry said. He'd become inquisitive and wondered where Philip's story would head.

'I called up the Director of Public Prosecution at the CPS, someone I've known for some time, and persuaded him to drop all charges against Amie.'

Harry placed his hands on the worktop. He pushed himself against the back of his stool and gazed at Philip in amazement. 'What? Just like that?'

'Not quite. I had to do a little embroidery.'

'Like how?'

'I told him that Ray Faulks had been on our radar for some time. I said he was part of a massive drug-importing syndicate, and had murdered several people who hadn't paid him. I also told him that Jimmy Ali, who's being held at Brixton for committing drug offences while on probation, was one of our informers, and had been watching Faulks for some time.' Philip took a sip of coffee.

'I said Jimmy had no doubt that Faulks would have raped and killed Amie, had she not got the better of him. I told him we couldn't say that in court, but let him know, most definitely, that unless they dropped all the charges against Amie, an innocent woman would go to jail.' Philip twisted his head to look directly into Harry's eyes.

'He agreed with me, and said he'd deal with it immediately.'

Harry bit and sucked on one of his thumbnails, and stared at Philip for several seconds. He felt speechless. He had been an investigative journalist for ten years. He'd reported on several nasty, criminal cases, but had never heard anything remotely like Philip had just recounted.

'How much of that is true?'

'Most. You know Jimmy was an informer.'

Yes, I do. But the bit about Faulks being on your radar; surely that was an invention?'

Philip smiled. 'Yes, it was. But it worked, didn't it?'

Harry shook his head. He felt staggered and flabbergasted, and stood up. He picked up another of the croissants, and started to pull and eat pieces from it while he paced around his kitchen. After several seconds, he stopped and stood in a corner. He faced Philip.

'Well. You've certainly pulled a blinder. I have to congratulate you.' He put the remains of the croissant down on the work surface. He spread out both his arms in a reverse V-shape behind him, and grabbed hold of the rolled edges of his worktop. He stared again at Philip.

'Tell me the truth. What motivated you?'

Philip emptied the remains of the cafetière into his cup and drank it down. 'Two things really.'

'They are?'

'I like Amie. She's a great girl. It was pretty clear she was innocent, and I wanted to do whatever I could to get her free. So I did.'

Harry scratched his neck and looked at Philip. 'Thanks.'

'That was the first thing,' Philip said as he looked into Harry's eyes.

'Go on,' Harry said. He picked up the empty coffee jug and moved towards his sink to replenish it. He had his back to Philip.

'I did it also for you.'

Harry left the jug in the sink, and turned around to face Philip.

'You see, I felt guilty about how we treated you over Operation CCC. At the time, you were so fired up I was worried you'd do something silly like publish everything we told you on the Internet or somewhere, and end up in prison.'

'I almost did,' Harry interrupted. He felt unsure as to how to react. Philip's admissions had come as a surprise.

'I know. That's why I came to see you that afternoon – to make sure you didn't. I understand how you felt at the time. I guess I would have done the same. So, apart from doing my very level best to get Amie free, I wanted to do it also for you.' Philip stopped and looked across the room at Harry. 'That's it.' Philip shrugged his shoulders.

Harry, who still stood with his back to the sink, put a hand up to his chin and started to rub his cheek. He thought about what Philip had just said, and recognised that it must have taken quite something for him to say it.

'Thanks. I appreciate that.' Harry noticed that Philip seemed to be fidgeting as though he wanted to leave. 'Here, hold on. Let me make some fresh coffee.'

'Not for me. I need to go. But there's one more thing I have to tell you.'

'What's that?' Harry moved back to sit opposite Philip.

'You'll read in the papers tomorrow that Richard Morecombe has killed himself. As you know, he'd been awaiting trial for having sex with minors. Well, while he'd been in prison, his company, The Morning News Group, was sold to Global Communications. You know, the massive American media company with tentacles all over the world. I know someone there. I called him. He said if you want you can have your job back at *The Morning News*.'

Harry screwed up his eyes and looked at Philip.

'Thanks. That's great. But I'll think about it? I've plans to write a book.' He shrugged his shoulders. 'But, I admit the money would be useful.'

'Okay.' Philip stood up and made for the door. 'Do as you wish, but the offer is there.' He stood with one hand on the door handle, and tilted his head a little to catch Harry's gaze.

'Why don't Amie and you come round for some dinner? Penny's always talking about you.' He held out his hand to Harry and opened the front door. 'Let me know.'

'Thanks.' They shook hands. 'I'll call you. But I don't think Amie will come.'

'No?' Philip looked into Harry's eyes. 'Why's that?'

'She has a new man.'

Philip shrugged his shoulders. 'That's life. 'Bye for now.'

Harry closed the door on Philip, and started to walk back to his kitchen.

So Philip's delivered, he thought. He knew Philip's admission about the CCC thing and how MI6 had treated him was the closest he would come to apologising. Harry felt pleased. Philip's actions had freed Amie and gone a long way toward repairing Philip's and his fractured friendship. He started to clear up the coffee things.

Closure

Chapter Thirty-Two

Harry opened the door to Amie at ten minutes past five. He hadn't been sure what time she would turn up, and felt glad when she called at four-thirty and said she'd be about half an hour. The wait for her had been strange and unsettling. He experienced emotions ranging from anticipation and excitement, to sadness and recrimination. She'd come to say good-bye. It would be the end of a long relationship, however much they promised to stay friends.

'Hello,' he said. He was unsure of what to say. 'Come in. It looks cold out there.' A few flakes of snow had settled on Amie's scarf. 'I've lit a fire.'

'Thanks.' Amie looked up at Harry. She smiled in the warm, friendly way that he remembered.

'Here, let me take that,' Harry said. He smiled back, and held out his hand to take her coat. 'Let's go in here.' He pointed to the open door to the living room.

'Have this,' Amie said as she walked through the door. She thrust a bottle of champagne into Harry's hand. 'It's been chilled. I bought it from the shop at the top of the road.'

'Great. I'll get some glasses. Go and sit by the fire and warm yourself up.'

Harry went off to the kitchen. He felt relieved to see Amie look so different. Her hair was clean, and sparkled. She seemed refreshed and at ease. She wore navy jeans and a white T-shirt with a dark-blue, abstract motif splashed across it. She looked great, he thought. Much like he'd always remembered her. But, like himself, he sensed she felt hesitant, not sure of the things she wanted to say or how to say them. He decided to fill the glasses in the kitchen and take them back to the living room on a tray.

'Here you go,' he said as he passed one of the glasses to Amie and sat in the chair opposite her. He raised his glass. 'Cheers. Here's to you. So glad to see you out of that awful place and looking so good.'

'Cheers.' Amie chinked her glass with Harry's. She smiled again, and took a large sip. She put the glass down on the small, wooden coffee table with six small drawers that she'd bought for the house when she'd lived there. She turned back to look at Harry.

'I don't really know where to start. I've so much to thank you for.' She brushed her hand through her hair. 'You saved my life, and then, somehow, you got me out of that hell of a prison.' Amie turned and took another sip of champagne.

'I really thought I would spend the rest of my life there. I don't know what came over me, but I was so shocked at being arrested that I just gave up. I killed a guy and reckoned I'd be imprisoned for years to pay for it. It was awful in there. I can't possibly begin to explain how bad it all was.' Amie stopped and had another drink and turned back to face Harry.

'What did you do to get me released?'

Harry sat back and rested his hands on his thighs. He tucked a little of his shirt into his belt. 'I didn't do anything.'

Amie looked surprised. 'Surely you did? All I was told was that the CPS had dropped all charges and I was free to go. I guessed you'd spoken to the police, or found Jimmy and got him to make another statement, or something like that.'

Harry shook his head. He picked up his drink and took a sip. He held the glass in his hand and rested it on his thigh. 'Nope, not me. But guess who?'

Amie shook her head. 'I have no idea. Who?'

Harry finished his drink. He picked up the bottle and held it over her glass. 'This is good. Here, have some more.'

'I will, thanks. I agree, it is good. I'd never heard of it before.' Amie blushed. 'A friend bought me a bottle last night.' She held her glass up for Harry to fill. He looked at her as he poured and guessed the 'friend' was Simon, the man she'd come to tell him about.

'But, come on. Tell me who it was who got me free?' Amie said.

'Philip Stacey.'

'Philip? No way.' Amie looked astonished. 'What, after everything he did to you?'

Harry stood up. He held the half-empty bottle of champagne in his hand. 'He's a big shot in MI6 now, and has influence. I'll tell you all about it. But first, let me get another bottle.' He returned within minutes, topped up their glasses again, and started to tell Amie everything that Philip had said and done.

'I still have you to thank,' Amie said when he'd finished. She stood up and took off her blazer, and looked down at Harry. 'I'd forgotten how warm and cosy it gets in here.' She smiled, and put her blazer on the back of her chair. She sat down, leant forward with her hands on her thighs, and caught Harry's attention.

'You must have said some pretty powerful stuff to get him to do all that.'

Harry took another large gulp of champagne. He reckoned it was time for him to say what he'd planned. He turned to face her.

'Maybe I did.' He looked away and put his glass down. He straightened up, sat back in his chair, and turned his head a little to catch Amie's eyes.

'I want to say sorry for the way I have treated you in the last eighteen months. There's no excuse for how I behaved. I truly apologise.'

Amie leant back and clasped her hands in her lap, and stared at Harry for a couple of moments. 'That's quite something. Thanks. I hadn't expected it, at all.

'I guess I owe you an apology as well.'

'Why?' Harry asked. He looked surprised.

'For bugging you so much, and going to your house uninvited.' Amie stopped and leant down to her bag. 'Oh, hang on a minute. I've just remembered something I have for you.' She picked her bag up, reached into it, and seemed to search around for something. Harry looked on. He had one hand clenched against his chin and just below his mouth. He had no idea what Amie looked for.

'Ah, here we are,' she said after a moment. She held a small parcel. It was wrapped in an artistic way in red tissue paper with a yellow ribbon around it. A bow had been tied on the top. She gave it to Harry and smiled. 'Something you've wanted for some time.'

Harry became puzzled. He took his time to undo the bow and unwrap the tissue until he was left with just a couple of sheets around a small, uneven object. He felt it. He thought it was metal, and seemed to have several ends to it. He tore the last two sheets away. A bunch of keys fell into his hand. He laughed, and looked across at Amie with a broad grin.

'Sorry, I should have given them back to you ages ago.' She reached into her bag again, and pulled out another present. 'Here you are. This is your real one.'

'What do you mean? I'm not entitled to a present.' Harry held back from taking the small package she pushed towards him.

'Go on – take it. Call it what you like. A late birthday present or whatever.' Amie ran her fingers through her hair and looked at him 'I wanted to buy you something to thank you for everything you've done.'

Harry felt taken aback. He hadn't expected anything. He stretched out his hand to take the parcel from her.

With care, he undid the tasteful outer paper until he came to a rectangular object wrapped in a double sheet of red tissue paper. He undid the paper and found a book. An old, leather-bound book with the title embossed in faded gilt. He lifted it up to his eyes to inspect: *Crime* and *Punishment* by Fyodor M Dostoyevsky. He laughed again and looked up at Amie.

'You haven't read it yet, have you?' she asked with an anxious expression.

Harry shook his head. 'No. You know I haven't.' He turned the book over several times to look at it.

'I thought so. You always said you wanted to read it, but I wasn't sure if you'd gone and bought it. You might have picked one up in the last year or so. I found it in an old, second-hand bookshop this morning. I loved the condition it was in, and thought you'd like it as well.'

Amie tilted her head a little, and caught Harry's gaze. She smiled. 'Open it.'

'Wow,' Harry said as he looked inside. 'This copy was printed in the early 1920s. Thanks.' Harry stood up. He held onto the book, and took a step forward to where she sat. He leant over, and gave her a kiss on the cheek.

'Thanks again. I'm sorry: I haven't a present for you.' He took a step backwards, and shook his head a little and looked down at Amie. 'You didn't have to do that.'

'Well I did.' Amie looked on as Harry, who still stood, opened the book and read the message she'd put inside.

Thanks, Harry, for everything
All the best for the future
With love
Amie.

He took his time to close it. He fingered the soft, leather cover, flicked through the pages, and admired the quality and condition of the paper.

'It's wonderful,' he said and looked across at Amie. 'I shall start reading it immediately.'

'Take your time. Enjoy it. There's no rush.'

Harry sat down. He still kept hold of the book and continued to examine it. He felt overjoyed, but had become uneasy. He wondered when or if Amie would tell him about Simon. He looked at his watch. It was six-thirty.

'So you going back to work at the university?' he said.

'I hope so. I'll go in tomorrow and see what they have to say. They've been very supportive up to now. How about you?'

'I'm going to write a book.' Harry stared at the ceiling for a moment.

'Philip told me this morning that he'd spoken to the new editor of *The Morning News* and they want me back.'

'Harry, that's great news. You going to go?'

'I'll think about it a little, but I guess I will. I need the money.' Harry paused and looked away for a second.

'Philip asked me something else.'

'What?'

'He asked us both round for dinner.'

Amie smiled. 'That's nice. I'd like to see him to thank him, and Penny as well. What did you say?'

Harry covered his mouth and rubbed his chin for a few seconds, and then looked at Amie. 'I said I didn't think you'd want to go.'

'Why?'

'Because, I think Simon, who I met last night, is your man now, and I didn't think you'd want to go along with me.'

Amie blushed again and stared at Harry. She smiled in a way he would always remember. 'Yes he is. I met him about ten weeks ago, and he's wonderful and I am in love with him.' Amie stopped talking. She tilted her head to one side and touched her hair while she still looked at Harry.

'I know it's quick, but he's asked me to marry him.'

'And?'

Amie looked down at the embers in the fire. It needed another log. She turned back to face Harry. 'I said yes. I would.

'But I'd still like to go to Philip's with you. If that's okay?'

Harry nodded a few times and pursed his lips a little. 'Yeah, I guess that'll be okay,' he said after several seconds. 'I'll call him in the morning.' He looked at the fire and suddenly felt cold and shivered.

'I must put another log on. It's about to go out.'

~~~***~~~

Notes from the author

I'm a crime writer. I write about people involved in sinister deeds like murder, extortion and retribution.

I've worked in a seaside arcade, as a record salesman, a decorator, a merchant banker, a marine and a retailer. I was once shot by terrorists, winched from the jungle into a helicopter, and flown to hospital. I live with my wife in Buckingshire.

If you enjoyed *Playing Harry*, you might like to try my other books – all e-books.

~~~

Electronic Crime in Muted Key, about a man who buys a dead body and fakes his death.

~~~

Murder He Forgot, about a man who forgot he tried to kill his wife, twice.

~~~

The Wrong Menu. Murder, drug-dealing, and adultery behind a famous restaurant.

~~~

Killing Sam Forever, about a man who is revisited by the person he thought he'd killed thirty years previously.

~~~

The Bloodied Black Heart. Terrorists threaten to nuke London.

~~~

Death in the Fishing Net, about a man who pulls his wife's body from the sea.

~~~

Short Stories

Oh, What a Night. A wacky, urban fantasy, where the author invites the characters from his book. Hilarious, a touch violent.

~~~

Harry and His Unfinished Business. Harry Fingle goes to Istanbul to relax after his near death, in *Playing Harry*, and finds his enemies are still at large.

~~~

Love, Life, and Loss. Fifteen shorts about life's highs and lows. All royalties donated to Médicien Sans Frontières/Doctors Without Borders

~~~

I'm in the process of writing a follow-up to *Playing Harry*.

~~~

http://www.nickwastnage.com
http://twitter.com/@nickwastnage
http://nickwastnage.blogspot.com/
http://www.facebook.com/Nicwastnage